## PLAYING WITH THE BIG BOYS . . .

"Hello, Andrea . . ." There he stood, just to the left of a young maple. Leather cap, denim jacket and broad, merciless smile. "What's that in your hand there?"

His eyes sparkled in anticipation. I could sense the progression of his thoughts. Dark night. The lovely lady realtor all alone.

I lashed out at him, swinging the gaff with all my might, trying to put a two-inch dent in that mobster skull. He ducked beneath my speeding gaff, then popped up again like some leering jack-in-the-box. Never had I seen a human being move that fast. I had a split-second glimpse of his grinning face, followed by a fleeting closeup of this big clenched male fist. And then a fireburst of agony exploded on my chin.

Spectacular pain! It mushroomed like a nuclear blast, extinguishing every last iota of consciousness.

Next thing I knew, I was floating in absolute darkness, listening to the roar of Tahquamenon Falls.

As my consciousness began to crystalize, I tasted bleeding gums, winced at the excruciating pain emanating from my chin. I realized that I wasn't floating. I was draped facedown over something warm and muscular. I recognized another sensation as well. A warm pressure across the back of my knees. A man's arm. I was being carried.

I tried squirming a bit, just to see what bodily parts were still operational. And his voice admonished me. "Hold still. If I drop you now, it's a helluva slide into the lake."

# AN ANGELA BIWABAN MYSTERY
# TARGET FOR MURDER

## J.F. TRAINOR

## ZEBRA BOOKS
### KENSINGTON PUBLISHING CORP.

*"To offend me is to court calamity."*
*Martha Jane Cannary*
*1871*

ZEBRA BOOKS

are published by

Kensington Publishing Corp.
475 Park Avenue South
New York, NY 10016

Copyright © 1993 by J.F. Trainor

First Printing: February, 1993

Printed in the United States of America

# Chapter One

I knew I was in trouble the minute Paul Holbrook walked into my booth.

Tall fellow, that Paul. His curly, wheat-colored hair brushed the canvas ceiling. He has sort of a long face, highlighted by low, thick eyebrows. He smiles a lot.

I guess I like him. Even if he is my parole officer.

I was working the Digger game. You've probably seen one at your local Kiwanis picnic. It's the little toy shovel that scoops up jackknives and Kewpie dolls. As carnival games go, it's the cleanest on the midway.

Why was I working there? Well, if you're a parent, where would you send your toddler? To the beetle-browed fellow who looks as if he just finished doing five to ten for armed robbery in Q? Of *course* not! You'd send your little darling to the Digger game, which is run by that lovely girl with the bright obsidian eyes, slim aquiline nose, and long, straight hair the color of a raven's wing. The one who looks twenty or twenty-one and who probably spent last night babysitting for the Andersons.

Anyway, there I was, holding a squirming three-year-old on my hip and helping him win a package of toy soldiers. And in comes Paul Holbrook, his face alert and expectant, with just a trace of harshness around that thin-lipped mouth. "Hello, Angie."

I gave my toddling customer's hand a gentle twist. The shovel spit his toy soldiers down the chute. After setting him down, I showed Paul my prettiest smile, a

5

nice spread of white orthodonture against copper brown skin. "Hello there, Mr. Holbrook. Did you have a nice drive down from *Peeeeee-aire?*"

"Knock it off, Angie." Paul's stern tone was almost affectionate. "You've been in South Dakota long enough to know we call it *Peer.*"

"Don't remind me!" I accepted a dollar bill from another youngster and shoved quarters into chocolate-stained hands. "How'd you track me down?"

"Wasn't hard. I know this state police sergeant. We were in the same platoon in Panama. He put the word out."

Aware of Paul's disapproving gaze, I hoisted the next three-year-old onto the stand. "I notice you didn't turn me in."

"No, I didn't." Paul tried to make himself heard over the prekindergarten clamor. "If I had, you'd be back in Springfield right now."

The word *Springfield* conjured up a host of unpleasant memories. Chainlink fences and electric bells. Laundry duty and bed checks. Smirking screws and ice-eyed lesbians. The memories seethed just beneath the surface of my mind, like mold blossoming in the darkness of an abandoned refrigerator.

My customer shrieked with delight as the shovel grabbed a miniature jackknife. Paul flinched at the noise. "I can't hear myself think in here. Can we go somewhere else and talk?"

My smile struggled against the bad memories. "Buy a lady a Pepsi?"

"You've got it. Just so we can be alone and hear ourselves speak."

I peeled back the canvas tent flap, spied our resident Fat Lady on her way to the cooktent, and asked her to spell me for a while. After handing over my change apron, I drew my silken black hair over my shoulders and followed Paul into the heat of the day.

It was one of those warm May days that offers a preview of summer. A prairie sky with more blue than the

6

New York Police Department. Cottonball clouds crowding the ridgeline of the Black Hills. A relentless hot breeze rattling tent flaps, parching the buffalo grass, and turning nearby Box Elder Creek into an alkali-rimmed ditch.

So we wandered through the midway, Paul and I. Tall, resolute Marine veteran turned Department of Corrections bureaucrat. A Panamanian grenade had ended Sergeant Holbrook's promising career in the Corps and had sent him back into civilian life with a fifty percent disability and veteran's preference.

And then there was yours truly—Angela Biwaban, good-looking, fun-loving, loyal, and true. Raven-haired lady casually clad in an aquamarine T-shirt and clingy white jogging shorts. Formerly the toast of the Lady Trojans, the championship volleyball team of Central High School in my old hometown of Duluth, Minnesota. And now, sad to say, a recent graduate of the South Dakota correctional facility at Springfield.

Screaming children and exhausted parents hurried past us. I was beginning to feel like a boulder in the middle of a spring freshet. Paul and I stopped at the popcorn wagon. A skinny kid in a white vendor's cap drew a pair of tall Pepsis for us. I saw Paul go for his wallet and put my hand on his wrist. "Keep your money. Employee discount." I grinned at the kid. "He's with me, Tommy."

We found a shady spot beside the animal wagons. Rajah, our Ferocious Eight-Hundred-Pound Bengal Tiger, lay on the scrubbed floor of his cage, tail flicking, watching me with bored, sleepy eyes.

Paul handed me a Pepsi. "I suppose you know what today is."

"May seventh, the last time I looked at a calendar."

"Does the date March the twenty-fifth ring a bell?"

My face tensed thoughtfully. I shook my head no.

"It was your last regularly scheduled appointment with me, Miss Biwaban!"

Uh-oh! I took a long sip and said nothing.

"You know the terms of your parole, Angie. Do I really have to read you the Department of Corrections rule book?"

"We can skip that part. I don't mind—"

"No, I think we'd better review them." Paul drummed his fingertips on the side of his paper cup. "First, you must report to your parole officer once a month—*in person!* Second, if you are unable to report, you *must telephone* your parole officer and reschedule your appointment. Third, if you change your address, you must—*without fail*—get in touch with your parole officer immediately." He shook his head in exasperation. "There are nine Indians in my caseload, Miss Biwaban. And, I swear, there isn't one of them who gives me half the headaches you do."

"Point of clarification, Paul," I said, raising my hand. "I am not an Indian. I am a Native American. Indians are people who wear turbans and live in places like Varanasi and Calcutta. They're very nice people, I'm sure, but I'm not one of them."

"My apologies. I forgot you were a full-blooded Chippewa princess."

"Paul, there is no such thing as a Chippewa. That's a nonsense word invented by white people who were too lazy to learn our language. Our name is Anishinabe, and it means people. Repeat after me. Ah-nish-ih-nah-bay . . ."

"All right, all right. Anishinabe princess. You made your point, Angie. You're not an Indian. Now, can we get back to business?"

Brushing the hair away from my eyelashes, I cast a doleful look around. "You know, sometimes I wish I was in Calcutta. Just for a change of pace. No offense, Paul, but there isn't a whole lot to this prairie state."

"Well, I'm afraid you're going to have to put those travel plans on hold, young lady. You have a sentence to complete."

"Pretty steep sentence, too. Five years for embezzlement."

"Your embezzlement was a little steep, too, as I recall. Three hundred grand."

My face warmed in indignation. "You know damned well why I took that money."

"For the trip to Hawaii?"

My open palm was halfway to Paul's cheek before I realized what I was doing. Trembling all over, I folded it into a white-knuckled fist and forced it back to my side. I couldn't afford the luxury of fury. Slapping one's parole officer is the express ticket back to the Big Dollhouse.

"Damn you!" Sudden welling of tears. "My mother was dying, Holbrook. What was I supposed to do . . . let her die?"

I left him standing beside the tiger cage and took refuge in the shade of a nearby cottonwood tree. There I sniffled and hiccupped and brushed away the tears. Mother's death, not Paul's tactless comment, was responsible for the sudden weep. She had passed away while I was still in prison, doing time for that embezzlement. I'd stolen the money from the Cameron Tax Assessor's office to pay for Mother's surgery.

Among our people, the bond between mothers and daughters is extremely strong. Mother and I were closer than most. I haven't gotten over losing her. Sometimes I don't think I ever will.

Just then, a pair of broad masculine hands gave my shoulders a brotherly rub, and Paul's voice whispered in my ear. "Sorry, Angie. That was hitting below the belt, wasn't it?" He let out an apologetic sigh. "Okay . . . so maybe I can understand how you felt. You were inside for over three years. That's a long time to be taking orders from correctional officers. You felt you had to assert your independence, and heading for the tall timber seemed like the best way to do that."

Paul sounded so sincere and so contrite that I couldn't stay mad at him. Sometimes he's like a big, graceless, energetic Saint Bernard puppy. Eyes shiny with tears, I turned to face him.

"Welcome to the nineties, Holbrook. These days, women are always asserting their independence—"

"All except those women who are still under the jurisdiction of the court!" he interrupted. "That's you, Angie. You seem to think that just because you're out of the slam, you're no longer accountable to the Department. That's not the way it works. You will remain under Department supervision until the day your parole ends."

"Did you come all the way out here to remind me of that?"

"No, I came all the way out here to find out what the hell your problem is. Look, Miss Biwaban, you have violated your parole up, down, and sideways. If it were anyone else but me handling this case, you'd be back inside right this very minute. I am way out of line on this. If old man Langston ever finds out I let a client go forty-five days without reporting, he'll have my ass!" Paul's slow, deliberate look made me feel like a little girl who had just pulped her favorite dolly in a tantrum. "Why'd you do it, Angie?"

I turned my back on him. "I'd rather not talk about it."

"I would. That's why I'm here." Paul finished his soft drink, crumpled the cup in his fist, and put it in the trash bin with a flawless hook shot. "Last time I talked to you, you were working waitress in Sioux Falls. What happened?"

"You don't want to know."

"Yes, I do. I got you that job."

Prairie breezes pushed strands of hair over my eyelashes. I peeled them away one at a time, showing Paul a small, hurtful look.

"I didn't like it, okay?"

"Not okay! I thought we discussed your need for positive work experience."

"That was *anything* but a positive experience! My feet were *killing* me! The cook was a bitch. The pay sucked. Nobody tips at a goddamned lunch counter, you know! You have to do your own bus work. You have to watch where you stick your ass because there's always some old

10

bastard who helps himself to a free feel. So I ran away and joined the carnival. End of story."

Paul shook his head slowly. "My sister worked waitress all the way through college, and it didn't leave *her* with any permanent scars."

"Gina didn't have to listen to that sour-faced old bitch yapping 'Pick up your feet, dear!' because she was a half second too slow in running to fetch the salad plate. Look, Paul, I had enough of that shit on the inside!"

"So you joined Finch Brothers when they played Sioux Falls."

"That's right."

"Doing what?"

By way of reply, I tilted my chin toward the row of sideshow posters just beyond the cooktent. One showed a garish painting of your Angie in a white deerskin minidress emblazoned with multicolored porcupine quills. Bold black letters proclaimed:

PRINCESS LILIONAH!

DEATH-DEFYING LEAP FOR LIFE!

FIVE HUNDRED FEET!

REENACTS AUTHENTIC SIOUX DRAMA!

I nudged him. "Looks just like me, don't you think?"

Paul blinked. "Five hundred *feet!?*"

I pointed out the slim highrise ladder between the Tilt-A-Whirl and the Skyrocket. "It's not really five hundred feet. More like eighty or ninety, I think. There are five hundred rungs in the ladder. Jack Finch encourages the skeptical to count them." Catching his astounded glare, I added, "It's perfectly safe, Paul. All I do is climb the ladder, sing a Lakota war chant, and backflip onto a mattress the size of a ranch house."

"Angie, I don't think this is the appropriate work experience for you."

"Yeah?" I struck a pose, pretending to be writing something on an invisible notepad. "Well, I like it a whole lot better than standing behind a stupid lunch counter all day. Feeling my feet swell up and muttering 'Whattaya *have?*' to a bunch of old men!"

Paul's disapproving gaze circled the midway. "I think you'd better come back to Pierre with me."

I kept my tone light. *"What!? And give up show biz!?"*

"I mean it. You're still on parole, Angela. And if you'll read the fine print, you'll notice a clause about consorting with other convicted felons."

"That's it, Holbrook. Be a pluperfect *shit!*"

"Will you please try to look at this sensibly?" Paul had adopted his counselor's voice—even and well modulated, brimming with fatherly wisdom. "You're not the only one here with a record. What's going to happen if one of your fellow carnies pulls a job and the sheriff finds you here? You don't even have to get arrested. If Langston finds out you're here, you'll be on your merry way right back to Springfield . . ."

I let him go on and on. I was wearing what Becky Reardon used to call my fussbudget face. Eyes narrowed angrily. Two vertical ridges just above the bridge of my nose. Tightly compressed lips. And a gaze looking rigidly to the left.

That's when I saw her.

She was a face in the crowd at the merry-go-round, a fleeting glimpse of lovely profile and cotton kerchief. The curling chestnut hair was shorter than I remembered. There were deep worry lines beside the soft, sad mouth. They hadn't been there the last time I'd seen her, a decade ago. But there was no mistaking that pert nose and imperial chin.

"Mary Beth . . . ," I mumbled out loud.

"Angie!" Fatherly wisdom retreated before Paul's sudden wave of irritation. "You haven't been listening to a word I've said."

I had to get rid of him.

"Yes, I have, Paul, and you're absolutely right." Hooking my arm around his, I steered him into the parking lot. "From now on, I'm going to follow the rules religiously. Starting with rule number two."

12

"Rule number two?"

"Yeah! I want to reschedule my appointment."

*"What!?"*

"Can we please continue this discussion tomorrow?" I kept my smile demure, humble, and contrite. "I have something to do, Paul. It's very important."

"Right now, complying with the Department's rules and regulations is the most important thing in your life, Miss Biwaban."

"Don't *do* that, Paul. You sound like one of those goddamned *screws!*"

"Correctional officers," he reprimanded, then sighed heavily. "All right. I'll bite. What is so important that you can't talk to me right now?"

"I have to get ready for the show." It was an easy lie. The ones based on truth always are. "I do three a night—six, eight, and ten P.M. I've got to get started on my limbering-up exercises."

"Angela . . ." he replied patiently. "You shouldn't even be working here. You know that, don't you?"

"Paaauuuuul!" My sweeping gesture took in most of the midway. "I just can't walk out on everybody, now can I? The Finch Brothers are depending on me. Look, all I'm asking for is a twenty-four-hour delay, okay? Come back at noon tomorrow, and I'll meet you right at this spot. You can yell at me to your heart's content."

Paul's expression turned thoughtful. I caught a fleeting expression of sympathy, like a solo cloud crossing Lake Superior, and I knew I had him. Like I said, Paul Holbrook is basically a nice guy. You can't say the same for his boss, Mr. Langston, though.

"Oh, all right." Paul gave me a no-nonsense look. "I'll be back at noon tomorrow. We'll go picnic at Bear Butte. You and I have a lot to discuss, young lady."

"Thank you, Paul."

I waited until Paul was well into the dusty pasture that served as our carnival parking lot. Then I double-timed it back to the merry-go-round. My gaze zigzagged through the crowd, dodging baseball caps and Shady

13

Brady cowboy hats, seeking the lilac kerchief I'd seen earlier.

And there it was, covering a wedge of chestnut brown hair and hovering over a sweat-stained, shortsleeved oxford cloth blouse and pale blue summer-weight slacks. I trotted up behind her. "Mary Beth!"

She turned and gasped. Familiar hazel eyes moistened.

And then it was no longer a searing May Thursday at a second-rate carnival in Medicine Tail, South Dakota. It was Labor Day again in my hometown of Duluth, with best friends Angela Biwaban and Mary Beth McCann rushing forward and laughing and hugging each other after the long summer apart.

Mary Beth and I first met in junior high. Seventh grade! She was from Duluth Heights, and her parents were quite a bit older than mine. Her father managed a ski lodge at Spirit Mountain during the cold weather months. Every summer, he took Mary Beth to Tilford, a town on Michigan's upper peninsula, where he owned a goodly piece of lakefront property on that pocket ocean my ancestors called Kitchi Gammi. I spent my girlish summers on Kitchi's north shore, at my grandfather's cabin up at Tettegouche.

I was born on the Fond du Lac Indian Reservation but grew up in Duluth, also known as the Zenith City of the Unsalted Seas. My mother's family hails from Ginonwabiko-zibi. That's the Split Rock River country, to those of you not conversant in Anishinabemowin, which is just west of Beaver Bay, Minnesota. Dad's family, the Biwabans, were living on Duluth's sandspit peninsula of Park Point when Daniel Greysolon, Sieur du Lhut, first beached his canoe there back in 1679.

Anyway, Mary Beth came into my life at just the right moment. My father had been killed a few months earlier in an accident at the taconite docks, where he was employed as a foreman. I was having a lot of trouble adjusting to junior high school. I really needed a friend. And Mary Beth McCann fitted the bill perfectly. She became

14

the sister I never had. The two of us were inseparable. We kept Northwest Bell in the black with innumerable after-school phone calls. We did the sleepover bit, alternating Saturday nights between her parents' house in the Heights and my mother's place on Park Point.

And yes, Mary Beth was there the day I made a complete bonehead of myself in junior high. The day I spilled cranberry juice all over my white jeans and sneaked out of school to get them cleaned at a nearby laundromat. Mary Beth covered for me that day. And on many occasions at Central High, as well.

These, and other, equally embarrassing memories, zipped through my mind as I embraced Mary Beth. Tears of happiness blurred my vision, and I laughed as if I had never left junior high.

Holding Mary Beth at arm's length, however, I found that I could not sustain the wonderful illusion of an adolescent Labor Day back home in Duluth. Worry lines bracketed her tense mouth. Her chestnut hair seemed limp and lifeless. There was a haunted, defeated expression in her eyes, a noticeable droop in the set of her shoulders. I could nor reconcile this cowed stance with my memory of the best backfield player in the Lady Trojans. I had to keep reminding myself that Mary Beth was only twenty-eight years old.

My gaze found the slender golden band on her left hand, then traveled up to Mary Beth's sad, tired face and down to the pronounced bulge that was pressing the front of her oxford cloth blouse. Her right hand rested protectively on it.

That I hadn't expected. The sight knocked open my mouth and emptied the tact from my brain. "You're *pregnant!*"

"Yes, Angie." Her mouth tensed several times. She looked as if she wanted to cry but was determined not to.

Myself, I was still groping with the reality of that swollen belly. Don't ask me why it hit me like that. After all, we were both ten years out of high school, and this is supposed to be the peak childbearing period. Still, this

15

was Mary Beth McCann, childhood chum and telephone confidante. Not too long ago, we'd been seated in
the rear of Mrs. McArdle's homeroom, giggling and
whispering about boys. It didn't seem, well, possible
that Mary Beth could be expecting. But there she was, a
good six or seven months along. Rotund reality in the
dry plains of South Dakota.

"What are you doing here?" I asked, squeezing her
hands in mine. "Where's your husband? I'd love to meet
him. I'd—"

I saw Mary Beth's eyes flicker with unquenchable
hurt. Lowering her head, she murmured, "He's dead,
Angie. They—they killed him."

Then her mouth twisted, and the first heartrending
sobs began.

I caught Mary Beth as she toppled forward, very
deftly put myself under her shoulder, and trundled her
off to the parking lot. Her soft, heavy body trembled
with each snuffling gasp. Once in a while, I felt the baby
kick.

At ease, Junior. Mommy's in good hands. Don't
worry.

I noticed something else, too. At that range, the scent
was unmistakable. Mary Beth had been in those clothes
for a couple of days.

Bracing her against my shoulder, I levered open the
passenger door of my mechanical steed, a 1969 Mercury
Montego affectionately known as Clunky. Tenderly I
eased Mary Beth onto the seat. She made no resistance,
weeping in that heartbreaking, keening, spiritless way,
surrendering herself to whatever dismal fate chose to
claim her.

I got behind the driver's wheel, feeling a queasy blend
of surprise, sadness and dismay. The Mary Beth Mc-
Cann I'd known was no more. In the place of my girl-
hood chum sat a weary pregnant woman whose
desperate sobbing chilled the walls of my heart.

Time enough for questions later. The first order of
business was getting Mary Beth away from the gawking

eyes of the fairgoers. What my old friend needed was quiet, good food, deep slumber, a hot bath and a competent laundry service. In that order.

I turned the ignition key. Clunky's three-hundred-and-fifty-one-cubic-inch engine rumbled to life. Eight cylinders roared at me for disturbing their rest.

In time I would learn what had brought Mary Beth McCann to my South Dakota carnival and why she had wept such bitter tears and what had happened to the young husband. But that could wait.

As I drove off the lot, I thought I could make an educated guess. Sometime between our graduation from Central High and her visit to my carnival, Mary Beth's life had gone totally, irrevocably wrong.

Believe me, Angela Biwaban knew all about that!

# Chapter Two

The motel I was staying at was called the Lariat. It was on the outskirts of Medicine Tail — six stucco cabins strung out behind a roadside central office. With a wonderful view of the Piedmont Valley, which resembled a glacier of buffalo grass snaking its way toward Sturgis. Not to mention the occasional rimrocked bluffs speckled with Ponderosa pine.

I'll say one good thing about the Lariat. It had a quiet little restaurant and bar. The Chuckwagon Room. After shepherding Mary Beth through a hot shower and a change of clothes, I installed her in an old-timey cedar booth and ordered lunch for us both.

To be perfectly frank, it felt strange doing this for Mary Beth. Back home in Duluth, it had usually been the other way around. I've only been in love once or twice in my life, but I've had lots and lots of crushes. Most of them ended with me flopped facedown on the bed, soaking my pillow with tears. Whenever I had my heart broken, it was always Mary Beth, my surrogate sister, who brought me out of it. She'd sit beside me on the bed, squeeze my hand, stroke my shoulder, hand me a fresh box of tissues and assure me that the object of my desire was a complete and utter fool for not wanting me. She never failed to assure me that there were millions of other, equally desirable men in the world.

So now it was my turn to play morale builder, and I

18

gave it my best shot. True to the traditions of Anishinabe hospitality, I pronounced her my luncheon guest and summoned the waitress to take Mary Beth's order.

Twenty minutes afterward, I finished my buffalo burger and daintily sipped Lowenbrau, watching with mild surprise as my childhood friend consumed a salad, sourdough rolls, french fries, black-eyed peas, a Cattleman's Choice medium-rare steak, and two tall glasses of milk. Over her protests, I ordered her a dish of chocolate ice cream. That, too, disappeared in a matter of moments.

"So how many days has it been since you've last eaten?" I asked, resting my chin on my fist.

Looking a little embarrassed, Mary Beth pushed the empty dish away. "Four. No . . . three, I guess. Miss Martinez at the County Aid bought me lunch the day I went there."

I studied her over the rim of my beer stein. "You want to tell me about it?"

She locked her fingers, sighed, laid her forehead against upraised knuckles. "Angie, thank you for the meal. I — I don't want to sound ungrateful, but . . . I don't want to be a burden."

"I believe it, McCann." The stein made a thumping sound as I replaced it on the hardwood table. "That stiff-necked Irish pride wouldn't let you. But you've got more than your precious pride to think about. You've got a little tenant downstairs, and he or she needs to eat every day. Even if Mommy's stubborn enough to think she can do without."

A faint smile touched Mary Beth's lips. "He. I had the ultrasound back in Tilford."

I was supposed to smile at that but didn't. Instead, I flashed my Paul Holbrook frown of concern. "So how come you're not eating lunch these days?"

Mary Beth lowered her gaze. I could see how distressing this situation was for her. Mary Beth was her father's daughter. And from what I remember of Brian Mc-

19

Cann, he had enough ego for two Hollywood screen-writers and all the politicians in Wisconsin.

"I don't have any money, Angie. I—I ran out a week ago. Linda Martinez at the County Aid told me I'd probably qualify for WIC and AFDC. But there was a problem. All my papers . . . you know, birth certificate, Social Security card, like that . . . they were all back home in Duluth. Linda tried to get me emergency food from the Child Welfare Board. Only they're down in Rapid City, and I don't even have a *car!*"

Her mouth began to tremble. Reaching across the table, I smoothed my palm up and down her sleeve. "Hold it, McCann. Before we go any further, I think you'd better start at the beginning, okay? How did you get out here, anyway? Last I heard, you were living in Michigan."

And on that note, Mary Beth began her story.

Well, I was wrong about the last name. It wasn't Mc-Cann anymore. It was Tolliver . . . as in Mr. and Mrs. James P. Tolliver.

The last time I had seen Mary Beth was our graduation party on Park Point. I have vague memories of myself and Mary Beth, mortarboards askew on our heads, still boozy from the previous night's excesses, stumbling around in the brown sands, singing "Goodbye, Central!" with off-key enthusiasm, and doing our famous lampoon of the Rockettes.

After that, we went our separate ways. I, to Grand Marais and a summer job as a guide on the Gunflint Trail. Mary Beth, to Mackinac Island, in another great lake, where she doled out ice cream at a Dairy Queen and shared an attic loft with two other college-bound girls.

Mary Beth went to the University of Michigan with the idea of becoming a biology teacher. She changed her major twice. By the time graduation rolled around, she was majoring in dental health and was engaged to a nice

20

boy from Wisconsin. The career choice lasted—the engagement didn't. Mary Beth landed a job as a dental assistant in Traverse City and spent the next few years picking and flossing and scaling. Then, one autumn day, a tall marine engineer with an impacted wisdom tooth walked into her clinic. His name was Jim Tolliver, and he handled the harbor's dredging operations for the local office of the U.S. Army Corps of Engineers. The dentist's chairside manner left Jim cold. But he certainly was impressed by the dentist's pretty, chestnut-haired assistant. And a bonding of another sort took place.

In case you're wondering—yes, Mary Beth got in touch and asked me to be in the wedding party. By then, however, I was majoring in laundry and floor scrubbing at the South Dakota women's prison and was thus unable to attend.

The Corps transferred Jim, and he and Mary Beth set up housekeeping in Sault Sainte Marie. Six months afterward, Mary Beth's father retired and decided to put all his money into the development of his vacation property in nearby Tilford.

Jim was very much interested in his father-in-law's scheme. The two of them spent endless hours discussing plans for the property. They wanted to sink a few pilings behind Foxtail Point, put up a year-round boathouse, build a luxury motor inn with a twenty-berth marina.

Unfortunately, Brian McCann never lived to see his dream fulfilled. He died in an accident on the wharf the following March. Mary Beth moved down to Tilford to look after her elderly, grief-stricken mother. However, with her husband gone, the heart seemed to go right out of Margaret McCann. She passed away in her sleep about four months later.

That summer, Mary Beth and Jim made up their minds to finish her father's project. As the executrix of both estates, Mary Beth sold her parents' ski lodge and home in Duluth, put her own house in the Soo up for sale, and incorporated herself and Jim as the McCann and Tolliver Construction Company.

Actually, it was Jim who was the driving force behind McCann & Tolliver. He wanted to make the Tilford site as profitable as he could, build the marina and the resort, and then sell out to a firm like Best Western. With the money from the sale, Jim intended to buy a couple of ships and go into marine construction in a big way.

Mary Beth was definitely in favor of her husband's plan. She thought the finished resort would be a sort of monument to her father. As soon as their Soo house sold, they went shopping for a line of credit and presented their construction blueprints to the Finlayson County Planning Board. In no time at all, they had a pile driver anchored out there behind Foxtail Point, pushing those forged steel rods down into the bedrock.

"Then what happened?" I asked.

Mary Beth's face tightened with long-remembered anger. "A man came to see us — Jerry Carmody. A short guy, snappy dresser, going a little thin on top." She smiled acidly as if the memory of his baldness gave her pleasure. "He told us he was the vice president of Lakeside Development Corporation, Inc. He'd heard about our permit and had come out to have a look for himself. He was full of praise, Angie. Oh, you kids deserve credit for putting this thing together. First-class job on those specifications, too. You'll be as popular as all hell with the county, bringing in all those new jobs. And that's how he worked up to it, Angie. He kept telling us what a big job it was. Too big, really, for a couple of kids from the Soo. It was the kind of job an established company could handle best. By the time we finished coffee, Carmody got to the bottom line. Lakeside Development liked the marina idea and wanted to buy it all — Jim's blueprints, the existing contracts, title to all six parcels, everything."

"Did he quote a price?"

"Uh-huh. Two-point-two million dollars. A one-time offer only. Take it or leave it."

"And you left it."

"Damned right! Jim told Carmody that the completed project would be worth six times that much. Even at current real estate prices, my father's holdings would net, separately or together, a minimum of three-point-five million in the Tilford real estate market." I detected a note of pride in her voice. "My husband did his homework."

Naturally, Jim and Mary Beth hadn't seen the last of Jerry Carmody. He had visited their construction site again, uttering all sorts of dire warnings about environmentalist protestors. And, like Cassandra at the siege of Troy, the awful prediction came true. An environmentalist group from Washington persuaded a federal judge to issue an injunction against McCann & Tolliver. Mary Beth appealed at the federal district court in Traverse City and got the injunction lifted. But by then it was October, and further construction would have to wait until after the spring melt.

"Did you ever see your friend Carmody again?"

"Yes." Mary Beth's voice was barely audible. "He showed up at the house one day while Jim was at work. I stayed in the kitchen, gave him a cup of coffee, pretended I was busy as hell. I hoped he would take the hint and leave, but he didn't. He talked to me like a Dutch uncle. 'It's a great project, Mary Beth, but too many things can go wrong with it. Why do you think nobody ever bothered with it before? We can handle that sort of risk. It's too much for you and Jim. Now Jim's a mule-headed boy, and he's got too much of himself tied up in this thing. He can't see the pitfalls, but you can. A smart woman, Mary Beth, knows how to make her man do the right thing. You talk to him, honey. Show him those pitfalls.' "

"Must have been a memorable visit," I commented. "It sounds as if you memorized Carmody's speech word for word."

"It *was* a memorable visit, right up to the moment I leaned over . . ." Her voice dwindled. An expression of complete humiliation swept across her face. My loathing of Jerry Carmody was on the ascendant.

Touching her forearm, I murmured, "What did he do to you?"

"He—He tried to rape me." Mary Beth bit her lower lip. "When I leaned over, I—I felt something odd. I looked down, and there was my breast in his upturned hand. He showed me this jolly little smile. Said we were going to be real good f-friends. I couldn't believe this was happening to me. And in my own kitchen, too!"

"What did *you* do?"

"I told him no! He backed me up against the counter, smiling all the while. He kept joking about it, telling me how much fun it was to get taken at the kitchen counter. I thought I was going to throw up. Then my hand closed around the paring knife. I took a full-armed swing at him. He jumped back like a scalded cat. But not quick enough. My blade caught him right on the tip of the nose. Nicked him good."

I flashed a small grin. "Mary Beth the killer."

Her bleak expression vaporized my smile. "I wish I had killed him, Angie. If I'd known what was going to happen, I would have."

Taking her hands in mine, I whispered, "Listen, if you don't want to talk about this, we can go back to the cabin."

"N-No, I—I want to tell it." Tears glistened on her lashes. "It was like a nightmare, Angie. I ran to the phone and dialed 911. Carmody wiped his nose on a dish towel. Then he glared at me and said, 'You just bought the whole package, cupcake. You and lover boy won't be left with a dime. Next time I see you, you're going to be selling your ass at the Chain & Anchor. And on that happy day, I'm going to hand over a hundred bucks and do anything to you I fucking please!' I—I screamed at him to get out. The police dispatcher came on line. I begged them to send a patrol car. That's when Carmody left."

My gaze was cold and steady. "Cops do anything?"

"No!" The memory turned her mouth bitter. "After I mentioned Carmody's name, they backed off. It was as if they were just going through the motions."

"What did Jim do?"

"He wanted to go down to the Lakeside office and pound Carmody's face into pulp. I talked him out of it. I filed a formal complaint at the courthouse, but nothing came of it. Finally, Jim buttonholed Sheriff Hendricks, and the sheriff told him that Carmody had an airtight alibi. Apparently, he'd been in Congressman Burdick's office all that morning."

"Sounds like a very tight power structure down there. And they don't seem to care that Carmody's a Grade-A sleazoid." I ran my thumb around the rim of the stein, wondering how many other Tilford women had been unwilling participants in Jerry's kitchen games. Banishing that depressing thought, I said, "So how did it happen, Mary Beth? How did you lose all your money?"

During the next half hour, Mary Beth told me how the local establishment had greased the skids under McCann & Tolliver. A man named Sherman popped out of the wilds of Wyoming and challenged their quitclaim deed to one of their shoreside properties. As a result of that, the bank canceled their line of credit. Fearful of not being paid, their subcontractors began to file lawsuits. Then their lawyer called and announced he was dropping the case. The environmentalists had just charged Jim and Mary Beth with causing "permanent damage" to the littoral areas of Foxtail Point. The lawyer had four words of parting advice — sell out and scram!

Jim Tolliver, however, refused to quit. He hired a new lawyer, a very sharp young attorney named Andrew Capobianco, whom they'd met at the Soo's Stony Ridge Country Club. This proved to be a shot in the arm for Jim. He got a lot of his old verve back. Mary Beth had a feeling that her husband and Capobianco were cooking up something. But, for the first time in her marriage, Jim didn't confide in her.

"He used to come home from those Saturday conferences with a determined gleam in his eye," Mary Beth recalled. "He told me that he'd asked Andy to file a sub-division plan for the McCann properties. He said this was the only way out. Cut up my father's farm into lots, put up some nice gambrel homes, rake in the money, pay off our debts, and toddle back to Duluth." She gingerly stroked her forehead. "I don't know, Angie. I simply didn't believe him. That was as good as admitting defeat. Jim was up to something. I—I only wish he'd told me what it was." Her eyes closed painfully. "The n-night he d-died, it was snowing. The telephone rang. Jim got to it first. He—He never told me who it was. After he hung up, he said he had to go out. I pleaded with him to wait until morning, but he was too excited. He said, 'I've got you now, you bastard!' Then he pulled on his winter coat and rushed out."

I signaled the waitress. She wrote up the check and left it facedown beside my empty beer stein.

"I—I lay awake all night, waiting for Jim to come home. Just before dawn, I saw a red light flashing on my bedroom wallpaper. Knuckles hammered the front door. I found two state troopers out there. One asked if I was Mrs. Tolliver. I said yes. Then they both turned very solemn. The other one told me that . . . J-Jim was d-dead."

She uttered a sudden keening gasp but somehow managed to keep her composure. I thought I detected a leavening of fury in her grief, as if other angry memories were chipping away at that anguished scene of her husband's death.

"The troopers drove me to the morgue. Jim was . . . his face . . . his head . . . the whole left side! I—I turned away . . . oh, Jesus! I—I couldn't look at him, Angie. I—I *couldn't!*"

"It's all right, Mary Beth. It's all right," I crooned, my palm smoothing her forearm. I watched as she teetered on the brink of hysteria and pondered bringing this impromptu inquest to a close. But somehow she found the strength to go on.

"I—I asked the troopers how it happened. They told

me Jim's car was found by the side of the road. The engine was off. There was a Styrofoam cup on the floor. It was empty. I — I guess Jim stopped somewhere for a hot chocolate. Something to keep him warm while he waited. He liked hot chocolate." Her voice grew slightly shriller. "The window. Driver's side. Shattered, they said. There was blood on the rest . . . he was holding a gun . . . he —" Gritted teeth gave her a feral look. "They said he shot himself!"

"Take it easy, Mary Beth."

She stared at me in disbelief. "I told him he was crazy. Jim couldn't have . . . he wouldn't . . . he didn't even have a gun! Somebody else must have done it. I tried to tell them, but they wouldn't believe me."

"What did your friend the sheriff have to say?"

"I drove straight over to his house. I stood there on that snow-covered lawn and hollered, 'They killed my husband, Dave Hendricks! What are you going to do about it?' I'll tell you what he did. Our brave Sheriff Hendricks — he put *me* in the hospital. He bundled me into the cruiser and took me to Shea Memorial and had a doctor give me a shot. Calm me down, he said. I was in there three days. When they finally released me, Sheriff Dave was waiting for me in the lobby. He kept trying to convince me it was suicide. I told him Jim didn't even own a gun. He said it was a .22 caliber revolver. Serial numbers filed off. Could have picked it up at a pawnshop anywhere in Michigan. He said Jim was depressed because of all our money troubles. Took the easy way out. I told that man he was crazy. My husband would never kill himself, not with our baby on the way."

"Is that the last time you saw the sheriff?" I prodded.

She shook her head briskly. "I saw him again — the day he came to fetch me." Teardrops meandered down the curve of her face. "You see, the money simply evaporated after that. I had to sell Daddy's other holding for whatever I could get. All except our family farm, and I owed on that like you wouldn't believe."

27

"Back up a minute, Mary Beth. What do you mean — the money *evaporated?*"

"Jim and I borrowed heavily to get McCann & Tolliver Construction off the ground," she explained. "Loans for the construction work off Foxtail Point. Mr. Jaswell at the bank was so understanding. He said we had so much real-estate as collateral, there'd be no problem in lending us the money. Then, after Jim died, I got this letter from the bank. They were executing what Mr. Jaswell called a codicil in the loan instrument. Since there was little chance of the project ever being completed, the bank insisted upon the immediate repayment of forty percent of the face value of the loan. Then the other creditors got after me, too. I — I put McCann & Tolliver through the Chapter Eleven process, sold off the other five farms, and was forced to put the money into an escrow account. The creditors gobbled it up. I had a couple of thousand left to start over. I — I tried to make it last, but — but it was no use. By April, I was sitting in that farmhouse with no running water, no electricity, and no heat except for the wood stove." Her voice became a soft, shrill murmur. "But that wasn't the worst of it, Angie. Everybody in Tilford turned their backs on me. I'd go to the supermarket, and the checkout girls would whisper about me. I even overheard someone saying I *drove* my husband to suicide!"

Shaking all over at that vile memory, Mary Beth studied me with haunted eyes. "Sheriff Dave came out to the farm one afternoon. He seemed terribly upset about the way I was living. He asked if I had any people to go to. I told him about Jim's mother out in Oregon. Then he made me pack my bags and drove me over to the bus terminal in Newberry. He bought me a ticket to Minneapolis. Said I could catch a westbound Greyhound from there."

"Did you reach your mother-in-law?"

Mary Beth's shoulders slumped, as if bending beneath an invisible weight. She gave me a slow-motion nod. "E-Edith didn't want to talk to me. I — I guess she

28

blames me for J-Jim's death. I couldn't deal with that, Angie. I just couldn't! So I started drifting—"

"Enough." I helped her to her feet. "You don't have to tell me any more. Not right now."

After paying at the counter, I ushered Mary Beth out the door, her child-heavy body swaying from side to side. The parking lot was filling rapidly with the happy-hour crowd. Off-duty cowhands stopped to stare at the sniffling, sad-faced pregnant lady and the scowling Anishinabe princess.

One hand rummaged in my shoulder bag for the cabin key. "You need to lie down for a while, Mary Beth. Take a nap."

"Angie, I hate to impose on you."

"For Christ's sake, McCann, you're not imposing. You're my guest." A deft turn of the key unlocked the door. Pushing it open with my moccasin, I walked Mary Beth inside. "Now, do as you're told and get some rest."

Soon, despite her feeble protests, I had Mary Beth tucked into bed. Her quiet sobbing had a strange lingering echo quality. The sound seemed to follow me all around the cabin. It was loudest while I was in the bathroom, showering and washing my hair and getting dressed for the evening show.

When I emerged, Mary Beth was dozing. I told her I would be back after midnight. She mumbled sleepy words of assent. I looked back at her as I flicked off the light. Stringy chestnut hair on the immaculate pillow. Heavy tummy ballooning the sheet. Pregnant, penniless, and exhausted—that's my surrogate sister, Mary Beth.

So what to do now, Miss Biwaban? I asked myself, steering Clunky down the two-lane blacktop of South Dakota 382. Ahead, the Finch Brothers' ferris wheel peeped over a line of cottonwoods.

That's easily answered. Carnival entertainers cannot adopt pregnant women, even if they want to. On fifty percent of the Digger game's daily take, I was hard-pressed to handle the motel, gasoline, and food expenses for myself.

No, the most obvious and sensible course of action was to drive Mary Beth down to Rapid City and leave her in the capable hands of the state human services people. They would find a women's shelter for her, and a competent case-aid counselor would help her put her life together after the baby's birth.

So do it, Angie. Drive her down to Rapid City. Give her a hug and kiss her cheek and tell her to send you a postcard as soon as the baby's born. Send it in care of Finch Brothers' Carnival.

Scratch that! Better make it General Delivery, Pierre, South Dakota 5705. If Paul Holbrook had his way, your Angie would soon be living in the shadow of the Department of Corrections building . . . where he could keep an eye on me.

Yet, while I ran that mature, logical course of action through my mind, I could feel ancient genes stirring. I had a sudden crazy desire to paint three red stripes on my cheeks, to go shopping for a Bowie knife at Sears, to take a long, leisurely drive to upper Michigan.

I had a very satisfying vision of myself seated in front of a birchbark *waginogan,* artfully dressing three fresh scalps. Little nametags on each scalp. Jerry Carmody. Congressman Burdick. Sheriff Hendricks.

Oh, well, you can take Angela off the Fond du Lac reservation, but she is Anishinabe — first, last, and always!

Cool it, I told myself. That kind of thinking can get you in trouble. Do you really want to go back to Springfield for the full tour? Three more years of hefting laundry baskets and scrubbing cottage floors? Uh-uh, no way! I'd had more than enough of jailhouse grief.

Sure, Mary Beth had had a rough time of it. She'd buried her husband and her parents, all within the space of a year. Carmody and his pals had plucked her clean and run her out of Tilford.

So what? Life is tough all over. Angie Biwaban wasn't

30

exactly swishing her skirts and running barefoot through a field of daisies while Mary Beth was being shafted.

Without meaning to, I found myself comparing our respective life experiences of the past four years. Somehow, no matter how I presented the evidence, poor Angie just didn't seem to measure up.

So where were you, Miss Biwaban, while your surrogate sister was struggling to keep her sanity?

Oh, nothing to write home about, Your Honor. I graduated from Utah State University with a degree in business. Then I spent a year up in Bozeman, Montana, attending grad school by day and working nights and weekends at Lodgepole Realty. Shortly after earning my Master's from Montana State University, I took a job as an accounts receivable clerk at the Tax Assessor's office in Cameron, South Dakota.

At first I thought I had gotten in on the strength of my Master's and my 3.4 cume. Come to find out, the only reason they hired me was because the town was embroiled in an Affirmative Action hassle with Uncle Sam. By hiring me, they were getting a *minority* and a *female* in one size-six linen suit.

If it hadn't been for Councilman William H. Shattuck, I suppose I might still be in Cameron. Shattuck had a thing for Native American women. He always managed to drop in whenever I was at the filing cabinet. He had his own jolly little greeting for me. First the hearty "How's it shaking, Angela?" Then the spirited fanny whack or the discreet squeeze or the intimate pat. Once in a while, whenever his wife made him sleep on the couch, there was a whispered invitation to a fun weekend in Denver.

Yes, I realize that Mr. Shattuck's boorishness is no excuse for embezzling three hundred thousand dollars from the taxpayers of Cameron. But I needed the money. I needed it desperately and I needed it fast. When I was fifteen years old, my mother underwent an operation for cervical cancer. They thought they had gotten it all, but a few malignant cells had spent the ensuing nine years incubating in Mother's ventricular system. There was a new growth on her brain stem. Good neurosurgeons don't come cheap, and Mother's health insurance had expired when she was forced to give up her teaching job.

I could be very noble about it, I suppose, and tell you that I gladly donated three years of my life to the Big Dollhouse so my mother could enjoy an extra three years on this earth. But that's only partly true. I began embezzling for altruistic reasons and kept it up for totally selfish ones. You see, I enjoyed running my little scam under the noses of the Town Council. The unremitting jeopardy of my daily life, the ever-present danger of apprehension — they made the whole situation unbearably sweet. The thought that every time Big Bill Shattuck slapped me on the rear end it was costing the town three thousand dollars brightened my workday immeasurably.

So let's have some honesty here, okay? The truth of the matter is — after I saved my mother's life, I spent just about a year pampering myself with the hard-earned dollars of Mr. Shattuck's constituents. Then I got caught, and the state Department of Corrections took it upon themselves to unpamper me.

Had I been a good girl, I might have been out of Springfield in twenty months. Unfortunately, I was not a good girl. I was *difficult*, to use Miss Carlotta's lovely phrase. And so I spent an additional sixteen months at Miss Carlotta's School for Girls. That's one of the names we called the disciplinary unit out in Billsburg.

You see, when a woman misbehaves in South Dakota, they send her to Springfield. When she misbehaves at Springfield, they hand her over to Miss Carlotta.

I tried to adjust. Honest I did. I steeled myself to do the time . . . convinced myself that I could do it . . . and I believed that, I really did, up to the minute that cottage door slammed shut behind me.

The Department of Corrections does its best to ensure that every female inmate has the exact same unpleasant experience. They have a sign in the Springfield intake office. WE DON'T PROMISE YOU A ROSE GARDEN. And they don't deliver one, either!

So I tallied up the separate experiences of Mary Beth Tolliver and Angela Biwaban. If not for Mother's illness, Angie's woes would have had a slightly juvenile flavor. Male chauvinist fanny whacks avenged by clever embezzlement. Robin Hood in a miniskirt. A tasteless schoolgirl prank that ended in a well-deserved detention.

You can't say that about Mrs. Tolliver, though. There we see the grown-up woman dealing with the very real and pressing problems of life. Coming to terms with the death of parents. Coping with the end of the cherished dream of success. Burying the dead spouse.

And I had wondered why Mary Beth had looked so much older than me.

At that instant, I felt as if Mary Beth and I had somehow reversed roles. That she was the one looking after me. Tired, pregnant, chestnut-haired mama and impulsive, rebellious, raven-tressed adolescent. Behave yourself at the carnival, Angie. Mother's going to have a nap now.

So what do you do when your surrogate sister turns up on your doorstep with her husband possibly murdered and her possessions stolen by a pack of two-legged jackals?

Well, if you're a full-blooded Anishinabe, you track the bastard down, circle him four times in silence, and then shove your trusty blade into the depths of his putrid heart.

But we don't live under Anishinabe law. More's the pity, since we all know who originally owned this continent. No, we live under a system which loudly proclaims eternal fealty to the ideals of equality and justice and yet permits predators like Jerry Carmody, vermin armored by money and political influence, to grease

33

a young woman's slide into the ranks of the homeless.

Well, no one can say Angie's not adaptable. If this is the system I have to work within, so be it. I'm going to introduce my own brand of Anishinabe justice into the tangled skein of Tilford, Michigan. One way or another, my surrogate sister would be avenged.

Ah, but first there was Paul Holbrook to contend with.

# Chapter Three

"You want a *what!?*"

Paul's shout sent a pair of goshawks cartwheeling into the sky. I flinched a little myself. I didn't think he had the wind for it, not after that forty-four-hundred-foot hike up Bear Butte.

We were at the summit, Paul and I, standing on a wooden observation platform which the midday Dakota sun had turned into a solar-powered griddle. I endured it for all of fifty seconds, then ducked into the shade of the nearest ponderosa.

Paul's stern gaze raked me from headband to Reeboks. *"Angela!"*

Time to change the subject. Gesturing at an outcrop of limestone, I remarked, "Paul, did you know that Bear Butte is an old laccolith? That's a volcano that never got around to erupting. Of course, we Native Americans believe that it's a giant spirit bear. The same bear that clawed up Devil's Tower in Wyoming . . ."

"ANGELA!"

I shut up. Paul's face was the color of new brick. His chest was heaving. A dark V-shaped stain traveled down his Marine Corps T-shirt from collarbone to belly. He smelled like the locker room at Camp Lejeune.

"Really, Paul, there's no need to shout."

Hot sunshine seeped onto my shoulders. I moved deeper into the shade, parking the seat of my bike pants on a wooden railing. His scowl grew ever more impatient with each passing second.

"I want to make sure I heard you correctly. You want a *what!?*"

"A furlough," I answered. "I have to be excused from parole temporarily. I've got to go to Duluth."

"What for?"

"It's personal." I lifted the weight of my wringing-wet hair, then let it fall, rustling against my sweat-damp scoop top.

Paul stood his ground. "That's not good enough, Angie. Why do you need a furlough?"

"Look, it's personal. Okay?" I caught his skeptical expression and responded with a fussbudget face. "Come on, Holbrook, this is *important*. I'm not going to sneak off to Minneapolis and get laid. There's something I've got to do."

"Why do you need a furlough, Angie?"

"Paul! Don't be such a bureaucrat. Give me a break, huh?"

"Why don't *you* stop beating your head against the system, Angela? I need a more compelling reason to issue you a furlough than a blithe 'It's personal!' Tell me why you need it, and I'd be delighted to consider your request. Fair enough?"

"Welllll, since you're asking so nicely . . ."

I told him all about Mary Beth. Paul listened in silence through most of it, interrupting here and there to ask about the social services people Mary Beth had dealt with. I finished up by telling him my plans. Not everything, mind you. I deleted the felonious parts.

"Why Duluth?" he asked. "Why don't you and Mary Beth just find yourselves a place in Rapid City?"

I couldn't very well tell Paul that I'd chosen northern Minnesota because of its easy accessibility to Tilford, Michigan. He might suspect that I had felony on my mind.

To be perfectly truthful, I planned to commit two felonies. First, I intended to work a clever confidence game on the Lakeside Development Corporation, thereby stealing back Mary Beth's money. Second, I was going

36

to learn who killed Jim Tolliver and pin the fraud rap on him.

"Look, Paul, all of Mary Beth's documents are in Duluth," I said. "She needs them to sign up for those social programs. Believe me, this is the best solution. Mary Beth can stay at Tettegouche with my grandfather. We'll get her signed up for WIC at the clinic in Silver Bay. She'll be well taken care of."

"Uh-huh . . . and what about you, Angie?"

"Oh, I thought I'd stay with Mary Beth until the baby's born. Then I'll head back to Rapid City."

"But the baby won't arrive for another three months."

"So? I guess I'll need a furlough for three months."

Paul shook his head. "I have a much better idea. I'll give you a furlough for *one* month. You take Mary Beth back to Minnesota and get her squared away. Then you come straight back here and go to work at the Five & Ten lunch counter in Rapid City. I'll set up the job while you're gone."

"That idea *sucks,* Holbrook!"

Paul, who'd been carrying our picnic cooler under his good arm, hunkered down and set it on the pine needles. "Those are the conditions of your furlough, Miss Biwaban."

"Since when do furloughs come with conditions!?"

"Ever since a certain female parolee started traveling the countryside without informing her counselor." Resting on his haunches, Paul unlocked the lid. "Would you care for a beer?"

"Paul, that's not *fair.*"

"You know, I'm delighted to see you doing this for Mary Beth. That's the first time in all the weeks I've known you that I've actually seen you assume some responsibility. Let's see some more of that, Angie. Let's see you come back here and do a good job at the lunch counter."

"Paul, I don't *want* to be a waitress!"

He removed a couple of Tuborgs from the cooler. "I

37

seem to remember you telling me just the opposite back in February."

"I was only telling you what you wanted to hear."

"You *jumped* at the opportunity to work."

"That was *before* I knew how shitty it was!"

"Angela, you promised me—you swore up and down—that you were willing to work waitress at a lunch counter. Now I intend to hold you to that promise." Seating himself, he offered me a sweating bottle. "First you learned responsibility. Now you're going to learn how to finish what you start. You're going to be a waitress. Just like you promised me."

"Oh, you rotten *shit!*"

"Sticks and stones, princess."

Giving my nose a spoiled adolescent upturn, I snapped, "I won't do it!"

"Oh yes you will."

"Oh no I *won't!*"

Paul let his stern gaze sweep the misty panorama of farms and prairie. "Angela, have I ever told you about the Department's special halfway house for female parolees? It's a great, big, rambling, old Victorian house—right up there on the hillside—with a beautiful view of downtown Pierre. Nice, homey atmosphere. They offer a pleasant structured environment, just right for women who can't seem to handle the responsibilities of adult life."

Mammoth fussbudget face. "Holbrook, you are without doubt the biggest turd in South Dakota!"

Blithely ignoring me, Paul unscrewed the bottle's aluminum cap. "Enjoy your trip. Be sure to get plenty of rest. I'll see you in my office on June ninth—the day before you start your new job."

The morning of May eleventh, I drove Clunky into the parking lot of Min No Aya Wim. That's the Fond du Lac Indian Reservation to you people of Euro-Asian ancestry. The old place hadn't changed a bit in four years. Same gray gym building and long, windowless DPW building and lofty white pines and two-story social center. I was born in the center's cafeteria, right in front of the Coke machine, when a late-November blizzard kept my mother from getting to the hospital in nearby Cloquet.

While Mary Beth had breakfast, courtesy of my Bureau of Indian Affairs I.D., I jogged over to the library to meet and greet with old friends and to see if anyone could point me in the direction of my grandfather.

Turns out we missed Chief by about a week. He had already left the reservation and had gone up to Tettegouche to repair some minor snow damage to the cabin. I was more than a little nervous about seeing him again. In fact, the last time I had talked to Chief was a little over three years ago, right after I'd heard my sentence. Bye, Chief, I'm off to the Big Dollhouse. His response had been extremely loud, disapproving—and memorable!

I wondered if that *aneakokwun* was still hanging in the kitchen. That's the slim basswood paddle our people use to harvest wild rice. When I was younger, Chief found another use for it.

Two hours later, I was pushing Clunky up County Road Four, wending my way through the Sawtooth Mountains. Chief's place is on the northern rim of Tettegouche State Park. My grandfather, Charlie Blackbear, built that log house all by himself after he came back from World War II. "Blackbear" isn't really his surname, you understand. Whites can't seem to get their tongues around *Muckudaymakwah*, so Chief uses the English translation.

The house squats on a low shoulder of Pikwakon Ridge, facing south, a steep-roofed, two-story Alpine cabin fashioned entirely of hand-hewn white cedar. A fieldstone chimney warms the north wall. There's a small garage for the pickup and the snowmobile, an outdoor privy . . . well insulated, thank God! . . . and a leaning woodshed flanked by a cord or two of seasoned hickory.

If I hadn't known it was May, the blackflies on my face

39

would have clued me in. Last year's leaves crunched underfoot. I looked over my shoulder at Mary Beth, but she was doing just fine, thank you very much. Brows knit in determination, she followed me up the wooded slope without a single murmur of complaint.

My grandfather came out as we reached the front stairs. Chief is a heavyset guy, four inches taller than me, with a broad, square head, looking a bit like those century-old photos of Gall and Rain-in-the-Face. Deep-set obsidian eyes bracketed by wrinkles. Thin, white hair meticulously combed back. Small, flat ears. He was wearing a mackinaw shirt, its sleeves rolled back to the elbows, and a pair of faded work jeans that molded a couple of masculine thighs awfully robust for a man of seventy-five.

Putting my hands on my hips, I displayed a sad-eyed smile.

" 'Lo, Chief."

"I didn't expect to see you." Gnarled brown hands gripped the porch railing. "Them folks in Pierre change their minds about letting you come home?"

"Something like that." My grandfather's direct, questioning stare was mightily unnerving. *Have you been misbehaving, Angie?* I swallowed hard. Smiled. Tried again. "I've got a furlough. I can only stay a week or so."

Of course, Chief said nothing. He just kept staring at me in that irritating expectant way. I had a sudden irresistible compulsion to confess any and all wrongdoing.

*I did it, Chief. I'm guilty. I lied to my parole officer to get this furlough. I told him I want to help Mary Beth, and I do. But what I really want to do is go to Tilford and work a con on Lakeside. Which, yeah, is against the law. And if I get caught, the punishment is going to be a whole lot more painful than that old rice paddle. But I'm going to do it anyway. Your granddaughter is guilty, guilty, GUILTY! There, satisfied?*

But instead of voicing these thoughts, I turned to my companion and said, "Chief, you remember Mary Beth."

"Sure do. Took you swimming that time up at Nipisi-quit Lake." Heavy lips formed a wistful smile. Then his gaze zipped back to me. "What did you do with your luggage, Angie?"

Chief said it so casually that you might have thought I'd been to Minneapolis for the weekend instead of spending the last three years scrubbing floors in a women's prison. I showed him a monumental scowl. I didn't feel suited to playing the role of the Prodigal Grand-daughter.

If Chief caught my reaction, he gave no sign of it. Instead, he gallantly helped Mary Beth up the front stairs.

"Go in and make yourself comfortable. The fridge ain't moved since the last time you were here. There's cold goat's milk if you're thirsty. Cool you off good after that hike up the trail."

Mary Beth wiped the perspiration from her forehead. "Thanks."

Chief's hand circled my wrist as he reached the bottom of the stairs. "Come along, you. It's high time you made yourself useful around here."

We didn't speak all the way down the ridge. As we stepped onto the corduroy road leading through the marsh, Chief halted, about-faced, and put a knuckly hand on my shoulder. I lifted my chin defiantly. We were two grim and silent Indians on that moss-stained wooden trail.

"No bullshit." Chief's eyes narrowed somberly. "You're on parole. You're not supposed to leave South Dakota. What are you doing here?"

Taking a deep breath, I replied, "Look, Paul gave me the furlough. Honest! I've got the letter in the glove compartment if you want to see it. Nice and neat and on Department of Corrections stationery."

His gaze was skeptical. After twenty-eight years, Chief knew me better than anybody. "How much of that is bullshit, Angie?"

Warmth flooded my face. "None of it! Mary Beth was in trouble, so I brought her here. I thought we might be welcome. But since we're not—"

I turned away suddenly, but Chief was as quick as ever. Sinewy fingers clenched my wrist. His stern expression faded, replaced by one of concern. "You look like you're about to start crying."

I flicked a tendril of raven hair away from my eyelash. "So maybe I expected a little better from you."

"Like what? A handshake and a pat on the back? Did you *really* expect me to approve of what you did out there?"

"N-No." My throat clogged. Tears blurred his image. I held my breath, determined not to start bawling.

His tone softened a little. "What did you want from me?"

"I—I just wanted you to welcome me, that's all. The way you're acting, it—it's like you don't even care that I'm home."

Taking a raggedy deep breath, he smiled sourly. Then his broad hand lovingly stroked the nape of my neck. "Missed you a lot."

"Me, too."

"I'm sorry you were in jail. It hurt me some . . . when your mother came home and told me about it."

Sobbing, I buried my face in the hollow of his shoulder. "One visit . . . I didn't even get *one visit* from you."

"You didn't want me to come out there. You made that pretty clear over the phone that day."

"Couldn't you see that I didn't mean it?"

Looping his arms around me, Chief sighed. "Yeah, I suppose I could. Ah hell, that's what I get for listening to your mother. I was all for going straight out there, but Geraldine said wait. Said a young woman's dignity is mighty important to her. She thought you'd be shamed, having your whole family see you in that prison. So we decided that she'd do the visiting at first. Then we'd start coming around. But then they sent you to that place further west, and you weren't allowed to have visitors at all."

"Miss Carlotta's . . ." A rancid shudder rippled through me as I said it. I hugged my grandfather closer.

"I wish you had come. Mother was wrong. The first thing they do in there is rape you of your dignity."

"That bad, eh?"

"Worse!"

His voice tightened. "Angie, why didn't you come to us? I sure ain't rich. And neither is your aunt Della. But we could have worked something out."

"I—I don't know!" My tears made a sopping mare's nest of his shirt. "It was my problem, I guess. I—I wanted to handle it m-myself—"

"Stubborn," he chided gently. "Just like your mother." Blunt fingertips lifted my chin. "Well, Geraldine always said a young woman's got to make her own way."

"I guess I screwed that up pretty good, didn't I?"

"You won't hear any arguments from me." Cocking his head to one side, he asked, "When are you due back in Pierre?"

My split-second hesitation gave the reply a discordant note. "May the nineteenth."

If Chief caught it, he let it pass. Instead, he admonished, "You do what your Mr. Holbrook says, Angie. Don't you play any of your famous games with him."

"I won't. Girl Scout's honor."

We gave each other a fierce, lengthy hug on that corduroy road, then headed for my car. On the way, I filled him in on Mary Beth's situation.

Chief had no objection to Mary Beth's staying indefinitely at Tettegouche. He installed her in the upstairs guest room, remarking how nice it would be to have the meals prepared by a woman's hands. The arrangement appealed to Mary Beth's sense of personal pride. By doing the cooking and cleaning for my grandfather, she wouldn't be a burden.

It felt good to be back at Tettegouche. Despite the drudgery of the household tasks, I found the reality of Northland life to be just as pleasant as my daydream remininiscences back in the Big Dollhouse. I split seasoned logs for the wood stove, pumped fresh water out of our hillside well, shelled corn at the counter, seeded the

43

new garden with peas and gourds, basted venison roasts, baked corn bread muffins, and somehow found the time to visit old friends up and down the north shore.

It was a good time for Mary Beth, as well. She put on weight, much to her chagrin, and her face grew fuller, smoothing out the anguish lines. Once in a while, I found her singing to herself as she peeled potatoes. Day by day, she became more a part of our family. Evenings were our favorite time. Chief would march in with a load of hickory under his arm, then build a fire in the gabbro hearth. Nothing major—just enough to take the bite out of the chilled spring air. Mary Beth would brew us up a batch of that black, scalding McCann coffee. And then we'd all sit around on the throw pillows—Angie in her stonewashed jeans and moccasin boots—and sip from steaming mugs and talk fondly of old times and old friends.

I could feel myself being drawn more deeply into the family circle. Although I wanted more than anything to be a part of that, I put a little distance between myself and them. I hadn't forgotten about Jerry Carmody and the nice folks in Tilford.

While Chief took Mary Beth down to Silver Bay to see the local obstetrician, I gassed up Clunky and drove all over northern Wisconsin, cooking up the alternate identities I'd need for my upcoming scout. I stopped at small print shops in Rhinelander and Bayfield and Ashland, places where I was a complete stranger, and had sets of business cards run off. Ten cards to each set. They would come in handy when I started my campaign against Lakeside.

I also went back into full-time training, telling Chief and Mary Beth I was getting in shape for the carnival. I put myself through a regimen that would have taxed a Green Beret. Push-ups with my moccasin soles against the trunk of an elm tree. Torture sit-ups with my knees draped over a maple limb. Cross-country windsprints on the back trails of the Sawtooths.

44

When the mornings turned warmer, I took to running in Tettegouche State Park. I did ten miles every morning, finishing up at the High Falls of the Baptism River. After a workout like that, I felt the need to indulge myself. So, every morning, I treated myself to a leisurely soapy scrubdown in a lady-sized pothole near the edge of the falls.

One of these days, I'm going to ask the U.S. Geologic Survey to rename that formation Angie's Bathtub.

Then, one fine Saturday, I bounded into the kitchen after workout and found my grandfather deftly scraping sputtering sausages off the cast-iron skillet. Without giving me a look, he muttered, "Eggs'll be ready in a minute."

"Sounds good to me." Placing my palms on the table, I extended one leg in a glorious backward stretch, trying to get the kinks out. Calf muscles seemed to hum like bridge cables. I pursed my lips tenderly. "Where's Mary Beth?"

"Took your car down to Silver Bay. I told her we're running low on groceries." Chief cracked an egg with his thumb. "You and me have to talk, girl."

I'd suspected that this particular confrontation was on the way but had hoped to delay it until the nineteenth. Straightening up, I found myself looking at a tense male Anishinabe mouth.

"Why are you working out in the woods?" he asked.

"Hey, I've got to stay in shape for the act, you know?"

"Don't lie to me, Angela."

All at once, I was on the defensive. "Look, Chief, I make my living falling off towers. I have to be in shape to—"

"Don't lie! Mary Beth says you're not supposed to be in the carnival anymore."

I knew I shouldn't have mentioned that during the long drive to Duluth. But, dammit, I had to talk about *something*.

"Mary Beth has a great, big, flapping mouth!"

Chief's irate gaze swiftly circled the kitchen. "Now where did I hang that rice paddle?"

"Too old for that!" I shot back.

"Don't you push your luck!"

Now, the last time I'd heard that tone of voice, I'd ended up out in the woodshed, draped over a pair of grandfatherly knees. Instinctively, I put my back to the wall. That was one childhood memory I had no desire to live over.

"Mr. Holbrook said you can't be in the carnival anymore."

"And since when do I do what Paul Holbrook says?"

Judging from the scowl of disapproval on Chief's face, I might yet finish the morning tenderly rubbing the seat of my jogging shorts. Time for a little diversion. I flashed him a contrite and conciliatory Angie smile.

It had worked when I was eight years old, and time hadn't diluted its effectiveness. Chief's warpath scowl steadily diminished. "Mary Beth had a rough time of it," he remarked.

"Sort of."

"I know what you're thinking, Angie." Turning, he grabbed a quilted potholder and removed the skillet from the fire. "You're thinking of trying to get back at Jerry Carmody for her. You want to steal back the money she and her husband lost."

On came the fussbudget face. I looked rigidly to my left.

"Is that what you have in mind, girl?"

Uttering a quiet sigh, I relaxed, folded my arms, and gave him a wry grimace. "I never could hide anything from you, could I?"

"Not hardly." Chief slid a portion of those steaming scrambled eggs onto my plate. "What have you got planned?"

"I'm going to work a con game on Jerry Carmody. Get him to invest four million in a Big Store scam. At the same time, I'll be finding out who killed Jim Tolliver."

"And then?"

46

"Then I'll make it look like Jim's killer and I were partners in the scam. I grab the money and run. The killer does hard time in the Michigan state pen. Justice is served."

Ever the gentleman, Chief drew the chair for me. "You know, a grown-up lady would take Mary Beth and have a long talk with the police."

"Get real, Chief. Carmody owns that sheriff. The Tilford establishment would bury the whole rotten mess, and you know it."

"You don't know what you're getting into, girl," he muttered, tucking a clean napkin into the cleft of his shirt. "Maybe Tolliver did commit suicide. Ever think of that? Maybe he bought that pistol without Mary Beth knowing about it. Maybe he stopped to pick up a hitch-hiker, and the guy pulled a gun on him."

I sprinkled a little salt on my eggs, then sawed away with knife and fork. "Chief, a man who bolts from the house after receiving a mysterious phone call isn't going to stop and pick up hitchhikers."

"He stopped for hot chocolate, didn't he?"

I gave my grandfather a long, meaningful look.

"Mary Beth and I have done some talking, too," he said, then lifted a forkful to his mouth.

"That just underlines my point, Chief. The caller asked Jim to meet him outside of Tilford. Jim knew who it was. He knew the caller had to travel some distance to get there. It was cold and snowing. Jim knew he'd have to wait for a while. So he stopped for that hot chocolate on the way there."

"Got it all figured out, have you?"

Ladylike swallow, followed by a quick negative shake of the head. "Not exactly, Chief. Just the broad outlines. I figure Jim went there to meet somebody and got dry-gulched. It had to be one of two people. Either the caller himself or somebody who knew the caller was on his way there."

"Well, before you go taking any bows, missy, you'd better think that through just a little bit more." Glaring

47

at me from beneath a pair of bristling brows, Chief slapped fresh butter on a crumbling slice of frybread. "You're only half as clever as you think you are."

"What are you getting at?"

"The left side of Tolliver's head was shot away, that's what Mary Beth told me. That puts the muzzle on the right side of the head, about an inch above the ear—"

"Most would-be suicides aim for the temple," I interrupted.

"That ain't the point, Angie. Whoever did the shooting was sitting on Tolliver's right, in the passenger seat." He paused to take a bite of the frybread. "Think about it. Man gets a call to meet someone in the middle of the night. Meeting takes place on a lonely country road. Somebody gets into the car. Man doesn't suspect anything. Then the somebody pulls that gun, plants the muzzle right above the ear, and pulls the trigger. Now, do you suppose Jim Tolliver was going to open that passenger-side door to just *anybody?*"

My forkful halted in midair. I gave it a moment's thought, then flashed Chief a questioning glance. "The caller?"

He nodded emphatically. "The caller."

We finished breakfast in silence. Chief was right, of course. Jim Tolliver had definitely been set up. All I had to do now was find out who. And why.

As I ferried our empty plates to the sink, I remarked, "You been up to the Gunflint lately?"

"Yeah. Two days before you arrived. Why do you ask?"

I put the kettle on the stove, checked the firebox, grabbed a kitchen match, and scratched it sharply on the cast-iron. "Just wondering if Bob and Genn have left for the BWCA yet."

Bob Stonepipe and his wife, Genevieve, gave me my first job as a guide after high school. Every summer, they button up their Gunflint Trail home and head overland to Little Pancake Lake. And that's the last you see of them until Labor Day.

"They're still around," Chief said, scratching the side of his neck. "Can't leave till the school board turns their kids loose. You thinking of dropping by for a visit?"

"Uh-huh. And asking them if I can borrow their Mitsubishi for a bit." I thrust a sturdy hickory bough into the stove's mouth. "Clunky's a tad too conspicuous for what I have in mind."

"Those two ought to know better, but they'll probably give it to you. They think so highly of you." He stood slowly. "Anything else you need, missy, while I'm up and about?"

"Uh . . . two thousand dollars." I made my smile as sweet as maple sugar. "I need some costumes for the scam. Thought I'd pick up some linen suits at Frugal Fran's in Superior. How about it, Chief?"

Slowly the broad head came around. That warpath scowl was back with a vengeance. "How about I meet you in the woodshed in ten minutes?"

"Chief!"

"It ain't bad enough you're bound and determined to put yourself back in the calaboose. Now I'm supposed to pay your way there!"

"Look, Chief, I need money for operating expenses—"

"I told your mother years ago what *you* needed. But did she listen to me? No!" His broad palm thumped the table's edge. "Goddammit, Angie, will you open your eyes? If you go into the U.P. looking for trouble, you're going to find plenty. You steal that money, and the Michigan law's going to put you away. You're not exactly an ingenue, you know. You've done time. If you get caught, they'll have you doing laundry till there's gray in your hair."

"First they have to catch me."

"No, first you have to go to Tilford. And for that, you need two thousand bucks. Well, you're not getting it. Not from me."

I felt my mouth turning ugly. "And what about Mary Beth, huh?"

Uncertainty filled Chief's face, aging him, adding a frail cast to those proud features. He made a hapless gesture with one hand, then turned away from me. "I . . . I don't know about Mary Beth. We'll just have to find some other way to help her, I guess. Maybe if we talked to a lawyer—"

"Bullshit!" I snapped. "No law is going to touch Carmody. If Mary Beth wants that money back, she's going to have to *take* it from him. And she can't do it, Chief. She hasn't got the nerve or the skills. I do! I can take Carmody, Chief. I can smash him flat. Hit and git! It's the only way. You know that as well as I do."

I thought I saw a moistness in those gimlet eyes. "You're the only granddaughter I've got. I don't want anything to happen to you."

Giving him a bone-squeezing hug, I replied, "Nothing's going to happen to me. I'm going to go in there, grab Mary Beth's money, and scram! It'll be just like stealing war ponies."

"Serve you right if I repeated that, word for word, every visiting day." His shoulders slumped. A warm, knuckly hand reached up and patted my forearm. "I guess I ain't going to talk you out of it, eh?"

"Afraid not, Chief," I said, resting my face against his shirt. "And don't worry about the money. I'll pay you back. You know I will. I'll give you ten percent interest, too." I hugged him a little tighter. "Come on, Chief. For Mary Beth's sake. Please?"

"You helped Mary Beth when she was down. Found a home for her. Can't you be satisfied with that?"

"They took every cent she had, Chief. It isn't right. Carmody shouldn't get away with it."

"Aren't you ever going to grow up?" Chief's tone was severe, but I thought I detected an undercurrent of affection riding through it. And I knew I would get the money. "The world is full of Jerry Carmodys. People like him get away with it every day."

My smile was bitter. "Not *this* time, Chief!"

# Chapter Four

Among the interesting women I met in Springfield was an accomplished con artist named Maria Antonia DiNatale, alias Toni Gee. She'd been a grifter since dropping out of college and had worked scams from Atlantic City to Vegas. She was inside for trying to take a Hot Springs cattleman for a half-million. The cattleman bought Toni's scam all the way. Trouble was, he had a jealous wife with a cousin in the state attorney general's office.

Toni taught me everything she knew about the game. She detested the phrase *con artist,* preferring to think of herself as an actress entertaining an audience of one.

That's what ran through my mind as I drove into Sault Sainte Marie on the afternoon of May twentieth. I was no cold-blooded grifter out to bamboozle Mary Beth's old lawyer. Rather, I was a daring actress making use of a clever ruse to secure vitally needed information.

What a thought! All those years in the Big Dollhouse, and Angie was *still* Robin Hood in a miniskirt. Alas, the myth of rehabilitation.

Actually, I was very glad to be back in the Soo. This is a place dear to the heart of every Anishinabe. This is Bawating, the fishing place, and here it was that the Anishinabe people, for the fourth time in their history, erected the sacred medicine lodge and practiced the rites of Me-da-we, given to us by Kitchi Manitou, the Great Spirit.

51

Well, if you think the white-eyes have screwed up the rest of the continent, you ought to see what they've done to Bawating.

First they destroyed the original Soo rapids by building those four monstrous concrete locks. Then the diesel fuel leakage from their oreboats killed off the whitefish. Finally, they raised what has to be the most atrocious piece of architecture of all time. That's their two-hundred-foot Tower of History, which mushrooms beside the St. Mary's River like a concrete exclamation point.

I'd been pretty busy since leaving Tettegouche. Alternate identities are not concocted within the hour, you know. After borrowing the Stonepipes' Mitsubishi, I zipped down to Superior, Wisconsin and spent a delightful afternoon shopping at Frugal Fran's, the big discount warehouse on Hammond Avenue. Rack after rack of better label suits. Linens, crepes, poly-rayons, and gabardines. I spent a goodly portion of Chief's two thousand in there, choosing a balanced selection of traditional and contemporary outfits, all at sixty to seventy percent off the manufacturer's list price. Nothing too dressy. I wanted the simple yet fashionable look of the youthful lady realtor out showing nice gambrel homes.

Toni Gee once told me that a phony driver's license is the key to a new identity. And from my own brief career as Princess Lilionah, I knew that carnivals were the primary retailers of bogus ID.

I struck paydirt over the line in Bayfield County. A mud show was playing at the fairgrounds in Moquah. Gesner Brothers—The Biggest Little Show on Tour. I had my fortune told by an Italianate lady channeling the voice of Zsa Zsa Gabor, gave her the proper code phrase, and was immediately referred to the photographer's booth.

I then zoomed due east on Route 2 to Ironwood, Michigan. I left the Mitsubishi parked in front of a brownstone pharmacy on McLeod Avenue, walked downtown, got whistled at by a pair of High School Harrys, and located the branch office of the Department of Transportation. There a bored looking middle-aged woman in a periwinkle shirtdress listened with obvious disinterest to my tale of just moving to the U.P., accepted my fraudulent Wisconsin driver's license and equally fraudulent birth certificate, asked for fifty dollars, and then referred me to the end of the counter for an eye examination.

The license they handed me bore a spooky resemblance to my own. It was a laminated Michigan card, with your Angie's smiling face on the left and the pertinent information on the right. Reading it over as I left the building, I learned that I was Andrea Porter, age twenty-six, vision twenty-twenty, weight one hundred and five, formerly of Cable, Wisconsin, now a resident of Sault Sainte Marie. I yielded to a giggle as I tucked it away in my purse. Then frowned mightily when I drew another whistle from a construction worker smoothing cement in front of the old Soo Line depot. They sure are loud in Ironwood.

And so, Andrea Porter went into hibernation for the time being. I needed a whole new character if I was going to successfully pump Mary Beth's former attorney. Andrew J. Capobianco, attorney-at-law, would be a far more critical audience. Toni used to say that you can't con another con man. And lawyers are the biggest con men of all.

I did a lot of thinking during the long drive east. Selected and discarded various approaches to the lawyer. Ignored the vistas of aspen and birch, of roller coaster hills and peekaboo lakes, in favor of cooking up some plausible dialogue.

Concentrate on that new character, Angie. Try not to remember that every lawyer is an officer of the court and, as such, is duty bound to report a crime.

Shortly after ten o'clock on the morning of May twenty-first, I put the Mitsubishi in the parking lot of Andy Capobianco's sandstone office building on the corner of Portage Avenue and Osborne Boulevard. After killing the engine, I turned the rearview mirror my way and experimented with a darker, more subdued lipstick. Then, after brushing my long sleek hair, I gathered it into a demure bun and pinned it with a Spanish comb. I left a few stray tendrils around the hairline, seeking that intellectual, careless-groomer look. After rummaging in my shoulder bag, I withdrew a pair of costume glasses. Windowpane took the place of prescription lenses. I studied my mirror image. A militant, bespectacled brunette frowned back at me. Well satisfied with the results, I hefted my bag and marched indoors.

The honey-haired receptionist gave me the once-over as I strode in. Distaste flickered momentarily on her diamond-shaped face and was immediately eclipsed by a bland expression of secretarial efficiency. She politely informed me that Mr. Capobianco was busy and perhaps it would be best if I made an appointment. Scowling, I handed her one of the business cards I'd picked up in Ashland. One of my better productions, I thought. It read:

### ANGELA HOLBROOK
*Office of Equal Opportunity*
*Michigan Department of Human Services*

The receptionist perked right up. Traffickers in law, more than anyone else, are aware of the power of bureaucracy. I was from Lansing and therefore merited polite hospitality. She humbly asked me to wait a moment, then pressed Andy's intercom button.

Andy came out a moment later. He was a smallish, thin-shouldered man in his early thirties, with one of those longish Woodrow Wilson faces—narrow nose, high forehead, crows' feet, and a wide, downturned mouth. He was the only man I ever saw—other than Ronald Reagan—who could wear a brown suit and make it look stylish.

My own outfit was far from stylish. It came straight from Frugal Fran's bargain basement. I was your average intense, underpaid social worker in her oversized maize peasant blouse, sensible ballet flats, and a shirred dirndl skirt with the hem at mid-ankle. Today I was a woman who wanted her mind noticed and not her rear end.

Adjusting my costume glasses, I snapped, "I am Angela Holbrook." Quick presentation of the card. Add a note of officialdom to my pleasant contralto voice. "I'm with the Department of Human Services. I'm handling a civil rights complaint on behalf of Mary Beth Tolliver. I'd like to talk to you, if I may."

He pocketed the card. Concern softened his angular face. "This way, Ms. Holbrook." He levered open the door of his private office. "We can talk in here."

In no time at all, Andy and I were on opposite sides of his century-old desk. The file cabinets were fairly neat. Gauze curtains filtered out the dazzle of the morning sun. He smiled in invitation, gesturing at a soft, flare-armed guest chair on his right. I took a reporter's notebook out of my shoulder bag. Tapped a ballpoint's button with my thumb.

"Where is she?" he said simply.

Drawing myself erect, I became Angela the Efficient, arch-bureaucrat and defender of widows and orphans. "I'm not at liberty to say, Mr. Capobianco." I did a perfect imitation of the intake director at Springfield. *Take your shower, go to the caged window, and you will be issued a uniform, Miss Biwaban.* "Rest assured, however, that Mary Beth is in good hands and is currently receiving the best of care."

"The baby?"

"She's in our Prenatal and WIC programs. Everything's fine."

Andy looked at me as if I hadn't even spoken. "Where is she?"

His tone of voice told me everything. It spoke of his

55

continuing anxiety, his regret at not having done more, his helplessness and anger.

I softened my bureaucratic stance a bit, exchanging the intake officer for the warmth of Paul Holbrook. "She's with friends, Mr. Capobianco. That's all I can tell you. I'm sorry."

Miserable brown eyes sought mine. "Can't you at least tell me *how* she is?"

"Believe me, she's fine. She had a rough time for a while after she left Tilford. Then she met some old friends from Duluth, and they took her in—"

"Mary Beth's in Duluth?" The hopeful note in his voice gave me a start. It was like a clash of cymbals.

"No, she isn't." I put those slipping glasses back on the bridge of my nose. "Please, Mr. Capobianco, I didn't come here to be cross-examined. I wish I could tell you, but the regulations are quite specific." I flipped open my notebook. "I simply need a few facts from you. Mrs. Tolliver has filed a civil rights grievance against the sheriff of Finlayson County for having her hospitalized against her will. I understand that you were her lawyer—"

"*Am* her lawyer," he snapped. Elbows on the desk blotter, he gave me a scowl. "You don't know what I've been through these past two months, Ms. Holbrook. It's as if Mary Beth disappeared off the face of the planet!" His bony fist thumped the chair's armrest. "I went up there at the end of April. Know what I found? All the doors and windows boarded up and a NO TRESPASSING sign on the gate. The people in town told me what happened. How that son of a bitch sheriff shipped her off to Minneapolis. Bastard! He had no idea where she was headed."

I drew a Smile face on my notebook's blank page. "I understand the Tollivers came to you after their first lawyer advised them to sell out."

"That's right." All the angry tension flowed out of him. His smile was rueful, strangely nostalgic. "They lived here in the Soo when Jim worked for the Corps of Engineers. We played racquetball together at the club. Jim came up to see me right after Christmas. He told me he

56

was taking a real screwing down in Tilford from that environmental group. I agreed to look into the matter."

"Did you ever find a connection with Lakeside Development?" I asked innocently.

He cocked his head all of a sudden, seeing me in a new light. "You and Mary Beth had a long talk, I gather."

"She had a lot to say."

"Anything we can discuss?"

"We can discuss the whole ball of wax, Mr. Capobianco, if you're willing to be perfectly frank with me."

"Before I do that, Ms. Holbrook . . ." I caught the first faint glimmerings of suspicion in his gaze. My mouth went dry. Was the scam faulty? Leaning forward, he murmured, "Perhaps you'd better tell me a little bit more about Mary Beth Tolliver."

The game was still on. Andy thought I was one of Carmody's hired guns. Well, I knew how to dispel that notion.

I talked about Mary Beth's childhood in Duluth and our championship season at Central High. I mentioned her brief career as a dental assistant, the wedding to Jim, and their move to Tilford. The more I talked, the more open Andy's expression became. Finally, he lifted a palm and grinned at me.

"Okay, Angela, I'm convinced. You must be an easy lady to talk to. You know more about Mary Beth than I do."

Andy and Angela. We were on a first name basis at last. I scribbled more Smile faces in my notebook. "Tell me, in your considered legal opinion, was Lakeside playing dirty pool in the matter of the McCann properties?"

"Hell, yes! Jim and I just couldn't prove it, that's all. There was no direct link between Carmody and that environmental think tank."

"The think tank was in Washington, wasn't it?"

His smile was tart. "And where are you going with

57

that testimony, counselor?"

"Carmody made a very nasty pass at Mary Beth back in November," I told him. "She reported it to the police. When Sheriff Hendricks investigated, Carmody produced witnesses who swore up and down that he'd been in Congressman Burdick's office all morning."

Andy's mouth made a perfect upside-down U. I sensed his courtroom mask slipping into position, but not before catching a glimpse of his sudden rage. Then, all at once, he became very distant. He looked at me as if I were a stranger sitting across from him on a bus.

"What are you thinking about?" I asked quietly.

"Interesting supposition." Andy's forefingers touched the underside of his chin. "Carmody wants the McCann properties. Carmody tells Burdick. Burdick talks to the environmentalists. They file for an injunction. You know, Jim suspected a Washington connection. But it wasn't that way."

"How so?"

"Jim was thinking more in terms of the flawed title on the old Sherman place." Somehow Andy couldn't resist the opportunity to show off his legal expertise. "Our friend, Mr. Sherman of Gillette, Wyoming, was one of the heirs and assigns of the late Philip Sherman, the last owner of the farm. Old man Sherman died during the Depression, and his widow let it go for taxes. The original warranty deed was rendered null and void. That's what you call an interrupted title. Follow me so far?"

I nodded attentively.

"A man named George Quinlan bought the farm after the war. Finlayson County issued a quitclaim deed for the place. Twenty years later, Quinlan sold it to Mary Beth's father. Now it's a perfectly valid deed, but there is a long gray period stretching fifty years from the date of secondary acquisition. During this fifty-year period, the heirs and assigns of the original owner can pay the back taxes and petition the county to have the original warranty deed restored."

I did some quick mental arithmetic. "So Mary Beth's

deed to the Sherman place wouldn't have become completely kosher until the end of the century."

"In a manner of speaking, yes. Actually, at any time Mary Beth can go to the state Land Court and press for a disposition on the legality of her title. The process is costly. For one thing, she would have to have the land resurveyed. At the end, though, her claim would have been upgraded to a warranty deed. I've never heard of a judge denying title after a continuous acquisition of forty years."

"Where does Washington come into it?"

"Jim was wondering how a Sherman heir could have popped out of the woodwork after all these years. The farm wasn't for sale. There'd been no posting of any court notice calling upon the heirs and assigns. So how did friend Sherman find out about it?"

"What was Jim's theory?"

"Remember, Jim had worked for the federal government. He told me that the Internal Revenue Service controls the world's biggest database. It's chock-full of information on each and every taxpayer dating back to 1913. Jim thought it would have been a simple matter for the IRS to have pulled out old man Sherman's tax return for, say, 1933 and traced his heirs all the way to the present."

Intriguing circumstantial scenarios took shape in my mind. A Jerry Carmody could not turn the IRS into a private detective agency. But what if the search request had come from a congressman?

"So the IRS found the Sherman heirs, and Carmody took it from there," I concluded.

"Supposition, Ms. Holbrook. There's no evidence to suggest that Mr. Carmody encouraged Mr. Sherman to challenge the title to that farm."

"But you know damn well that that's what happened!"

He sighed heavily. "It was a multifaceted attack, Angela. They hit Jim and Mary Beth from all sides. The environmental issue. The disputed title. A squeeze by the local bank. Very thorough and very nasty."

"How does the title stand as of now?"

"Brian McCann left all six farms to his wife and daughter," Andy explained. "Margaret McCann's will hasn't been probated yet, although I understand from their former counsel that Mary Beth is the sole legatee. As the executrix of her mother's estate, Mary Beth had the power to sell five of those farms. I—I advised her against that. We could have fought it out. But I think Jim's death really demoralized her. I think she simply wanted to settle those debts and put an end to it."

"Could she have successfully fought it?"

"Hell, yes! We could have filed a counter suit against Jaswell. Proved the Deer Cove project was a going concern. We had EPA and state water quality officials do particle counts in the cove. The offshore area tested at well below federal pollution standards. The EPA had given us a clean bill of health. They would have testified in Mary Beth's favor at the Circuit Court of Appeals. And Jim had come up with—"

All at once, Andy cut himself short. That courtroom mask made him look like an old photo of Woodrow Wilson. His trust in me extended only so far.

What had Jim Tolliver come up with?

I went at it from a roundabout route. "Mary Beth still owns the original McCann farm, doesn't she?"

"Yes. She owns it free and clear, warranty deed and everything. There have been . . . *offers.*" I caught another glimpse of that hidden rage. "You see, without the McCann farm, you can't develop Deer Cove. It's right in the middle of those six properties."

"Offers stemming from Jerry Carmody?" I prodded.

His nod was curt. "They were made by two Tilford developers, but I would say . . . yes, it was Carmody."

"Andy . . ." My voice was warm and sympathetic. Angie the Kindergarten Teacher. "Would it be worth Mary Beth's while to come back here and fight it out?"

"*Yes!*"

Andy's vehemence made me flinch. I watched his courtroom mask shatter, spilling out all of his pent-up feelings. Oh yeah, Andy wanted Mary Beth back, but it had nothing to do with the legal tussle with Lakeside. I chided myself for not having seen it sooner. Andy Capobianco was in love with Mary Beth McCann Tolliver and had been for quite some time.

So now I had some leverage to use against the Soo lawyer, and I despised myself for having to resort to it. Oh, I could see how it had all happened. Those friendly racquetball games at the club. Cold drinks afterward and yuppie small talk and maybe a little lighthearted flirting. And then Andy began to look forward to seeing her sweating, smiling face, to feeling the warmth of her trim, soft, overheated body. Perhaps he had even been a little bit relieved when the Tollivers had moved to Tilford. If you can't see the cookie jar, you don't want any, right? Wrong! You want it more than ever. And when Jim Tolliver had asked for legal help, Andy had taken the nearly hopeless case, not for the sake of an old club buddy but for Mary Beth.

I could guess at the effect Jim's death had had upon him. He would have put some distance between himself and Mary Beth, staying away for appearances' sake, all the while telling himself that someday he and Mary Beth would get together again. But then she had vanished, and that had changed everything. Now I understood the echo of desperation behind his first words to me. *Where is she?*

What a nice girl you are, Angie. Using a good man's guilt to ferret out the information you need. I hastily buried those embers of quiet sympathy. I had to know what Jim had on Carmody.

"I think I could convince Mary Beth to come back." I hesitated, slowly closing my notebook. "But it would take some doing." Bait the hook like a good little fisherman. "If there's some ace in the hole, Andy — some bit of evidence that could guarantee success — I'm sure Mary Beth would want to return. Otherwise . . . well, I really don't think she could stand this kind of turmoil again."

Chin on fist, Andy sat there for several moments,

staring past me, weighing his revered legal ethics against the near-miraculous chance of seeing Mary Beth once more. Finally, his gaze dropped to my notebook. Steely frown. "This will remain off the record, understand? If any of it comes up at your civil rights hearing, I will categorically deny ever having said it. Got that?"

Nodding, I stuffed the book in my shoulder bag.

"Jim tried to find proof of that Washington connection." Without realizing it, Andy had lowered his voice. "He set a trap for Carmody. He asked me to draw up a subdivision plan and file it with the county planning board."

"Mary Beth told me about that. She thought Jim was planning to sell out and use the funds to settle the claims against them."

"Never happen! It was a ploy, that's all. Jim had a few friends in Washington. One of them used to be an accountant for the Corps. He's with the Comptroller of the Currency these days. Jim asked the guy to keep an eye on that environmental group's bank account. The effort paid off. Three days after I filed with the planning board, the bank account showed an outpayment of thirty grand."

"Who was the lucky winner?"

"The Veeder Gas and Oil Company of Tilford, Michigan." He caught my puzzled expression, adding, "It's run by Mike Veeder, the younger brother of Glenn Veeder, the chairman of the planning board."

"What a coincidence!"

"It gets better. I attended the board's next meeting. Brother Glenn buttonholed me and said the people in town had, quote, severe misgivings, unquote, about the Tolliver subdivision plan."

"My, my! Coincidences do seem to proliferate in Tilford."

Andy turned dead serious. "I told Jim we ought to bring this to the attention of the state attorney general's office. At the very least, the Veeder brothers would have gotten an all-expenses-paid trip to Jackson. But Jim was against that idea. He wanted to find out more. He wanted to corner Carmody and his Washington friends and stuff those harassment suits down their throats."

My memory was taking requests. Golden Oldie time. I asked to hear Mary Beth's story once more. It came through as smooth as an old Creedence Clearwater tune.

*". . . The telephone rang. Jim got to it first. He-he never told me who it was . . ."*

"Quick question, Andy—when was the last time you spoke to Jim Tolliver?"

He flipped through his desk calendar. "Let's see." His forehead tensed as he scanned the relevant page. "Jim was here on January twenty-eighth. We discussed the upcoming planning board meeting."

"You didn't call him on the telephone after that?"

"Not at all. Why do you ask?"

"Mary Beth told me that Jim got a phone call the night he died. Afterwards, he rushed out into the snowstorm to meet the caller. That wasn't you?"

Andy shook his head somberly. "Not me. Tell me, though, did Mary Beth mention that to Hendricks?"

"She did. However, the good sheriff was still convinced it was suicide."

I had taken the matter as far as I could. Any more questions, and attorney-at-law Capobianco would certainly be wondering why a mere social worker was so interested in her client's husband's death.

It was time for Angela the Bureaucrat again.

"Our office will be in touch, Andy." I stood, gracefully brushed the back of my skirt, and offered him a firm, sexless handshake. "I have a few more people to talk to. Then we'll schedule the grievance hearing. You're familiar with the statehouse, I trust."

"I've been there, Angela." He held his office door open for me. "Our receptionist will give you the number. Just send me the date and time. I'll look forward to seeing you there." A sudden, anxious shadow flitted across his long face. "Mary Beth . . . will she be—?"

"I'll be seeing her soon. Shall I pass on any messages?"

"Yes." For the very first time, Andy's smile was hopeful. "Tell Mary Beth I was asking about her. If it's possible, please have her call me. We—we have much to talk about."

My reassuring smile masked the flagrant lie. "I'll do that, Mr. Capobianco. Thanks again."

I started feeling the weight of that lie the minute I stepped on the sidewalk. As much as I would have liked to, I didn't dare put Mary Beth in touch with Andy Capobianco. I couldn't risk them comparing notes.

Sorry, Andy and Mary Beth, I'm going to have to ask you two to be miserable just a while longer. We all have to make sacrifices. It's for a good cause, you know.

As I turned the ignition key, I asked myself if it really was such a good cause. Just what was I trying to prove with all these clever impersonations and callous manipulation of good people's feelings?

Would it really be so terrible if Andy and Mary Beth got together? He was already in love with her. Mary Beth might even enjoy being a lawyer's wife. God knows she deserves a little happiness after all she's been through.

Sure. Everyone lives happily ever after. Even Jerry Carmody. And the Lakeside Development Corporation, completely beyond the reach of Michigan law, goes merrily on its way, stomping the little guys and occasionally slipping a troublesome opponent into the cold, dark depths of Lake Superior.

Uh-uh! No way, friends!

So I put the moccasin to the metal, sparing a thought for poor Jim Tolliver in his pine box, and steered Clunky up Maple Street, tooling past drive-in shopping plazas and a gauntlet of small, independent gas stations.

I could feel some of the hurt pride of the first-time businessman, and I could understand Jim's tight-lipped determination to take it all and shove it right back at his tormentors.

So Mary Beth's husband had gone looking for more shit to dump on Lakeside, eh? That was a pretty cute trick with the comptroller's office. Mary Beth had married a shrewdie. I had a feeling Jim's other amateurish probes had been equally effective.

I remembered what Jim had said as he had rushed out the door that snowy February night. *I've got you now, you bastard!* He must have thought one of his other boobytraps had gone off. Had provided him with the hard evidence he needed to challenge Carmody and Lakeside. It had been a trap, of course. A gimmick to get Jim Tolliver out on that darkened country road and into the line of fire of that .22 caliber pistol.

The caller had known just what buttons to push to bring Jim Tolliver on the run.

Which meant the caller was intimately involved with Lakeside and the hassle over the McCann properties.

Not a very nice place, this Tilford, Michigan.

But it was my next stop just the same.

# Chapter Five

Bright and early on the morning of May twenty-second, I set off for Tilford. I took the scenic route across the U.P., west on Route 28, then north on Michigan 123. Along the way, I collected pretty yellow Century 21 signs from the lawns of houses for sale.

Gone was the waspish social worker in her Gypsy queen garb. The ballet flats had given way to tall-heeled Bandolino pumps. Today I was Corporate Angie. Or, to be more precise, Andrea Porter, that bright young real estate sharpshooter from the Soo.

I picked up Michigan 678 just north of Paradise, cruising along Kitchi's rockbound shore. That stretch of shoreline is better known as the Sunrise Coast, one of the few places in the U.P. where the sun rises over water.

When I arrived in Tilford that afternoon, I had three Samsonite suitcases full of new wardrobe, a handsome leatherbound notebook, and eleven Century 21 signs. The luggage and the signs' wooden stakes occupied the Mitsubishi's trunk, along with Bob Stonepipe's Minnesota plates. The notebook and the realty signs rode up front with me.

Downtown Tilford wasn't much different from the other towns of the Upper Peninsula. The main drag, Armistice Avenue, runs parallel to the shoreline of Lake Superior two streets up from the beach, stretching from pineywoods Pontiac Park to the T intersection in front of the big Olsen lumber mill. A second major street, Catamount Boulevard, runs perpendicular to Armistice, reaching from the rocky lakeshore far inland, eventually linking up with Michigan 123.

My orientation tour acquainted me with Tilford's major landmarks. Three-story, century-old office buildings at the corner of Armistice and Catamount, all built of sturdy brownstone from the quarries of the Apostle Islands. Victorian monument to the town's Civil War dead. A charmingly tacky little place called T.D.'s Trading Post, which looked like Fort Apache but was actually a combination gift and hardware store. And, last but certainly not least, there was the Finlayson County building, one of those impressive, pseudomedieval, gray granite courthouses fronted by a grove of stately elms and a seventy-five-millimeter cannon left over from the First World War.

I already had a rough idea of the scam I was going to use on Carmody, and it involved a field that I know quite well. Real estate. Once again, I was grateful to the MSU Business School, which had gotten me that student intern job at Lodgepole Realty.

That was one of the most enjoyable times of my life, that year in Bozeman. It was the year I made the transition from college girl to career woman, trading in the worn denims for crisp blouses and houndstooth skirts, cleaning up my language a bit, and generally finding out that cash flow, not grades, makes the world go round. The owner, Ben Scoggins, let me build my work day around my classes, and I put in my forty-per-week on the computer, expanding Ben's Multiple Listing Service entries to include more information on the homes for sale.

By the time graduation day rolled around, I had two big decisions to make. Whether or not to join Lodgepole Realty on a full-time basis, letting Ben train me for my broker's license. And whether or not to kiss and make up with Rory McDaniel. I said no to both. Which is why today there is no Mrs. McDaniel, realtor, in Bozeman, Montana.

Sometimes I wonder if I screwed up my life long before I made that decision to pilfer the accounts at the Cameron Tax Assessor's office.

Falling back on my Lodgepole training, I made my first stop the Finlayson County Registry of Deeds. Their courthouse office resembled a German monastery with its tall ceilings, arched gabbro doorways, and century-old desks. Books the size of coffee tables warped the oaken shelves. Into this den of despond came Angie Biwaban, coolly professional in her brand-new off-white faille blouse, stylish wheat-colored linen blazer with matching slim skirt, and a pair of shiny black Bandolino pumps with three-inch heels. A warm, bright smile . . . a half hour of pleasant and gossipy conversation . . . the payment of a twenty-dollar fee, and I was on my way to the McCann farm with a pair of rolled-up Registry maps tucked beneath my arm.

Mary Beth's old homestead was five miles west of town, a sprawling two-story white farmhouse, shaped like an L and flanked by a grove of white birch. The mailbox read *Tolliver,* the bank's doorside sign read NO TRESPASSING — PRIVATE PROPERTY, and the farmhouse itself seemed to float on the windswept weeds of the broad, overgrown lawn. I parked in the narrow asphalt driveway, spread my Registry maps on the Mitsubishi's hood, and waited for the caretaker to show.

He did. Two hours later, by which time the offshore breeze had thoroughly mussed my perm. He was a gaunt, unkempt man in his middle sixties, crewcut hair and wrinkled brow, fatigued brown eyes and veined, potato-shaped nose. An old, old Milwaukee Braves ballcap rested on the back of his head, its navy blue matching his zipped-open jacket.

"Need any help, lady?" Whiskey had put a permanent rasp in his basso profundo voice. I scanned his jacket pockets and found the telltale pint bulge on his left side.

"Yes, I'm interested in this property." I let him get a good look at the lot plans, my leatherbound notebook, and the stack of Century 21 signs. After zipping open my brushed leather handbag, I handed him my latest business card. "I'm Andrea Porter. I'm a licensed real estate agent up in the Soo."

The caretaker took a sudden backward step. This went a little beyond the scope of his responsibilities. "Oh well, you'll have to talk to Mr. Jaswell in town."

"Mr. Jaswell?" I echoed, opening my notebook.

"Yes'm. Richard Jaswell. He's president of the First South Shore Savings Bank. Pays me to sort of keep an eye on the place." His gesture took in the farmhouse, the white sand beach, and misty, tree-lined Foxtail Point a quarter mile beyond. "Ain't too hard. Hardly anyone comes out here except them damn kids looking to raise hell. Burn the place to the ground if you give 'em half a chance. Damn kids."

I dutifully jotted down the information. Then, a hopeful tone in my voice, I said, "The bank owns the house?"

"Not exactly, miss. Mrs. Tolliver owns it, I guess. This was her daddy's place. The bank filed a—a . . . what do you call them damn things?"

"A lien?"

"That's it." His broad face brightened all over. "Bank filed a lien against the place. On account of the money Jim Tolliver still owed when he killed hisself." A knuckly hand massaged his whiskered chin. "Terrible thing, miss. Just plain terrible."

I agreed wholeheartedly that it was a terrible thing, and after a moment of awkward silence, began to roll up my lot maps. "You worked here long, Mr. —?"

"Killinen. Axel Killinen." The handshake was just as firm and warm as his smile. "Just since April, miss. I took retirement from the lumber mill last year and got to driving the woman crazy sitting round the house all day long. So when Mr. Jaswell offered me the job, I jumped at it like a hungry trout. And it ain't such a bad job, either. Except for them goddamn kids!"

Putting the maps in the front seat, I asked, "Would you mind if I took a stroll around the place?"

"Guess it can't do any harm, Miss Porter. Since you're the one set on buying it."

"Please, it's Andrea." Offering a brilliant smile, I tilted my head in invitation. Axel scampered right along. "And I'm not buying the place. My client is. You see, my office is representing a big developer from Detroit. He's interested in putting a luxury motel and a summertime marina just behind Foxtail Point."

"The hell you say!" Axel's startled gaze zipped out to the point. "That's just what Brian had in mind."

"Who's Brian?" I asked, tongue in cheek.

"Brian McCann. Mrs. Tolliver's father. He was a Tilford boy, just like me. He used to work the fish boats out in Whitefish Bay. His mother was a Shay. There's still a whole passel of Shays out there on the island. See, Andrea, this here used to be George Quinlan's dairy farm back when Brian McCann and I were just kids. After the war, Brian went out to Duluth and worked the taconite boats for a spell. Then he wrenched up his back some and had to take a job ashore. He started coming back to Tilford summers in the Fifties. I think he would've come back for good except his wife didn't like it. Maggie was a city woman, and you know how they are. No offense."

"No offense taken. I'm a South Dakota girl myself." I said it reassuringly, hoping that embarrassment wouldn't shut him up. I needn't have worried. Axel was so delighted with having someone to talk to on this lonely caretaker's job he would gladly have kept chatting all night.

By the time we reached the aging, weatherworn wharf, Axel Killinen had given me a pretty detailed history of the Deer Cove area. Apparently, old George Quinlan had really known how to turn a dollar. He had picked up five neighboring abandoned farms for taxes back in the Fifties. Just one of the many speculative ventures the old boy had dabbled in. About the time Mary Beth was born, old George had decided to retire and move to Florida. He sold his own dairy farm to Brian

70

McCann. He was very fond of Brian. Treated him like the son he'd never had. Over the years, he had sold the other properties to the McCanns one by one.

"That chicken farm old George picked up during the war — that's called Grenquist Acres now. They're always putting a new development in there. Them houses start at two hundred thou and go right on up." Axel aimed his thumb at the end of the dock. Grayish brown decaying wood peeped out of the placid water. "You know, if Brian hadn't had his accident, I bet he would've ended up just as rich as old George. Brian and that son-in-law of his — that Oregon kid — they were going like hell to lay the foundations for that marina. Then their luck turned bad in the worst way. Brian went and got hisself killed. Happened right out there, it did."

Slow, deep breath. I was going to have to play this very carefully, striking exactly the right balance between curiosity and polite interest. I wanted some more information about Jim's work on the project. I wanted to know if anyone else from Lakeside had been out to the construction site. But I couldn't afford to let Axel realize I was pumping him.

"When did this happen?"

"Oh, a year ago March. The summer before that, Brian had left Duluth and moved down here with Maggie for good."

"How did he die?"

"Well, it was March, like I said, right about the time the pack ice breaks up on the big lake." Pulling the ballcap brim forward, Axel shaded his face against the late afternoon sun. "The way I heard it, Brian went out in a rowboat to have a look at the pilings. Wanted to see how they'd weathered the winter. When he didn't come in for supper, Maggie came looking for him. She found him facedown in the water, just off the edge of the wharf, there. The boat was floating free. And there was a gaff on the dock. One hell of a shock for Maggie. Poor woman never got over it. They had to call her daughter up at the Soo and ask her to come on down to look after

71

things." Weary sigh. "You can take a look, if you want. But watch your step."

I manufactured a timid expression. "Is it safe?"

"Safer than in winter. Then it gets coated with six or seven inches of rime ice. It's them damned rotten planks you got to watch out for this time of year."

Together we strolled down the moldering wharf. Splintered planks vibrated beneath my feet. My caretaker friend had not been exaggerating. Docks don't last long on Kitchi Gammi. One more bout with the gales of November, and this one would be so many pieces of driftwood.

"Did McCann slip on the ice?"

"Well, that's what the *Gazette* said." Axel pointed out a stout rusted iron ring near the splintering end beams. "The way Sheriff Dave figures, Brian must have climbed out of the boat to fix something. Then he noticed the boat drifting away. So he turned and reached for its prow. That's when his foot slipped on the ice. He fell forward, cracked his head on the rowboat, and plumb drowned. Hell of a thing, miss."

I was about to steer the conversation onto the topic of Jim's construction project when my foot suddenly descended on a plank riddled with dry rot. My spike heel punched through it like tapioca pudding.

And over I went, plunging backward, my arms windmilling, doing a frantic watusi to retain my balance. It was all for naught, though. The other heel snapped, pitching me to the left, and, letting out a kittenish squeal, I tensed for an early season swim in the big lake.

Fortunately, Axel was right there. Quick as a weasel, he got his left hand around my flailing wrist, his right clutched the lapels of my blazer, and he yanked my hundred and five pounds away from the brink as if I'd weighed no more than a cat. Very strong and quick for an old timer. Never was there a more unlikely Lancelot.

"You all right, miss?" he asked, holding my biceps.

I nodded, managed the flicker of a grateful smile. "I am now. Excuse, please." Holding his shoulder for support, I lifted my right leg and removed the damaged pump. Then repeated the maneuver with the other leg. Brandishing the offending footgear, I treated him to a caustic smile. "Fashion Rule Number One — you must look glamorous, even if you break your fool neck." I resisted the impulse to heave both shoes into the lake. "I am thinking of writing Signor Bandolino and letting him know that his shoes are not appropriate for the waterfront."

Patting my shoulder, Axel let out a hoarse chuckle. "Miss Porter, you're damned lucky you didn't sprain that ankle." His forefinger picked out the skewered plank. "That's what Brian was looking for when he came out here that day. Dry rot. Makes the wood as soft as cotton candy." His hand sweep ran the length of the wharf. "Take a good look. You can see where he was jabbing away with the tip of that gaff."

Sure enough, I spotted several tiny circular holes here and there. My gaze lingered on a pair a couple of feet away. Two perfect little craters, side by side, about a half-inch deep. That wood looked reasonably firm. Brian McCann must have thrust pretty hard with the gaff when he made those two.

Taking my arm, Axel said, "Come on. I'd better put you back ashore. Where it's safe."

"No need for that, Axel. I'll be all right."

"Please, Miss Porter." Shaking his head, Axel ushered me toward dry land. "Dick Jaswell'd grind my ass into hamburger if he ever found out I let one of his lady clients land in the drink. You be careful where you step. Okay?"

Yielding to the inevitable, I let Axel walk me back to the beach. The dock's weathered wood felt cold, damp, and scratchy against my stocking feet. Here and there I snagged myself on a splinter and winced as each run began its liquid upward slide. Back at the car, I glanced at both soles. Shredded nylon inspired the recitation of several naughty words. Fortunately, Axel Killinen was well out of earshot by then, so I departed the farm with my ladylike image still intact.

It's just as well. I had lost my taste for inquisition back there on the wharf. I had much to think about. Every time I replayed Axel's folksy story in my memory, I extracted yet another interesting question which I would have loved to have put to Sheriff Dave Hendricks.

Such as . . .

Since when does an experienced Great Lakes sailor like Brian McCann climb out of a rowboat onto an icy wharf when it would be just as easy for the said Mr. McCann to walk down the wharf?

And why would experienced sailor McCann squat down and reach for the prow *with his hand* when he had a gaff lying nearby?

Most of all, why would Brian McCann, who had left the taconite fleet because he'd "wrenched up his back some," bother with such awkward acrobatics in the first place?

I could think of an alternate explanation, one that made me very glad that Mary Beth was far and away and safe at Tettegouche.

Brian McCann goes out to check his wharf one fine March afternoon, gaff in one hand, rowboat tether in the other. He uses the gaff's steel tip to probe for rotten spots in the wharf. The boat will be used later, to help him survey the underside.

At the end of the dock, Brian sets down his gaff and makes fast the rowboat line to that steel ring. Maybe he's found a patch of dry rot similar to the one I put my heel through. He kneels, slips out a pocketknife, and begins to probe the wood.

And that's when the visitor arrives. The visitor comes walking down the wharf, pauses, leans over and picks up the gaff. Gets a good grip on the metallic end. Brian looks up. The visitor swings like he's going for a homer. The wooden staff strikes Brian just above the eyebrow, sending him sprawling into that ice-strewn water. He is most likely dead. But even if he isn't, immersed in that

74

thirty-five-degree water, he will perish of hypothermia in three minutes.

So now I was glad I hadn't discussed Jim's project with Axel Killinen. I didn't want it generally known that Andrea Porter was morbidly interested in the Tollivers. At least not until I had a chance to feel my way around a bit.

There was so much about Tilford I didn't understand. I had thought the Deer Cove conflict was basically a case of the big developer dumping on the little guys. But now it seemed as if Lakeside's interest in the cove predated the arrival of Jim and Mary Beth.

I wondered if Carmody's company had ever done a land-use survey of the Quinlan/McCann holdings.

It was beginning to look as if Brian McCann had been murdered, as well. Someone at Lakeside was extremely eager to get his hot little hands on that shoreline. And he wasn't averse to speeding up the acquisition process with a little murder.

My thoughts turned to Mr. Richard Jaswell of the First South Shore Savings Bank, who had been so quick to slap a lien on Mary Beth's property. I remembered that tiny codicil—that emergency call provision—in the loan instrument. A remarkable piece of foresight, that. If Jim and Mary Beth had had that much collateral, then why had such a fortuitous escape hatch been needed? It was almost as if Richard had expected something bad to happen to McCann & Tolliver Construction.

Not to mention the fact that Jass's codicil had given him the leverage he needed to force Mary Beth into a disadvantageous sale of the other five properties.

I decided to have a little chat with Axel's boss. For two compelling reasons. First, I wanted to see this prophetic banker with my own two eyes. And second, I needed some camouflage for my stalk of Jerry Carmody. The Lakeside honcho wasn't going to open his door to just anyone. Not even to a lovely, bright and charming Anishinabe princess like your Angie.

Nope, I needed someone to bring me and Carmody together. And who fit the bill better than the president of First South Shore Savings?

Jass ol' buddy, you're going to be my entrée to Jerry, so let's see if we can't come up with a creative tale for you.


The First South Shore Savings Bank was on Armistice Avenue, three blocks down from the county courthouse, a one-story cinderblock structure with narrow Polaroid-tinted windows and a facade that looked like slapped-on Florida coquina.

I got there promptly at nine the following morning. It had rained heavily overnight, leaving threatening batteries of thick gray cumulus brooding above the town. The air had that thick, moist, lacustrine feel so peculiar to northern Michigan. Occasional flashes of morning sun tinted the cloudtops a bright salmon pink and dried the parking lot asphalt between the large rain puddles. After leaving the car, I picked my way between the puddles, not wanting to ruin my brand-new Amanda Smith dress pumps. I probably looked like the world's oldest hopscotch queen.

That wasn't the impression I gave when I strolled into the bank. Andrea Porter gave up hopscotch long ago. Nowadays she's into crisp peach-colored business suits, sateen blouses, and heels. When she marches into a bank, chin up, leather notebook tucked professionally under her right arm, you know she's not there in search of a second mortgage.

I walked into the nearest glass-walled office and struck a career woman pose. You know the kind. All the weight shifted to the left heel. Right foot forward. Right hand extended in a graceful gesture. Big cheery smile. "Good morning. I'm Andrea Porter. I'm with Century 21. I have an appointment to see Mr. Jaswell."

"He's in conference, Ms. Porter." She was a full-figured matron in a burgundy twill suit, permed grayish brown hair, and noticeable lipstick, tired, tough, and rigidly schooled in First South Shore protocol. I put her at ease with a formal presentation of an Andrea business card.

She nodded approvingly, then picked up the phone. "I'll let him know you're here."

"Thank you." I kept my smile cool and professional.

Dick Jaswell came out a few minutes later. He was a lineman who had broken training twenty years ago. Huge shoulders and forty-four-inch waistline. Thick, wavy, rust red hair, stubby Dublin nose, and faintly freckled face and hands. He moved with surprisingly athletic grace, and his handshake was that of a true sports enthusiast. I felt as if I were back at Tettegouche, trying to get water out of our hillside well.

"Come into my office, Ms. Porter." Dick's smile betrayed a touch of silver back there in the molars. And he buttoned his navy blue pinstriped jacket, unconsciously trying to hide the unbecoming gut from the eye of the attractive female.

Jaswell's office reminded me of an ad in a stationery catalog. Low, comfy furniture, thick shag rugs, gleaming teakwood desk. There were plaques on the pastel blue wall, testimonials from the Bankers' Association, Rotary, Kiwanis, Jaycees, and a couple of color photos of Jaswell with the Tilford High Tigers, circa 1965. His was a sparsely populated desktop—just the blotter, the calendar, the computerized phone, and a photo cube displaying lots of devilish ruddy-haired children. My guess was that Dick Jaswell did most of his wheeling and dealing away from the office.

Smoothing the back of my skirt, I seated myself in the plush guest chair, declined his offer of cigarettes, and smiled thankfully as he ordered a tray of coffee. I decided to start him off with the con game and then, at just the right moment, sidetrack him into a disquieting chat about Jim Tolliver. It would be interesting to see his reaction.

We went through two cups of coffee and assorted conversational pleasantries, feeling each other out, and then got down to business.

"I'm curious about that Deer Cove shorefront, Dick." I slid my cup and saucer onto the corner of his desk. "I've studied the lot specifications at the Registry of Deeds. It's a little over three square miles, with direct access onto State 678 and navigable waters on both sides of Foxtail Point. Frankly, I'm surprised. I thought it would have been marketed as a single unit long before now."

"Several of the individual properties have changed hands during the past year. It's a high-demand area."

"If I may be so bold, what's the going rate for a property that size?"

Jaswell ran his large palm over his chin. Watery blue eyes narrowed in deep thought. "Well, we're talking undeveloped rural land, Andrea. No sewage, no roads, no platting. My ballpark guess, for one of those farms, would be seven hundred grand."

"And for the entire area?"

"Oh, I'd say four to four-point-five million. The larger the parcel, the greater potential for maximum utilization."

"Has anyone attempted to develop the area?"

"Just a retired businessman from Duluth. He passed away last year. The sale of the individual farms began shortly thereafter."

I looked at that big, bluff, earnest, condescending face, squelched a surge of anger, and forced myself to display a coy smile. Well, well! No mention of the Tollivers, eh? I guess you forgot all about them, Jass ol' buddy, after you forced Mary Beth to declare bankruptcy and sell off those other farms.

I wondered if he had a more pressing reason for avoiding a mention of the Tollivers but kept my voice as innocent as a schoolgirl's.

"Has the bank funded any of those transactions?" I asked.

Jaswell cleared his throat suddenly. His face became more earnest than ever. "I'm not at liberty to say, Andrea. However, First South Shore Savings is always interested in productive loans from reliable clients. We have the utmost faith in the growth prospects for this particular area. Real estate has long been a part of the bank's investment portfolio."

Bravo, Dickie, nice bit of footwork. That speech probably brought the audience to its feet at the last Chamber of Commerce dinner. Translated from the bullshit, what Dickie was saying was, First South Shore was playing fast and loose with the local real estate market. A goodly portion of the bank's assets were probably tied up in real estate investment trusts. A situation that undoubtedly gave severe acid indigestion to the chairman of the nearest Federal Reserve bank.

My nonresponse made Jaswell a bit nervous. But that was the whole idea. The key to a successful con game is convincing the mark that you're going to make him wealthy beyond his wildest dreams. To do that, you have to put him in a receptive mood. I had Dickie wondering what I was doing there, why I was so interested in Deer Cove. My sudden moody silence made him want to hear my pitch.

"Andrea, are you representing someone?"

Time to play on the banker's paranoia. Thoughtful frown. Cross the legs very demurely. Open the notebook. Draw a Smile face. Close the notebook. "You might say that."

"I understand you've expressed interest in a luxury motel and marina at the site of the McCann farm."

Oooooooh, very good, Dickie. You got in touch with Axel Killinen right after I phoned you yesterday, as I'd hoped you would.

"That's a possible option." I lowered my voice in a conspiratorial manner. "There are several others."

My evasiveness confused him. I was a vague threat, but he couldn't quite define the parameters of that threat. A tone of mild anxiety crept into his voice. "I thought you were representing a client from Detroit."

"He's the firm's client, not mine."

Jaswell shot me a puzzled look. "I'm afraid I don't quite understand."

"It's very simple, Dick. You're looking at one of the bright young stars of the Soo's real estate market. I have a very large and satisfied clientele. The gentleman from Detroit would like to build a combination luxury motel and marina similar to the one in Superior, Wisconsin. I will find him a suitable site. My firm will be immensely happy. I will draw a modest commission. And my boss will pat me on the head and steer me at the next client." The thought of how he'd treated Mary Beth made my smile tart. "I'm a forward-looking woman, Dick. I like my job and I do it well, but let's face facts. This is sales. And we're both grown up enough to know that sales is not where the money is. I don't want to be here ten years from now, showing single-family homes to first-time buyers. So you might say I have two jobs—one for the firm, the other for myself. I have my own string of clients, people I've met in the trade. They trust my judgment and they will avidly consider any proposal I put in front of them. Deer Cove is a very special piece of merchandise. Too special to share with the gentleman from Detroit."

I'll say one thing for Dickie. He was a fast study. Eyeing me thoughtfully, he responded, "Let me ask you a theoretical question, Andrea. How would you develop Deer Cove?"

I pantomimed several phases of construction. "I'd capitalize on the road and water access. Have the entire parcel rezoned for industrial usage. Set up a corporation to run it as an industrial park. Dredge out the bottom off Foxtail Point. Build loading wharves and a rail spur. Then begin the process of subdividing for industry." I broadened my smile. "It can't miss, Dick. Route 678 taps right into the interstate highway system. And water barge is still the cheapest way to transport bulk goods. An industrial park would generate a lot more revenue than a lousy marina, wouldn't you say?"

Jaswell didn't say much of anything. He was looking

at me as if I'd just planted the money tree. The adding machine between his ears was busily calculating the return on construction loans to all the companies moving into this shiny new industrial park.

"You have a client interested in a development effort of that scope?" he asked, his voice cautious.

I nodded slowly.

"May we discuss names, Andrea?"

"I'd rather not." Looking very smug, I leaned back and sank into the marshmallow softness of that leather guest chair. "Suffice to say that they're a large banking consortium back East. They're looking at a number of sites in the U.P. They were a little surprised when Deer Cove wasn't marketed immediately after the death of the owner. I heard of their interest and offered to study the problem for them."

"Well . . . ah, speaking as a community representative, I'm certain that you can assure your clients that any acquisition offer on their part would meet with favorable consideration here in Tilford."

"Not so fast, Mr. Jaswell. I'm a broker, not their messenger girl. I can sell them Deer Cove, but it's going to cost." I rubbed my thumb and forefinger together, my smile widening in triumph. "I'm not looking for a ten percent commission and a pat on the head this time."

"Now, Andrea, I'm sure any such arrangement would take your vital interests into consideration."

"Shall I discuss my requirements?"

"Please do."

"My needs are modest ones, Dick. I'll settle for one percent of the common stock of the industrial park development corporation. And I want a seat on its board."

Jaswell's face turned expressionless. I had really put him on the spot. He had no authority to grant such terms. He had to take it to Carmody. Which would put me another step up the ladder, bringing me closer and closer to a successful sting.

Jaswell knew that if he rubbed me the wrong way, I might flounce out of the office in a girlish snit, seriously jeopardizing his own personal financial future. The prospect of a multimillion dollar industrial park rendered him extremely willing to humor me.

"You're an ambitious young lady, aren't you?"

"It's a hard world out there, Dick, especially for women. And frankly, I think my talents are wasted in sales."

"I couldn't agree more." Making a steeple of his blunt fingers, Jaswell wallowed in his swivel chair, cocked his head to the left, drew in a long, anticipatory breath. "Andrea, could you give me some sort of time frame for your client's decision making?"

"That depends on the actual status of the Deer Cove properties," I replied, tugging at the hem of my skirt. "I understand there's a flawed title on the Sherman farm."

"That's correct. However, I'm sure Mr. Sherman would be amenable to an out-of-court settlement."

Meaning he's owned by Lakeside. But I already knew that. I was more impressed with Dickie's intimate knowledge of the inner workings of that development firm. I was suddenly envious of Jerry Carmody. It must be nice having your own pet banker.

Consulting my notebook, I added, "I understand a few of those properties have recently been sold. Two to a South Shore Enterprises, Inc. And another two to Whitefish Bay Associates, Inc. Both sales took place within the last month. That parcel looks primed to move, Dick."

Jaswell smiled as if he had just scored a touchdown. "Don't concern yourself on that point, Andrea. Once the industrial park corporation has been chartered, I'm sure both firms will respond positively to an acquisition offer."

I was certain they would, too. Because they were both fronts for Lakeside. Andy Capobianco's instincts had been right on target. Carmody was behind the recent moves to gobble up the cove.

Now that I had Dickie in a mellow mood, it was time to heft the brass knuckles.

"That leaves the Tolliver place. Which could be a problem, right, Dick?"

He blinked at me uncomprehendingly. "What do you mean?"

"You slapped a lien on that property."

"That's the least of our problems, Andrea."

"Is it?" Snapping my notebook shut, I flashed him a bristly smile. "I did my homework, Mr. Jaswell. You loaned Mary Beth Tolliver a lot of money to develop that area. A year or so down the road, you take it all back and scuttle out the contractual escape hatch. How come?"

His broad hand clenched the teakwood edge. He struggled mightily to maintain the mantle of financial sobriety. "My dear young woman, the bank's dealings with Mrs. Tolliver have absolutely nothing to do with the marketability of her late father's farm."

"Really?" I replied, folding my hands on the notebook. "Well, let's just say I have some very skittish clients, Mr. Jaswell. The merest hint of impropriety—"

"Impropriety!" he echoed, flabby chin aquiver.

"Come on, Dick, it's a can of worms, and you know it. You loan Jim Tolliver a few million, and then he winds up dead. That's not the kind of situation my clients want to become involved in."

I waited for his reaction, but instead of a nervous blink or a flush of alarm or an instantaneous tightening of guilty lips, all I got was a haughty, deadpan stare and a momentary tug on the knot of his club tie. I hit him with it cold, and Jaswell reacted with no more emotion than if he'd been listening to the evening news. Either Dickie was an innocent or he had the brass of a television game show host.

Fabricating an ingratiating little smile, he reached over and lightly patted my hand. "My dear, you have nothing to be concerned about. Mr. Tolliver's demise was a tragedy, of course. But we'd had misgivings about that particular project long before then."

"Did you ever discuss those misgivings with the Tollivers?"

"Now and again."

"Did you and Jim Tolliver ever discuss it over the telephone?"

No reaction. But Jaswell chose not to answer my question, either. Drumming his fingertips on the armrest, he said, "Andrea, if you're worried about the title, forget it. That farm can be sold. I will personally guarantee that First South Shore Savings will lift the lien in anticipation of Mrs. Tolliver's impending sale to the new corporation."

I feigned a look of concern. "There's just one more thing that bothers me, Dick."

"What's that?"

"Why didn't Mrs. Tolliver sell that last farm?"

He uttered a small dry cough. "Sentimental reasons, I suppose. I understand it was her vacation home when she was a child."

"Surely an offer was made?"

"Oh yes. Several, in fact. Mrs. Tolliver chose not to respond to them. She's a headstrong young woman. She can't always see what's in her best interest."

I thought of a clever way to beat a retreat and, at the same time, to send Dickie speeding to Carmody with the news of my wonderful moneymaking scheme.

"And you think she'll sell out *now?*"

Mouth working, Jaswell tried to salvage his argument. "I — I think she may have . . . perhaps . . . changed her mind. Certainly we could make a more generous offer."

At this point I was really beginning to enjoy myself. "This needs a woman's touch," I said, obsidian eyes a-twinkle. "Why don't you give me Mrs. Tolliver's phone number? I'll have a talk with her."

Perspiration beads sprouted at his hairline. "Uh . . . Andrea, I really don't think that's wise."

"Why not? I am a saleswoman, you know. Listen, you give me ten minutes alone with Mrs. Tolliver, and I guarantee I'll have her signature on a purchase agreement for you."

"That's very kind of you, Andrea. Still, I think it'd be better if we waited."

"Why wait? Dick, what if some operator gets to her first? Do you really want to pay top dollar for that property? Let me have a crack at her."

"Believe me, Andrea, it's the wrong time for—"

Wary expression. "Mr. Jaswell, somehow I get the feeling that you're trying to keep me away from Mrs. Tolliver."

"That's silly, Andrea. I'd do nothing of the sort."

How right he was! If anything, Dick Jaswell would have moved heaven and earth to bring me and Mary Beth together. But he had no idea of where Mary Beth was, and the nature of that particular impasse was fraying the edges of that banker's aplomb. Without Mary Beth's concurrence, he couldn't help Carmody put together that industrial park package for my nonexistent clients.

To help speed him on his way, I treated Dickie to another display of feminine pique. "Mr. Jaswell, is there some *problem* with Mary Beth Tolliver?"

"No! No problem." He stood up the same moment I did, lifting one hand in a conciliatory gesture. "Nothing of the sort, my dear."

Flashing him an icily polite smile, I replied, "I'd feel a lot better if I could hear that from Mrs. Tolliver's own lips." Shouldering my bag, I adopted a touch-me-not stance. "Thank you for your time. I think we've taken this discussion as far as we can for the moment."

For a hairy moment there, I thought Jaswell was going to forcibly prevent me from leaving. But he recovered beautifully. Squared those footballer shoulders and said, "Will you be in town long?"

"A few days." I paused at the door. My expression stayed wary. "I'll be at the Edgewater. You can leave a message at the desk."

"I have to talk to a few people. You understand."

I nodded briskly. "And I hope one of them is Mrs. Tolliver. It would be reassuring to hear from her. Good day, Mr. Jaswell."

And on that note, I made my exit, performing my famous Mary Queen of Scots imitation. All patient endurance and supreme dignity.

Soon I was back in my Mitsubishi, but I didn't feel much like smiling. I was troubled by Jaswell's reluctance to talk about his dealings with Jim Tolliver. He'd kept mum, even after I'd dangled a multimillion dollar profit in front of his ruddy nose.

Mine had been a sterling performance in what we Anishinabe call *ikwekazo odaminowin*. Woman's make-believe. But I wished I had more to show for it. This never happens on television, you know. When confronted by the seemingly all-knowing heroine, the bad guy is supposed to squirm in his seat, exude trickling beads of sweat, stammer without sound, and then bolt for the nearest exit.

I just wasn't cut out to be a stalwart policewoman on CBS.

I could have sat around the motel pool, waiting for the inevitable phone call. But I had business downtown. Mary Beth had told me that Jim's silver gray Toyota Corolla had been impounded by the sheriff after his death. Mary Beth had never gotten around to reclaiming it, so presumably it was still in the custody of Finlayson County. And I definitely wanted a look at that particular vehicle.

Returning to the Edgewater, I doffed my business togs in favor of a short-sleeved blouse and a most flattering black twill mini and headed for Catamount Boulevard.

I have a confession to make. I've always secretly loved tacky little tourist traps like T.D.'s Trading Post. It's a compulsion dating back to kindergarten, when I used to haunt the gift shops in Canal Park. I had a great time at T.D.'s. I wandered the aisles, ducking under mobiles and studying the bric-a-brac. I purchased a book of baby names for Mary Beth and a porcelain coffee mug for Chief. It had a little painting of Tahquamenon Falls on the front.

On my way to the checkout counter, I spotted a lovely T-shirt tacked to the wall. The shirtfront showed a teen-aged girl with her nose in the air and a legend reading PRINCESSES DON'T DO THE LAUNDRY OR TAKE OUT THE GARBAGE.

Well, I just had to have that one!

A few minutes later, I was in the Conoco station across the street from T.D.'s, playing out a little one-woman drama for the benefit of the gas jockey. With my shopping bag in one hand and the telephone receiver in the other, I called the local automatic weather report and told my nonexistent sister to kindly haul her ass downtown to pick me up.

The gas jockey was very cute. Smoky gray eyes, high cheekbones, wiry brown hair, and a forthright chin. His tan coveralls fit tightly in the neck and shoulders. I treated him to a truly Academy Award performance, but he was far more interested in my legs. His smiling gaze slithered up both calves every time he came into that cluttered office to ring up a sale.

While he was outdoors filling a cranberry Buick, I hung up the phone and struck a languid pose. Arms folded. Fanny resting against the drygas display counter in a way that added an inch of altitude to the mini's hem. Then I crossed my legs at the ankle, shaping my mouth into a frustrated adolescent pout.

He came sauntering into the office, wiping greasy hands on a burnt orange chamois rag. "Got a problem, honey?"

"Yeah! My sister Cindy was supposed to give me a ride to the courthouse. Got to get there before they close." Mild look of sudden anxiety. "The goddamned sheriff impounded my car the other day. My insurance sticker had lapsed." Cozy pat on the shoulder bag. "I've got the payment right here. But if I don't get to the Registry in time—"

"Hey, relax!" His smiling gray eyes held mine for a few

seconds, then fled south to the miniskirt hem. This con was going to be a whole lot easier than I'd expected. "Judge Lund doesn't adjourn until after four. The courthouse stays open until five. You've got plenty of time."

"Are you sure?"

I slid my left calf back and forth over my right knee. A discreet ladylike scratch. The wattage of that gas jockey's smile easily doubled.

Don't overdo it, I told myself. You don't want a date with this guy. You just want to find out where Jim Tolliver's car is.

"I wouldn't want them to sell my car at auction," I added.

His fond gaze never left my legs. "No problem, hon. Sheriff Hendricks holds the cars for at least ninety days."

"What happens to the cars after that?"

"The county sells them at book value to Pete Densmore over at Miskegin Motors. Ol' Pete, he sells them as used cars. He'll take anything."

"Done much business with him?"

"Oh, a bit." The aging cash register chimed as he tapped it open. He peeled the rubber band off a tightly-rolled wad of bills. "I've hauled a couple of junkers over there myself. Total losses from a head-on crash on 678. Don't you worry, honey. I'll bet that car of yours is gathering dust behind the courthouse right this minute." An elbow sweep slammed the cash drawer shut. "Are you in town for long?"

"Mmmmmmm . . . could be."

Now that I knew where to find Jim's car, I gave my rusty flirtation skills a mild workout, kidding around with that cute Conoco attendant. I let him know I was single and not averse to a little moonlight hot-tubbing. That grin of his grew wider and wider. He asked me eleven different ways where was I staying. I fielded each query with a coy pleasantry and made my escape as soon as the next car rolled in.

When that little pneumatic bell went *ding,* it was the saddest moment of his career.

88

No sooner had I returned to the Edgewater and kicked off my high heels than the telephone rang. Flopping back on the double bed, I scooped up the receiver. "Hello?"

"Andrea Porter?" The voice was masculine, slightly adenoidal. Breathless urgency softened its normal hard-edged tone.

"Yes. Who is this?"

"Ms. Porter, my name is Jerry Carmody. I'm with Lakeside Development Corporation. I, ah, understand we have a mutual interest in Deer Cove."

Play it cozy. "Mr. Carmody, I don't know what you're talking about—"

"Ms. Porter!" Impatience added a shrill note. "I know you've been to see Dick Jaswell at the bank. You say you'd like to talk to Mary Beth Tolliver. Shit, so would I! So what do you say the two of us have some lunch tomorrow?"

"Is this Dutch?" I asked, tongue in cheek.

That adenoidal chuckle grated on my ears. "I'm a generous guy, Ms. Porter. But only with those who don't take advantage. Shall I pick you up at noon?"

"I'd rather meet you somewhere, Mr. Carmody."

"My office?"

"That's fine with me. Where is it?"

As if I didn't already know!

Jerry gave me explicit directions. Lying on the bed, I repeated them word for word in a monotone, as if I were actually writing them down. I crossed my legs at the ankle, turned my toes to catch the chilly blast from the air conditioner.

"Got it!" I said perkily. "I'll see you promptly at noon." My teeth set in a tigerish grin. "Oh, and Mr. Carmody . . . ?"

"Yes?"

"Believe me, I'm looking forward to this."

"So am I, Andrea. See you tomorrow."

Hanging up, I let my weary gaze drift to the ceiling, wondering if I ought to select my outfit now. Interesting question. What does one wear to a luncheon meeting with an animal who enjoys raping women at the kitchen counter?

Put the fashion strategy on hold for now, Miss Biwaban. You'd be better off concentrating on Miskegin Motors. Since I was lacking both badge and warrant, Pete Densmore wasn't about to let me conduct a fine-toothed search of that Toyota. I needed a new con game, something that would get me into that car without even a mention of Jim Tolliver.

I thought back to my recent interview with Dick Jaswell. Remembered how he had completely ducked my question. Had Jaswell been dealing with Jim on the sly? Mary Beth and Andy Capobianco had had no inkling of that. I began to wonder just how deeply Jim had gotten involved in the affairs of Lakeside and First South Shore Savings. He had shielded Mary Beth from the knowledge of his subdivision gambit. Had he also been working another clandestine operation without his lawyer's knowledge? Something involving Jaswell?

I was beginning to feel like the frisky wolf pup who had just bounded out of the den for the very first time. I had had so much fun wandering down the trail that I'd never taken the time to notice just how dark and perilous and threatening the forest really is.

Brian McCann's unlikely death gave the whole situation a complexity far beyond my abilities of comprehension. I was going to have to burrow a whole lot deeper to make sense of all this. So deep, in fact, that I might not be able to get out.

Decision time! I didn't have to stick around, you know. I could change clothes, pack my bags, check out, and be on my way to the Soo in just over an hour. Jerry Carmody might scratch his head in puzzlement, and Dick Jaswell would certainly wring his hands over the loss of all those juicy industrial park loans. But other than that, I would be home free.

Uh-huh. Yeah. And Mary Beth and her infant son

would have a lovely time adjusting to life in a shabby, cold-water apartment in Duluth.

So you stay, Angie, and you be a lot more careful than you've been heretofore. Keep your eyes open and your ears perked, and you just might get out of Tilford with your fur intact.

Remember what Chief said. "You're only half as clever as you think you are."

No arguments here, Chief. I'll watch my step. Only a fool ignores trail sign.

# Chapter Six

I left the Edgewater shortly after ten o'clock the following morning. I had two hours to kill before my luncheon meeting with Jerry Carmody, and I could think of no better way to spend them than in a thorough examination of Jim Tolliver's Toyota.

Last night's rain had put a noticeable chill into Tilford's moist maritime climate. A miniature lake occupied the far side of the motel's parking lot. Wisps of mist drifted upward from the neighboring pastures. I felt the mild offshore breeze on my bare ankles.

This morning I was doing an applause-worthy impersonation of your average college coed. Oversized southwestern-style intarsia sweater. Blue spandex Capri bike pants. Ballet flats from the ten-dollar shoe rack. Aviator sunglasses. Raven hair uplifted in the eye-catching style made famous by Elvira.

And so we meet Jenny . . .

Jenny what? Memory conjured up the image of a nearly forgotten classmate. Okay, say hello to Jenny Sanderson, newly transferred to South Shore Community College. Jen is from Logan, Utah, where your Angie spent her undergrad days, and, with a slight twangy accent, I knew I could pass for a Mormon princess. Provided, of course, that Pete Densmore didn't hail from the Wasatch Front.

Miskegin Motors filled a rhomboid-shaped corner lot at Catamount and Felsen. I could see that the dealership had passed through many hands. The showrooms were more suited to a laundromat. The garage building itself was vintage Depression, all red bricks and sharp corners. Triangular vinyl flags fluttered gaily from a sagging rusty cable out in front. The cars were all parked at an oblique angle to the sidewalk. Sunlight winked off their windshields, making me feel a little bit warmer.

I found Jim's four-year-old Toyota close to the repair shop's entrance, parked with its tailpipe to the chainlink fence. Flabby tires. Fine layer of dust on the padded dashboard. Exposure to direct sunlight had bleached the windshield's inspection sticker into near transparency. Both side windows were open slightly to assist in ventilation.

I paused on the driver's side, noting the shiny new amber coloration along the window's edge. Pete Densmore had obviously replaced the original window. Which meant it had been shattered by that .22 caliber gunshot. Leaning forward, I shaded my sunglasses and peered inside. The car's interior looked as if it had been cleaned. I frowned dismally. Maybe I wasn't going to find any important clues.

Well, there was only one way to find out.

So I went into my act. I circled the Toyota with a determined stride, kicked its front tires, wiggled the antenna, glowered at the low-slung black grille, sat on its trunk, and bounced up and down. In short, I did all the things coeds do when they purchase used cars.

Within minutes, a Lincolnesque fellow of indeterminate age came striding across the lot. The breeze plucked at his loose-fitting, wrinkled, battleship gray, summerweight suit. Wiry mouse-colored hair. High, peeling, lobster-hued forehead and cadaverous blue eyes. His sudden appearance would have scared the shit out of Vincent Price. As he closed in on me, however, the initial frightening sepulchral expression yielded to a salesman's shrewd-eyed look and an incongruous Howdy Doody grin.

"Hello there!" A very rich and mellow baritone voice.

93

Some stage or operatic work in his background, unless I missed my guess. "And what can I do for you, young lady?"

Showtime! On came the scintillating Angie smile. I radiated an aura of bubbly college cheerleader enthusiasm, awkwardly pumping his extended hand. "Hi, yourself! Are you Pete?"

"Yes, ma'am! Peter B. Densmore, at your service." From the stance and the flourish, I gathered that Peter was a fixture in Tilford community theater.

"I'm Jenny . . . Jenny Sanderson." Beaming aw-shucks shrug. "I'm majoring in business over at South Shore. And I am definitely in the market for a new car. A new *used* car, that is. You see, Guidance just placed me at a personnel office in Trout Lake for the summer. Student intern, you know? And I'm sure going to need a car to commute every day. My roommate, Kerry Anne, tells me Japanese cars get some really good mileage. And"—my fingertips affectionately stroked the silver-gray fender—"I sort of like this one."

"Jenny, if it's a good car you're looking for . . . a good car with good gas mileage at a good price . . . well, you've sure come to the right place. That you have. Miskegin's got the best deals on the South Shore. Easy financing. Take six months off before the first payment. Fact is, we've got a special rate for college students that can't be beat in the whole blamed U.P. Why, it's so low—"

I had the weird feeling I'd heard this all before, and then it came to me. I'd been sitting in my room at the Holiday Inn a few nights ago, watching cable TV, and I'd seen a used-car salesman all decked out like Abraham Lincoln. I put an imaginary beard on Pete. Yup! It was him, all right. An honest deal from Honest Abe. My confidence came back with a vengeance. No one is more gullible than a frustrated actor.

Pete ran through the whole spiel, took a deep breath, then gasped, "You ever owned a car before, Jenny?"

"Oh sure! Back home in Logan. I had this old

94

bomber, a sixty-nine Mercury Montego. My dad wouldn't let me bring it with me to Michigan, though. Says I belong in the dorm, studying. Not out cruising with the townies. You know how it is."

Pete commiserated with me for a few moments, then asked, "Would you like to go for a test drive?"

That's just what I'd been waiting to hear. Up on tiptoes. Squealing gasp of excitement. "Oooooooh, you bet!"

Stepping past me, Pete fished a jangling keyring from his pants pocket, selected a stubby one, and unlocked the driver's side door. Humidity smothered me as I slid onto the smoldering vinyl bucket seat. I had a tough time keeping my Mormon princess smile intact. I was experiencing too many mental images of a .22 caliber pistol blowing Jim Tolliver's head into raw meat.

"Just give me a minute or two, honey, and I'll be right back with the registration and a plate," he promised, gently pushing the door shut.

"Take your time," I sang, then slumped in the driver's seat. My cheerleader grin evaporated. Sharp obsidian eyes circled the car's stifling interior.

Got to do this quick, Miss Biwaban. The gentleman scents a prospective sale.

The driver's seat was new. That figured. Jim's bleeding had hopelessly stained the old one. I ran a fingertip along the ceiling just above the window. Found several faded spots where the detergent had blotted out the spray patterns of blood and brain tissue.

Hasty check of the glove compartment. Nothing! Not even a dog-eared copy of the owner's manual.

Bending at the waist, I pillowed myself on the padded steering wheel and lifted the rubber floor mat with my fingertips. Bile tickled the back of my throat. I had to force myself to look. Dried rivulets, a shady coppery brown in color, meandered down the carpet, ending in an oval blotch of the same hue.

Suddenly the air in that car got very thick and stale. Face simmering, I wobbled on the seat, then quickly rolled down the window. The influx of fresh air settled my stomach. I took several deep steadying breaths. Grimaced sourly and looked again.

A pretty slipshod cleaning job, Mr. Densmore. Your maintenance people didn't even bother to shampoo the carpet. They expunged the ceiling stains, replaced the side window and the driver's seat, and that was it.

That employee sloppiness actually worked in my favor. I was seeing Jim's Toyota pretty much the way it had looked that fateful night back in February.

My gaze swiveled toward the showroom. There was Pete, clutching his dealer's plate, giving some last minute instructions to his master mechanic. I only had a minute or two left, so I had to make them count. With the utmost reverence, I replaced the floor mat.

Make it fast and thorough, Angie. Run the fingertips between the seat and the padded backrest. Feel the grit of dust and lint. Lean forward, cheekbone on the passenger seat, and study the rubber mat on that side. See the abrasion at the foot of the firewall. A woman's heels will do that. Hello, Mary Beth. So you still like to ride with your legs stretched out, eh?

As I lifted the edge of the mat, a tuft of feathery material drifted away from its underside. I snatched it in midair, then rolled it carefully between thumb and forefinger. A wisp of material no bigger than my cuticle. Sand-colored with a slightly oily feel.

Sitting upright once more, I frowned at that tiny tuft. The filmy texture was disturbingly reminiscent, and I wondered where I had touched fabric like this before.

Of course! Utah! I should have known the moment I spied that tawny color. Camel hair. My Aunt Della had gotten a camel hair coat one Christmas. She'd been delighted with it. I distinctly remember watching her hold the lapels shut and promenade in front of the hallway mirror. And I seem to recall numerous complaints about it shedding a tuft or two whenever she sat down.

What do we make of this, o trailwise Anishinabe princess? Well, for starters, we can safely assume that this

96

shedding fell from the coat of one of Jim's passengers a while back. Static cling had anchored it to the underside of that rubber mat.

This wisp of camel hair is a shade on the thick side, so it's a safe assumption that it came from a winter coat.

Camel hair also resists moisture pretty well. A camel hair coat is just what a person might wear if he or she expected to be outdoors in a February snowstorm.

Those coats are pretty expensive, too. Just ask my Uncle Matt. But they're affordable if you hold a management position in a successful firm like Lakeside Development Corporation or the First South Shore Savings Bank.

My imagination took over. I could see the mysterious telephone caller, clad in a brand-new camel hair coat, stepping up to the Toyota's passenger window and brushing the snowflakes off and rapping a knuckle on the glass. I visualized Jim Tolliver leaning across the seat and unlocking the door. The caller opens the door and slides onto the passenger seat. A tuft of hair is inadvertently scraped off and spirals to the floor. Jim finishes his hot chocolate. The caller draws his pistol. The Styrofoam cup slips from Jim's grasp. And then—

I flicked off the imagery the second I saw Pete Densmore heading my way. Artfully tucked the wisp of camel hair behind the cuff of my sweater. So maybe now I had some idea of who to look for. Someone in top management at Lakeside or First South Shore who was the proud owner of a camel hair coat. And who may have been dealing with Mary Beth's husband on the sly.

"All set, Jenny." The passenger door swung open, and Pete's lugubrious face beamed in at me. He put a newly minted aluminum dealer's plate in the front windshield, clambered into the empty bucket seat, and dangled a ring of car keys in invitation. "She's all yours."

"Neato! Thanks, Mr. Densmore." I snatched them away, pumped the accelerator a few times, selected the proper key, and gave it a rough twist. The Toyota kicked right over, emitting a throaty exhaust bark, raising a plume of acrid, oily smoke. "Let's see what she's got under the hood!"

I sent Jim's ghost a telepathic message. No disrespect meant, Mr. Tolliver, but I have to convince this guy I'm a teenager.

No sooner had Pete gotten his bony knees behind the padded dash than I punched the gas pedal to the floor, listening in satisfaction to the crescendo roar of the engine. Then, twirling the stickshift, I sent the Toyota hurtling across the asphalt in a shrill, tire-screaming gallop.

Well, as you've probably guessed, my Daytona takeoff seriously dampened Pete's enthusiasm for a sale.

Fact is, when I opened the passenger door for him, he was green around the jowls and doing an awful lot of ragged breathing. He advised me to heed my daddy's advice and forget about keeping a car on campus. I'd live a whole lot longer, he said.

I had about forty minutes left to return to the Edgewater and shower and change clothes for my luncheon date with Jerry Carmody. And I got out of that motel with sixty seconds to spare.

Lakeside Development Corporation was located in the 5500 block of Armistice Avenue. That put it a good four miles from the center of town, on the gray granite shores of Kitchi Gammi, right where the avenue turns into four-laned Route 678. Carmody's home office was an L-shaped, one-story, beige-brick structure that could have been a professional building. Seeing its tall chainlink fence for the first time, I mistook it for the state public works depot and drove right on by.

I found a stretch of pebbly beach a quarter mile beyond, nosed the Mitsubishi into it, wet my front wheels in Kitchi surf, and performed a looping left turn that put me back in the inbound lane. Minutes later, I had the car neatly tucked away into a visitor's space and was heading for the tinted-glass door of the Lakeside personnel office.

I was at my fashion best on this sunny May forenoon — tailored windowpane plain jacket and slim tweed check skirt, both in a soft gray — virginal white silken tank — shiny black patent leather pumps with three-inch heels and a handbag to match. Adios to Jenny Coed with her Capri pants and Elvira hairdo. I was Andrea Porter again, dressed for success and on my way to a typical Yooper power lunch.

Carmody's outer office terminated a long pastel blue corridor. As I opened the teakwood door, I glimpsed Swedish blond furniture, a lush carpet, well-upholstered lounges, a coffeemaker, IBM computer equipment, and a pair of framed wall sketches, the kind they sell at the popcorn stand at Showcase Cinema. Somehow I doubted that Claudette Colbert had ever been a Lakeside client.

I heard the computer printer's banshee squeal and saw Carmody's sandy-haired receptionist handling the runoff. I hailed her, but she didn't hear me. With an absentminded nod, she studied each perforated sheet as it rolled out. I tapped her on the shoulder.

"Excuse me."

The receptionist nearly came out of her spectator pumps. She cast me a frightened doe look, dropped the runoffs, and, brushing a sandy blond spitcurl away from her eyes, smiled awkwardly. "I'm sorry. You startled me." Curiosity flitted across her oval face. "May I help you?"

Show the jumpy lady a reassuring woman executive smile. "Hi, I'm Andrea Porter. I have a luncheon appointment at twelve with Mr. Carmody."

"Have a seat, Ms. Porter. I'll announce you."

Two minutes later, I followed the receptionist into Jerry's inner sanctum, wondering all the while why she was so skittish. And then a familiar adenoidal voice boomed. "Andrea Porter!"

There he sat — Gerard F. Carmody, according to the gold-embossed nameplate on his leather-rimmed blotter. He filled the padded swivel chair like a jovial troll king, left ankle resting on the opposite knee, arms outspread in welcome, grinning at me from behind an oak-wood desk the size of an aircraft carrier.

Well, Mary Beth had been right about the hair. It was lank, reddish brown, and baby fine, and he was losing it rapidly. Jerry's part was on the right-hand side, an inch above the ear, leaving a lengthy sweep to cover the balding crown.

But she had said nothing about Carmody's striking animal assurance. Jerry was by no means handsome. His face was a long oval, ending in a slightly recessive chin. His heavily lidded eyes had a vague Oriental cast. An Irish Fu Manchu. That Sandinista moustache may have been popular in the Age of Disco, but it did nothing to help his looks. I could still make out the gap between his two front teeth. Yet, in spite of these defects, Jerry Carmody radiated an almost palpable aura of masculine aggression. He looked me over with the frank appreciation of the veteran woman slayer, and his insolent troll king slouch seemed to suggest that our presence in bed together was merely a matter of time.

Jerry was out of that chair in an eyeblink, charging around the corner of that mammoth desk, putting out a leathery hand. Chalk up another accuracy for Mary Beth. My heels and his lifts put us nose to nose.

"Molly, I'm taking Ms. Porter to lunch. Take messages." Jerry was one of those bosses who operates on the assumption that all of his employees are hearing impaired. "If it's MacKinnon on the horn, blow smoke up his ass. I'll be back around three."

I had hoped to make it a firm, friendly handshake, but Jerry held on until he'd given Molly her marching orders. His thumb drifted lovingly back and forth across my knuckles. "What do you say? Do you like ribs? Yeah? Ribs it is then."

As he hustled across the room for his suit jacket, I studied his desktop. Bound reports, half-folded blueprints, computer-generated cost estimates, an old-fashioned accounts ledger, six well-chewed pencils, and a heavy-duty adding machine. Unlike Dick Jaswell, Jerry kept his own books and made all the crucial Lakeside decisions right here in his own office.

"You ever been to the Caribou?" Using both hands, he carefully donned a leather Irish cap. A necessary precaution, this. A stiff lake breeze would have spelled disaster for that painstakingly cultivated hairstyle. "Shit, no. You're new in town, right?"

My smile was sweet. "Arrived just this week."

"Hey, you'll love it. It's up there on the lake. Grade-A class." He shooed Molly out of the office, then showed me a sidelong grin. "I can't keep calling you that. Ms. Porter. I had a teacher back home by that name. You're Andrea. I'm Jerry or Jer. Take your pick."

And so, Jerry and Andrea departed for the rustic hideaway Caribou Lodge. He even let me drive his sporty low-slung BMW. For reasons which soon became apparent.

You see, Jerry was a toucher. He believed that fanny pats were a legitimate form of steering. It had started on our way out of the building. "Head left, babe." Four-fingered whap on the left buttock. "My car's over there."

Now I understood why Molly was so jumpy.

It was an interesting ride to the Caribou. The BMW's bucket seats were parallel with the gas pedal. Once inside, I found my knees bracing the steering wheel. My skirt began its downward slide. And I couldn't drive one-handed, not with that stickshift.

By the time we got to the Caribou, Jerry's hand was undoubtedly an expert on the texture of No Nonsense pantyhose. I was beginning to wish that Mary Beth had been a little more competent with that paring knife.

The Caribou's setting restored my good humor somewhat. It was a late Victorian hunting lodge that someone had turned into a cozy backcountry restaurant. Small, circular, linen-covered tables for a quartet filled the oak-beamed dining room. The unknown master carpenter had done a superb job on the hand-hewn molding. Antique French doors offered unimpeded vistas of placid Tamarack Lake.

The Cambodian waiter was crisply efficient and charmingly attentive. I was Mr. Carmody's lady, a rank equivalent to a duchess in the Tilford social order. Which meant I got the best table in the house, a cut-glass centerpiece adorned with two American Beauty roses, and a well-endowed Mai Tai that numbed my smiling lips.

Watching Jerry eat was a strange experience. He hunched over his food, his left arm curled protectively around the plate. It was as if we were two refugees in a bombed-out Third World village, fearful that some soldier might snatch our meals away.

It was the table etiquette of the underclass, and I was more than a little surprised to find it in the head honcho of one of the South Shore's leading corporations. Jerry's voice told me he was a native Michigander. But that's not the way you learn to eat in Grand Rapids or Saginaw or Alpena. It is, however, socially acceptable politesse in certain tenement neighborhoods of Detroit.

I had already decided on the con I was going to use. It's an old favorite of Toni's called The Big Store, and it goes something like this. The con woman visits the mark, claiming to represent a fabulously wealthy developer. The con woman knows of a pending real estate deal that will make the mark as rich as Donald Trump. Because of sundry reasons, the con woman cannot possibly swing this deal by herself. So she offers to go partners with the mark in a brand-new corporation. She offers to put a hefty chunk of financing into this new corporation if the mark will do the same. The mark eagerly forwards the money, then sits back and waits for the Big Store to shower him with riches. It never happens, of course. Ten minutes after the mark deposits his share, the con woman cleans out that bank account and skips town.

It's a great scam, and it's kept Toni in silks and satins for many a year. But it does generate a lot of heat. Six years ago, Toni skinned an Atlanta banker in a Big Store game, and the Georgia Bureau of Investigation is still looking for her.

Somehow I had to convince Jerry Carmody to team up with me in a corporation to develop Deer Cove. I was going to con him into thinking I represented a well-heeled New York banking consortium. My nonexistent clients would be willing to put up four million to buy bloc shares in the Deer Cove firm if Lakeside would do likewise. I'd arrange for the money to be held in an escrow account at Jaswell's bank.

While working for this Deer Cove firm, I would be looking for Jim Tolliver's killer. Once I'd identified him, I would ransack that escrow account, disappear with Lakeside's four million, and leave behind a letter proving that the killer and I had planned the theft together. The Michigan law would take it from there. It would be the greatest frame job since *Whistler's Mother*.

First, though, I would have to sell Carmody on the scheme, and that wouldn't be easy. A Motown refugee wouldn't bite at the same bait as a graduate of Harvard Business School. I was going to have to add a little embroidery to my Big Store tale.

"Did you enjoy the meal?" Jerry asked, dabbing at his moustache with the napkin. He left the linen in a crumpled heap beside his plate.

"Very lovely. Thank you." I fingered my long-stemmed cocktail glass. "But I insist that we split the bill."

"Hey, not a chance. Consider it the compliments of Lakeside, Andrea."

I felt his knees close around one of mine. Intimate rubbing of polyester against nylon. I remembered Mary Beth at the counter and wondered if I ought to tote along that steak knife as protection.

I drew my captive knee away. Flashed him a warning frown. "That's not what I'm here for, Mr. Carmody."

"Then you may have had a wasted trip, Andrea. The word is, the McCann farm is not for sale."

"That's not what I hear from Dick Jaswell."

"Mary Beth Tolliver isn't available to sign."

"And where is she, Jer?"

With a grunt, he leaned back, laced his knuckly fingers together, and showed me a petulant look. "Who the fuck knows? She went flippy after her old man died. Skipped town." His face betrayed a shadow of momentary anger. "It shouldn't have happened. I pay people good money to keep things like that from happening." All at once, remembering my presence there, he pasted on a confident smile. It reminded me of a lopsided painting. "Don't worry about it. I put the word out. The Tolliver woman has to surface sometime. When she does, I'll have her brought back. We'll get that signature for you, Andrea. And then we'll see that she goes away for a nice, long rest. Flippy broad like that, she needs lots of peace and quiet, right?"

Put the word out. Boy, did that give me a queasy chill. I didn't think Jerry was referring to his chums in the Chamber of Commerce. The moustachioed fellow was wafting a decidedly underworld smell. Fearful questions began to emerge. Just who was going to get "the word?" How hard could it be to find a chestnut-haired pregnant lady? Had Mary Beth and I made ourselves memorable while passing through Duluth? I wondered if I ought to get in touch with Chief. Tell him to use the eight-round combat extension load in the Remington 870 and to be wary of strangers.

"Deer Cove will be a single marketable unit, Andrea," he continued. "Now, why don't you tell me just why it's so important to you?"

Just then, a vibrant male baritone rang out behind me. "Jerry! Hey, Jer!"

Turning, I saw a couple standing in the foyer. The man caught my eye at once. Light brown hair, tiny cleft in the chin, good nose, and eyes the color of a South Dakota summer sky. Mmmmmmm — cute! I liked the set of his shoulders, the lanky length of his arms and legs. He shepherded his brunette companion through the maze of tables.

"Saw your car in the lot, Jer. Figured we'd come in and say hi." I liked Mr. Cute's profile even better close up. That grin made him the perfect candidate for a TV commercial. I was looking at a five-digit orthodonture bill. "You folks had lunch yet?"

"We just finished, Donny. But stay for a drink, why don't you?"

"Business lunch?" The brunette had an evenly modulated contralto voice, just a shade deeper than mine. A lot of ice-cold class there. Diamond-shaped face, narrow chin, classic cheekbones, a slim nose, a Cupid's bow mouth, and eyes the color of Dutch chocolate. Wavy, shoulder-length hair swirled down from a high part on the right, obscuring part of her forehead, framing her delicate olive-tinted face. Flawless makeup and golden hoop earrings. Wet-look lipstick and oversized khaki chambray workshirt and form-fitting white gabardine slacks. She let Donny draw a chair for her, then rewarded him with a wrist squeeze and a coy smile.

The gesture was a message to me. Formal notification of possession. This one's taken, darling. Go find your own.

Jerry introduced them as Donald Winston Pierce and Monica Lonardo. Donny was a local boy, the son and heir of Tilford's leading industrialist, Keith Pierce, a gentleman whose name was always spoken in reverential whispers. Donny ramrodded the Junior Chamber and handled public relations for his father's flagship company, Pierce Saw and Steel. Continual presence in the office was not required. Here it was, one-thirty in the afternoon, and Donald was fresh from his daily tennis game at the Lynx River Country Club.

Monica told me that she hailed from New York but would say nothing more about that. I guessed that she had come out to the U.P. on a modeling shoot, fallen head-over-heels for her handsome Northland prince, and was now happily living in sin with her lucrative consort. It had been quite a while since Monica's exquisitely manicured nails had punished a keyboard.

Naturally, the three of them wanted to know all about me, so I invented a plausible biography for Andrea Porter, complete with a fondly remembered childhood in Madison, South Dakota. I'd done my Princess Lilionah high dives there back in April and could pretty accurately describe the town. Right down to all the flagpoles in the Bicentennial park. Add to that college in the Twin Cities, a hectic real estate apprenticeship in Sioux Falls, a recent move to the Soo, and you had a fairly comprehensive background for the mysterious Ms. Porter.

Donny was the only one who made it a conversation. Jerry merely sat back and listened, not missing a word. Monica sipped a highball and made no effort to conceal her boredom.

"Andrea, I would have thought you could have done a whole lot better in the Falls," Donny commented.

"Not really. The competition in Sioux Falls is too intense. You're really under the gun to move houses," I replied. "Besides, let's face it. The commercial sector's heavily overbuilt out there. You can only have so many malls for two hundred thousand shoppers. People aren't going to drive all the way in from Chamberlain. I like the U.P., Donny. This area's primed to move, and I want to be in on the ground floor. I'd much rather work in this market."

Donny's eyes gleamed with interest. "That's what I keep telling my dad. And the other old-timers in the Chamber. Tilford missed out on the construction boom in the middle eighties. Industry's moving out of New York and Pennsylvania. Aging plants. Union problems. The area that can get its act together can pick up some choice plums."

Jerry snorted. "More of that shoulder-to-shoulder shit, eh?"

"It's the only way to go, Jer." Donny looked irritated, but he kept his voice down, as if unwilling to antagonize the other man. "Look, if you want to deal with these guys, you have to have your house in order. That means they can come in and build. And not have to worry about a jump in tax assessments next year." His glance was rueful. "The Old Guard wants it both ways, Andrea. They want to bring in new industry. Yet they also want to maintain Finlayson County exactly the way it was when they were kids. You should've seen the fuss when I was in junior high, when the state turned 678 into a four-lane road."

I cleaned my lips and dropped the napkin. "I'll see what I can do to convert them to the true faith, Don."

"That's the spirit! Andrea, I'm drafting you into the ranks of the progressive. Lord knows we could use a few more forward-looking women in this community."

Jerry looked as if he had gas. "Please! There's enough of those already."

"How sexist can you get!" Monica turned a tart smile on him. "Where have you been for the last forty years, buster? Whether you like it or not, we're in the work-place to stay."

"Hey, come on, Monica . . ." Jerry went into his act. Mr. Charm. Silly smile and outspread arms. "You know I've got nothing against women in *business.*"

I caught Jerry's subtle, deliberate emphasis on the word, heard Monica's gust of sudden laughter, and puzzled over the knowing gleam in her dark brown eyes. An in-joke, of course, its meaning known only to the two of them.

I turned my gaze on the heir. I was growing quite fond of that endearing little cleft in Donny's chin. And I liked the way his polo shirt fit snugly in the chest and biceps. Donny's open-hearted sincerity and diligent interest in the county's well-being added up to pluses in my general ledger. I had a feeling I was chatting with Congressman Burdick's eventual successor.

Then Donny's gaze met mine, and I experienced a deep, warm shiver. The forthrightness of his stare was a little disconcerting. I made my smile polite. His seemed a bit eager.

"Do you like to play tennis, Andrea?"

"Once in a while."

107

"Have you ever played up at Stony Ridge?"

The name threw me for a moment, and then I remembered Mary Beth telling me about her married life in the Soo. She, Jim, and Andy Capobianco had played many a racquetball game there. Awkward, tentative smile. "Uh, Donny, Stony Ridge is a little beyond the income range of us poor, hardworking real estate ladies."

"That's going to change." Grinning at me, Donny leaned back in his chair. "Jer, I move that we obtain a guest membership at Lynx River for your lovely luncheon guest."

"Shit, yeah! Seconded. You'll love the place, Andrea."

Monica's smooth hand alighted on her consort's wrist. "Good idea, *querido*." The smile she flashed me was friendly enough, but its warmth didn't quite reach her eyes. "We'll have to have a game some time. I hate playing with Donny. He never lets me win."

"The game isn't any fun, Monica, unless it's for real."

Moist lips made a moue of disappointment. "*Querido,* I'm out of cigarettes."

Donny's tone was teasing. "If you quit smoking, your tennis game would improve."

"*Don*-neeeee . . ."

"No problem, hon. We can pick some up on the way back to—"

Monica tilted her head toward the foyer. "There's a cigarette machine over there," she snapped.

Their gazes met, locked, and identical frowns appeared. There are some couples who can fight like that, using wordless glares. Rory and I were shouters. Square off and bellow at each other for fifteen or twenty minutes. This pair did it all with looks.

Sixty seconds later, Donald, that soul of politeness, let out a hushed sigh of frustration, excused himself, and departed on his errand. His shoulders were tense as he sauntered between tables. Monica aimed a well-satisfied smirk at me. See my obedient puppy.

There would be more discussion between those two on the way back to town. Of that I had no doubt.

Monica permitted many things within the context of their relationship. Unfortunately for Donny, offering guest memberships to comely lady realtors was not one of them. There would be punishment.

On our way out, I noticed an antique mirror hanging above the stalwart brick fireplace. While Jerry saw to the check, I gave myself the once-over, reviewed the status of the lipstick, ran my fingers through the cascade of raven hair. I saw motion within the reflection. Glancing at the upper corner, I found a rearview image of Jerry and Monica at the cashier's counter.

All at once, Jerry's hand grabbed a quarter pound of feminine derriere and gave it a loving squeeze. I was hoping Monica would plant a resounding wallop on the side of his face, but she disappointed me. Instead, she flashed a quick look of annoyance and muttered, "Christ! Is that all you ever think about?"

"What else is there, babe?" He gave that well-shaped seat a jolly smack, just for luck, and was still guffawing when I rejoined them.

We said good-bye to the lovely couple in the Caribou lot and drove back to Lakeside. I had intended to get Jerry talking about Jim Tolliver. But somehow I couldn't get Donny and his lady love out of my mind. Monica's placid acceptance of the fondling bothered me. She couldn't be involved with a sleaze like Jerry — could she? What kind of handle did Jerry have on her? And was Donny aware of it?

I'd expected a tightly knit establishment when I first arrived in Tilford. But this crew was downright incestuous.

I hoped Jerry was in a talkative mood.

"So what about those two?"

"That's Tilford's great romantic tragedy, kid. Romeo and Juliet. With Donny as Juliet!" He uttered a short, harsh laugh.

"Come again?"

"Ahhhhh, old man Pierce is standing in the way of true love. He doesn't want any chili-bean grandchildren." Jerry's gaze flitted between me and the front windshield, but he kept both hands on the wheel. "Donny can marry that Jane if he wants. He's of age. But the minute he does, he can kiss Pierce Industries good-bye. The old man will cut him off without a dime."

"He could tell dear old Dad to take a flying leap."

"He could. But he won't. Donny may be lovesick, but he's no fool. Pierce Industries' aggregate worth is in the neighborhood of eighty-five million." Jerry nodded in sincere appreciation. "So things are at an impasse. Donny would dearly love to be fucking the Spic. But Monica's got him on starvation rations, holding out for a wedding ring." He laughed as if that was the funniest thing he'd heard all year.

This time, I let my natural distaste gush forth. "You are one romantic bastard, Carmody, you know that?"

"What's the matter with you?"

"Has it ever occurred to you that Donny may truly be in love with that woman?"

"What is it with you broads, anyway?" Jerry's look of incomprehension was quite real. "That guy's supposed to flush his life down the shitter for the sake of true love? Take it from me, babe. No piece of ass is worth eighty-five mil."

"If Donny wanted to marry her badly enough, I'm sure he'd find a way to make it on his own."

"Don't kid yourself, babe. The old man casts a long shadow up here. All he has to do is give the word, and Donny's an orphan. The kid couldn't even get a job flipping hamburgers."

"Does that go for everyone in Tilford, Jer?"

"Cross him and find out, sweetie. Tell you one thing, though" — Jerry slid two fingers over my knee — "You get on old man Pierce's bad side, and it'll be a long, long time before you can afford another pair of those hundred-dollar shoes."

I gave the insinuating hand a stinging rap. "What's Monica doing about all this?"

"Turning up the stove heat one notch at a time." He shot me an affronted look, but the hand kept its distance. "Monica lives out on Houk Point. She gets Donny so steamed up, he doesn't know if he's on foot or horseback. Just when he thinks he's spending the night, Monica gives him a chaste little kiss and ushers him out the door. I saw him at the Birchbark one night. Monica had given him the gate, and he was trying to get looped enough to forget that hard-on between his knees."

Jerry laughed at that one all the way back to Lakeside.

Well, what can I say? Some, like Donny Pierce, are born to be gentlemen. And some turn out like Jerry Carmody. Among the Jerry-predators of this world, you'll find neither belief in nor desire to find the something that transcends the physical act of copulation. They are cheerless hunters, the Jerries, and theirs is an endless search for the nerve-tingling rush of climax. The partner is merely a sexual receptacle, whose goodwill is necessary for the achievement of orgasm. Love words are verbal currency redeemable in ass.

I considered rigging my Big Store game in such a way as to ensure that Jerry took a hard fall, too. I wanted Jerry to do a little prison time in Jackson. I wanted him naked in front of a shower wall, experiencing the same terror as Mary Beth.

Yet, for Jerry to appreciate the irony, for him to feel the weight of such punishment, he first had to possess a sensitivity that, in him, was completely lacking. The glass bottle has no way of knowing whether it's filled with milk or urine.

So forget the fervid dreams of vengeance, Angie. Stick with the mission. Merry Jerry is a member in good standing of the Tilford establishment. He has squirreled away plenty of markers from area politicians. He may even own his own congressman. No way will he ever be back-door pussy in Jackson. You'll never get him near a courtroom.

So go in cold and take him for every penny of that four million. Leave him flat-busted broke, with everyone at the Lynx River Country Club laughing their socks off at him. And be satisfied that it's all you can possibly do.

# Chapter Seven

I spent the remainder of the afternoon in the Lakeside conference room. Jerry called in his civil engineers, his accountants, and the company's legal counsel. Helpful aides spread site maps of the Deer Cove area on the table in front of me. Molly the Skittish occupied the corner seat, legs primly crossed, dutifully recording the minutes of this planning meeting.

I gave them all a rerun of my presentation to Dick Jaswell. The Lakeside people were sharp, and they hit me with a flurry of questions. Developmental costs, marketability, bond issue, incorporation, scope of the project. Striking a realtor's pose, I fielded the questions as best I could. Just as he had at the Caribou, Jerry leaned back in his padded chair, tilted his head slightly, and let his shrewd gaze drift between me and the inquisitors.

Shortly before six, Jerry called it quits. "That's enough for now. Molly, I want those minutes typed up for tomorrow. Copies for me and Ms. Porter."

They all trooped out of the conference room.

I watched Jerry swing his swivel chair about and gaze out the drapery-rimmed window. The building's lengthy, late-afternoon shadow discolored Superior's windswept surface and cat's-paw waves.

"You all talked out, Andrea?"

"Not quite." I rolled up the site maps.

"Good! Because I've still got a few questions." He

swiveled back to face me. "Number one, what do I get out of all this?"

Jerry's strategy was perfectly clear. A detailed cross-examination at the end of an exhausting meeting. Ferret out the weak points in the lady's arguments. But I was ready for him. If anything, that three-hour inquisition had been the greatest dress rehearsal an actress could have asked for. By now, I literally *was* Andrea Porter, real estate sharpshooter.

"I thought that was obvious, Jerry. Title to Deer Cove will be held by the new corporation. You'll control that corporation. The industrial park will be your baby all the way."

"Next question — if it's that simple, babe, why do I need *you?*"

"Why haven't you done it already?"

"I have a number of plans for that area. Lakeside's first task has been acquisition of all six parcels. I hadn't really thought about an industrial park, though." He reached into an inner pocket, withdrew a pack of Marlboros, shook one out, and stuck it between his lips. Big wicked smile. "But now that you've pointed out the potential benefits . . ."

I placed both palms on the table. "And who's going to finance it, Jer?"

"Lakeside has an excellent line of credit."

"Don't try to shit me, Jerry." I flipped open my leather notebook and scanned a few notes I'd taken at the Registry of Deeds. "You haven't got anywhere near the funding needed to undertake a project of this magnitude. Since January, Lakeside has been working on an eleven-million-dollar town house development at Nijonik Beach. One hundred and sixty-four units. You've also started a seventy-two-unit project in Seney valued at six-point-five million. You're drawn to the limit, and you'd need double those amounts to cover a loan. If you don't go in with at least twenty-five percent down, the bank's loan committee won't even let you take your coat off."

113

"Jaswell will do it. No problem."

Jaswell, eh? It was so nice to have official confirmation of my earlier suspicions.

"Sure he will. Because he's your boy. But you know as well as I do that First South Shore Savings can't possibly handle that kind of financing on their own. Jaswell's board of directors would boot him out tomorrow if he so much as suggested it." Tall heels clicking on the well-polished floor, I circled the table. "The only way Dick Jaswell can help you is if he puts together a loan package composed of several banks. And you know damned well what'll happen if he does that."

Only those lidded eyes betrayed him. "You're a smart girl. Why don't you tell me?"

I leaned against the table's edge. "Jaswell won't be able to call the shots if he's just one banker in a consortium. That means you'd lose control of the financing. You'd have to compete with other development firms for construction contracts within the park. No more guaranteed gravy for Lakeside. Another developer might outbid you, Jerry, and then you'd be holding your ass."

"And you're the lady with the financing."

I nodded slowly.

"Next question—why are your banker friends so interested in the U.P.?"

I took a deep breath, knowing I had to play this very carefully. Jerry was a bit cagier than your average mark. To convince him that I had access to all that nonexistent money, I had to cook up a very plausible cover story.

"Some very smart people made some very bad mistakes, pouring all those billions into the Third World. The money was supposed to build up industry. The bandidos running those countries pissed it all away on trips to Disney World. End result—the banks' paper began to lose its value. Those Third World loans weren't worth shit, and everybody knew it. The banks had to start moving investment capital into some really solid loans. They needed to show their bondholders lists of nice, productive, income-generating loans. Loans with a good probability of being repaid. So the word went out. Find us economically healthy projects in the advanced countries."

"Where do you fit in?"

"I'm a bird dog, Jer. Like I told Dick Jaswell, I've built up my own clientele within the industry. I heard of some interest in the Great Lakes area, so I put together a list of potential sites. Deer Cove made the list."

"How many sites have you lined up?"

"Four. If Tilford goes under, I'm on my way to Ludington next." I showed him an expression of utter determination. "This is a once-in-a-lifetime opportunity, Jerry. My ticket out of sales. I'm not letting it slip through my fingers."

"Interesting . . ." With thumb and forefinger, he smoothed the ends of his moustache. "I've got my hands on a site and no access to money. You've got the money but no site. That's about it, isn't it?" He sent me another doubtful look. "What's to stop me from going right over your sweet little head, babe?"

"But you won't, Jer."

"And why not?"

"Because you don't have all of Deer Cove. Mary Beth Tolliver still owns the McCann farm."

Thin lips tightened. "We'll find her."

"Good hunting then." I gave him a jaunty little wave on my way out. "I'll send you a postcard from Ludington."

"Wait a minute!" Ten quick strides put him between me and the door. "Let's cut the bullshit, okay? I want to hear the bottom line. All right, so for now I can't move that fucking farm. How's this industrial park of yours supposed to get off the ground, eh?"

"Why, Jerry, I wave my magic wand. Just like my fairy godmother taught me."

Color flooded upward from his shirt collar, and I immediately regretted the witticism. Poking sticks into the animal's cage is not very smart. Particularly when there are no bars between you.

"I said, cut the shit!" Jerry ground it out between clenched teeth. "Why did you come to me?"

I watched his color recede, shivering at the memory of that sudden rage. And wondered if Brian McCann had seen the same thing, too, that March day on the wharf.

"You're the only one who can make it happen, Jerry. You can charter the industrial park corporation and get me a seat on its board."

"And if I do that?"

"Then I go to New York and sell the consortium on Deer Cove."

"Deer Cove isn't marketable yet."

"But they don't know that, do they?"

Comprehension brightened Jerry's features.

"You've got it." I nodded slowly. "You give me that seat on the board, and the consortium gets the all-clear."

"Clever, babe."

The prospect of imminent success made me tingle all over. I'd dangled the possibility of fabulous wealth before those bestial eyes, and Jerry had lunged for it with both hands. It was time for a glorious Angie smile.

"It's all settled then?"

Jerry's good humor abruptly vanished. In its place was a grim thoughtfulness. Putting a proprietary arm across my shoulders, he ushered me out the door.

"It's not as simple as that, Andrea. I can't give you a firm answer right now. I have to talk to a few people. You know how it is."

Unpleasant reality obliterated my smile. "Not exactly, Jerry. How is it?"

His quick paranoid glance zipped up the corridor, seeking eavesdroppers. "Could you put off that Ludington trip for a few days?"

"If I have to."

Jerry's attempt to build a confident expression wilted under the pressure of an all-too-apparent anxiety. "This is too goddamned big, Andrea. We need time to think it over. We'll be in touch."

And that was it. Jerry closed the door, and I found

myself looking at my reflection in his polished brass nameplate.

*We* . . .

That single word knocked down the whole elaborate theoretical structure I'd built on the basis of my talks with Mary Beth. Up until now, everything I'd learned about Tilford seemed to have affirmed my original assumption that Carmody was the main man at Lakeside.

And I was wrong. Merry Jerry wasn't the bold business buccaneer I had loved to hate. He was a team player, a front man for the real Lakeside boss. Whoever he was. Or she.

Complications! My Big Store game was geared to a false assumption. As Lakeside personified, Jerry was supposed to snap at the bait and give me a shot at Mary Beth's stolen legacy. Instead, front man Carmody had chickened out and shoved it all right back at me.

More complications! Jerry might not have murdered Brian McCann and Jim Tolliver to get his hands on Deer Cove. Oh, I couldn't exactly rule him out yet. There was that interesting comment about "putting the word out" on Mary Beth. And Jerry had just told me that he'd had long-term plans for Deer Cove. And, judging from that flash of rage a few minutes ago, Jerry was perfectly capable of splitting an old man's skull with a gaff.

On the other hand, Jerry's silent partner might have killed them. Or perhaps the silent partner had ordered Jerry to do it.

Then again, the murderer might be someone else entirely. Perhaps someone hoping to win the favor of either Jerry or the silent partner by doing away with the McCann/Tolliver nuisance.

I frowned at my nameplate reflection. What now, Miss Biwaban?

Well, there wasn't much I could do at this particular moment. Jerry was undoubtedly carrying the word to his clandestine boss. All I could do was sit tight and hope

117

that the boss found my scam as alluring as did Jaswell and Carmody. Sit and wait.

Attention, boss. Come out, come out, wherever you are. Here I am. Come out and take your best shot at Angie.

Just what I've always wanted to be. Little Miss Target.


Friday, May the twenty-ninth, plastered the U.P. with sunshiny mugginess more suited to Panama. I spent that sweltering morn in the outdoor pool at the Edgewater Motel, doing slow crawls up and down its sparkling length. There is something deliciously decadent about splashing around in sun-warmed waters while the majority of your fellow citizens are gainfully employed. Picking up the pace, muscles stretching and tightening, I performed a graceful dolphin turn and headed for the low board once more.

I heard a man call my name. Halting in front of the swim ladder, I treaded water up to my chin and swept the soaked tresses from my face. A tall masculine shadow appeared on the sun-dappled surface of the pool. "Hello, Andrea."

And hello to you, Donald Winston Pierce, president of the Junior Jaycees, standing by the ladder with my big fluffy towel in your tanned, willing hands. I like the light gray blazer. And I hope you like my French-cut navy blue tank suit. At the very least, I am heartily glad to be wearing it at this auspicious moment.

Up the slippery ladder, streaming water like a seal. Laughter and surprised greetings. Brisk but gentlemanly rubdown with the towel. Ruffle the raven hair. Drape the towel over womanly shoulders. Thank you, kind sir. Affectionate hug. More joshing and silly smiles and relaxing sprawls in poolside deck chairs.

"You're going to get canned, young lady." Donny rested his elbows on the bleached wooden armrests, showing me a broad smile. "Goofing off around the pool when you ought to be out moving two-hundred-thousand-dollar homes. Wait till Bosso finds out."

"Tell me, does your employer know just where you are at this particular moment, Mis-ter Pierce?"

"Right now I'm wearing my Jaycee *el presidente* hat. So I get to be my own boss. At least until nine A.M. tomorrow."

"Self-employment is an important goal of mine, too."

I liked that teasing smile of his. "So you're not too worried about getting fired?"

"I just might have something else lined up."

Swinging his long legs over the side of the chair, Donny faced me, his expression somber. "The deal with Jerry Carmody?"

"Leading question, Mr. P."

"I talked to Ed Salvucci this morning. Civil engineer with Lakeside. He told me all about an exhaustive meeting in the conference room yesterday afternoon. The star performer was a bright, young, black-haired lady realtor. The subject was the theoretical development of the McCann properties on Route 678."

"The key word is *theoretical*, Don."

"And the other key words are *acquisition, subdivision,* and *industrial usage*." He leaned an inch closer, forearms resting on his knees, jaw muscles tightening with resolve. "I like the concept. It's exactly the kind of kick in the ass this area needs. So I'd like you to consider this an audition, Andrea."

"Donny, there's nothing to audition for. Not yet, anyway."

Clenching his fists impatiently, Donny knocked opposing knuckles together. "Look, I've got investment capital of my own set aside. Just let me know when the first issue of shares takes place. I want in on the ground floor."

"The whole thing may never get off the ground. You realize that, don't you?"

He nodded grimly. "But we'll get it off the ground, Andrea. The two of us together. I've been waiting for a chance like this for a long time. If I play my cards right, I could wind up with a seven-digit income."

I couldn't resist smiling. "I thought you already had one of those."

Donny assumed the gravity and dignity you find at college graduations. At least among the guest speakers. Rule Number One in How to Marry a Millionaire: Never kid the rich about their money.

"Most of my inheritance is tied up in trust, with the exception of a pair of mutual funds. Interest on the trust accounts generates my venture capital. Salaries take care of the living expenses. I have the money, Andrea." I found a glint of desperation in his eyes, the forlorn look of the baseball hopeful who's been condemned to riding a bench. "It's the most important thing in my life. I need to make my own money. For my own reasons."

I remembered what Jerry Carmody had said and wondered if Donny's bid for financial independence was fueled by that stalwart desire to marry Monica Lonardo. Perhaps old man Pierce's threat was in earnest. Big dividends from investments in the proposed industrial park would certainly take some of the sting out of losing that eighty-five million. In addition, his association with the Deer Cove development effort would serve Donny well should he ever make a political bid for Burdick's seat.

Just then, a cleaning lady in a khaki shirtdress came out onto the sundeck. Shading her forehead, she leaned over the wooden railing and said, " 'Scuse me! Are you Miss Porter?"

I sat upright. "Yes, I am."

"Phone call for you. You can take it at the front desk."

"Thanks!" Draping the towel over my neck, I stood up. Donny rose as well, showing me a lopsided smile.

"I told you Bosso would be looking for you."

I pursed wry lips. "Listen, fella, I just might wind up asking you for a job."

Donny walked me to the sliding glass doors. "Tell me, are you busy tomorrow?"

"Not particularly. Why?"

"I thought you might want to give your new guest membership a workout. Kathy Veeder's getting married tomorrow. We're having the reception at the club around two. Care to come?"

The name rang an immediate bell. "Veeder Gas and Oil, right?"

Donny looked at me strangely. "You know them?"

Oh, Angie, when will you learn to keep your big mouth shut? Flashing a tepid smile, I added, "Kathy and I were in the same sorority." Desperately quick change of subject. "Besides, Don, don't I need an invitation to attend that reception?"

Halting at the doorstep, Donny took a ballpoint pen and a small white business card from his breast pocket. He jotted a hasty message on the back of the card, then handed it to me. "There's your invitation. I'll see you at two." Then, squeezing my hand, he gave me a solemn look. "Don't forget what I said. I can be a big help to you, Andrea."

"Donny, I'm a big girl now. I don't need a chaperon."

"I know the local real estate market—"

"Fine! We'll get you a broker's license."

"Honey, I'm not kidding around. It's a pretty choppy swimming pool. I can warn you if Carmody tries to pull anything cute."

I'm not sure what impressed me more—Donny's sudden anxiety or the endearing way he said *honey*. It made me want to hear it again. Trying to keep my poise, I went for the jovial approach. "Hey, I think I can handle Jerry Carmody."

"You don't know what kind of man he is." The harsh tone startled me. I'd thought Donny too much the gentleman to let such distaste show. "Andrea, you have no idea what Jerry Carmody is capable of."

I felt a cold spot on the back of my spine, just above the lumbar region. Was Donny trying to tell me about the Tollivers? I decided to give him an opening.

"Give me a for-instance, Mr. P!"

121

"It's nothing to joke about, Andrea," he said sternly. "There was a lot of labor trouble here three years ago."

"Labor trouble?" I echoed.

"Lakeside Development had many good years farming out construction to little outfits here in the county. Like Glenn Veeder's crew. Then the Michigan Pipelayers' Union, Local Number 357, began organizing Lakeside construction workers. Four crews went on strike. Lakeside was in deep shit. They had due dates breathing down their necks and four condominium projects in varying stages of completion. Then Carmody showed up in town. Wayne Burdick told me he'd hired him as a labor consultant. Right! You know what Carmody used to do in Detroit?"

Ladylike shake of the head.

"He kept the books for the International Federation of Toolmakers," Donny added, his features tense. "And they are *not* AFL-CIO. Carmody was under indictment in Detroit. While he was their head accountant, the Toolmakers' pension fund somehow mislaid three million dollars." He exhaled heavily. "Look, Andrea, my father and I aren't exactly union fans. But there are better ways of solving problems than bringing in a leg breaker like Carmody. It was a dirty business all around."

I could understand Donny's indignation. I had heard of the Toolmakers, courtesy of the TV show *Sixty Minutes,* and their affiliation was definitely Ehm-Oh-Bee. Retired Federation officers had a tendency to wind up buried in supermarket parking lots.

The underworld smell was getting a bit stronger. Now I understood the framework of Jerry's remark "put the word out." So he was connected. And capable of killing Mary Beth's men. But what intrigued me most of all was the information that Congressman Burdick had brought Jerry to Tilford.

The forest was growing darker and nastier all the time.

Show the heir a masterful smirk. Run my fingertips

122

along his crisp lapel. Puckish smile. "Don't worry about me, Don. If Carmody tries anything, I'll give him a good skinning and send him toddling home in a barrel."

"Andrea, please listen to me. Don't underestimate him!"

"Donald . . ." I looped my towel around his neck, drew his face within an inch of mine, flashed a crooked Angie smile. "You're a very sweet guy, and I like you a lot. But let's get something straight right now. I am not your kid sister. *Capisce?* I can take care of myself."

"Maybe I'll ask you to prove that to me."

"How?"

No sooner had I spoken than I felt the warm pressure of Donny's muscular forearm behind my spine. My startled gaze met his, and a whole lot of subliminal communication went on. I was just getting it all sorted out when Donny's lips touched mine. And then my diligent effort at reconstruction collapsed in a surge of delightful emotions.

Lovely kiss. My first in a long, long time. Easily on a par with the pre-Springfield smooches. Definitely well worth waiting for. Delicious! Donny's kiss left me with tingly lips and a triphammer heartbeat, giddy breathlessness, and a cozily warm all-over glow.

If Rory had known how to kiss like that, I never would have left Bozeman.

Somewhere in the motel, that sadistic telephone jangled. Donny reluctantly broke it off. I began wishing that Alexander Graham Bell had been drowned at birth.

"You have a call waiting," Donny murmured, sliding open the glass door for me.

"I'm tempted to let them wait."

"It might be Bosso. Better go answer it, honey."

"I despise practical men." Waggling my fingers in farewell, I strolled into the air-conditioned lobby.

"For the record, Andrea, I never considered you my kid sister."

I glanced over my shoulder, saw him smiling at me through the glass, then very unwillingly hotfooted it across the lobby's plush carpet. I turned my radiant smile on the desk clerk. He showed me an impatient look and handed me the beige telephone receiver.

"Andrea Porter?"

Feminine voice. Brisk, no-nonsense, throaty contralto. Familiar flat tones of the U.P.

"This is Andrea," I replied.

"Ms. Porter, are you available for a late lunch?"

"That depends on who's offering the invitation."

Sharp intake of breath. Annoyance at the sassy black-haired minx. "Ms. Porter, I haven't time for silly games. You're invited to lunch at the Shoreliner Hotel. The Birney Room. Three o'clock. Be there."

"Who is this?"

"If you're still interested in that seat on the board, I'd advise you to come. Please don't be late. I'm not the sort of woman who likes to be kept waiting." *Click!*

I replaced the receiver. Well! What do we make of that?

The accent makes her a Yooper, and the tone drips with authority. She reminded me a lot of the screws at Springfield. *Shake your ass, Biwaban!* Sounds to me as if our mystery lady has some military service in her background.

The lady knows about Andrea's behind-the-scenes maneuvering. That means she knows what Jerry and I discussed after yesterday's meeting. Which probably means that Jerry reported the gist of our conversation to her.

Was I just talking to Jerry's silent partner?

Only one way to find out.

Precisely at two-fifty-five, I crossed the marble-floored lobby of the venerable Shoreliner Hotel. It was a gracefully aging dinosaur from the Grant presidency, built when Tilford was still a lumberjack camp. My heels made no sound on the Persian carpet. The clerk gave me directions to the Birney Room, and then I set off down a long, narrow, oak-trimmed corridor. My swimsuit had given way to a midnight blue double-breasted jacket, a white mock-turtleneck blouse, and a slim gray dirndl skirt. As I walked along, my gaze took in the beeswaxed oak and the velour drapery and the antique eight-piece chandeliers. Lumber and railroad money had built the Shoreliner. The continued patronage of the Pierce family and their affluent peers had helped to maintain its old-fashioned elegance. I could easily visualize Donny coming here as a kid for Sunday dinner.

The Birney Room had once been a reception parlor. I counted no more than eight dining tables in there. Pink brick Victorian fireplace, polished brass light fixtures, and plenty of cherrywood trimming.

Welcome, Miss Porter, and here's your table—right next to the colored glass window offering a view of the sunlit town square and its Civil War monument. I was seated with minuscule fanfare, offered a clothbound menu, and informed that my luncheon guest would be joining me shortly.

At two minutes past three, I heard the tock-tock of stiletto heels on the oakwood floor. Turning, I saw a woman heading straight for me. She was perhaps an inch over my five-foot-four, a round-faced matron with short, stiff brownish blond hair. At first I put her age at thirty-five. Then I noticed the telltale grooves on either side of the plum-colored mouth, the parallel forehead lines, the poreless look of pancake makeup. A matron, all right, but one on the far side of forty. Beige velveteen suit and ivory Crepe de Chine blouse. She offered me her long-fingered hand, beaming at me as if I were her long-lost daughter.

"Andrea! How do you do? I'm Mavis Heisler."

Her accent was pure Yooper. With a firm and friendly smile, she shook my hand and gave me an approving nod. I didn't have to fake a look of confusion. I couldn't see how this woman was tied in with Jerry. Unless, of course, the mob was now doing its recruiting in the League of Women Voters.

Play it cozy. "Excuse me, do I know you?"

"We have a mutual friend named Carmody."

"Correction, please. *You* have a friend named Carmody."

"Jerry said you have a mouth on you." Mavis lifted her soft chin, and a red-vested waiter came rocketing all the way across the room to draw the sycamore chair for her. Radiating an aura of Hollywood intrigue, she seated herself. "Try to remember your manners, child. After all, I'm your hostess."

I showed a toothy smile. "I don't respond well to imperious telephone calls, I'm afraid."

"A necessity, Andrea. And I apologize." Her expression changed all at once, shifting to a kissy-kissy, how-marvelous-you-look-dear smirk. With deft touches, she unfolded the linen napkin. "We have much to talk about. But we can do that later. I don't know about you, but I'm putting my diet on hold this afternoon." Picking up the menu, she gave me a shrewd once-over. "I can see you're not the diet type. Very fit. You're a runner, I'll bet. Aha—I thought so. Tell me, are you married?"

And so it went all through lunch. Mavis showed me photos of her sons and her cherished grandchildren and bombarded me with all sorts of chatty personal questions. She taxed my storytelling ability to the limit, forcing me to embroider childhood reminiscences on the spot. On and on I babbled, interweaving real-life memories of Madison, South Dakota with outright fiction. Through it all, Mavis smiled and listened and nodded. And there was no doubt in my mind that she was sifting every word, relentlessly searching for the slightest contradiction.

The boeuf bourguignon was superb, but I couldn't really enjoy it. I had a hard time reconciling Jerry the legbreaker with this grand-motherly refugee from the D.A.R. Obviously, Mavis was an emissary from Lakeside's true owner, and she had been sent to look me over. But what was Mavis's place in the enemy chain of command? Was she Jerry's immediate superior? And who was the boss man at the top?

When we finished, the waiter cleared our table and refilled our glasses with sparkling Chardonnay. Mavis opened her kidskin purse and rummaged for cigarettes. I watched her withdraw a thin pack of Virginia Slims and a Spartan battleship gray lighter.

I was intrigued by the way Mavis lit her cigarette. White tube between clasped lips, forehead crinkling, left shoulder protectively hunched, left hand cupping the lighter flame. I recalled her authoritative telephone manner. Okay, so Mavis was in the Navy.

And how did I come to that conclusion? Well, when your Angie was a bright-eyed papoose, her grandfather told her many, many stories about the war they used to call the Big One. I vividly remembered Chief's tale of that wartime cruise from Honolulu to the Saipan beachhead. Breaking the wind with the hunched shoulder, sheltering the tiny flame — that's how swabbies light up aboard ship.

"Let's get right to the point, Andrea." Quick inhalation. Jet of wispy gray from pursed lips. Remorseless dark brown eyes. "Where can we find Mary Beth Tolliver?"

The question hit me right between the eyes. It was the last thing I had ever expected to hear from the neighborly Mrs. Heisler. I flinched inwardly, hurriedly trying to come up with a defense strategy. Masking that wave of astonishment, I offered a slightly puzzled smile and reached for my glass of Chardonnay.

"How should I know?" I lifted my shoulders in a baffled shrug. "Mrs. Tolliver left town months ago. Jerry told me he's still trying to locate her."

"Don't bullshit me!" I've seen friendlier eyes in an alligator den. "You wouldn't go public with that industrial park unless you had access to the Tolliver woman. I repeat the question — where is she?"

"I haven't the foggiest idea."

"Andrea dear, you're a smart girl, but you are way out

127

of your league. You know perfectly well that Deer Cove's no good without the McCann farm. Keeping that fact from your consortium gives you leverage over us and them. However, you cannot possibly make this pay off unless you can push through that final sale. Therefore, you either have Mrs. Tolliver, or you know where she is. Which one is it?"

"No offense, Mavis, but you're out in the back pasture on this one."

She took a dainty sip, then smiled coldly at me over the rim of her wineglass. "I can see right through you, kiddo."

That chilly, omniscient smile of hers was beginning to irritate me. I wanted to see if I could erase it.

"Tell me, Mavis, did you develop that X-ray vision in the Navy?"

The smirk vanished, replaced by deepening wrinkles, a startled expression, and a new respect.

"So you did your homework, eh? As a matter of fact, I had four years in. WAVE lieutenant. ROTC put me through the University of Chicago. I ran the public information office at Alameda." She rapped the cigarette on the ashtray's blunt rim. "You know, you remind me of one of the girls in my outfit. Bright girl, very cheeky, but a little too impertinent for my taste. Word of advice, dear. Bright and sassy little girls who irritate the wrong people sometimes have much to cry about."

"Personally, Mrs. Heisler, I've always considered a ready wit to be a sign of irrepressible charm."

Mavis was too much the professional to waste time in a fruitless game of repartee. Stubbing out her cigarette, she said, "I'll be honest with you. We've looked all over for that Tolliver girl. The situation was handled very badly. Carmody should have come to me earlier. With the proper motivation, I'm sure Mrs. Tolliver could have been persuaded to sign."

"Proper motivation?"

"An out-of-court settlement. A generous cash payment for the bereaved young widow in exchange for a

128

transfer of title. There are civilized ways of handling these matters."

"Like having the sheriff put the roust on her?"

"So you know about that, too." Weary sigh. "I'm afraid that was the sheriff's idea, Andrea. David couldn't resist the impulse to play the good samaritan. His actions complicated matters needlessly. In fact, I was *quite* displeased about it." From the expression on her face, I gathered that Sheriff Dave had received a proper naval ass-chewing. "That is neither here nor there. The problem facing us both right now is the final disposition of the McCann farm. Once the Tolliver girl sells, Deer Cove will become extremely lucrative property. And that will be to our mutual benefit, am I right?"

Yes indeedy, Lieutenant ma'am. And I am quite disturbed by your savage avidity. You are very, very eager to get your hands on Mary Beth. How come?

Mavis finished her wine. "How quickly can you arrange funding?"

I needed a second or two to get back into the role. "Three days. The consortium is poised to bid on the first issue of the common."

Her smile warmed a bit. "We like your idea, Andrea. It'll be good for us. For our area. For you, too, I think."

"Then you're willing to charter the corporation?"

"Within the next few days. We'll contact you."

"Suppose I have to get in touch with you, Mavis."

"I'd prefer that you didn't. But if it's absolutely necessary . . ." She gave her fingers a brisk snap. The waiter hustled over with our check. Taking a pen from him, she dismissed him with a nod and a frown. She scribbled numbers on a napkin, then pushed it across the tabletop at me. "If you need to reach me, call that number and leave your name. I'll phone you at the motel later on. Understood?"

I nodded. "When do I get my seat on the board?"

"Not so fast, dear child." Mavis's gaze turned brittle. "First you come up with Mary Beth Tolliver's signature on a bill of sale. Then we're open to negotiation."

"And how am I supposed to accomplish that?"

Small gust of silvery laughter. Rising abruptly, Mavis shouldered her purse. "If you have Mrs. Tolliver stashed away somewhere, no problem! If you don't . . ." She took a few steps, halted, and glanced over her shoulder at me. Plum-colored lips curved in a tart smile. "Well, I'm sure a bright little girl like you will be able to come up with something." Another condescending head tilt. "Don't worry about the check, Andrea. I'll take care of it. Thank you so much for coming to lunch."

And off she went, shoulders squared, pudgy bottom trembling the narrow skirt. Lieutenant Heisler rushing off to a white-glove inspection. I sure felt sorry for those WAVES at Alameda.

Frowning, I fingered my long-stemmed glass, pondering my next move. Enlisting Andrea Porter into the hunt for Mary Beth was a smart play on Mavis's part. It widened the scope of Lakeside's search, and it tested Andrea's resolve to close the industrial park deal. And if I screwed up, they had a ready-made excuse to deny me a seat on the board.

The luncheon had still left me with some very queasy questions. First I'd heard it from Jerry, now from Mavis. Lakeside was tearing up the Midwest in search of Mary Beth Tolliver. I had the uneasy feeling that there was more at stake here than my friend's signature on a purchase agreement. Could be that someone's bound and determined to finish her off, too, like her husband and her father.

A very odd funhouse, this Lakeside Development Corporation. The visible honcho is a fugitive mobster from Detroit. I lay my Big Store tale on him, and out of the woodwork pops Mavis Heisler, who outwardly resembles my eighth grade math teacher but is easily Jerry's match in sheer ruthlessness. There was something decidedly unnatural about the whole thing. When you shake the coconut tree, you expect a coconut to fall out, not a rutabaga.

My frown deepening, I glanced at the napkin. Maybe

it was time to learn a little bit more about the cold-eyed Mrs. Heisler.

I found a wall-mounted public phone at the end of a side corridor, across from the steamy hot solarium. After popping in the coins, I tapped out the number. One ringy-dingy, then a woman's nasal alto came on line.

"Good afternoon. Congressman Burdick's office."

I blinked at my reflection in the solarium's frosted-glass window. Well, well, the world of Tilford grows ever smaller.

Impatience did not improve the nasal voice. "May I help you, please?"

"Uh, hi there." Improvisation time. "I'm a Native American single mother with three kids, and I just drove up from the L'Anse Indian Reservation, and I called up to find out if I'm eligible for the Department of Education's special retraining program for unemployed single mothers of American Indian ancestry. I've got my high school diploma, and I'd really like to go to college, and—"

"Ma'am, would you please slow down?"

"Huh? Oh, sorry. It's just that I'm parked here in front of Osco's, and I left the motor running, and the kids are playing in the back seat with the dog. Well, anyway, my social worker told me about this program, and she said to call Congressman Burdick's office and ask for somebody named Mavis."

"Mavis Heisler, you mean?"

"That's her. Is she the education coordinator?"

"No, ma'am, Mrs. Heisler is the congressman's aide. She's out to lunch right now, but I would be delighted to give her your message. Would you please give me your name?"

"Certainly." I yanked an amusing alias out of the depths of memory. "It's Charbonneau. Mrs. Charbonneau. See-haitch-ay-are-bee-oh—" Horrified intake of breath. "Oh, my God! My kids are climbing into the

131

front seat! Don't touch that brake! Listen, I have to hang up. Thank you. Bye!"

I replaced the receiver, hoping that Sacajawea, my fellow Native American of Lewis and Clark fame, would forgive my frivolous use of her married name in a telephone con. I didn't worry too much about Mavis learning of my call. Mrs. Charbonneau was merely one of the dozens of constituents calling that office daily to inquire about federal programs. And she had to be legit, right? She had even offered to spell her name. If I was remembered at all, it would be as the harried young mom with the three unruly kids.

I hurried out of the Shoreliner. At that moment, I sincerely wanted to be elsewhere. Pick the spot. Why, I'd even settle for sitting in Paul's office, listening to yet another Holbrook lecture on personal responsibility. I vehemently disliked this close proximity to the federal government. As a congressional aide, Mavis had access to Uncle Sam's police agencies. She's the one who could have sicced the IRS after the Sherman heirs. And she could have asked the FBI, as a personal favor to the congressman, to get a line on Mary Beth Tolliver.

A cold invisible fist closed around my heart. For all I knew, at this very moment, gray-suited Feebees with mirrored sunglasses were knocking on doors in good old Medicine Tail, making inquiries about a pregnant lady named Tolliver.

I have the utmost respect for the Bureau. Bright and sassy little girls who mess with Uncle Sam are liable to spend the best years of their lives sorting laundry in Alderson, West Virginia.

Whoa, Angie. Don't let your imagination run away with you. Didn't Jerry say he'd have his old mob buddies in Detroit do the looking? Since it was highly unlikely that the Feebees would team up with the Outfit, Mavis would have to refrain from calling the *federales* in. She couldn't afford to have them find evidence of collusion with Carmody's old pals in Detroit. The Bureau's organized crime division would have a field day with that kind of information.

I slowed my pace on the way back to the car. I began to wonder if Lakeside's top management was only using me. I mean, what if they really did believe that I had Mary Beth squirreled away somewhere? They could be waiting for me to lead them to her. Sign on the dotted line, Mrs. Tolliver. Then you, too, can have a bullet hole in the middle of your forehead, just like the black-haired minx over there.

Cheerful thought. Maybe I should have come right out and asked Mavis if she was the proud owner of a camel hair coat.

Courage, Miss Biwaban. You're an Anishinabe warrior on the scout, remember? With pluck and daring, you have infiltrated the enemy encampment and slipped into their sagebrush corral. Their finest war ponies are yours for the taking.

There's just one teensy-weensy question remaining. Now that I'm in here, how do I get out *alive?*

# Chapter Eight

Finding the Lynx River Country Club that Saturday was easy. Choosing the proper outfit for Kathy Veeder's wedding reception was not. I must have spent the better part of the morning with a white blouson dress in one hand and a romantic, long-skirted, floral print in the other. Decisions, decisions!

The country club was right where its name implies, way out there at the end of County Road Seven, overlooking the boulder-strewn streambed of the Lynx. Summery heat had reduced the river's flow to an ochre trickle. Six weeks earlier, those rapids must have been something to behold — surging, spring-melted white water gushing and foaming all the way down to the big lake.

The clubhouse was a pavilion-style structure, not more than ten years old, with wall-sized windows offering panoramic views of rhyolite bluffs and steep, pine-covered hills. The parking lot was full, so I ended up putting my rental Ford on the grass, right next to the cars of all the other latecomers.

I was wearing my last-minute fashion choice — the pale pink floral print with its free-flowing skirt, ruffled, off-the-shoulder neckline, and elbow-length sleeves. I wished I had a hat to go with it. Something broad-brimmed and ribboned to match my white midheel mesh pumps. These days, a wedding reception is the only

134

place where a woman can safely wear one of those silly ro-
coco hats.

At the door, the club manager asked to see my invitation. I picked through my white handbag and fished out
Donny's business card. The heir's signature brought a
surprised smile to the manager's lips, and he waved me in
with a gracious flourish.

I was impressed by the jumbo-sized wedding cake in
the foyer. Apparently, Glenn Veeder was willing to spare
no expense to make his daughter's wedding day a memorable one.

I arrived in the reception room just as they were clearing the tables. There was Kathy at the head table, radi-
antly lovely in bridal white, tête- à-tête with the new
husband. They both looked as if they couldn't wait for the
honeymoon to start. The mother of the bride sat on
Kathy's right, a hefty, reasonably attractive, graying
blonde, her round face exceedingly flushed. I was more
interested in her husband, though, the beefy fellow on
her right. Glenn Veeder was a good four inches over the
six foot mark. Broad square head and Marine Corps
crewcut. Small, hard, porcine eyes and a face like a Lake
Superior cliffside. His gray-green eyes flitted from side to
side, missing nothing, and the champagne glass touched
his lips with methodical precision.

My, what big hands you have, Papa Veeder. Broad and
thick, with pushed-back knuckles, noticeable tendons,
and veins the size of soda straws. Very much in keeping
with your construction livelihood. I remembered Donny
telling me about the Pipefitters' strike three years ago and
wondered if Papa Veeder had taken up any of the slack as
a favor to Lakeside.

"Hey, party girl!"

Donny Pierce meandered his way through the crowd,
unfurling a toothy smile of welcome. His was not a
rented tuxedo, and he wore it amazingly well. Warm,
strong hands descended on my bare shoulders.

"For a while there, I didn't think you were coming. Andrea, you look lovely."

135

Before I could respond, Donny's lips nudged mine with a startling intimacy. It started out as a welcome kiss and turned into something else entirely. I very nearly lost myself in it, but the realization of where I was put on the brakes real fast. Pushing against his broad chest, I disengaged myself. "Umm, is this some kind of warm-up for when you kiss the bride?"

He grinned. "Don't need one. I already know how to kiss Kathy."

"Oh really?"

"Do I detect a glimmer of green in those dark eyes?"

"Fella, in about two seconds, you're going to detect my palm on the side of your face!"

"Take it easy, honey." Thumb and forefinger gave my chin a playful tweak. "Listen, Kathy and I had our fling years ago. We were high school juniors. She dumped me for Dave Kiernan. Ancient history." His grin widened. "Hey, are you hungry?"

"I could maybe nibble something."

"Please do so. I left Mike Garceau hanging in midconversation. Let me get things squared away, and I'll be right back. Okay?"

Nod of agreement. Watching Donny zero in on a trio of earnest, middle management types, I made my way over to the buffet table. Always conscious of calories, I gave the moist roast beef and ham and turkey slices a skip and settled for a sliver of bland American cheese. Nibbled on the corner like a shy little Anishinabe mouse.

Looking around, I saw Mavis Heisler, glass in hand, being utterly charming with the groom's mother. Off to the left stood Jerry Carmody, shoulders hunched, lit cigarette dangling from loose lips, having a quiet conversation with an elderly man in banker's blue pinstripe. Three steps behind Jerry stood an anxious-looking woman my height or thereabouts, with a delicately hewn face and moderately short sandy blond hair. She wore a black-and-white leopard-print, twisted-front, V-neck dress and stood there with the kind of poise they drum into girls at the best finishing schools. Stood there and rapped nervous fingertips on her cocktail glass. Rap-tap-pety-tap. She stared at Jerry with the submissive anticipation of the well-trained geisha. Mrs. Carmody?

Turn to the right. More familiar faces. Dick Jaswell with a comradely arm around the broad waist of the missus. She was a florid matron flying on Dom Perignon. Sometimes after you've had that fourth baby, it takes a while to get your figure back. Right, Mrs. J? The Jaswells were sharing a joke with a vaguely familiar woman. Oh yeah, my old friend from the bank, Mrs. Burgundy Suit.

And then I spotted Monica Lonardo, over there by the bandstand, trying to rival Jerry's woman for sheer poise but not quite succeeding. Looking darkly ravishing anyway in a sleeveless capelet-collar blouse and a lengthy, curve-hugging, eggshell-colored skirt.

Monica reacted instinctively to my stare. Her chin came up, her eyes narrowed in recognition, and that lipsticked Hispanic mouth settled into a thin, hard line. Oh, she wasn't pleased to see me at all. I gave her a cool, polite nod. Her response was a hateful glare, followed by a sudden anxious search of the reception crowd.

Well, now I understood why Donny hadn't brought me to the reception. He'd had a previous date. I half hoped that Monica would find him. I wanted those two to have a good shouting quarrel out in the parking lot. Break up that romance for good. Whenever possible, I prefer not to be the other woman in any kind of triangle.

Then the band struck up a slow tune, and Glenn Veeder took his daughter for a turn on the dance floor. At just that moment, I felt a familiar pair of masculine hands on my shoulders. "When they're finished, Andrea, it's our turn."

Slipping out from under Donny's grasp, I turned and flashed him an arch smile. "Are you certain Monica won't mind?"

He cast a sidelong glance in the direction of the bandstand. Frowned a little. "Look, Monica and I are both over twenty-one. And we're not engaged." He tilted his head toward the tall windows. "Come on. I want you to meet the folks."

"I'd mind if it was me," I said, letting him take my hand.

Burgeoning smile. "Why am I always drawn to jealous women?"

"Fair warning, Mr. P. Get involved with me, and I'll show you what jealousy *really* is."

His palm rested lightly at the base of my spine. "You know, I'm not sure if that's a threat or an invitation."

"Take it any way you please."

"Then I'll take it as an invitation."

And so I met the parents of Donald Winston Pierce. His mother, Elaine, was a pert, vivacious, gray-haired lady on the high side of fifty, who fingered a matched pearl necklace and questioned me at length about my pedigree. She seemed a little disappointed to learn that I was not one of the Porters of Cheboygan but made me welcome anyway.

Keith Pierce was something else again. He came from the same Yooper aristocracy as Donny's mother, but his physical presence was more suited to a longshoreman. Forthright, hard-chinned, eagle-eyed, broad Jovian forehead and deep-set pale blue eyes. At first I pegged his age at fifty-five. Then he took my hand in his, gave it a firm shake, and, seeing the liver spots behind the knuckles, I revised my estimate upward a good fifteen years. All at once, I understood Donny's desire to strike out on his own. Standing beside the old man, Donny seemed to become inconspicuous, indistinct, inconsequential, as if he might suddenly fade away into the wallpaper.

Halfway through our chat, Mavis Heisler came over to meet and greet. Elaine offered her cheek for the obligatory peck. I did the same. And then Mavis made a great show of fussing over me, acting as if I were her favorite niece.

"Andrea, what an adorable dress!" Quick fingers smoothed my sleeves. "My, you do know how to shine, don't you?" She turned her megawatt smile on old man

Pierce. "We're going to be seeing a lot more of this young lady in Tilford, Keith. Bet on it."

"Andrea tells us she's thinking of opening her own realty office here in town," he replied.

"Among other things." Mavis threw me a knowledgeable smirk.

"I'm surprised Wayne didn't make the wedding." Keith took his wife's empty champagne glass and set it on the table.

Mavis reacted as if an admiral had just barked at her. Shoulders back. Chin up. Tennn-hut! Her smile became fragile. "The appropriations committee scheduled a meeting for last night. Mr. Burdick couldn't get a flight out of Washington. I'm sorry, sir."

"Don't apologize to me, Mavis. It's Kathy's wedding."

"He'll be in town tomorrow, sir."

"Fine!" Keith signaled a club waiter, then pointed at the empty glass. "We'll be dining here around seven or so. Please tell Wayne he's welcome to join us. There are a few aspects of the new tax legislation I'd like to discuss with him."

Offering us all a radiant smile, Mavis assured Donny's father that the congressman would be delighted to attend, praised Elaine's matched pearls, complimented me on my hair, and headed for the next circle of unsuspecting wedding guests. I watched her slide effortlessly into their group. Plenty of handshakes and how-are-yous. I could see why Burdick had hired her. She was the perfect congressional aide, stroking the home folks and making them feel like the most important people in her life.

"Charming woman," I observed aloud.

Elaine showed me a look of mild reproof. "Perhaps we should have asked her about her husband."

Donny cleared his throat. "Ex-husband, Mom."

"Running a fishing camp near Rockland, isn't he?" Elaine fondled one of her pearls. "That's quite a comedown from being Lakeside's public relations director. Well, at least Mavis is still with the company."

My ears perked at that. So Mavis was moonlighting as a Lakeside honcho, eh? Very interesting.

Keith sighed. "That's just gossip, dear."

"Oh, come now. Lena Rolofsen told me she's there practically every day. That woman is running the place for Wayne Burdick, and everybody knows it—"

"How did she get started with Lakeside?" I asked innocently.

"She went to work there twelve years ago. Her husband hired her. She put together one of those little company newspapers. Wayne really liked it. And when he made his first run for Congress, he invited Mavis to take over his campaign."

Donny winced at her disapproving tone. "Mom, you make it sound like an ax murder."

"Well, I'm sorry, Donald, but I'm afraid I'm just hopelessly old-fashioned." Elaine's annoyed gaze picked out the congressional aide. "Where I come from, you don't trade in a perfectly good marriage for a career in politics. It simply isn't done."

Donny's father scowled. "Elaine . . ."

"I'm entitled to my opinions, Keith."

Donny deftly turned the conversation into a discussion of the groom's background as a ski instructor. The parental tension subsided. Only children are quite good at that. Take it from one who knows.

Somehow I really wasn't surprised to hear that Mavis had ditched her hubby after he'd provided her with an *entrée* to the company. I suppose it was the feminist counterpart of the Jennifer-for-Janet exchange that goes on amongst successful members of the other gender. You know, when a guy hits forty-five and divorces good old Janet to marry a sleek, blond, beautiful, twentyish Jennifer, the kind of woman he lusted after twenty years ago but couldn't afford back then.

That sort of thing doesn't go on too often in our gender. We cast our spouses adrift, too, but for deep personal and emotional reasons, not monetary ones. The fact that

Mavis Heisler was capable of it tended to set her apart, to put her in a ruthless class all by herself.

There was a lady in a big hurry, the kind who would let nothing stand in her way. It looked as if my first impressions at the Shoreliner had been dead on target.

They certainly made for an unusual triangle — Jerry Carmody, Mavis Heisler, and Congressman Wayne Burdick. Just where did the congressman fit in? I wondered. Was he just another front man? Was he the man at the top? Or did everything originate with Mavis?

Soon they opened the dance floor to couples. Donny whisked me away from the folks, assured me that I had made a good impression, and, to the music of the five-piece band, showed me how well he had mastered the Arthur Murray course.

And then we were into one of those slow, moody Glenn Miller pieces from long ago. I snuggled closer to him, resting my head in the hollow of his shoulder, feeling the warm pressure of his arm on my lower back. Mellow music and languid ambulation. Worsted wool against my cheek. Slight tangy whiff of aftershave. Mmmmmm — nice!

Donny nuzzled the nape of my neck. "Do you want to get out of here?" he murmured.

Purring, I closed my eyes. "Don't tempt me."

He kissed the nuzzle spot. "I'm serious. Let's wish Kurt and Kathy bon voyage and take off." Affectionate pat on the seat of my skirt. "Or are you one of those women who has to be the last to leave the dance floor?"

"Donny, I have the sneaky feeling that if I leave this dance floor, I just might wind up a fallen woman."

"There is that possibility. What do you say?"

"Ohhhhh, I hate temptation!"

All at once, a trombone brayed. Donny and I found ourselves surrounded by applauding couples. I engaged in a few half-hearted claps, furious at the interruption, and was partially consoled by the presence of Donny's arms around my waist.

Taking the mike, the bandleader asked us to clear the

floor. Then he asked all of the single women to line up in front of him. I saw Kathy leave the head table, bouquet in hand, and realized what was up. I tried to back away, but Donny laughed and ushered me forward. "You heard the man, Andrea."

"No!" I shook my head decisively. "Not this! I hate this!"

Laughter from the guests. Hollers of encouragement. Embarrassed single women in party frocks formed a crooked line. Two bridesmaids came for me with feral grins and outstretched hands.

"Come on, honey! *All* the single women!"

I made no resistance as my bridesmaid captors marched me out there, to the great enjoyment of everyone present. The three of us doffed our shoes beside the cake table, then joined the rows facing Kathy. Happy, eager women crowded me on either side. It was like being back in the Lady Trojans again. All I needed was a net in front of me and Mary Beth in the serve position.

The bouquet missed me by six or seven feet and landed in the delighted grasp of a teenaged Veeder cousin. Entering the spirit of things, I squeezed the winner's shoulders and cried, "You caught it!" And added in a teasing tone. "And we all know what that means! *You're next!*"

Leaving the winner surrounded by a giggly clamor, I skulked away to retrieve my shoes. Mavis Heisler caught me by the sleeve, however, and led me over to my bridesmaid captors, introducing them as Kim Draper and Trista Petersen. Trista was the shorter, noisier one, a chestnut brunette with a ready chipmunk smile. Together we formed one of those female conversational clusters which never seems to break up. It just gains and loses chatters. We lost Mavis after the first ten minutes. Kathy's aunt took her place, followed by another Veeder cousin and Kurt's younger sister. Through it all, I stood there in my stocking feet, listening and fibbing, sipping enough frosty Dom Perignon to make my party smile permanent.

It was just as well, though. The single guys had lined

up, Donny included, and I had no desire to watch a frilly lace garter flying around the room.

Finally I got back to the cake table and found my mesh pumps in a pigeon-toed stance on the floor. I looked around for Donny, but he was nowhere to be found. As I was slipping on my pumps, I suddenly felt the pressure of someone's steady gaze. That old prison awareness of hostile intent. Going with the instinct, I glanced over my shoulder.

There was a man standing beside the bandstand, hefting a plate of potato salad. He was fiftyish, a lean and rangy six-foot-one, with bristly hair that had once been the color of Dutch chocolate but was now rapidly going gray. He had a Teutonic nose that had been broken some years ago, close-set brown eyes, jughandle ears, a pistolero moustache, and a narrow, downturned mouth. He wore an aging but still presentable houndstooth suit. Gave me a hooded look, smiled a little, and dipped his plastic fork into the creamy mound.

I didn't like being all alone out there. Not in enemy territory like Tilford. And especially not in front of a total stranger who was eyeing me as if we shared some weird little secret. My mouth dry, I looked around for sanctuary. An Angie without friends is ripe for serious trouble.

So I made a beeline to the head table. I thought of a clever way to secure some instant protection and advance my clandestine investigation at the same time. Glenn and Doris Veeder loomed just ahead of me. I grabbed a folding chair, complimented Kathy's mother on the wedding, chatted for a bit, and then placed a delicate hand on the forearm of her hulking spouse.

"Oh listen, Doris, do you mind terribly much if I steal your husband for a while? Every time I attend a wedding, I make it a point to dance with the bride's father."

Flushed with champagne and good humor, she replied, "Oh no, I don't mind . . . Andrea, isn't it? Just don't forget to bring him back." Burst of tipsy laughter.

"How about it, Mr. Veeder?" I stood, placed my hands on my knees, and displayed an ingenue smile. Daddy

Glenn gradually became aware of my presence. He was one of those stolid, silent drinkers, the type that will frown and drink, frown and drink, until, like an alligator trapped in a refrigerator car, all physical motion ceases.

"Whuzzat?"

Why don't you get up and dance with the young lady?" Doris suggested.

Shrug of massive shoulders. "Ahhhhh, I can't dance worth shit."

"Nonsense! You're just out of practice." Tugging at his arm, I glanced over my shoulder. Sure enough, Old Potato Salad was still over there, watching me with extreme interest. Gooseflesh rippled up the undersides of my arms. I tugged a bit harder. "Come on, Mr. Veeder."

"Go on, Glenn. Get up and dance."

"Who do I look like — that jigaboo Michael Jackson!?"

"You know, Glenn, if you practiced . . ." I made my smile elfin. "You'd be able to take Doris, here, to those hot new dance clubs every once in a while."

Kathy's mom responded favorably to that. "She's right. When's the last time you took me out, Glenn Veeder?"

"What am I — made of money or some damn thing!?"

"Oh, you've got more money than you know what to do with. We never go *anywhere*. We haven't been down to Grosse Pointe since Kathy was a child."

"It ain't around the corner, Dorrie."

"I've never met anyone so antisocial. They ought to give you a TV with the Sports Channel and stick you in a cave." Doris poked him repeatedly behind the armpit. "Go on! Dance with her, Glenn. For heaven's sake, it's your daughter's wedding."

Realizing that he was to have no peace at the table, Glenn growled and muttered and escorted me onto the dance floor. I let Mr. Potato Salad have a real eyeful of me on Papa Veeder's arm. Give him something to think about, whoever he was.

Well, Daddy Glenn hadn't lied about his aptitude. Fred Astaire he wasn't. His sole dance step consisted of a cross between a Forties foxtrot and the lumbering stride of the Frankenstein monster. Leading him, I felt like one of those sequinned lovelies in the bear cage at the Moscow Circus.

Glenn's mammoth hand swallowed mine. "So what brings you here to Tilford, Andrea?"

"A little project of mine."

"Deer Cove?" Slyness gleamed in those champagne-dazzled eyes. I noticed that he was beginning to lead.

"And how did you know that, Mr. Veeder?"

"You made a lot of friends at the Registry the other day. And Dick Jaswell tells me you were out at the McCann place." His hard-muscled forearm pressed my spine. "You're wasting your time, you know."

"Mavis Heisler doesn't seem to think so."

"Come on, Andrea. Mavis ain't got the kid's signature. Nobody does. The cove's worthless without that farm."

"Kid?" I echoed.

"Yeah, you know. Brian McCann's kid. Mary Beth. Hard for me to think of her as a missus." His size fifteen shoe crushed the mesh protecting my toes. I choked back a shrill yelp.

"Sorry," he mumbled.

Somehow I managed to build a flaccid smile. "Tell me, Glenn, why are you opposed to developing Deer Cove?"

Startled, he whispered, *"What!?* Who told you that?"

"Jerry Carmody." Might as well sow a little dissension in the enemy ranks. "Jerry told me you arm-twisted the Planning Board into turning down a number of projects."

Crimson crept upward from his too-tight collar. "That lying little son of a bitch — !"

"Glenn," I murmured. "I read the board's minutes at the Registry. Jim Tolliver's lawyer submitted a subdivision plan back in January. You expressed misgivings about it."

He calmed right down. "I'm not opposed to develop-

145

ment, Andrea. I just want to be certain it's the right kind, that's all."

While he was off balance, I decided to go for broke. "Why did you turn down the Tollivers' subdivision plan?"

"It wasn't well thought out. The board found flaws—"

"It didn't seem that much different from the other plans approved by you and your fellow members."

"We . . . ah, we were against any more housing in that area."

"Just when did the Planning Board change its mind, Glenn?"

"The board didn't change its mind, Andrea."

"Well, it must have! In January, you were against development. Now you're in favor of it."

Glenn floundered a bit. "We, uh . . . decisions are made on a project-by-project basis."

I made my mouth a little loose, as if the champagne were having its full effect, and blundered on. "But didn't Jim Tolliver get in touch with you just before he died?"

"Hell no!" Glenn's denial was just a shade too loud.

"Well, he must have wanted to discuss the board's negative vote." I added a tipsy giggle for a plausible stage effect.

"I never spoke to Tolliver."

"You didn't talk to him the night of the snowstorm?"

"Of course not!"

And how would you know what snowstorm I was talking about, Mr. Veeder, unless you were intimately aware of the exact circumstances of Jim Tolliver's death?

Frowning, Daddy Glenn gave me a shrewd, suspicious look. I couldn't let him realize I was pumping him. Two mentions of Jim Tolliver would have to do for the moment. It was showtime again. Toss the hair. Laugh lightly. Give the mark a big glassy-eyed smile and show him how happily plotzed I am.

"How do you feel about industrial parks, Glenn?"

"That's the word I hear from Jaswell. Where do you fit in?"

"Right in the middle of the financing, Mr. Veeder."

"You working for Carmody?"

"No way! Jerry's just another customer."

After a moment's dour consideration, Glenn lowered his head until we were cheek to cheek. But his words were anything but romantic. "I have to talk to you. Soon. Alone. In private. You won't regret it."

"Why, Mr. Veeder! And you a married man."

"I'm talking about Deer Cove, dammit! That motherfucker Carmody is fixing to sell you out. We can help each other, Andrea."

"We'll see, Glenn. We'll see."

As I rhumbaed across the floor, I reflected on this new wrinkle. Judging from the venom in his voice, I gathered that there was no love lost between Kathy's dad and the one-time mob accountant from Detroit.

Glenn Veeder was uncommonly ready to parlay my industrial park proposal into a move against Jerry Carmody. Why?

Another uncomfortable thought. I was pretty sure Veeder had lied about not talking to Jim Tolliver that snowy night. I was beginning to wonder if Glenn Veeder was the person Jim had run off to meet. And if, in some yet-unknown way, Papa Veeder would have benefited the most from those two murders.

Just then, I spotted Donny Pierce doing a praiseworthy rhumba over by the bandstand. Praise, however, was the last thing on my mind. Particularly when I recognized his dance partner — Monica Lonardo!

I glared at those broad Jaycee shoulders, stifling a sudden urge to splatter that handsome, treacherous face with a slice of Kathy's wedding cake.

My fussbudget face drew a chuckle from Glenn. "You had your little head turned by the heir, eh? No future in that."

"I *don't* know what you're talking about."

"Kathy was sweet on him once. I'm glad she got over it. He's a mama's boy. Me, I don't understand the attraction. That Donny's never starved for female companionship, though."

"Donald cuts quite a swath, does he?"

"Not at all. Donny's strictly a one-woman man. He'll meet some gal and go out with her for a year or two. We'll all figure — this is the one. Then they'll break it up. He'll date around for a bit and latch on to another one. Monica's setting a record with him. Two years."

"How did they meet?"

"Monica met him at the Chamber. Went in there one day to ask about setting up a business here in town."

"*She's* in business for herself?"

"You bet. And doing very well at it. She owns one of them women's walk-in fitness joints. The Form Fantastique. It's over in Shoreside Plaza."

I shot the lady a hasty appraising glance. "Hmmmmm . . . pretty well dressed for a fitness instructor."

"Nahhhhh, she ain't hurting for bucks. Owns a piece of the Chain & Anchor, too, I hear."

Now that rang a bell, but for the life of me I couldn't remember exactly where I'd heard that name before. And then it came to me. Mary Beth. Something to do with Mary Beth.

Glenn laughed. "Once Donny pops the question, though, Monica will be able to retire."

"What did she used to do in New York?" I asked. Curiosity is an irresistible affliction.

"New York!?" Glenn flashed me an astonished look. "What the hell has Carmody been telling you, anyway? Monica's from Detroit. Just like him."

But it wasn't Jerry who had told me that. It had been Monica Lonardo herself, sitting across from me at the Caribou Lodge. I glanced her way once more, blinking in confusion. Why had Monica lied about her background?

And why hadn't Jerry called her on it?

I thought back to their strange little in-joke. *Women in business*. What had Jerry meant by that? Was it a veiled dig at Monica's ownership of that fitness center? Or was there some hidden message?

The music stopped before I could ponder the matter

further. Both Glenn and I heartily applauded the song's end. He wished to get off the dance floor, and I wished to spare my feet further torment. Smiling stiffly, I looked around for a vacant chair. I wanted to sit down, slip off my shoes, and tenderly massage those mashed toes.

Keith Pierce joined us before I could make my getaway. Slapping my ursine partner's shoulder, he said, "Glenn, I never figured you for a dancing fool."

Gesturing at me, Kathy's dad went red all around the ears. "Aw hell, Keith, the kid wanted to dance."

Turning to me, Keith pulled a slim cigar from his blazer pocket, then unwrapped the plastic with surprisingly agile fingers. "I never thought you'd get him out of that chair, Andrea."

"Believe me, it wasn't easy, Mr. Pierce."

Smiling puckishly, I straightened Keith's club tie for him and tried my hand at some spur-of-the-moment flirting. He laughed out loud, delighted to be considered a philanderer at the ripe age of seventy. In no time at all, the three of us were surrounded by a phalanx of Lakeside junior executives. The Boss was in a jovial mood, and it was time for all good upwardly mobile brown noses to make themselves noticeable.

I listened politely to all the corporate chatter, clung to Keith's arm, and basked in the reflected glory, enjoying the status of a substitute Mrs. Pierce. I noticed Mr. Potato Salad's eye on me once or twice. And took a perverse delight in that troubled look on his Teutonic face.

I had a close call back at Mr. Pierce's table. Elaine was chatting with Kathy's aunt, and she offhandedly mentioned that I had been in Kathy's old sorority. Well, it turned out that Aunt Susan had been a Rho Delta, too. I had an extremely hairy ten minutes, playing off the garrulous aunt, improvising a tale on the basis of the few names she mentioned. I sincerely regretted telling Donny that little bit of untruth. Aunt Susan looked like the talkative type. I had a feeling that story would be all over Tilford before sundown.

Okay, so I felt very nervous about that. And with good

reason. Those impromptu tales are the very ones that come springing back at you when you least expect it.

No sooner had I left the Pierces' table than I felt a fore-finger tap me lightly on the nape. Turning, I came face to face with Jerry Carmody. Oily smile. "Your health." He handed me a brimming champagne glass. "I need to talk to you, babe."

"So talk."

His gaze wandered around the club's posh interior. "Some joint, eh?"

"Very nice. I'm grateful to you and Donny for the guest membership."

"Bet they've got nothing like it in Cowflop, South Dakota or wherever it is you're from." For a second, Jerry's expression reflected genuine admiration. "Sure as hell nothing like it on Livernois Avenue."

"Livernois Avenue?"

"Never mind. You wouldn't know it."

But I do know it, Jerry. It's on the south side of Detroit. One of my fellow inmates at Springfield grew up there. Hell, she probably knows you. She told me your old neighborhood has a nice scenic view of the railroad yards. An exceedingly rough neighborhood in an exceedingly rough town. A place where gunshots are as common as freight trains headed for the River Rouge plant.

I thought of Tulip's description of the gangs at Chadsey High, and then I understood the forces that had molded Jerry's psychotic aggressiveness and ice-eyed stare. A boy of his stature must have had it rough at Chadsey. I wondered what he had done before joining the Toolmakers. But I knew better than to ask.

"So what did you want to talk about, Jer?"

"Tomorrow. It's decision time, Andrea. The man wants to meet you."

All at once, I remembered that Congressman Burdick would be in Tilford on the morrow. "What time?"

"One-thirty. We're meeting at my house. Evvie and me'll be hosting a nice friendly afternoon cookout.

You're supposed to casually drop by. Don't bring any company."

"Is Mavis going to be there?"

He nodded. "You really impressed the old girl, Andrea."

"Who else?"

"You don't need a fucking guest list." Jerry gave me a sharp look, then followed up with a tepid smile. "Look, this is top level. Just the few of us. Here's where you get your answer — yes or no. Me, I hope it's yes. But there's no telling what the man will say."

"Where do you live?"

Jerry gave me his Butternut Lane address and made me repeat it a few times.

"You only get one shot at it, babe. If he's not impressed, you'd better head down to Ludington."

Nodding, I turned away, but Jerry's insistent hand caught my wrist. I really didn't think he would try anything. Not with better than seventy people in the room. I should have known better.

A pair of utterly cold eyes found mine. "What did that asshole Veeder say to you?"

I swallowed hard. "Nothing much."

The look Jerry gave me must have given nightmares to certain dissident members of the Toolmakers union. "What was he telling you, eh? Was he telling you how to fuck me up?"

My knees quivered beneath the flowing skirt. I forced myself to look bored and slightly irritated. Get sassy, Angie. And do not, repeat, do not let this Livernois shiv artist suspect how truly frightened of him you really are.

"Veeder asked me to run away with him to Tahiti. And he hates your guts. Otherwise, he'd ask you to be the best man."

Jerry burst into laughter. I steeled myself for his touch, and he didn't disappoint me. A tender stroking of the cheek. A proprietary smile that let me know where I stood in the Carmody scheme of things.

"Joke about everything, don't you, Andrea?" He pol-

151

ished off his champagne with a fast swallow. Aimed a stubby forefinger at my nose. "Stay away from that asshole. Got it?"

"If you say so, Jer."

Leaving my glass on a linen-clad table, I watched Jerry saunter back to the cowed yet elegant sandy blonde. She welcomed him with a strange facial expression. Half relief and half apprehension.

Well, now I had my crack at Lakeside's top dog. And, if all went well, I would soon have that four million for Mary Beth. I didn't think the main man would back out now. Not after all those sterling testimonials from Jaswell and Carmody and Heisler. That's the beauty of a Big Store scam — it practically sells itself.

My main task now was to nail down the identity of Jim Tolliver's killer. And I had to work fast. My con game would soon be reaching its conclusion, and I needed the killer in place to take the rap.

I was pretty certain Brian McCann and Jim Tolliver had been murdered to facilitate the sale of those properties to Lakeside. But I did not yet understand the why of the why. I had a strong feeling that the ultimate motive had something to do with Lakeside's internal politics. Someone stood to benefit from those two deaths. But who?

Jerry's was the first name that came to mind. After all, he'd made the first offer to Jim and Mary Beth. I wondered if Jerry was dissatisfied with his current status as a caretaker. Perhaps gaining control of the McCann/Tolliver holdings would enable Jerry to oust the top man and seize control of the company for himself.

Then again, the same motive could just as easily apply to Mavis Heisler. Mavis seemed awfully upset about the fact that Mary Beth had slipped out of their grasp. Acquiring the properties just might make Mavis the head honcho at Lakeside. And perhaps killing Mary Beth would ensure that no one ever unearths the truth about Mavis's rise to prominence.

For a moment, I considered Dick Jaswell, then

dropped him in favor of another line of reasoning. Something Glenn Veeder had told me rushed to the forefront of my mind. Glenn said Dick Jaswell had told him about my visit to the McCann farm. Kathy's dad had also mentioned my visit to the Registry of Deeds. Papa Veeder knew a lot about my comings and goings, didn't he?

How close to Jaswell was Kathy's father? I wondered. Did Jaswell phone Glenn Veeder as well as Carmody right after my visit to the bank?

Now there's a scary thought. Daddy Glenn lied about not talking to Jim Tolliver the night of the snowstorm. Then I show up in town, making noises about the McCann farm. And, all of a sudden, Glenn Veeder wants to meet with me . . . *alone*.

Hmmmmm, I think I'll pass on that invitation for a while.

At that moment, I experienced that same strange shiver of awareness. I fired a discreet glance to the rear, and, sure enough, there was Mr. Potato Salad getting an earful from garrulous Aunt Susan.

Mellowed by a sizeable dose of champagne, Aunt Susan babbled away. Mr. Potato Salad listened very politely, occasionally shooting me a quick, wary glance. Then, ever so casually, he turned his wrist, gestured at me, and mumbled a short question. Aunt Susan nodded with enthusiasm. And he flashed me a small, tight, merciless grin, the kind I used to get from the screws at Springfield.

Time for a ladylike retreat. Resisting the sudden onslaught of blind panic — that irresistible urge to run for the nearest exit — I drifted backward through the reception crowd. Nod and smile with the Lakeside staffers. Exchange hellos with Veeder relatives. A stop at the silvery pail for a champagne refill. In no time at all, I was out of Mr. Potato Salad's line of sight, a situation which made me feel a little bit better. Tilting the glass to my lips, I spied Doris Veeder with the orchestra and wondered if I could con her into telling me who Mr. Potato Salad was.

153

Four sinewy fingers latched on to my upper arm. I recognized that familiar tangy aftershave even before I heard Donny's voice. "I've been wondering where you ran off to."

And there he was—Donald the heir apparent, silken tie loosened, tuxedo jacket unbuttoned, unruly hair curling across the forehead. I had expected a cocky smile. Instead I found myself facing a firm, solemn, tight-lipped, utterly masculine expression. No locker-room smirk with this guy. Just a somber look of invitation and a posture brimming with barely restrained urgency. I hadn't seen that look in quite a while. Indeed, after Bozeman, I had never expected to see it again.

Things were moving just a tad too quickly for my liking. I was feeling an uneasy urgency myself. Sudden breathlessness and a flood of warmth in a very private place. I sipped a little Dom Perignon. Showed Donny a coy smile.

"Social butterfly, that's me!"

Donny's hand closed around mine, and he tilted his head in the direction of the dance floor. "How about one more before we go? I haven't danced with you in over an hour."

That slow-blossoming smile of his chiseled away at my resolve. I made a valiant effort to resist temptation. Yanked my hand out of his grip. "No thanks! You've had your dance lesson for the evening."

"Beg pardon?"

"You know damned well what I'm talking about!"

"Andrea, there are many things I'm good at. Finance. Management. And a halfway decent tennis game. Mind-reading, however, isn't one of them. How about an explanation? Please?"

I was thinking very evil thoughts about a certain Hispanic fitness instructor, so I gave him a bright-eyed smirk, following up with a momentary bump-and-grind. "Aiiii, gringo, you wan dance el rhumba?"

"I think that's *la rhumba* in Spanish."

"Bastard! You should know!"

Unfazed by the outburst, Donny stroked the side of my face. "If you ask me, green-eyed people ought to go easy on the champagne."

"Don't be such a fucking gentleman, Donald." My expression was one of high indignation. Not an easy thing to accomplish when you're steamy under the silk.

"Were I a gentleman, Andrea, I'd spare you the coming lecture on how jealousy and alcohol don't mix."

"Are you saying I'm drunk?"

"Slightly inebriated would be the more accurate term." Playfully he tweaked my chin. "And definitely in need of a breath of fresh air. Come on."

"I'll be the judge of what I need, Mis-ter Pierce!"

Oblivious to the curious stares of the guests, Donny put a comradely arm across my shoulders and steered me toward the French doors. I knew we were on our way to the terrace, and, to be perfectly honest, I didn't really mind. However, a woman's self-respect demands at least one strong show of resistance before the surrender. Sliding out from under his arm, I snapped, "Don't touch me!"

"You are spoiling for a fight, aren't you?"

"I can find my own way out. Why don't you go babysit the fitness instructor?"

Donny's arm circled my waist instead. "Suggestion noted and rejected. I'll be the judge of what I need, honey."

Balking at the French doors, I muttered, "Look, I am *not* a consolation prize."

He lifted the brass latch. "You're a prize, all right."

And out we went.


Okay, so maybe I should have put up a little more resistance.

It's not like I do this sort of thing all the time, you know. Compared to some of the girls I shared the dorm with at USU, I was a regular Vickie Virgin.

On the other hand, if Grandma Biwaban knew the intimate details of my love life, she'd be after me with a hairbrush.

Boy, do I have fond memories of that night. Donny's tongue masterfully circling the inner rim of my mouth, pouring fresh kindling on those deep-seated emotional fires. Broad hands tenderly smothering my breasts, sliding back and forth over the soft, moist undersides. Nipples growing firm and erect and straining against his palms. Rasp of chest hair against my skin. Tense interplay of powerful masculine muscles. Heightened scents tickled my nostrils — fading aftershave flavored with fresh sweat, the sour smell of male arousal, the faint aroma of my own musk.

We might have been a pair of playful dolphins at sea. Nude bodies slick and glowing with perspiration, rolling over and over on the dampened, tangled sheets. I straddled his hard-hewn thighs, looked down at the burgeoning, blood-weighted phallus, and noted the expression of flushed animal urgency on his handsome face. Then I impaled myself on the upright spike, feeling the plum-shaped knob burrow into my dripping aperture, savoring the sliding motion of his shaft between my quivering labia. Uttering a soft groan, I placed my palms on his heaving chest and let my own pelvis begin its rhythmic, rocking motion. Within seconds, the cadence of his thrusts matched mine, and our lovemaking began in earnest.

Each grinding spasm triggered a flash of fire. I sat upright, bumping and thrusting away, waves of pleasure radiating through me, all too cognizant of the impending rush prodding me toward the edge. Higher and higher, faster and faster. Angie the demented hobbyhorse buckarooing on the pleasure pole, riding her way to climax.

My initial orgasm was just like overinflating a balloon. Up, up, up and *pow!* I arched my spine, teeth bared and clenched, expelling my breath in a prolonged sigh. Ooooooh — lovely!

I was ready for sleep, but Donny gave me no respite. Our coupling assumed a frenzied, juggernaut intensity of its very own. My disobedient body welcomed every prod, greedily clutching his swollen manhood. My second orgasm came out of nowhere, filling me with a joyous incandescent rush. I kept hearing these strange noises. Sort of an *oooooooooh-oooooh* traveling up and down the musical scale. Only afterward, when I lay limp and spent on Donny's broad chest, did I realize that those noises had been coming from me.

Cool night air chilled my perspiration-soaked body. Feeling me shiver, Donny wrapped both his arms around me. Dry lips brushed the top of my forehead. I twirled a tuft of chest hair around my forefinger. Hearing him chuckle, I whispered, "What's so funny?"

"I was thinking about the reception." His hand slowly glided up and down my spine.

"What about the reception?" Lifting myself on both forearms, I looked him right in the eye.

"I knew you were spoiling for *something*."

Mammoth blush. "Oh, shut up!"

"Why so mad, Andrea?"

Pillowing my head on his collarbone, I murmured, "Not mad. Just embarrassed, I guess. I've never been vocal before."

"Here's hoping you'll be vocal again. And in the very near future."

"How near?"

"Not *that* near."

Showing him an elfin grin, I fondled the slack tubular tumescence. "Old Faithful is closed for the season, eh?"

"For the evening only."

"Mmmmmm—I always love to have something good to look forward to."

Donny ruffled my hair. "Get some sleep, honey."

My darling heir apparent was snoring within minutes. As for me . . . well, a strange bittersweet sense of longing kept my eyes open. And kept them moist with unshed tears. I tried to be cold-blooded about it but failed. I couldn't quite shake this queer feeling of remorse and dissatisfaction.

157

At that moment, I wished I had never come to Tilford. I wished I'd been looking the other way when Mary Beth walked by that carnival merry-go-round. I wanted to turn back the clock four years. Go back to being Angie the Tax Assessor's clerk again. I knew exactly how I would have rewritten my life. It would have been a much happier scenario this time around. Mother finds the new cancer a whole lot sooner. Angie punches the lecherous councilman in the nose, quits her job, and comes home to Minnesota. And then, maybe a year or two later, she goes to a Chamber of Commerce convention in Minneapolis and shares an elevator with Donald Winston Pierce.

Why did I have to meet you now, Donald? Why *now*, when I'm trapped in this false identity, and there is no way for you to ever get to know the real me? Poor Donny. You've made love to a woman who doesn't exist. A woman who can't afford to level with you. But one who would dearly love to try.

I couldn't ignore my feelings for Donny. I wanted very much to expand our relationship, to take it all the way. I wanted the whole thing, I guess—long nights of love-making at his place or mine, moonlight strolls along Superior's rockbound shore, tennis at Lynx River, smiles and kisses in office doorways, quiet talks about careers, coffee together in the morning, cuddles on the bearskin in front of the fireplace, squabbles about the clothes closet and the dirty dishes in the sink and the relatives, his side and mine. I wanted to follow our road wherever it led, whether to the final break-up or to that white clapboard Episcopal church on the edge of town.

But it would never happen. Never! I felt cheated. Angie was the ultimate victim of her own cleverness. Too much was riding on the outcome of my scout for me to abandon it now. There was Mary Beth and her unborn son to think of. I was the only one who could retrieve her stolen legacy. Not to mention the fact that her husband's murderer was still out there somewhere. He had already killed two good men, and, if I didn't take him down, he might start adding to that total, beginning with Mary Beth. No, I had to see it through. The reality of my situation dispelled all those pleasant fantasies of a happy home life as Mrs. Donald Winston Pierce.

So, blinking away the tears, I glanced at Donny's sleeping face. In repose, he looked all of fourteen years old. I kissed that endearing chin cleft, fighting off the lunatic urge to shake him awake and make confession. By the way, fella, the name is Angela, not Andrea. Angela Biwaban. And I'm not a lady realtor. I'm a thief. I'm here to bamboozle Lakeside and pin the frame on Jim Tolliver's murderer. I'm not sure if I love you, but I would certainly like to find out.

Uh-huh. Right. And I'm sure Mr. Pierce won't mind waiting, Angela, while you're doing time at the Huron Valley Women's Institute in Ypsilanti for attempted fraud. Ouch! What a thought. In that event, Donny and I could look forward to a very long engagement.

Donny had it right the first time, princess. Get some sleep.

So I did. I nodded off with Donny as my mattress, drowsily riding the ebb-and-swell of his chest, thinking of how nice it would be to do this on a regular basis.

Hey, I can dream, can't I?

I awoke to the hammering of an authoritative fist on my motel room door. Sitting upright slowly, I kicked the sheets aside and glanced at the draperied window. Sunlight blazed around the rim, a rectilinear incandescence that scorched my retinas. The sudden influx of light triggered a pinprick of pain just behind my eyeballs. Within a heartbeat, it blossomed into an excruciating hangover headache. Moaning in whispers, I tenderly touched my forehead. Too much Dom Perignon at the Veeder reception.

The knocking continued.

"Just a minute," I called, scrambling out of bed.

I made myself presentable in ten seconds, slithering into a fresh T-shirt, pulling on a pair of snug black bike pants, and grooming my wild raven hair with my hands.

My head felt like a soap bubble about to burst. Grimacing, I padded barefoot across the room and answered the door.

He looked like the motel gardener. Lightweight brushed flannel shirt, utilitarian blue Levis, thick-heeled work boots, and a khaki baseball cap set way back on his head. But then I caught a glimpse of that familiar fiftyish face with its broken Teutonic nose, and a fearful chill shuddered through me.

Mr. Potato Salad leaned against the doorjamb. He lifted his cap's brim in greeting. "Miss Porter?"

"Oh . . . yes?"

"Pleased to make your acquaintance, miss." He flipped open a deerhide wallet. Pinned to the leather was a noticeable silvery badge. "My name's David P. Hendricks. I'm the sheriff."

# Chapter Nine

"Mind if I come in?" asked Sheriff Dave.

I thought of Donny snoring facedown on my mattress and, yielding to impulse, tried to preserve the remnants of my reputation. Closing the door behind me, I offered the sheriff a wan smile. "I'd rather talk out here if you don't mind."

"Suit yourself." Sheriff Dave leaned against the pastel blue corridor wall, folding his arms casually.

"Why were you following me yesterday, Sheriff?"

"You interest me, Miss Porter. Career girl like you comes to town. Very bright and well spoken. First you're studying lot specifications at the courthouse. Next thing you know, you're having private meetings with Jerry Carmody and Mavis Heisler. So I ask myself . . . what's it all about?"

"We're all in the same industry, Sheriff. Development. I'm always checking up on potentially marketable properties."

Speculative look. "Real estate didn't draw you to Kathy Veeder's wedding reception."

"I was invited."

"By Donny Pierce. And I find that just a little bit strange."

"How so?"

"I'm surprised Kathy didn't invite her old Rho Delta sorority sister."

For a moment there, I forgot all about my thundering

161

hangover headache. I had a very vivid mental image of the sheriff and Kathy's aunt chatting at the reception.

Quick save. "Kathy didn't know I was in town, Sheriff."

"You didn't look her up?"

"I've been busy."

Tucking his thumbs behind that thick brown belt, he asked, "How did you like going to school here in Tilford?"

A tricky fellow, this Sheriff Hendricks. Had Kathy Veeder attended South Shore Community College? I had no way of knowing. So that gave me a fifty-fifty shot at the correct answer. And if I blew it, the game was over.

Sometimes you have to act as if your life is a Princess Lilionah high dive. Just close your eyes and step into space.

"Lots of fun, Sheriff. You know, I've really missed the South Shore.

His eyes narrowed slightly. "How long were you in town?"

"Two years."

"I don't remember you."

"You know every kid in town, Sheriff?"

"No record of an Andrea Porter in that graduating class."

"Who says I graduated? I transferred to the University of South Dakota at the end of my sophomore year."

A smile of reluctant admiration tugged at his Teutonic mouth. "Girl, we could go round and round like this all morning. You dance divinely."

"Thank you, kind sir."

"You really aren't going to tell me what you're doing here in Tilford, are you?"

Polite and ladylike smile. "I really don't see where it's any of your business, Sheriff."

"That remains to be seen, young lady." He touched the brim of his ballcap. "Maybe we could have another dance one of these days. When you get yourself a free minute, drop on by my office."

"Any particular reason, Sheriff?"

"Just being neighborly."

Sure, I thought, a nice neighborly chat. And when we were finished with our coffee, Sheriff Dave would have my cup dusted for fingerprints, make copies on the official FBI form, and fax them to Washington. Where, as a convicted felon, I'm on file with the other seven million Americans who have done time. No thanks! That's one dance I'd be happy to sit out.

Just then, I heard the door creak open and Donny's sleep-blurred voice mumbling, "Mmmmmm . . . Andrea?"

And there he was, Donald Winston Pierce, all six-foot-plus of him, newly roused, his eyes barely open, running a hand through his unruly locks. Normally I would have welcomed the sight of all that glorious masculinity packaged into a single, wrinkled pair of BVD briefs. But not now. Not in front of Sheriff Dave. And certainly not with that wake-up erection disturbing the front of Donny's shorts.

The sheriff flashed me a meaningful look, as if to say, "Oh, so that's how it is. The heir is boffing the realtor." I blushed like a fifteen-year-old. It started as a deep warmth at the base of my throat, then swept across my face like a gasoline blaze.

"You're up kind of early, aren't you, Hendricks?" Blinking rapidly, Donny scratched the back of his head. "What're you doing here?"

"Hullo, Mr. Pierce. Oh, just routine." He stepped away from the wall. "You look like you could do with some black coffee."

"Maybe later." Donny rubbed his eyelids. "When I stop tasting sand."

The sheriff turned to me. "Thank you for your time, Miss Porter. I look forward to seeing you again."

He ambled down the corridor, moving with a lazy, duckfooted stride, looking very much like the motel gardener on his way to assault the weeds. I was mightily thankful for Donny's presence. If not for him, Sheriff Dave might have pressed me for a response to his invitation. And I could only bob and weave for so long.

Donny's arms encircled me from behind. I felt a kiss at the top of my head: "Hmmmmm — been wondering where you ran off to."

"I've been entertaining." Slipping out of his embrace, I beckoned with my index finger. "Get in here before you embarrass me completely."

Donny feigned a look of astonishment. "Andrea Porter, is that a sunburn I see on your face?"

"Never mind!" Holding the door for him, I deliberately ignored that swelling in his underwear.

Well . . . at least until I got the door closed.


A couple of hours later, I was sitting on the rumpled bed, vigorously toweling my newly shampooed hair. A tropical downpour hammered the frosted glass of the shower. Donny's voice came drifting out of the bathroom. "Hey! I thought I saw two bath towels in here last night."

"You did. They're both in use. Sorry." I squirmed uncomfortably in my makeshift sarong. With swift, sure strokes, I fashioned a turban with the second bath towel. "Can you get by with hand towels?"

"Looks like I'll have to," he said ruefully. The downpour noise faded into a loud showerhead trickle. "What did Dave Hendricks want, anyway?"

I winced. Sorry, but I'm not the type who can make love to a man one minute and lie to him the next. And I was finding it harder and harder to prevaricate in front of Donny Pierce.

Hopping off the bed, I padded over to the dresser Opened my lingerie drawer. Tried the truth for once. "He wanted to know what I was doing in town. Why I was meeting with Carmody and Heisler."

"What for?"

"You've got me." I chickened out. My foray into truthfulness hadn't lasted very long. I peeled the towel sarong away, then donned a pair of lemon-colored panties. I thought of a new way to extract some background information from Donald. And despised myself for resorting to it. "Maybe it has something to do with Deer Cove."

"Why would Hendricks be interested in that?"

Hammocking myself into a matching sports bra, I responded, "I don't know. Maybe it has something to do with the owner's death."

Donny emerged from the misty bathroom. Two hand towels formed a makeshift loincloth. I loved that Tarzan look. Mopping his dampened face, he remarked, "I thought Tolliver shot himself."

"Did he?" I tore open a fresh package of No Nonsense.

"Well, that's what I heard. There wasn't too much about it in the *Gazette*. The editor never plays up suicides."

"Maybe he's afraid it'll give people ideas," I said, seating myself on the edge of the bed. "What's the word at Lynx River?"

Donny frowned. "They say Dick Jaswell did a hell of a number on those kids. He went to see them right after they filed their marina plan with the Zoning Board of Appeals. He dazzled them with tales of widespread community support and easy financing. Then he got their signatures on that loan agreement. The way I heard it, Jaswell was prepared to execute the call provision all along."

Keeping my personal reaction to myself, I flavored my voice with mild curiosity. "Pretty dirty pool for an upright banker."

"He's not so upright, Andrea." He slipped on his wrinkled dress shirt. "Jaswell got called on the carpet last year. The Federal Reserve's annual audit turned up a few irregularities in the books."

"Can you give me a for-instance?"

"First South Shore is required by law to maintain a minimum reserve requirement. That means they can't lend out every cent in the bank. Or pour the depositors' money into speculative ventures," Donny explained. "Jaswell had been claiming delinquent loans as productive assets, fraudulently listing those amounts as the bank's reserves. To quote the auditors, First South Shore's reserves were 'minimal.' "

"And he's still working there?"

Donny cracked a smile. "He has friends on the board, my dear."

"Like Congressman Burdick?"

"I thought you were supposed to be a stranger in town." Tightening his cufflinks, Donny did a mild double-take.

"It stands to reason, love. You usually find the biggest men in town on the bank's board of directors. You, your father, Wayne Burdick —"

"Biggest men in town," he interrupted, his grin widening. "Tell me, Miss Porter, are you using that phrase in the anatomical or the financial sense?"

Another colossal blush. "Shut up! You know, you are getting as raunchy as Jerry Carmody."

"Heaven forbid!"

"Did you and your dad sit in on that particular board meeting?"

Looping his tie, Donny faced the mirror and hummed in assent.

"Was there any talk about Jaswell making large, unsecured loans to Lakeside?"

"No comment." He fastened his tie clip, stood fully erect, and shot me a serious glance. "Sorry, hon, but I don't discuss board business with outsiders, no matter how pretty they are."

"But you think he really sandbagged them — the Tollivers, I mean."

"Damned right. Jaswell encouraged those kids to climb out on a limb. Then he sawed it off." Donny slipped on his suit jacket. "That guy is bad news, Andrea. If I had my way, First South Shore would have had a new president long ago."

"Did you know Jim Tolliver?" I asked.

"Hell, sure. I met him at Rotary. He really impressed me. For a while there, I was thinking about getting into offshore development myself. I asked Tolliver if he was interested in signing on. No thanks, he told me. He was bound and determined to make it on his own."

"Think he would have succeeded?"

Buckling his belt, Donny frowned. "I don't know, honey. I think if Jaswell hadn't sandbagged him, somebody else would have."

"What do you mean?"

"I mean Wayne Burdick has been after that area for years. Right after he formed the Lakeside Development Corporation, he made old George Quinlan — the original owner — an offer for all six parcels. Burdick was thinking in terms of high-rise, shoreside condos, I hear. But it fell through. Old George never forgave Burdick for blocking the permit on a proposed subdivision on Meadowrock Road."

"What about the second owner — whatzisname — McCann?"

"Brian McCann?" Donny tightened the knot in his silk tie. "Actually, nobody really expected him to do much with them. People figured McCann would sell the parcels one at a time to finance his retirement. When the word got out he was going to develop the cove, Lakeside offered to buy it all."

"Burdick made the offer?" I prodded.

"Not hardly. Wayne was in Congress by then. His business dealings are supposed to go on hold for the duration. No, I heard it was Mrs. Heisler who made the approach."

"The price was unacceptable, I take it."

"Well, Burdick didn't get where he is by paying top dollar for real estate. So it was no deal."

"Did anybody make an offer to the Tollivers?"

"Not that I know of." Donny's face had a sudden, world-weary look, a somber expression which gave me some idea of what he would look like as an old man. Handsome, grave, and dignified. "They're the ones I really feel sorry for, though. The Tollivers. I don't think they ever had a chance, really. Burdick would have found some way to pull the rug out from under them. Either him or someone eager to do him a favor.

And there's no shortage of those people in Tilford."

"Or anywhere else in the world."

"True enough." Restless and moody, he went to the window and parted the drapes. Sunlight cheered him a little. He gave me a sidelong smile. "Why don't you climb back into those bike pants, Andrea?"

"Why?"

"Well, for one thing, you look terrific in them."

"Thank you. But I need a more compelling reason than that."

"They'd come in handy on a trail ride up around Tamarack Lake," he replied, crossing the room. "How about it? We'll stop at the Caribou for lunch. Rent a pair of mountain bikes and spend the afternoon in that bracing fresh air. What do you say?"

I had no need to fake an expression of disappointment.

"No can do, Donald. I have a previous appointment for lunch."

"On Sunday!?"

I nodded in dismay. "Duty calls. I'm making a presentation at the Carmodys' this afternoon. To your friend Burdick."

"This is it, eh?" Leaning over, he gave me an affectionate one-armed hug. "Knock 'em dead, Miss Porter."

"I'll try."


Butternut Lane was just east of town, a winding asphalt road zigzagging into a quartet of forested, glaciated, smoothly rounded hills. Many, many ledges of brownstone and rhyolite. And not so many houses. They were mostly two-story Colonials with gambrel roofs — starting price, two hundred big ones. The Carmody place dominated the crest of a low hill, facing southwest, with a broad lawn ending in a high retaining wall made of dressed fieldstone.

I parked the Mitsubishi out front, beneath a tall, middle-aged elm, reflecting on my recent conversation with Donny. I didn't like the progression. Burdick offered to buy Deer Cove from old man Quinlan. Mr. Quinlan shot him down. Then, when it looked as if Brian McCann might develop the area instead, Mavis Heisler paid a call. Again the answer was no. And then Mary Beth's dad wound up in Lake Superior, floating facedown beside the wharf.

It certainly looked as if Dick Jaswell had intended to deep six the Tolliver loan all along. I knew from my initial conversation with Jerry Carmody that Jaswell was Lakeside's tool. And Donny had just as good as told me that Jaswell's banking future was intimately related to Lakeside's financial well-being. So it was a pretty safe bet that someone from Lakeside had sent Jaswell after the Tollivers. But who?

I still had much digging to do, so I strolled up that long cement walkway in my Sunday best. Corn yellow linen jacket with puffed shoulders, bright brass buttons, and elbow-length sleeves. Glossy black slim skirt and matching pumps. Cream-colored challis scarf and golden clamshell earrings. A bumblebee rose suddenly from the flawlessly trimmed forsythia bushes, attracted by my perfume and jacket. He probably thought I was the world's biggest marsh marigold. Sidestepping his flight path, I shooed him away with a wave of my hand, then climbed the front step to ring the doorbell.

A woman answered. It was the sandy blonde from Kathy's reception, the one who had so carefully watched my conversation with Jerry the previous day. Watery blue eyes, high delicate cheekbones, pert tip-tilted nose, and a soft, expressive mouth. She reminded me of Jerry's secretary, Molly the Skittish. They might have even been sisters, had Molly attended Smith or Vassar as this one obviously had. She regarded me with a polite, level, dullish stare.

Classic Angie smile. "Hi, I'm Andrea Porter. Jerry asked me to drop by."

"Oh yes, he's been expecting you." Her voice was a clarion alto, very precise and well modulated. Stepping to one side, she made a gesture of invitation. "How do you do? I'm Evelyn Carmody." She added after a moment's hesitation, "Jerry's wife."

It's not something a woman brags about. Her smile was faint, sickly, and apologetic.

I watched Evelyn's hand dart unerringly toward the half-empty cocktail glass waiting atop the living room table. The heels of her slingbacks wobbled a bit as she slowly, deliberately led me through the house.

Evelyn was smashed. She had the functioning alcoholic's obsession with total control. Each and every step was an exercise in disciplined balance. She wore a curve-hugging coatdress—a very expensive little number in turquoise voile jacquard—that would have been the envy of Cheryl Tiegs. Her short, tousled hair gave her a strangely juvenile air, as if she were a little girl dressing up in Mom's finery, an aura of unhealthy vulnerability.

The living room had a distinctly feminine touch. That made it Evelyn's fantasy, not Jerry's. Old-fashioned grandfather clock in one corner. Plush flare-armed sofa in a bold silver floral pattern. Chippendale table bordered in burl wood. Paintings enclosed by hand-finished antique gold-leaf frames. To quote Jerry, there was nothing like it on Livernois Avenue.

Evelyn escorted me out to the broad redwood sundeck. Jerry was playing bartender in the corner, wearing a chef's apron emblazoned with a skull, its eyes rolled upward and its tongue extended. With the amusing notation "Army Cook—Death From Within." Mavis Heisler was seated on the bench of the picnic table, pudgy legs crossed, beige spike-heeled sandals slipping off. She tried to be casually stylish in her bright red jersey wraptop and loose, Aztec-print skirt, but the image was ruined by the masculine way she gripped her beer bottle.

I was far more interested in the man Mavis was talking to. Wayne Burdick was taller than I'd expected. An inch over six feet, unless I missed my eagle-eyed Anishinabe guess. Dark brown hair with distinguished-looking threads of gray in his sickle-shaped sideburns. Impeccable styling camouflaged a noticeably high hairline. The face was blunt, vaguely Scandinavian—broad, intellectual forehead, long nose with a tip that curled slightly downward, thin lips bracketed by tiny slanting folds of flesh.

Burdick's face brightened the instant he spotted me. "You must be Andrea Porter." Out came the hand for the politician's hearty shake. "I'm glad you could make it."

If anything, Burdick was better at meet-and-greet than his aide. He shepherded me to the table, summoned the Carmodys' elderly cook, and suggested I sample the roast lamb.

All in all, it was a lovely back-porch luncheon. The congressman acted as if he wanted to hear my whole life story. Mavis took personal responsibility for my presence there. And, wonder of wonders, Jerry even managed to keep his hands away from my rear end.

When we finished eating, Burdick went to the ice chest and withdrew a damp bottle of Coors. Leaning back against the redwood railing, he unscrewed the bottlecap and let his smile turn chilly. "Andrea, you have five minutes to convince me. Begin!"

So I did a rerun of my presentation in Jerry's office. Burdick took many long sips from the bottle. His facial expression never changed. It was shrewd, skeptical, tough, and authoritarian. I had no further questions as to who was the real boss of the Lakeside Development Corporation.

When I concluded, Burdick remarked, "This consortium of yours . . . how high are they willing to bid?"

"Five million."

"That's a pretty hefty investment, kiddo." He placed the empty bottle on the picnic table. "Are you sure there are no dissident voices in the group?"

"Mr. Burdick, they're sitting on a big pile of money. They're on the prowl for projects here in the Midwest. If I don't sell to them, somebody else will."

"And you think you can sell them Deer Cove?"

"I *know* I can sell it. It's exactly what they're looking for. An industrial park in the upper Midwest with water access and high-growth potential." Looking both sincere and anxious, I twisted my paper napkin round and round. "Only I can't deliver on my own. They're not interested in raw land. There has to be a development firm in place, ready to begin construction. You issue the common — they'll buy in. It's as simple as that."

Mavis began to speak. Burdick silenced her with a wave of his hand, then jutted his chin in the direction of the kitchen. "Why don't you and Jer see if Evvie needs any help?"

Displaying a docility I wouldn't have believed possible, Jerry nodded, doffed his comedy apron, and obeyed. Mavis, on the other hand, balked a little. "Wayne, I'd really like to sit in on this."

His congressional smile held no warmth. "No need. Andrea and I are going for a little walk."

And so we did, the congressman and I. Down the wooden stairwell, across the well-trimmed lawn, and all the way to the edge of the backyard. Jerry's land fell away abruptly, leading downhill into a stony ravine. Standing at the brink, looking straight ahead, I could just make out the azure glimmer of Lake Superior between a pair of converging evergreen hillsides.

Burdick's smile warmed a bit. Pointing to his small, wrinkly ear, he said, "What I want you to do right now, Andrea — what I'd really like you to do — is whisper a name in my ear. The name of the heaviest hitter in your consortium."

"I'm afraid that's not possible, Mr. Burdick."

"This could be the end of it right here, kiddo."

"In which case I'll be on my way."

I started back to the sundeck. Burdick let me go fifteen steps before setting off in pursuit. His hand clutched my shoulder.

"What's the matter, Andrea? Afraid I'll go over your head and deal you out? No way. We can be very helpful to each other, little lady."

"I haven't heard any terms yet."

"Make me an offer."

172

Thumbing the unruly bangs away from my left eyebrow, I said, "I'm offering the same terms I discussed with Jaswell. A seat on the board. And one percent of the common."

"Too high." His chuckle was affable. "The seat's yours. But one eighth of one percent is as high as I'm prepared to go."

"One half," I snapped.

"One quarter. Zero-point-two-five. That's my final offer. And to sweeten it a bit, I'll let you draw full salary and perks as a vice president of the Deer Cove Enterprises Corporation."

Slowly widening Angie smile. "You've already got the name picked out, eh?"

"Jaswell's legal staff is working on the formal incorporation papers right now. We sign at First South Shore at nine A.M. tomorrow. From that point on, you're working for me. I'm going to have you hustling new industry for the park. I fully intend to press that cute little ass to the grindstone." The stiffening lake breeze raised a cowlick on the right side of Burdick's head. "Now I have a question for you. Why so secretive with the name?"

I rubbed my chilled forearms. "It was their idea. Tilford is a highly desirable site. However, there was some hesitation in the consortium, particularly after what happened to James Tolliver."

"You're a very naughty girl, Andrea. You got poor Dick Jaswell all upset with that kind of talk. He's back on Tums again."

"Mr. Burdick, my clients would prefer not to be associated with any sort of scandal. There are too many eager beavers at the SEC ready to haul someone into court."

"What scandal!?" Amused chuckle. "The man shot himself. It happens every day. And to people with less reason to kill themselves than Tolliver."

"You really believe that?"

"I read the coroner's report," he replied, quite sure of himself. "A man in my position has to stay aware of . . . potential threats. I went looking for information that

173

would have been damaging to my—'to Lakeside." His cold-eyed gaze swept over me. "I didn't find anything. It was an open-and-shut case, kiddo."

"Any mention of Jaswell's boobytrapped loan to the Tollivers?"

"Where'd you hear that one, Andrea? From Mary Beth Tolliver?" Flashing a contemptuous smirk, he suddenly put himself between me and the house. I couldn't help noticing how large and muscular his hands were. "You know, Mavis seems to think you have that girl hidden away somewhere."

"Don't be an idiot." Every smidgen of my acting ability went into the construction of my languid, nonchalant pose. "If I had the Tolliver woman, do you think I'd show up here without a signed purchase agreement? One of those in my purse would have made this sales job a whole lot easier."

He considered that for a few moments. I willed my knees to stop trembling. Get real, Biwaban. Congressmen don't murder people at the side of the road. They pay someone else to do it.

"Yeah, that makes sense." His gaze was shrewd. "Tell me, how'd you hear about that loan?"

"No one can keep a secret in that bank, Mr. Burdick."

"I'm sorry to hear that, Andrea. I was under the impression I was paying for confidentiality." Feral smirk. "Jaswell's going to have to toss a few asses out the window."

Smoothing my collar, I added, "In any event, you can see why my clients do not want to become involved in any sort of situation—"

"For Christ's sweet sake, will you get off that kick!? There is no *situation*." His sharply annoyed glance skewered me. "We don't even own those tracts. Deer Cove Enterprises will have to negotiate for purchase. And who knows where that Tolliver girl went—"

"You could ask the Bureau," I interrupted.

Burdick's exasperation vanished in a twinkling, replaced by a cool, wary look. "Jerry's handling that end of it. You needn't concern yourself."

174

Oh, but I was concerned. The thought of Jerry's pals out hunting for Mary Beth made my stomach curdle. Naturally, they would try Cottage Grove, Oregon first — Jim's hometown. If Mary Beth had hit the road unobtrusively, there was a slim chance they'd be stalled there. But not for long. Sooner or later, they'd dig up a clue pointing in the direction of Medicine Tail.

The congressman had as good as told me that he was well aware of Jerry's mob connections. His strange reluctance to use the FBI hinted at some incriminating dealings between Burdick and his gangland majordomo.

Patting down his cowlick, he muttered, "Why do you keep harping on that loan, Andrea?"

"It makes my clients back East very uncomfortable. Jaswell loans the Tollivers money. The young husband turns up dead. Then Jaswell arm-twists the young widow into liquidating those properties."

Thinking it over, he sighed. "All right. I can see where your banker friends might get antsy about that. Well, tell them not to worry. There's no conflict of interest involved. Jaswell knew the Tolliver project would never get off the ground. That's why he built himself an escape hatch."

"I didn't know ol' Jass was psychic."

"ESP had nothing to do with it, Andrea. Jaswell had heard that Glenn Veeder was out to scuttle the Tollivers. He knew Veeder had enough back-pocket votes on the Planning Board to make good that threat. So he built himself a storm shelter."

I took a sudden deep breath. Papa Veeder had just jumped into the front rank of Mary Beth's enemies. I thought back to our brief conversation at his daughter's wedding. Remembered his flipflop on the Deer Cove development issue — his chumminess with Jaswell. Why had Glenn Veeder wanted to sandbag the Tollivers?

"Was Veeder interested in the cove?" I asked.

Burdick let out a gust of laughter. "Honey, *everybody's* interested in Deer Cove."

"Including you?"

"Me most of all." Taut savage smile. "Years ago, I was this fucking close to getting title." He held his thumb and forefinger an inch apart. "That old son of a bitch Quinlan cut the ground right out from under me. I had contracts signed. I was all ready to build. And that old bastard, he sold out to McCann. I flew down to Sarasota personally . . . offered him top dollar, too. Turned me down flat! And for what? For spite. 'Cause I once gave him a screwing on that Meadowrock Road deal. Crazy old bastard!" Hands in his pockets, he turned back to the Carmody house. "Maybe this time I'll make it pay, eh?"

Then he halted, looking back at me, checking to see if I was dutifully following. "Anything else I can do for you?"

"Just one thing more, Mr. Burdick." I spied Jerry up on the sundeck. He was leaning against the rail, carefully watching us both. "Keep that animal away from me."

Burdick flashed me a hasty ingratiating smile, one that was completely devoid of sympathy. "What can I say? Jerry likes the ladies."

"Make him understand that *this* lady is off-limits."

"Now, Andrea . . ."

"I'm not fucking around, Burdick. Tell Jerry to keep his hands to himself." My voice held enough real indignation to be totally convincing. "The next time he tries to play grab-ass, the deal is off! Understand?"

The congressman sighed. This was simply one more in a long line of Jerry-related difficulties. He gave my shoulder a comforting pat.

"I'll have a talk with him, Andrea."

"See that you do!" I snapped.

And then we rejoined the others on the sundeck.

# Chapter Ten

Promptly at nine o'clock on Monday morning, the first of June, I formally rejoined the world of work. Not as a minimum-wage waitress in Paul Holbrook's work experience program but as the vice president in charge of site development for the newly incorporated Deer Cove Enterprises. The job promised me a salary of eighty-five thousand per year, fringe benefits, stock options, Blue Cross/Blue Shield, and a pension payable at age sixty-five. In addition, I got my very own small but cozy private office at First South Shore Savings Bank, complete with a gold-embossed nameplate on the door. First South Shore would serve as our company's temporary quarters until we found a lease of our own.

Others did considerably better. Dick Jaswell, for one. Ten minutes after the signing, he was voted in as CEO of Deer Cove Enterprises, a position that paid a whole lot more than eighty-five grand.

The board also voted to turn over a hefty share of the common — fifty-two percent — to Northern Horizons, Inc., which I soon learned was a corporate front for Wayne Burdick. Indeed, Jaswell's first official act as Deer Cove CEO was to award Northern Horizons a two-hundred-dollar contract for unspecified "legal services."

Our first board meeting closed with a rousing little speech from Burdick full of misty-eyed tributes to all of the people who built up the U.P. The French *voyageurs* and the Cornish miners and the Irish railroad workers and all the other misplaced Europeans who crapped up my people's ancestral homeland. In between kudos to Tilford and stouthearted exhortations to pursue the holy grail of industrial development, he managed to squeeze in a mention or two of his upcoming reelection campaign. Make those checks payable to Burdick for Congress, folks. But all things come to an end, even congressional speeches, and by ten-thirty we were all having coffee and danish in the conference room. The gentlemen found your Angie absolutely charming. The same cannot be said of Mr. Burdick, who came up behind me, gave the seat of my skirt a proprietary pat, and told me to quit flirting with the old geezers and get to work.

And I did. For two solid days, I was Dick Jaswell's shadow. Little Miss Helpful. I managed his paper flow, made appointments for him, quizzed him on local companies who might wish to buy into our industrial park, hand-delivered every memo I typed up, brewed his coffee, and snarled at all the tellers.

Oh, those tellers didn't like me. I had the nasty habit of delegating every task that wound up on my desk. Every time I emerged from my office, I could feel the weight of those resentful female glances. All those catty unspoken remarks. Who is that woman? Why is she working here? Is she fucking old man Jaswell? Who the hell is *she* to be giving *me* orders!?

The tellers' mascaraed eyes really popped on Tuesday, June second. That's the afternoon Donny Pierce walked in and took me out to Lynx River for lunch. A long lunch. Later that day, as I strolled past the employees' lounge, I heard a torrent of gossipy conversation. It dried up the moment I stuck my face in the doorway.

Today's hot topic — mystery brunette chases the boss and romances Tilford's most eligible bachelor at the same time. Soap opera deluxe!

Actually, my pursuit of Jaswell had a more practical

178

objective in mind. By clinging to his blazer sleeve, I managed to learn where he hid the access codes to the First South Shore computer. He kept them taped to the bottom of the photo cube on his desk. Once I had them memorized, I was definitely in business.

The afternoon of Wednesday, June third, found me lounging in my padded swivel chair, thumbing through an old Chamber of Commerce industrial survey. Perched atop the side table was my brand-new IBM station—keyboard, monitor, hard disk, printer, and all. Putting aside the report, I slumped in my chair, legs demurely crossed, one midheeled pump dangling from my instep, faced the amber monitor screen, and ever so casually tapped in the access code with my pencil's eraser tip.

First entry . . . Lakeside Development Corporation.

Now isn't that interesting. Lakeside routes all of its bill payments through its accounts at First South Shore. A mammoth parade of Lakeside dollars marches through the bank's general ledger. No wonder Dick Jaswell was so interested in Lakeside's well-being.

Oh-kay, let's have a look at the subcontractors. Tappety-tap on the keyboard. Kaleidoscopic shift of the alphanumerics. Ooooohh! Lakeside certainly does a lot of business with Glenn Veeder's construction outfit. Concrete foundations at the Nijonik Beach project. Roofing and flooring in Seney. Plumbing at the Diplomat Motel way out there in Ontonagon. All in all, as Lakeside's favorite subcontractor, Daddy Glenn was dependent upon Burdick's firm for just over one-point-seven million in construction work.

Veeder Construction appeared to have a passable cash flow. However, business had peaked a year ago. There was a noticeable slump in new construction. Glenn Veeder needed a spurt of development in Deer Cove to maintain his profit margin.

So add Glenn Veeder's name to the roster of people likely to benefit from Lakeside's acquisition of the cove. Daddy Glenn was in distinguished company, right up there with Mavis Heisler and Jerry Carmody and Dick Jaswell and Wayne Burdick.

And I was pretty sure Glenn had lied about not speaking to Jim Tolliver just before the shooting.

Something to think about, eh?


For about a week, I trailed Dick Jaswell around the office like an eleven-year-old on her first crush. This activity came to a screeching halt the morning Mrs. Jaswell unexpectedly walked into the bank. I guess someone had told her about the brunette who was young enough to be her daughter. To be perfectly honest, I didn't help matters, either, with my habit of sitting on Jaswell's desk with my hem at midthigh. You should have seen the look on Mrs. J's face. Ouch!

Anyway, when I got back from lunch, there was a memo on my desk. From Dickie, of course. The memo coolly informed me that he would be out of the office for a few days and henceforth all matters dealing with Deer Cove Enterprises would be channeled through Mrs. Eleanor Hartshorn, his administrative assistant.

Eleanor Hartshorn turned out to be Mrs. Burgundy Suit, the battleax who had greeted me at the bank that first day. Eleanor never felt comfortable with the notion of me as an equal. I was not a proper Katie Gibbs girl. Eleanor wanted a week or two to whip me into shape. She longed to yank my shoulders back, seat me upright in the chair, disconnect my telephone, put a pencil in my grasp, and set me to work scribbling on all the paper I'd delegated elsewhere.

Of course, some paperwork I didn't mind doing. Such as setting up the joint escrow account for Deer Cove Enterprises and my nonexistent consortium. Once this was brimming with moolah, I would be able to flush four million out of the system and transfer it to my newly opened savings account at Pontiac Bank and Trust in Detroit.

On Tuesday morning, June ninth, at the precise moment I was supposed to be starting my new waitress job for Paul Holbrook, I decided to drop in on Eleanor and impress her with my diligence. So, leaving my midheeled pumps beside my desk, I rolled up the lot maps, grabbed our draft application to the Zoning Board of Appeals, and padded down the hall to her office.

To my surprise, I found Evelyn Carmody in the guest chair. Jerry's wife was looking very Vassar this morning in her snug sage green Aran sweater and white double-pleated silk pants. A lengthy emerald scarf bound her fine hair in a simple but chic ponytail. She reacted instantly to my presence, turning my way, flashing a hesitant smile. Bright red threads spoiled the white of her eyeballs. I was uncomfortably reminded of my own head the morning after Kathy Veeder's reception. So I kept my smile sympathetic and my voice down. "Hi, Evvie."

"Er . . . hello, Andrea." Her fingers moved with a curious life of their own, twisting the fabric of her stylish trousers. "Eleanor, could I have a peek at the monthly statement of accounts first?"

Polite and serene, that's our Mrs. Hartshorn. Always defer to the customer. "Of course, dear." She reached for the intercom button. "I'll have Audrey print it up for you."

"If it would be easier, you could fax it to our house." The lady Evelyn was in a fidgety mood today. "I don't want to take up any more of your time. I'm sure what Andrea has is much more important."

"It's no trouble at all, Mrs. Carmody." Expectant glance from the matron. Sort of reminded me of the principal's office at Central. "What do you have there, Andrea?"

"Just the ZBA draft application. I figured you could look it over, then bounce it up to Dick."

"The industrial park?" Evelyn was on her feet in a twinkling, snapping her purse shut, casting gracious smiles at me and Eleanor. Any old excuse for an escape, I guess. "Well, that's certainly more important than our household finances. I'll leave you two to your work. Good day, Eleanor . . . Andrea."

And out she went, her stride just a shade too urgent to be carefree. Back to the ever-faithful brandy bottle. Just a little nip to take the edge off her headache. I've known too many people like that. Thoroughly depressed, I watched her country-day-school departure. And then Eleanor's muted *ahem* captured my attention.

Eleanor seemed genuinely pleased to see my ZBA application. But her expression changed the instant she spotted my shoeless feet. Penciled brows came together. A classic Hartshorn glare. A young-lady-this-is-a-place-of-business look.

I spread the lot maps across her desktop, and Eleanor settled down to some serious study. Thoughtful Iron Lady with her customary stiff grayish brown hair and roses-in-June lipstick. She sported her favorite corporate uniform, too. Tight-fitting linen jacket and slim skirt in a glossy Mediterranean blue. Crisp white satin blouse with a frothy throat rosette.

While Eleanor looked over the proposal, I wandered her office, my hands clasped behind me, admiring the framed photographs on the cinnamon-colored walls.

One captured my gaze instantly. It was a convivial Christmas scene, with the rustic interior of the Caribou Lodge as a backdrop. Jerry and Evelyn Carmody, Dick Jaswell and the missus, Mavis Heisler, Glenn and Doris Veeder, Monica Lonardo, Wayne Burdick and Eleanor Hartshorn, all with champagne glasses aloft for a toast. But I was far more interested in the empty chair to Eleanor's left. A tawny garment lay strewn over the backrest. I blinked in recognition, remembering that Christmas at Aunt Della's. A camel hair coat.

"Andrea."

Eleanor's voice sounded as if it were coming from Detroit. I studied the cheerful faces of the little group, wondering which one was the owner.

*"Andrea!"*

I spun at once. "Yes, ma'am."

"You'd better make a copy of this." Eleanor waved a bulky manila folder. "Our legal counsel will want to look it over as well as Mr. Jaswell."

"Okay." Accepting the folder, I nonchalantly tilted my head at the photo. "Say, who took that picture?"

"Dave Robineaux. He's a staff photographer for the *Tilford Gazette.*"

"The congressman always gets press coverage, eh?"

"Something like that." I received my second wordless glare of the morning. "Andrea, don't you have work to do?"

"Loads! Know something? I saw the loveliest camel hair coat in that picture. Yours?"

"That's a little too rich for my taste, dear."

"Any idea who owns it? I'd like to ask where they bought it."

"I haven't the foggiest," Eleanor replied, reaching for a blank worksheet. "Dave took that photo as we were leaving. There were coats all over the chairs. *He* carried them in from the cloakroom."

I caught the subtle distasteful chill in the word *he*. Decided to play a hunch. "I guess that was probably the only gentlemanly thing Jerry Carmody ever did in his life, eh?"

"Indeed it was!" Eleanor's weary eyes lifted. "Now, will you *please* make yourself useful, young lady, and get back to work?"

On Wednesday afternoon, I met Jerry Carmody for lunch at The Greenery. Jerry wasn't particularly happy with my choice. He had wanted to go to the Caribou, but I'd nixed that. For one thing, I had no need of another leg massage. The Greenery was an open-front restaurant right on Tilford's main pier. Plenty of white tables with huge beach umbrellas and lunchtime shoppers milling around. Our table was in a corner of the large weather-beaten sundeck, with a nice view of blue sky, gaily painted gift shops, herring gulls, and fishing boats.

While I munched away on my lettuce-and-celery special, Jerry lounged in his chair and thumbed through my status report. Mirrored sunglasses offered no clue to his reactions. Chewing the succulent greens, I tried to think of a clever way to ask him about the camel hair coat in Eleanor's photo. One that wouldn't earn me a burial at sea in Kitchi Gammi.

Frowning, Jerry closed the folder. His sunglasses showed me twin reflections of my pretty face. "So your friends back East came through, eh?"

After a fashion. The previous afternoon, I'd made a quick run out to the Soo and commissioned a print shop to run off ten blank checks. Earlier that morning, using a First South Shore checkwriting machine, I'd run off a check in the amount of four-point-five million. That check was now paperclipped to the inside of Jerry's folder.

"The check arrived this morning," I replied, reaching for my glass of lemonade. "Registered mail. My team held up its end. It's up to you and Burdick now."

Slow grin of pleasure. Handing back the folder, Jerry said, "Have Jaswell deposit that in the escrow account. Let me huddle with Wayne. Then I'll kick in my share tomorrow."

Suddenly, there was a disturbance at the gate. My reaction time is pretty good, but Jerry made me look like an arthritic old lady. A dismayingly quick and agile fellow. He was out of that chair in an eyeblink, fists clenched, shoulders tense, ready to meet an oncoming Glenn Veeder.

"I want to talk to you, Carmody!" The look on Papa Veeder's face would have sent grizzlies scurrying into the nearest den. "What the fuck is going on, anyway?"

Only Jerry's chin moved. "Have a seat, why don't you?"

"No thanks! I'd rather have some answers." Quivering with suppressed anger, Glenn raised a mammoth fist. "What's with this *new corporation* shit!?"

I didn't like Jerry's slow-blossoming smile. "Who you been talking to, pal?"

"Never mind! They say there's a new firm developing the cove. You're on the board. And Jaswell. And the little girl there. And I don't get an invite. What gives?"

"The board's open to anybody who can buy the shares."

"Yeah! Right!" Veins popped out on Glenn's temples. "Five thousand shares at twenty-two-fifty a whack!? I haven't got that kind of money."

For the first time, Jerry's tight little smile showed genuine pleasure. "I guess you're out, guy."

"You son of a bitch! You dealt me out on purpose!" Glenn shouted. "I stuck my neck out plenty for Wayne Burdick!"

"Maybe you ought to talk to him, asshole."

"Damned right I will! Burdick *owes* me! Maybe we'll have a nice talk about those Tolliver kids, eh? You think you're hot shit, you little bastard! No way am I letting you fuck me over, Carmody!"

The magic word — *Tolliver.* It prodded Jerry forward, stoking the fires of rage. Whipping off his sunglasses, he hollered, "You've got a big mouth, Veeder. One of these days, it's going to get shut — *permanently!*"

"You want it shut? Do it yourself!" Purpling in fury, Glenn waggled his big hand in invitation. "Come on! What's holding you back, you pint-sized faggot!?"

Eyes wide and bulging, Jerry lunged at him. Fortunately, the maître d' and a quartet of customers managed to keep the two separated. High-decibel profanity assaulted my ears. The poison level would have wilted The Greenery's potted ferns. Jerry's leg sprang upward, seeking his opponent's crotch, but Glenn backpedaled out of range. While the maître d' and the others restrained Jerry, an anxious manager got behind Glenn Veeder and labored to push his huge form through the gate.

Spraying spit, Jerry screamed, "That's the last time you'll ever mouth off at me, asshole! You know what I mean? You know what I'm saying to you? The last fucking time!"

"I ain't scared of you, you little shit, or that Detroit guineawopper you used to work for!" Glaring over his shoulder, Glenn balked at the gate. "This ain't over—not by a long shot! I'll be dropping by Lakeside to see you, motherfucker! Count on it!"

Then he vanished into the noontime crowd of pedestrians.

Shoving the maître d' aside, Jerry kicked an empty chair and marched back to our table. "Pay the fucking tab, Andrea!"

I did as I was told, charged everything to our new Deer Cove Enterprises account, and graciously accepted the manager's apology. I've had quieter lunches at Springfield. I took my time getting back to our table. Wanted Jerry to settle down. When I returned, I found Jerry sitting in the deck chair, blazer rumpled and features still ruddy with anger, possessively clutching the folder with the bogus check for four million.

Together we strolled uptown to the municipal parking lot. For once, Jerry was silent. He seemed to have forgotten my presence. And then, with no warning, he halted abruptly and turned to me.

"Find yourself a ride back to work, babe. I'm headed for the Chain & Anchor."

"I could do with a drink myself, Jer."

"Forget it. You've got work to do." Rubbing the back of his neck, he gave me a no-arguments look. "I've got me a phone call to make."

I gestured at the Rexall pharmacy across the street. "There's a pay phone over there."

"Sorry, babe. This is a private call." He straightened his tie, lifting his chin proudly. "Veeder I can handle. And I'll prove it next time. But not Veeder and a trio of his cement-mixing asshole buddies. I'm going to even the odds a little bit."

"What's so private about the Chain & Anchor?"

Wolfish grin. "I own the joint."

And with that, he strolled away, angling kittycorner through the block-sized parking lot, heading for Catamount Boulevard.

As for me, I was very thankful to Glenn Veeder. He

had just put a few troubling matters into perspective for me.

Such as Monica Lonardo's lukewarm reaction to Jerry's pinch. And the knowing gleam in her eyes when Jerry made that remark about *women in business*. And Monica's determination to conceal her Detroit origins.

Why? Because Monica was connected, just like Jerry. The two of them were co-owners of the Chain & Anchor.

Now I understood the hidden meaning of Jerry's strange little in-joke. There were *women in business* at the tavern, all right. Members of the world's oldest profession, operating no doubt on a franchise granted by Jerry's old boss in Detroit.

You'll find a lot of places like the Chain & Anchor in the U.P. Seedy pubs with a hard-hitting madam, equally rough bouncers, and a gynecologist on call. Monica herself had probably made her debut in a place just like it. A mob underboss had probably discovered her before she had become too shopworn. Coached her and groomed her and put her to work on the high-class call circuit, where the ladies earn fifteen hundred per night, minimum, and the gentlemen have some decidedly peculiar tastes.

I should have tumbled to it sooner. Mary Beth had inadvertently clued me in back in Medicine Tail. After all, it was Jerry himself who'd told Mary Beth that he'd one day see her selling her ass at the Chain & Anchor.

I began wondering if Jerry had planned to murder Jim Tolliver all along. Kill the husband, grab control of Deer Cove, and let mob buddy Monica put the young widow to work in the brothel.

Remembering what Donny had told me, I thought I could see the faint outlines of a motive. Jerry had originally come to Tilford to dodge that probe into the finances of the Toolmakers. But perhaps Jerry's old boss didn't trust him. Maybe the old man feared Jerry might cut a private deal with the feds. That would explain Monica's presence here in Tilford. She might be the capo's personal watchdog, keeping an eye on the exiled wiseguy.

Wayne Burdick might be able to shield Jerry from Uncle Sam. But who was going to protect him from the old man in Detroit? Particularly if the capo decided he couldn't trust Jerry to keep his mouth shut.

All of this would give Merry Jerry a mighty compelling reason to develop Deer Cove, that is, to lay hands on some money of his very own.

Four million dollars would purchase an ironclad cover identity down there in South America.

Just after five-thirty, I strolled into the bar at the Lynx River Country Club. I was meeting Donny for dinner at seven, and I definitely needed a touch of Happy Hour. In addition to pondering the parameters of the Jerry/Monica relationship, I had spent a hectic two hours at the bank, crouched over the telephone, trying to sell a prime lot site to a cement firm in Rogers City.

The bar's decor consisted of frosted glass, recessed muted fluorescent lights, a few potted plants, and well-upholstered stools. A thin-faced Mexican bartender with a soulful expression and noticeable eyebrows diligently wiped a Collins glass and offered me a welcome smile.

The after-work crowd was predominantly male. Which is probably why the sound level dropped a bit as I sauntered in. Climbing onto the barstool, I felt the pressure of surreptitious masculine stares. Woman alone at the bar. Target of opportunity.

Look elsewhere, fellas. Angie's taken.

The bartender brought me an exceedingly fine Beachcomber—tart and chilled and as smooth as brushed suede. Daintily sipping the frosted rum, I settled back in my seat and waited for Donny to arrive.

A few moments later, I was hailed by a familiar-looking brown-haired lady with a pert chipmunk grin. Trista Petersen, whom I'd met at Kathy Veeder's reception. She captured the empty stool at my side, put in her order for a margarita, and began complaining about her job at the

Olsen lumber mill. I deftly changed the subject to clothes, and we had a marvelous time evaluating the local boutiques. Trista complimented me on my outfit — a short, sailor-style white twill jacket and matching sheath dress with brass buttons and standaway pockets — and asked where she could find a pair of gorgeous T-strap shoes just like mine.

By the time we returned to the topic of work, Trista's mood was much improved. "So, Andrea, what gives? Is old man Jaswell running you ragged or what?"

"Actually, I hardly ever see him. Dick has me working for Eleanor Hartshorn these days."

"Oh God! That's even worse." Trista sent a sympathetic glance over the rim of her cocktail tumbler. "My sister worked for First South Shore when she got out of high school. She said that Hartshorn bitch used to stand outside the ladies room door with a stopwatch. True?"

"Absolutely." I took a ladylike sip. "Eleanor's keeping close tabs on my phone calls. She thinks I'm chatting with guys on company time." Putting down the glass, I added, "As if I had the chance! I am swamped with queries about the proposed industrial park."

"Think it'll sell?"

"Like tartans in autumn, Trista."

"I believe it." Trista nodded. "That's the choicest land in Tilford, I hear. When that Mr. McCann moved down here from Duluth, a lot of people were after him to sell. Kathy's dad even made him an offer."

Sitting erect, I glanced at her. "Glenn Veeder?"

"You bet. Right here in the bar. It was a Sunday, I think. I met my parents here for dinner, and we came in for a drink afterward. Mr. McCann recognized Dad. They were Tilford Tigers together . . . oh, a long, long time ago." Trista's features softened in reminiscence. "Mr. McCann introduced us to his wife. She was very nice. Then he was telling us all about himself, how he'd just retired and all. Then Mr. Veeder came in and joined us."

"And made a pitch for Deer Cove?" I prodded.

"Uh-huh. He offered to buy all six farms. Really urged Mr. McCann to sell. He said Mr. McCann could have a mighty fine retirement down in Florida if he signed. Mr. McCann said thanks but no thanks. He said he had his own plans."

I puckered my lips thoughtfully. So Papa Veeder had made the first pitch for those properties, eh? That meant Veeder must have had advance knowledge of Wayne Burdick's plans to develop the cove. By purchasing the McCann farms early, Veeder would have put himself in the perfect position to dictate terms to Lakeside.

"How did Veeder take the turndown?" I asked.

"He sure looked disappointed. But he was pleasant enough. He had a drink with us. He's not always that sociable, but at least he's a gentleman." Trista wrinkled her tiptilted nose. "Not like *some*."

I could think of only one person in Tilford who could generate that tone of distaste. "You talking about Jerry Carmody?"

Trista looked at me as if I'd suddenly grown another nose. "How did you hear about that?"

"Hear about what?"

"Carmody's fight with Mr. McCann."

"What fight?" My voice was an eager whisper. Come on, dear, let's gossip.

"Well, I don't know all the details." Her brown eyes gleamed with inspiration. Lifting a forefinger, she said, "Oh, Jorge . . ."

"Yes, Triss?" He stopped in front of us, both slim-fingered hands on the mahogany bar, the left caterpillar-shaped eyebrow arching in expectation.

"You know Mr. Carmody, don't you?" Trista said.

I sensed a sudden standoffishness in the bartender. "Of course."

I had a feeling Trista was going to blow it, so I took steps to keep the bartender attentive. Hooked the heel of my T-strap on the stool's aluminum rail. Swiveled my chair ninety degrees to the left. Flashed a bit of leg as I rummaged through my shoulder bag.

Jorge remained interested, and his interest grew when I slipped a wrinkled twenty beneath my glass. "Lovely Beachcomber," I said, "from now on, this place gets all my business."

He palmed the bill like a seasoned stage magician and gave his utmost attention to Trista.

"Do you remember that time Mr. McCann had that trouble with Mr. Carmody?" she asked.

"Sure, Triss. I'm the one who got them separated."

I eased my way into the interview. "Who was at the bar?"

"Mr. McCann, señorita. It was snowing that day. He stopped in for a drink on his way home. I poured him a brandy." Jorge touched the front of his snug-fitting red vest. "There was hardly anybody here in the bar."

Snow, eh? That made it wintertime. Brian McCann had moved to Tilford the previous July. This meant he had met his death six or seven weeks after his run-in with Jerry.

"How did it start?" I asked.

Jorge shrugged. "I'm not sure. Mr. Carmody came in and saw Mr. McCann here at the bar. He offered to buy Mr. McCann a drink. Mr. McCann looked as if he wanted to get up and walk away. Then Mr. Carmody started kidding him."

"Kidding him?" I echoed.

"Yes. He says, 'Hey, don't you believe in telephones? When am I gonna get an answer?' After that, the two of them talked for a while." Reaching for a worn dishrag, Jorge tilted his head to the right. "I didn't see it start. I had a customer to take care of. I remember, I heard the sound of breaking glass. I turned, and the two of them were on their feet. Mr. Carmody was swearing. They were pushing and shoving each other's shoulders. Believe me, I got right over there."

Quizzical smile. "Before Carmody lost it completely?"

"I wouldn't know anything about that, señorita." Avoiding my gaze, Jorge dutifully mopped the bar-top, removed my empty glass, and flashed Trista a servile smile. "Will there be anything else, Triss?"

"No, Jorge. Thanks again."

To me, it sounded as if Jerry had finally gotten an answer. And it was an answer he didn't like. I wondered what he had been doing the day of Brian McCann's death. Made up my mind to find out.

While she finished her drink, Trista began talking about the town's most eligible bachelors. She left me many long and breathless openings, hoping I'd take the bait and discuss Donny Pierce. With much weaving and dodging, I circumvented her trap and got her talking instead about her favorite topics — food, posture, diet and exercise.

"Are you thinking about joining a health club here in town?" she asked.

"Perhaps. But I plan to do some shopping around first." Deciding to dig up some more information on Monica, I added, "What about that place in Shoreside Plaza? The Form Fantastique?"

All at once, I felt a small, warm pressure on my shoulder. A familiar smoky contralto purred, "What about it?"

I turned. Monica Lonardo showed me a tight, cool smile. "We have very reasonable rates, Andrea. I'm sure you can afford them on a vice president's salary."

"I'll think it over," I replied. That woman had given me a nasty turn, sneaking up on me that way. How much of my conversation with Jorge had she overheard?

Monica aimed an elegant magenta fingernail at the rear exit. "If it's exercise you're looking for, dear, the club has a fully equipped gym. I was on my way there myself."

"To do what?" I asked, regaining my composure.

"Tennis, I hope." Her cool-eyed gaze ran from me to Trista. "Either of you ladies interested?"

"Sorry, Monica." Trista sighed with regret. "I have a ton of laundry waiting for me back at the apartment. And I would really like to finish the ironing before midnight. Thanks, anyway."

"How about *you*, Andrea?"

I prickled at the insolent challenge in her tone.

"Sorry, hon. I left my tennis togs back in the Soo."

"You're a club *member*." The sharpening tone informed me that Monica distinctly remembered the circumstances of my enrollment. "Why don't you rent an outfit in the sports shop?"

I gave her a long look, knowing full well what the proposed tennis game was really all about. Think of it as the feminine equivalent of two guys stepping outside of the bar for a minute.

"All right, Monica. See you on the court."

Twenty minutes later, your Angie was on her way out to the tennis court, pleated skirt twirling about her thighs, taking practice swings with a big, unwieldy Wilkinson racket. I greatly enjoyed the smell and feel of that freshly laundered cotton tennis dress. Fading sunlight illuminated the upper branches of the maples and aspens. I halted before the tall gate, tucked my towel through a gap in the chainlink, wound my black hair into a ponytail and bound it with a strand of yarn, and then stepped onto the clay to do battle with the fitness instructor.

Monica's opening serve was a low-flying fireball into the rear court. She clearly intended to whip my ass for showing an interest in Donny. I did a speedy crabwise backpedal to the right. Too slow! The ball bounced on the clay just short of the white line and rattled the chainlink. Big wicked smile on Monica's face. Always the good sport, I scooped up the ball and tapped it back to her.

She kept up the pressure all through the first set, sending me one lightning-fast net skimmer after another. She ran my ass back and forth across the clay, double quick time. I was well and truly whipped, forty-five love.

Ah, but those of us who do our jogging in the rugged Sawtooth Mountains of northern Minnesota don't exhaust quite that easily. Midway through the second set, I was still going strong. Moreover, I'd learned where Monica's fastballs were likely to land, and I got there in plenty of time to guarantee a full-power return. We volleyed back and forth, no quarter asked or given.

193

Gradually I took the initiative. Monica's serves had the same zip as before, but a steadily growing fatigue was sapping her aim. Too many of hers went out of bounds.

As for me, I was startled by her catlike reflexes and sudden surges of speed. Monica bounded back and forth like a she-panther, bold, quick, silent, deadly intent upon winning. That silence of hers bothered me more than anything. I'd played a lot of tennis at USU in Logan, and I was used to girlish chatter, squeals of laughter, groans of disappointment. *Good shot! Oh shit!* That kind of thing. Monica had no time for commentary, however. She hammered that tennis ball without mercy, her dark eyes widening with fury as I took the lead.

I let my thoughts wander for a moment, and then I was the one crying, "Oh shit!" She faked me out perfectly, coming in with what looked like a power backhand. Instead, she bunted and sent the ball dropshooting over the net. Galloping forward, I whacked it high and to the right. She got under it easily and drove it into my back court. I really had to hustle, but I won that set, forty-five, thirty.

Fortunately, I did a whole lot better on the last set. Back and forth, back and forth, high and low — your Angie was in her prime. I had it all together — speed, balance, and swing — and I dictated the pace of the volleys, returning each and every one of her net skimmers with a solid forehand. I blew away Monica with a final score of forty-five, fifteen. And the match was mine, three to one.

At the net, we were both breathing heavily, our faces gleaming with perspiration. Women in combat. With a weary smile, I gasped, "Good game!"

She didn't answer. She tried to smile, but it came out a sickly rictus. Then she tapped my racket, a little harder than necessary, and trotted off to retrieve her towel.

My hand stung from the impact. I glanced at the edge of my Wilkinson. Monica's racket had split the lacquer. I watched her storm back to the clubhouse, shoulders tense, hair tossing angrily. Temper, temper, dear. Nobody likes a sore loser.

* * *

I took my time in the shower. I wanted to give that woman plenty of time to dress and clear out. Next time, she might try to swat my face instead of my tennis racket. And then I would have to smack hers. Slap it redder than a South Dakota sunset. It was a prospect I might heartily enjoy.

I expected to find the locker room deserted. Figured I was the last woman Monica would ever want to chat with. But I was wrong. She was waiting for me when I emerged from the shower. She stood in front of the wall mirror, uncapped a bronze lipstick tube, and proceeded to make up her mouth.

I let her make the first move. She waited until I had slithered into my slip, then closed the lipstick and turned my way.

"So, Andrea, how's the real estate business these days?"

"Never better."

Monica stuffed the lipstick into her purse. "You know, a lot of people are pretty excited about that Deer Cove industrial park."

"Tell me about it. I'm just about buried in options to purchase."

Her tall heels tapped the floor tiles. "But it all hangs on that McCann farm, doesn't it?"

Fastening brass buttons, I shot her a sweet smile. "Have you been talking to Jerry?"

"I've been talking to a lot of people. And they all say the same thing. Mrs. Tolliver still owns that farm. Unless she sells, your industrial park is going nowhere."

"Jerry says he has some people out looking for her."

"They haven't had very much luck."

"Well, that's Jerry's problem, not mine. My job is marketing lot sites."

"Wrong, *querida*. Our problems are your problems, *no es verdad?*" The silkiness of her tone gave me pause. Looking up suddenly, I saw her leaning against a beige locker door, her arms folded, her head cocked inquisitively.

195

"Come on. Level with me. Do you know where Mary Beth Tolliver is?"

I could easily understand Mavis Heisler's interest in Mary Beth's whereabouts. She was a Lakeside honcho and Burdick's stand-in. But why was the fitness instructor so interested?

Pulling on my sailor-style jacket, I replied, "What's it to you, Monica?"

"I-I have a-a friend who wants to buy into Deer Cove Enterprises. But it has to be a sure thing. The only way that project will ever get off the ground is if the Tolliver woman signs over that farm. And that is by no means a sure thing." Her expression grew testier. "Nobody knows where the hell that bitch is. Except maybe you."

At first I thought she was talking about Donny Pierce. If Donny invested his money, and it became known that MaryBeth was not going to sell the farm, the face value of Deer Cove stock would plummet lower than the Italian lire. Donny's bid for financial independence would go up in smoke. But then I remembered that Monica was the co-owner of the Chain & Anchor. As the procuress of a mob stable, she had plenty of money of her own. Perhaps she, like Jerry, was intent on pulling together her own personal fortune. At first I had thought she was just another fortune hunter using my Donald as her ticket to a seven-digit income. Now I wasn't so sure.

I took my T-strap shoes out of the locker. "I'm afraid your friend is going to have to take his chances. Just like the rest of us."

Dark eyes glistened. "Then there's no certainty the deal will come off, is there?"

"There's no certainty in anything, Monica."

That wasn't what the lady wanted to hear. She took an angry step forward, her hands folding into fists. Tendons stood out.

"Jerry thinks you have that Tolliver bitch stashed away somewhere."

"So does Mavis Heisler. And they're both wrong."

Monica's fingertips drifted down the curve of my neck.

196

That silky tone was back, and it sent a weird shiver up my spine. "If I asked him to, Jerry would get the truth out of you."

I avoided that insolent hand, slapped it away, cast the woman a stern don't-touch look. She seemed amused by my reaction. Her breathy tone unnerved me. I'd seen enough of the lavender set in Springfield to know it wasn't a lesbian come-on. It was something else. Something eerie. Menacing and invitational at the same time.

I gave it no further thought. I had to change Monica's mind about running to Jerry and change it fast. Feigning a look of exasperation, I said, "Look, I am really getting sick and tired of this Tilford paranoia. What have I possibly got to gain by hiding this Mrs. Tolliver in a motel? Use your head. If this farm is so fucking valuable, wouldn't it make more sense for me to try to purchase it for myself?"

Monica's feral smile faded. Her eyes displayed a touch of uncertainty. I took the ball and ran with it.

"If I knew where Mrs. Tolliver was, I'd run to the nearest bank, take out a loan, and hand that woman a purchase agreement. Once I had the title, I'd do some *real* negotiating with Jerry and Mavis!"

Mulling it over, Monica gave me a thoughtful nod. "You've got a point there. Perhaps Mavis was wrong about you." Tucking her purse under her arm, she added, "What will happen if Mary Beth Tolliver doesn't turn up?"

Broad grimace. "I don't even want to think about that!" Lifting one leg, I gingerly smoothed pantyhose nylon with my fingertips. "Besides, it's not our department. Jerry said he'd handle it."

"And he will. Don't you worry on that score." As I put on my shoes, Monica remarked, "Hey! *Muy bonita!* Where did you buy those?"

"The Soo." Fastening the strap, I cast a glimpse at Monica's spike-heeled black pumps. "Oho! Another Bandolino woman heard from."

Striking a model's pose, she beamed down at them.

197

*"Caramba!* What sharp eyes you have, little girl. And how did you know they were Bandolinos?"

"I had a pair myself." The memory of my near-spill on the McCann wharf made me giggle. "Just make sure you stay away from boat docks."

Monica tensed all at once. Her dark eyes zeroed in on me. "What is that supposed to mean, eh?"

Nice going, Biwaban. First Aunt Susan, now the fitness instructor. You must be setting the world's record for mousetrapping yourself.

"I had a little accident on a wharf." I didn't want to tell her I'd been poking around the McCann farm, so I neglected to mention the locale. "I put my heel through a rotten plank."

Her merry laughter punctuated my reply. "Serves you right. Shoes like these have no place on the waterfront. I hope you learned your lesson."

"And an expensive lesson it was, too." Standing up, I reached for my shoulder bag. "Now, if you'll excuse me, I have an appointment for dinner."

"Have fun."

"I will. I most definitely will," I replied, thinking of Donny.

I headed for the door, expecting her to follow me. Instead I heard only the tappety-tap of my own small heels. I aimed a hasty sidelong glance at the wall mirror. Found a warped image of Monica, like a character in an El Greco painting. There she stood at the bench, gripping her purse and staring coldly after me. The lady was royally ticked off about something. But what? The tennis match? My parting statement? Or something else I'd said.

Feeling the pressure of her cold, hostile stare, I hastened my stride and hurried out of the locker room.

# Chapter Eleven

Shortly before midnight, serenaded by a multitude of chirping night insects, Donny wheeled me into the Edgewater parking lot. After killing the Corvette's engine, he gallantly opened the passenger door for me. I exited with my usual grace, smiling my thanks, and led the way up the walk.

Halting on the doorstep, I peeked through the lobby window. The overhead lights were dimmed. No sign of the night clerk.

"What are you doing?" Donny asked.

"Force of habit, I guess." I poked through my shoulder bag in search of the key. "Back in my coed days, whenever I got home, I always checked to see who was still up." Smile broadening, I unlocked the door. "Usually, it was my Aunt Della."

Coming up from behind, Donny cradled me in his warm, firm embrace. I felt his breath on my ear. "Tell me about her."

"Right now? That could take all night."

Spanning my waist with his hands, he murmured, "I'd like to hear all about her. And the rest of your family, too. I want to know everything there is to know about you, Andrea Porter."

Even in the dim light, there was no mistaking that sudden determined ardor in his eyes. Rubbing my palms up and down his sleeves, I cracked a brittle smile. "Hey! Let's not rush things, okay? We have plenty of time. I've

199

got to get up bright and early—"

"We'll leave a wake-up call at the desk."

"Look, I do not want to show up for that eight o'clock meeting with some goofy well-laid expression on my face."

"Quiet, honey."

His lips descended on mine. I luxuriated in the pressure of that warm, insistent masculine mouth. Donny's kiss kindled a sweet fire in my innermost being. Perhaps it wouldn't really be so terrible if I showed up for that meeting in a slightly bedraggled state.

For shame, Biwaban. You have no willpower at all.

And then I thought of Mary Beth and the Big Store scam, and I realized that this might be the very last time for me and Donald Winston Pierce. He was kissing me as if he really meant it, as if our romance would never come to an end. But I knew differently, and that heartbreaking knowledge carved away at my soul. Soon I was going to have to grab the money and run. And I would never be able to come back to Tilford. Not ever.

When he released me, my eyes swam with tears, and I made a fearful grimace to keep from sniffling out loud. Spying the waterworks, he instantly clasped my shoulders. "Andrea! What is it? What's wrong?"

I blotted a stray teardrop with my sleeve. "Nothing."

"But you're crying." Donny's face wore that strained, panicky, helpless expression men assume whenever they're confronted with a woman in tears. "Andrea . . . honey, what's the matter?"

"It's a personal problem. I'll be fine. Honest."

I started to ease myself away from him, thought the better of it, and flung myself into the warm circle of his arms.

"Andrea, if I can help—"

"You can." My face found the comfort of his shoulder. "Hold me!"

He did. In the lobby and in my room. Through the hours of passion on those tangled, sweat-dampened sheets. Until the moment we both slipped down the pre-

200

cipitous slope into the depths of sleep.

Late Thursday morning, June the eleventh, following a truly dull meeting with Dick Jaswell and the Deer Cove Enterprises board, I was poised over my desktop IBM computer at the bank. My telephone receiver nestled in a modem. And the glowing alphanumerics on the monitor screen informed me that I had just made contact with the Pontiac Bank and Trust Company of Detroit, Michigan.

Outdoors, beyond my slitted venetian blinds, summery sunshine dazzled the brightwork on the cars in the parking lot. The bank's first-rate air conditioning kept my office a comfy seventy. I was wearing a white embroidered Foxcroft blouse and a brick-red slim skirt. The skirt's matching jacket, with its cute black velvet collar, dangled from the back of my padded swivel chair.

A week earlier, I had opened a savings account at Pontiac by mail, using the amusing alias of Mary Anne Medicine Horse. The Pontiac computer asked me to identify myself. I typed in the ID number for First South Shore and then explained that I wanted to open a transfer link with an existing Pontiac account. After completing the entry format, I tapped out the proper account number. Mary Anne's bank balance magically appeared onscreen. One hundred dollars. Pert Angie smile. If all went well, I would soon be adding to that.

Just then, my office door flew open. "Andrea! I want to talk to you."

Never one to stand on ceremony, Eleanor Hartshorn made a beeline to my desk, her lipsticked mouth crinkling in disapproval. "I was just talking to Charlie Soderberg on the phone. He says you haven't even set up a meeting with him yet. What is the problem, dear? You know Mr. Jaswell wants to see those advertising proofs tomorrow."

My hand darted to the Escape tab. But the old girl caught my sudden expression of alarm. Quickening her stride, she rounded the corner of my desk two seconds before the display vanished.

Suspicious eyes stared down at me. "What was that?"

A fearful tremor ran all the way down to my black *peau de soie* shoes. Caught in the act! Frantically I tried to dream up a plausible alibi.

"Andrea, that was an accounts spreadsheet."

I made myself smile up at her. "Uh-huh. One of the board members wanted to see a balance sheet for Big Bay Molding & Casting."

Features troubled, Eleanor rested her hip against my desk. "Are they on your list of potential clients?"

Innocent look. "Well, no. They phoned me yesterday to ask about lot prices."

"Andrea," she said sharply, "all requests for financial information must be personally approved by Mr. Jaswell. The bank handles all fiscal matters pertaining to Deer Cove Enterprises. I thought Mr. Burdick *and* Mr. Jaswell made that perfectly clear to you."

Rolling my chair back, I scowled. "Come on, Eleanor. Big Bay had the information ready, and they offered to zip it right over. What was I supposed to do? Say forget it?"

"You are supposed to follow the procedure, dear."

"Look, I don't have time to chase Dick Jaswell all over Tilford."

"You are paid to *make* the time, young lady."

I raised my hands in exasperation. "Okay, okay, you're right. I fucked it up perfectly. I'm a nitwit. Mea culpa, mea culpa."

Eleanor managed to keep her temper in check. "Miss Porter, I think it's time you, me, and Mr. Jaswell had a little meeting."

Fussbudget face. "Oh hell! What's the problem now?"

"You're not authorized to access financial information. You shouldn't be looking at spreadsheets." Eleanor drew herself erect, looking very, very smug. "So we're going to talk about that. *And* your frivolous attitude. And we're going to clear up, once and for all, the question of who you take orders from." She permitted herself the luxury of a smile. "I am looking forward to this meeting."

"Better make it later in the week, Eleanor." I switched off my modem. "I'm up to my ass in site queries."

"I expect you to hold your schedule open, dear." Pausing in the doorway, she threw me a disdainful glance. "You can be relied upon for *that*, I hope."

My response was typically juvenile. The second the old girl had her back turned, I stuck out my tongue.

Well, I was really in deep shit now. Knowing Eleanor, she was already running after Jaswell, eager to tattle on me. She no doubt expected him to reorganize the Deer Cove chain of command, putting me squarely under her supervisory thumb. And then, boy, would there be punishment for past Angie impertinences.

Eleanor was the least of my worries, though. I was far more concerned about Jaswell. He would be furious with me for accessing confidential financial information. At the very least, he would have my computer station removed. And that would cripple my ability to withdraw Mary Beth's money.

I was half tempted to call Pontiac Bank and Trust, put the Deer Cove ledger on my computer screen, deduct four million, and transfer those funds to Detroit. But I couldn't do that. Folding the show immediately might restore Mary Beth's stolen fortune, but it would also result in Jim's killer getting away scot-free. And I still wanted to nail that bastard.

Right now, Glenn Veeder was the front runner among the suspects. He had made Mary Beth's dad the first offer for those farms, and he would have benefited handsomely from their sale to Lakeside. He had also arm-twisted the Planning Board into blocking the Tollivers' subdivision plan, thereby forcing the sale.

So, did Papa Veeder meet Jim Tolliver on that country road? Mmmmm — strong possibility. If Jim was as knowledgeable about Lakeside politics as I think he was, then he wouldn't have been surprised by Glenn Veeder's eagerness to sell out Jerry Carmody.

On the other hand, there was still the unexplained

matter of that Washington environmental group. According to Andy Capobianco, they had paid Glenn Veeder thirty thousand dollars. That didn't make sense. If Veeder had wanted the Tolliver properties so badly, then why had he waited around to be paid a bribe? Why hadn't he gone ahead on his own and used his personal influence to swing the board?

That bribe suggested that someone other than Glenn Veeder was far more interested in obtaining those Deer Cove farms. I could think of only two people intimately connected with Lakeside who had contacts on the Potomac — Wayne Burdick and Mavis Heisler.

I studied my glum reflection in the monitor screen. Maybe I simply ought to transfer those funds and be done with it.

If only I could find out who had called the Tollivers the night of that snowstorm . . .

Sudden inspiration! Leaning forward, I tapped into First South Shore's master loan list. I found the loan instrument signed by Jim and Mary Beth. Grabbing a number two pencil, I jotted down all the pertinent information. And then I was ready.

It took me all of eight seconds to make contact with the proper person at Northwest Bell.

"Hi! I'm Andrea Porter, and I'm with First South Shore Savings Bank here in Tilford. We have an ongoing claim against the estate of a James P. Tolliver, soon to be heard in court. We were given a list of the defendant's financial transactions, including all telephone bills. However, the record appears incomplete. We're missing the Tolliver phone bill for the month of February."

The telephone lady had a voice like a songbird's trill. "We're a little swamped at the moment, Miss Porter. Please give me your phone number, and I'll call you right back."

So I rattled off the bank's number, adding my office extension for good measure, knowing that this was merely a security procedure on the Bell lady's part. They don't hand out information to just anyone, you know. She had

204

to make certain I was with the bank.

The Bell lady returned my call five minutes later. I rattled off the ID numbers on the Tollivers' loan instrument. She seemed delighted to learn that I had a modem and offered to send the Tollivers' February statement clear on through.

And there it was — a detailed listing of all February calls at Mary Beth's old number, both incoming and outgoing. I ran my pencil's eraser tip down the screen. One line appeared to blaze greener and brighter than all the rest.

*Itemized Calls: Incoming*
*Date*
FEB 07
*Time*
0938PM
*Place*
TILFORD
*Area/Number*
MI 906 555-3396
*Min:Sec*
7:22
*Charge*
$1.87

I lifted my receiver from the modem's cradle, then tapped out the telephone number. Might as well go for broke.

Five ringy-dingies. Then there was a soft click at the other end of the line, followed by a tinny Sinatra tune and a woman's authoritative voice. "You have reached 555-3396. If you wish to leave a message, please begin when you hear the beep."

I hung up at once.

The taped recording hadn't told me anything new or important. But then again, it had no need to. I had recognized the voice.

It was Mavis Heisler.

"Early lunch, Andrea?

I paused at the bank's front doors, brushing back a wing of raven hair, glancing over my shoulder at the pert black typist at the mortgage desk. She was a shrewd-eyed lady, my age or thereabouts, with meaty shoulders and hollow cheekbones, Oprah Winfrey suffering from anorexia. Toying with her pencil, she showed me a quizzical smile.

"I'm meeting a client in Shoreside Plaza." Surreptitious wink. "It could be a long lunch, Audrey."

She had a keen imagination. "Say, isn't there a sale at Wahl's this week?"

Thank you, Audrey, for a truly lovely alibi. And may you have a pleasant time spreading it all around the employees lounge.

"Is there?" My grin hinted at just such a destination. "First I've heard of it."

Audrey's hearty chuckle ushered me out onto the sidewalk. I spent a few hectic seconds zigzagging the noontime customers, then turned left and headed up Catamount.

As I strolled past a navy blue van, I became aware of a huge shadow coming up behind me. Peripheral vision gave me a glimpse of evergreen coveralls, huge hands, a taut mouth, and close-cropped gray hair. I reacted instantly, starting to flee, but Glenn Veeder had anticipated that. His oversized mitt captured my forearm.

"You and me have got to talk, cutie."

"Let go of me!" Halting, I tried to shake free of that grip.

"Behave yourself."

"Let go, Veeder! What do you think you're doing!?"

I stamped down hard on his instep, grinding away with the spike heel. Veeder's reaction consisted of a sudden sharp gasp and a tightening of the skin around his eyes. And he endured. So I tried kicking. It always worked in high school. Pointed toes hammered his shins. I would have had better luck trying to boot that nearby van over a goal post. Tightening his grip, he tried to hustle me up the street. Looking around at the puzzled faces of pedestrians, I hoped they would respond to a shrill holler of *Rape!*

As I drew breath to shout, Glenn snapped, "Don't bother yelling for your boyfriend Carmody. He's nowhere around. I made goddamned sure of that." Pausing at the deserted street corner, he gave the crowd an anxious look and said, "You going to behave yourself? All I want to do is talk."

The last thing I wanted was a private chat with Glenn Veeder. The existence of that bribe didn't automatically disqualify him as a murderer. Baring my teeth, I put on a brave front. "Mr. Veeder, I'm going to find a policeman. And then I'm going to make you very, very sorry you ever put your hand on me!"

"Oh, for—!" His jug-handle ears actually began to redden. "Look, I'm sorry, okay? Christ, *that* has nothing to do with it."

"Oh? So you always grab women on the street when you want to talk to them? I'm sure your *wife* will find that interesting reading in the *Gazette*."

He let go of me as if I were a crackling wood stove on a January morning. Stepping away from him, I straightened my brick red jacket, smoothed its black velvet collar, groomed my tousled hair with my fingertips. Lofty glance of reproach.

Frustration tightened the big man's mouth. "Dammit, Andrea, I have to talk to you. Privately. You pick the spot."

I began to feel a little bit safer. Had he really wanted to hurt me, he wouldn't have been dissuaded so easily. This seemed like a golden opportunity to do a little more information-gathering. So I pointed out a wooden bench in the town square, an island surrounded by the noonday pedestrian and auto traffic. My trust of Veeder extended only so far.

207

"That's private enough," I told him. "Over there."

I crossed the street at the next orange light, very much aware of Daddy Glenn's bulk a step or two behind me. He followed me past the white oaks and the sugar maples, into the cool shadow cast by the granite Civil War monument. The bench itself was vintage John Philip Sousa, with a cast-iron frame and wooden planks for the seat and the backrest. I took a seat. Veeder rested his size fifteen workboot on an iron armrest well coated with decades-old paint.

Demurely crossing my legs, I said, "I'm listening."

Moody glance. "The word is, your asshole buddy is out looking for the McCann girl. Is that right?"

"Are we discussing Jerry? If so, your description is only half right. The first half."

Glenn cracked a smile. "You didn't answer my question, Andrea."

"Burdick assigned that task to Mavis, and she turned it over to Jerry. I hear he's put his old pals on it. Up until now, though, they haven't had any luck."

"You got to tell Burdick to pull him off it."

"Why?"

"You want that industrial park built, don't you? You need the McCann kid to okay the sale. If she don't sign, you're screwed." He looked down at me in somber satisfaction. "Mary Beth is no good to you if she's dead. Right?"

A tingly feeling of foreboding washed over me. Sort of like the shiver I get dipping my toes in Lake Superior. "What are you trying to tell me?"

"Carmody ain't looking for Mary Beth to get some goddamned signature. He's planning to kill her. You know why he's up here, don't you? Why he had to leave Detroit?"

"I think you've been watching too many DeNiro movies."

"Bullshit! Use your head, Andrea. After giving Jerry a lot of grief, Tolliver winds up shot out on Rollstone Road. Then Mary Beth up and vanishes. What do you think

208

happened?"

I knew the reason for Mary Beth's sudden departure, but I was curious to hear Glenn's interpretation. Mild puzzled look.

"Mary Beth saw him do it." He kept a wary eye on the circling traffic, fearful that Jerry might show at any second. "She saw Carmody shoot her husband."

"And she didn't go to the sheriff?" I challenged.

"Would you? Knowing how connected that little shit is?" Glenn made a fist and rubbed it against his whiskered chin. "I bet Mary Beth followed her husband at a distance. Saw him get whacked. She must have figured Carmody was on to her. So she skipped."

Suppressing a laugh, I replied, "There's only one thing wrong with that, Glenn. How did Jerry find out she knew?"

Shrug of ursine shoulders. "Maybe she let something slip. She was in the hospital right after the shooting. Pretty near hysterical, I heard. She made a lot of wild accusations. Maybe it got back to Carmody and got him thinking."

Had I not heard the real story from Mary Beth's own lips, Glenn's reconstruction might have given me pause. Why was Jerry so eager to find Mary Beth? Did he kill her husband? Or was someone else using him as a cat's paw?

I continued prodding. "You sound pretty sure of yourself."

"I ought to be." As he removed his foot from the armrest, Glenn left a smudge cake of reddish dirt behind. "Carmody ain't the only sharpie in this town. Sheriff Hendricks is pretty thorough, too."

I caught the definite note of conviction in the big man's voice. It went beyond his usual hatred of and paranoia about Jerry. I wondered what kind of dirt he had on him. And took a shot in the dark. "Did Hendricks question Jerry after the Tolliver shooting?"

Glenn showed me a gleeful smirk. "Damned right he did. Way I heard it, there was some kind of trouble between that asshole and Mary Beth Tolliver. When her husband got shot, Carmody's office was the first place Hendricks went."

In my mind, I was listening once more to Mary Beth's description of her near-rape at Carmody's hands. "What did the sheriff find out?"

"He did some nosing around the Chain & Anchor. That's where Jerry usually goes on Saturdays. Five, six people told Hendricks that your pal hadn't been there on February seventh. At first Hendricks thought maybe the snowstorm had kept him home. But the wife said Jerry left well before six o'clock." Cherished memories made him smile. "Your asshole buddy didn't take too kindly to the questioning. He kept dropping Wayne Burdick's name. In the end, though, he told Hendricks he'd been in Detroit that night. Some Toolmakers get-together. So Hendricks called the union president, and the top wop vouched for Carmody, natch. Dead end."

"Hendricks didn't push it?"

"What for? He was licked, and he knew it. If it ever came to trial, Jerry would've had at least ten guineas on the stand, swearing up and down he'd been munching pasta with them when Tolliver got shot."

Warming to the game of Tilford conspiracy, I added, "Just what is your interest in all of this, Mr. Veeder?"

"I've got that little bastard by the balls, Andrea." He made a palm-up clawing motion with his right hand. "My crew chief used to be a Toolmaker. He told me where the union usually meets on weekends. Guinea restaurant called Taliaferro's. February seventh was a routine night there. I called and checked. Just your usual Eye-talian mom-and-pop couples. There was no Toolmaker banquet that night."

Which leaves Jerry Carmody unaccounted for the night of Tolliver's death, I realized.

Papa Veeder awaited my reaction. I gave him the last one he ever could have imagined. Thinking of my favorite dirty joke, I manufactured a presentable laugh.

Porcine eyes widened. "What's so funny?"

"Sorry," I gasped. Taking a quick breath, I hit him with it cold. "It — it's too funny. Jerry said the same thing about *you*."

Ham-sized mitts grabbed my shoulders. No need to fake an expression of alarm. Glenn's grip was all the motivation required.

"What did he say!?"

"Th-That you weren't around the day of McCann's death."

Staring in sudden apprehension, Papa Veeder relinquished his grip. "I had nothing to do with that." Darkening brows. "He's a fucking liar!"

"But you weren't around—"

"Big deal! I was in the Soo, getting my transit-mix truck repaired. The radiator sprung a leak. I got witnesses, too."

"So does Jerry."

"I can prove where I was. The Conoco station in the Soo. Where was he on February seventh? Eh? That's what I want to know!" Daddy Glenn soon lost interest in a debate. "That little son of a bitch! I'll bet he told Wayne Burdick the same damn thing. Christ! No wonder Burdick's been so cool to me lately." Thinking aloud, he added, "Yeah . . . now things are beginning to make some sense. Carmody whacked McCann when he wouldn't sell. And when Mary Beth balked, too, he blew away the husband."

"I'm curious, Glenn." Standing up, I shouldered my bag. "Why haven't you shared that information with Hendricks?"

"What for? A lousy sheriff isn't going to nail Carmody. I'm saving that info for a very special occasion." His voice thickened with anger. "If not for me, Burdick would have sunk without a trace years ago. I kept the work going on Pinewood Acres when his crews walked out. He was mortgaged up to his neck on that deal. I saved his ass. He owes me—"

"But he relies on Jerry," I interrupted.

"That's because he has no other choice. Carmody's figured out that Wayne has a lot more to lose if their relationship ever goes public. He has a handle on Burdick." Sly secretive smile. "That situation won't last forever, you know. Carmody's a loose cannon, and everybody knows it. He's going to fuck up big—sooner or later. Some day that little fucker's going to go down, and I'm going to use that info to grease his slide all the way."

Forcing myself to relax, I remarked, "I have a feeling this is an offer of partnership, Mr. Veeder."

"Bet your ass, kid. Play your cards right, and I can make you the richest little lady realtor in the whole goddamned U.P."

There was no such thing as a proper moment for the next question. But the bear was in a jovial mood, so I let fly. "Did you make Jim Tolliver a similar offer"—his pleased grin vanished—"when you spoke to him before his death?"

"Jesus!" He took a sudden backward step, looking askance at me. "Where'd you hear that?"

"Let's just say I'm one hell of a guesser."

"Lower your voice goddammit!" Again with the hasty, furtive look around. I think if Jerry's BMW had tooled by the square, Papa Veeder would have gone into cardiac arrest.

My voice was an obliging whisper. "When did you talk to Tolliver?"

"I ran into the kid at the Farmer's Coop that Saturday." Alarmed, he hastened to add, "That morning. Before the snowstorm. Tolliver accused me of putting the squeeze on the Planning Board. He showed me some printout. Said he could prove me and my brother, Mike, took a bribe from those fucking tree-huggers."

"I wonder what Sheriff Hendricks would make of that."

"Nothing!" Rosary beads of sweat glimmered on his broad forehead. "Look, it was all Burdick's idea. He asked me how much I wanted to sandbag the Tollivers. He funneled us the money through that group. I got half. God only knows how Tolliver tumbled to it." Nervously he wiped his lips. "My ass was hanging out there at the end of the limb, you know? I couldn't exactly declare that fifteen grand to the IRS. So I says to the kid, 'Look, what do you want? Board approval? You got it.' And that Tolliver — he says, 'I want Carmody.' "

Sudden surge of excitement. I felt as if I'd been wandering in a trackless Montana ponderosa forest and had suddenly come upon a logging road.

"So you told him all about Carmody and Burdick, didn't you?"

"Look, I had no choice. It would've been one helluva conflict of interest mess, with me on the board and all. I wasn't going to jail for a lousy fifteen grand. So I told Tolliver how Carmody had fucked him over. That little shit was really eager to run those kids off."

Very interesting, I mused. Perhaps Mary Beth had been right all along. And I understood Veeder's eagerness to sell out. No doubt Wayne Burdick would have been most grateful to Papa Veeder for resolving the Carmody dilemma.

"You really think Carmody killed him?"

"I don't *think* anything, Andrea. I *know* he killed him. I told that Tolliver kid where, when, and how Carmody had sandbagged him. That kid was pissed. He probably went looking for Carmody, couldn't find him, and left a message. Carmody called him back that night and lured him out to Rollstone Road."

It was all very neat and logical. I was tempted to hurry back to the bank, complete my four-million-dollar withdrawal, and leave a little love letter incriminating Jerry. But there was one thing wrong with it. The telephone call luring Jim to the ambush site had come from Mavis Heisler's house.

Somehow I doubted that Mrs. Heisler would have given Jerry Carmody free run of her place.

Glenn cleared his throat. "Well? Are you in or out, kid?"

Thoughtful glance. "Can I get back to you on that, Mr. Veeder?"

"Sure!" With one fatherly hand on my shoulder, he escorted me all the way back to the sidewalk. "Think it over. You're going to see it my way. You'll see. You can be a great help to me, Andrea. You're in tight with Carmody. Next time he lets something drop, pass it on to me. I take good care of my friends."

"I don't doubt it, Glenn. I'll be in touch."

"Good girl." He gave me a head pat reserved for his favorite hunting dog. "Be seeing ya."

Leaning against an old-fashioned lamppost, I watched him amble across Catamount. Good old Papa Bear, bustling along in search of his next meal. He seems genial enough. Just don't get within a roundhouse sweep of those grizzly claws.

Okay, so Glenn Veeder would never be invited to join Mensa. Accepting bribe money with a provable paper trail was proof of that. Yet he had a shrewd animal slyness about him, a survival instinct that had served him well in the labyrinth of Lakeside politics. He just might topple Jerry . . . if Jerry didn't target him first.

Once I retrieved the Mitsubishi from the bank's parking lot, I tooled out of town on County Road Seven. I wanted to get to Mavis's before she returned home from work. As I drove along, I wondered if Veeder had set me up somehow. Perhaps he wasn't as dumb as he seemed. He might even be deliberately steering me in Jerry's direction, hoping to trigger some scheme that would get rid of us both.

Let's assume Veeder is telling the truth up to a point. Maybe he really did squeal on Lakeside to Jim Tolliver. Veeder might have had second thoughts after that morning meeting. Shooting Jim Tolliver would have removed the only person capable of putting him in prison for taking that bribe.

As I neared Tamarack Lake, I spotted the country club coming up on my left. And thought of a quick way to test Papa Veeder's veracity.

After parking next to the tennis courts, I hurried indoors. Five or six businessmen loitered in the Lynx River lobby, talking in low tones, waiting to be seated in the dining room. A fortyish, big-bellied type recognized me from Kathy Veeder's reception, and we exchanged polite hellos. Then I ducked into the nearest empty phone booth.

No impromptu striptease to transform me into Supergirl. Just a breathless grunt and a hoist of the ponderous Yellow Pages onto the venerable varnished lectern. Flip open to Automotive. Look for the Conoco in the Soo. Hope there's enough spare change in my purse.

I lucked out on my very first try.

"Good afternoon. I'm Angelique Atkins at Knowles Insurance in Marquette. We just received an itemized statement of repairs from one of our clients, and I have to confirm them. Do you have a minute to talk?"

Gruff male voice. "Yeah, yeah. Make it quick, will you, honey? I've got a Ford Escort on the lift."

"Thank you. Are you familiar with Glenn Veeder, the head of Veeder Construction in Tilford, Michigan?"

"Veeder? Yeah, sure! He's in here off and on."

"Did you do some repair work for him a year ago March?"

Thoughtful hum. "Lemme think. March, March . . . oh yeah! I replaced a truck radiator for him. Two hundred and thirty bucks, parts and labor. Totally preventable, too. You see, somebody replaced the original radiator hose, and they didn't tighten the clamp enough. All summer long, it was spritzing steam on the back of the radiator. Goddamn thing rusted through from the outside. Was old man Veeder pissed off! Somebody got their ass reamed when he got back to Tilford. Bet on it."

"Two hundred and thirty," I murmured, pretending to be looking at a statement of the account. "Ah, here it is. Sounds like a pretty sizeable repair job. Did Mr. Veeder wait around for it?"

"He didn't have any choice, hon. He drove it down from Tilford. He didn't get out of here until after seven. And don't think he wasn't riled about *that!*"

"Thank you very much, Mr. . . . ?"

"Rousseau. Bob Rousseau."

215

"Mr. Rousseau, would you be interested in our low-cost fire-and-theft coverage? If you wish, I'd be happy to arrange for a sales representative to visit—"

*Click!* I winced at the sound. Then, yielding to a giggle, I replaced the receiver. Memo to all con artists—a sales pitch is the surest way to blow off a mark.

As I closed the Yellow Pages, I reflected on Glenn's tale. I was reasonably certain that one person had killed Brian McCann and Jim Tolliver, with the same motive for both murders. Veeder might have had a compelling reason to bushwack Jim, but there's no way he could have murdered Mary Beth's father. The Soo was just too far away, especially for an irate contractor deprived of his truck.

You have an unshakable alibi for the McCann killing, Mr. Veeder. So down you go to the bottom of the suspect list. At least for now.

Which left me with Jerry Carmody, a leading candidate if ever there was one.

And Mavis Heisler, who may or may not have made that fateful telephone call on February seventh.

Time to narrow it down.

# Chapter Twelve

As I left the phone booth, a club waiter stepped into my path. He was an inch shorter than Donny, lanky and stoop-shouldered, with a neatly trimmed Van Dyke and a furtive, servile smile.

"Miss Porter?" Gentlemanly gesture in the direction of the bar. "Mr. Keith Pierce requests the pleasure of your company."

Well, I suppose I could have pleaded Mother Nature and rushed off to the ladies' room. But I was curious. What did Donny's dad want with me? So I decided to be polite and ease my curiosity at the same time. "Lead on, MacDuff."

I followed the waiter into a very private booth at the far end of the bar. The decor was what I call Yooper baronial—plush oxhide cushions, polished cedar table, hand-chiseled oak ceiling beams, and a multitude of potted plants. Nestled in the cushioned seat was the baron himself, suitably attired in a gray houndstooth sport coat, slim-striped dress shirt, and a burgundy-colored foulard club tie. His taut lips turned upward in greeting.

"I swear, Andrea, you look lovelier and lovelier every time I see you." Peering past me, he leveled an imperious forefinger. "Robert, fetch the young lady a drink, would you?"

"Miss?" Impatience flavored Robert's glance. Nobody kept the great man waiting.

"Rock and Rye," I said, sliding gracefully onto the opposite bench.

Robert must have set the world's speed record, returning with my brimming highball glass. Keith's blunt fingers toyed with the stem of an empty liqueur glass. He snapped a fingertip against its rim, making the glass chime.

"I saw you making a phone call when I came in," he said. "Now that I'm officially *retired*"— ironic smile — "my day starts at noon. Which is an excellent time for a pick-me-up. Robert!" The waiter obediently removed the empty glass. "My wife won't serve alcohol before four o'clock. She's a Methodist, you know." Sudden sharp look at me. "Is Dick Jaswell keeping you hopping down at the bank?"

"You bet. The minute I arrive, he drops phone messages on my desk and tells me to start calling all those prospective new clients."

"How close are you people to Zoning Board approval?"

And so it went. Keith Pierce gave me a pretty thorough grilling on the status of the industrial park. Plenty of sharp questions about long-term leases, utilities costs, and right-of-way easements. I had a feeling old man Pierce was going to walk into the Pierce Industries boardroom one of these days and personally decide the issue of their participation in the cove project.

Midway through my drink, however, I heard him artfully shift the topic of conversation to my — well, *Andrea Porter*'s background.

"So you grew up in Madison. Where did you go to school?"

I suspected that he'd already had a chat with Aunt Susan, so I made sure the stories meshed. "Actually, I did the first two years right here in Tilford. Business major."

"I suppose a pretty miss like you led a rather active social life."

Lifting the chilled glass to my lips, I grinned. "Only on weekends, Mr. Pierce."

"How active?"

I nearly choked on my mouthful of rye and lemon juice. I shot him a quick glance of annoyance, wondering

218

if the remark was a feeble attempt at geriatric humor. It wasn't. He sat there in perfect composure, patiently awaiting my reply

"That's a pretty personal question, Mr. Pierce."

That steely gaze never wavered. "I consider it relevant. You are seeing my son."

I felt my face steaming. "True enough. And I don't need your permission to do it."

"There's no need for impertinence, young woman."

"Mr. Pierce . . ." I set down my drink. "I don't even discuss my love life with my *mother*. I sure as hell am not going to sit here and chat about it with *you*."

"Hold your horses there, girl."

"Thanks for the drink." I rose suddenly, slinging the leather bag over my shoulder. "It was lovely. I can't say the same for the conversation, though. Good day."

"Goddammit — *sit down!*"

He sounded just like Chief after one of my adolescent misadventures. I reacted instinctively to the tone, dropping my shoulder bag, resuming my seat.

"That's better."

"Mr. Pierce," I said, remembering that I was an adult and his equal. "I don't mean to be rude. But your son is a grown man, and he is perfectly capable of managing his own life. Our relationship is, to be perfectly frank, none of your business."

"I'm afraid I have to disagree with you on that, Andrea. Some day Donald is going to have to carry on for me. And that makes it very much my business." He looked at me for a long moment, as if trying to find the right words. "Donald isn't like me. He has too much of his mother in him. Like Elaine, he's always looking for the good in people. He just doesn't seem to realize what people are capable of." Tapping his thumbs together, he added, "When I came home from the war, I was a lieutenant j.g. with two years' sea duty behind me and damned few illusions left about the basic decency of man. I inherited a brokendown sawmill and a pile of debts taller than the Porkies. If that mill is slightly more marketable these days, then it's because I had to be just a little bit rougher, just a little bit meaner than all those two-legged sharks around me. So let's just say I'm sadly knowledgeable about the nature of people. More knowledgeable than Donald or Elaine will ever be." Devious glance. "Have you ever heard of Ramsay-Norrie Corporation?"

I wondered where he was going with this. "Can't say that I have."

"They're a rather large development firm in Chicago. They handled that riverfront rehabilitation project a few years back. I happen to own a sizeable percentage of that firm." His tone turned mischievous. "How would you like to walk into Ramsay-Norrie a month from now as a vice president? The very same work you're doing for Wayne Burdick. But for two hundred thousand per year, after taxes. What would you say to that?"

I stifled my initial reaction. I thought of Donny and his other women, those who came before Monica. Wondered if they, too, had been invited to a quiet chat with the old man. How many had had Pierce money waved under their noses.

Chin up. Ladylike smile. "I would say . . . Mr. Pierce, kindly take your offer and shove it up your ass."

To my surprise, he cut loose with a sudden burst of warm, hearty laughter. His lumberjack hand walloped the tabletop. That reverberant laughter lured a very anxious-looking Robert to the doorway.

"Andrea, Andrea, Andrea . . ." Keith dismissed the nervous waiter with a nod. "You know, your eyes didn't even flicker when I mentioned that two hundred grand. I'm beginning to think you're in love with my son."

I gathered I had passed the Pierce Golddigger Test. "No comment, Mr. P."

"You're not afraid of me at all, are you?"

"Not one single bit, sir."

"Well, well. My admiration of Donald has just gone up a few notches." Blue eyes twinkled with reluctant admiration. "I have the feeling you'd make an interesting daughter-in-law."

"Are you sure you don't want to pry my lips apart? Examine my teeth? Make certain I have good strong bones?"

Leaning back in his seat, Keith replied, "Don't worry. I'll have you checked out. Quite thoroughly, too."

I didn't doubt it. Eighty-eight million can buy a lot of diligent private detectives. I wondered if he had done the same with Monica Lonardo. Only one way to find out.

"Sounds like a tough gauntlet to run, Mr. Pierce. How did Monica do?"

His lips stiffened suddenly. "We won't discuss that, if you don't mind. Let's just say Miss Lonardo wasn't . . . *suitable.*"

Cheery grimace. "Ouch! Too many wild weekends with Jerry, eh?"

*"What!?"* Disbelief and consternation made those elderly jowls quiver. "What did you say? Monica and *Carmody!?*"

Uh-oh! You really did it this time, Princess Big Mouth. Donny's dad doesn't know about Jerry and Monica, their co-ownership of the Chain & Anchor, their playful camaraderie. Those detectives did a sloppy job of backtracking. Or perhaps Jerry sicced some mob muscle on them.

Expression of startled innocence. "I thought you knew. Glenn Veeder told me they knew each other in Detroit. Monica's a Motown girl."

His stern gaze skewered me. "Really? She told *me* she was from New York."

Interesting, I thought. Another county heard from. Why was Monica going to such lengths to conceal her Detroit background?

The old man's eyes narrowed in concentration. "Her and Carmody. Damn! No wonder they missed it."

"Missed what, Mr. Pierce?"

Summoning the waiter with a brisk waggle of fingers, he said, "Monica Lonardo didn't come here from Detroit. Wayne Burdick brought her up here from Washington."

"Burdick!?" I echoed.

He nodded crisply. "When Donald began seeing her, I made certain . . . *inquiries*. I was told she'd been doing some television work in Washington. Modeling clothes on cable TV. That sort of thing." All at once, he looked lost and uncertain. Reaching across the table, he squeezed my hand. It was a token of reassurance for himself as well as for me. "You see, when you have as much money as I do, you lose the luxury of supporting the political candidate of your choice. You donate to both parties as a matter of economic necessity. If you don't, you run the risk of retaliation from the side you didn't support." Slowly he drew his hand away. "Two years ago, I was approached by Wayne Burdick's opponent. He wanted me to organize a political action committee here in Finlayson County. He showed me . . . shall we say, *convincing evidence* . . . that Burdick was unfaithful to his wife. When I first met Monica, she seemed familiar somehow. I remembered that videotape, and I asked to see it again. There was no mistake. It was her. She was Burdick's mistress in Washington."

Three years ago, I thought. About the same time Jerry Carmody left the Toolmakers and went to work for the congressman.

Now I understood the rationale behind Keith's ultimatum to Donny. A very clever move on the old man's part. Had he come right out with the sordid tale of Monica's past, Donny might have accused him of making it all up. Even worse, knowing Donny, there might have been an ugly confrontation with Burdick. That would have meant some major embarrassments all the way around.

Instead, old man Pierce had found a way to maintain the Tilford status quo while at the same time making his son a whole lot less attractive to the acquisitive Monica.

And then I realized that Jerry Carmody had lied to me during our drive home from the Caribou. Alluding to Keith's opposition to his son's romance, Jerry had made that racist crack about "chili-bean grandchildren." As the congressman's majordomo, he must have known about

222

the affair between Burdick and Monica. Another chilling thought. What if Jerry had aimed Monica at the congressman in the first place?

I'll bet those two went back a long way. It was probably Jerry who had found Monica among the Outfit's platoons of hookers. He was the underboss who had hoisted her out of a Livernois Avenue bar, groomed her for the big time, and installed her in a plush studio apartment on the Potomac. And I wouldn't be at all surprised if they had had or still enjoyed an intimate relationship of their own.

Sounding a bit like a diesel truck, Keith cleared his throat. As if by magic, Robert the waiter appeared, humbly offering a green plastic tray adorned with the check.

"Andrea, I'm afraid I have to run." He pulled a hand-tooled leather wallet from the interior of his sport coat, withdrew a pair of crisp tenners, and left them on the tray. "I appreciate your taking the time to talk to me. And I look forward to seeing you at the house." Genuine smile. "Don't be a stranger, eh?"

"I'll try not to, Mr. Pierce."

And off he went, making a beeline to the lobby. Taking one last swallow, I watched Robert surreptitiously slide one of the tens into the pocket of his plum-colored vest.

I had a strong hunch where Keith Pierce was headed. The old gent had a few phone calls to make. He wanted to test my information, bounce it off some old friends in Tilford or Detroit. He might even put a discreet query in Sheriff Dave's ear, as well. If Monica had an arrest record for prostitution, the sheriff would be able to access it.

All of this added up to bad news for Wayne Burdick. If Monica was still working for Jerry, and if she was still servicing the honorable member of Congress, then it was indeed Jerry Carmody who controlled Wayne Burdick and not the other way around. And Keith Pierce was not about to place his economic fortunes in the hands of a man dominated by a mob hooker.

Look for a big upset in the primary, folks, with a political unknown taking center stage. Read all about it next September in the *Tilford Gazette*.

Me, I still had a farmhouse to visit.

County Road Seven ended in a circular cul-de-sac at the foot of a low, grass-covered hill. After bringing the Mitsubishi to a halt, I cut my front wheels to turn around. Forty yards behind me, the Heisler farmhouse squatted on its well-trimmed lawn, baking in the three o'clock June sunshine. Three elms shaded the north side of the house, and a spindly windmill flanked the crushed-stone driveway, its propeller blades turning slowly in the mild lake breeze.

I had made two careful drive-bys of the place, both ending here at the cul-de-sac. No energetic German shepherds. No skittish, whinnying horses. Nothing but a small herd of white-faced Herefords taking their ease in a mudhole behind the fence, in the shadiest corner of the front pasture. The farmhouse looked deserted. But your Angie was taking no chances.

I found a twin-rutted dirt road about sixty yards past the Heisler front gate, on the way back to the country club. The road zigzagged through a field of buffalo grass, vanishing into a thick grove of aspen. With my head out the driver's side window, I backed the Mitsubishi all the way into the grove, then got out and camouflaged the brightwork with blown-down aspen branches.

I peeled off my brick red jacket and tossed it in the front seat. Off came the ouch shoes. Bandolino spikes with three-inch heels are not made for stomping around in muddy pastures. Fortunately, I had picked up a pair of Minnetonka moccasins in Trout Lake, and these were handy in the Mitsu's glove compartment. I pulled my blouse out of the waistband. Wished I hadn't worn such a snug skirt. Always wear loose-fitting, comfortable clothes when you're breaking and entering.

Turns out I didn't have to climb any fences. The white wooden rails were far enough apart for me to slip through. I was less than enchanted with the moccasins, though. They didn't shed water as well as my own hand-made mooseheide moccasin boots back home in Tette-gouche.

The front porch was straight out of Booth Tarkington — plenty of gingerbread trim, a two-seater ceiling swing, sculpted wooden pillars, and an ornate, chiseled front door with a curtained window. Quick check of the rim. No wires. That was a relief. I frowned, peering down at the doorknob. Only one keyhole. I made a fussbudget face. That meant there was no dead-bolt, either. What gives?

Mavis Heisler spent a lot of time away from home. Every would-be burglar in the U.P. was aware of that. It didn't make sense that she would leave the front door vulnerable to the first lockpick that happened along. There had to be another alarm. An electric eye, maybe, with a ten-second shutoff before the alarm was called in to the sheriff's office.

Quick peek through the front door's window. Nice view of the hallway but no sign of any wall-mounted alarm box. I danced across the porch to the parlor window. Now *this* glass was wired. Electronic spiderweb littered the top of the windowpane. Staying well clear of that glass — after all, you never know if it's hooked up to a pressure sensor — I studied the parlor's interior. Lengthy sofa upholstered in a floral print. Big-screen TV, glossy VCR array, and handsome chestnut sound-system cabinet. But no sign of that damned alarm box, though. Nor could I see one in the dining room beyond.

I knew the box couldn't be in the kitchen. Mavis had a lively step for her age and weight, but she couldn't possibly reach that kitchen in less than ten seconds. Which meant the alarm box had to be camouflaged nearby.

Returning to the front door, I let my gaze roam every inch of that hallway. Oho! Since when do interior decorators put Andrew Wyeth prints right across from an antique coatrack? And since when do picture frames come with hinges?

Crouching before the doorknob, I drew a bobby pin

225

from my hair. Now we would see how well your Angie had mastered the lockpicking course at the Big Dollhouse.

Forget all that TV crap about MacGyver busting locks in five seconds. Never happen, people. Lockpicking is long, tense, tedious, nerve-wracking work, yielding at least two gallons of cold perspiration. By the time I got that door open, I had quivering fingers, numb feet, stiff, aching shoulders, and thigh muscles shrieking from the strain.

Nevertheless, I zipped down that hallway like a spooked rabbit. Flipping aside the *Helga* frame, I found the recessed alarm and flicked off the power switch. With four seconds to spare.

I gave the downstairs closets a pretty thorough toss. No luck! Then it was up the carpeted stairway to the bedrooms. Mavis's lair boasted beige walls and a canopied four-poster bed. Her vanity table would have embarrassed Zsa Zsa Gabor. I couldn't believe how neat and tidy that room was. The Navy had taught Mavis well.

On to the closet. Fixed in my mind was that photo I'd seen in Eleanor Hartshorn's office, the image of that camel hair coat. I still had the tuft of camel hair I'd taken from Tolliver's car, and I dearly wanted to match it with the coat in that photo. It would be proof positive that Mavis did the shooting.

Feminine clothes filled the center rack. They were divided by seasons — summerweights on the far left, tartans next, spring ruffles and linen suits, and the winter wear tucked away in a shadowy alcove, smelling faintly of talcum and mothballs. My hands groped through the semigloom, identifying each garment by touch. Smooth mink, bristly fox, raggedy woolens. But no camel hair, dammit!

Thoroughly disheartened, I sat on Mavis's bed. Dead end! She might not even own a camel hair coat. Or perhaps she had it in cold storage somewhere.

Now *that* was an idea. If the coat was in storage, then Mavis would have to have a claim check on the premises.

Hopping off the bed, I galloped downstairs to the woman's study.

Minutes later, I was leaning over the government surplus desk, carefully picking my way through the open center drawer. Clutter galore. Receipts, parking garage tickets, telephone memos, a Kennedy Center brochure, and an unopened envelope from Publisher's Clearinghouse. The papery chaos made me feel better. My fading belief in the humanity of Mavis Heisler was restored.

Then the bright red logo of Northwest Airlines caught my eye. Brushing the litter aside, I unearthed a canceled airline ticket. My gaze skimmed over the computerized printout.

NW 1289    07FEB TFDORD 450P 700P
NW 439     07FEB ORDDCX 820P 1240A

The flight date gave me an invisible slap. February seventh!

A one-way flight, I realized. Tilford to Washington, D.C., with an hour-and-twenty-minute layover in Chicago. Peeling back that page, I went looking for cancellation stamps. I found two — one marked Tilford, the other O'Hare.

I replaced the ticket and closed the drawer. There was no need to search any further. Mavis couldn't have killed Mary Beth's husband. At the moment Tolliver had been shot, Mavis had been sitting in the first-class section of a Northwest Airlines 767, thirty thousand feet above Ohio.

And yet the telephone call luring Tolliver out to Rollstone Road had come from this very farmhouse.

All at once, I heard the crunch of tires on gravel. Dousing the desk lamp, I fled the study and hurried to the kitchen window. My ears detected the twin slams of car doors. Muffled female voices.

Peering around the drape, I saw Mavis and Monica Lonardo strolling toward the back door. I looked around for sanctuary. Had a sudden horrifying glimpse of *Helga* scowling at me from the hallway. Idiot! I had left the picture-frame door wide open.

Quick like a bunny, I covered the intervening distance, flicked on the alarm, eased the cover shut, and wiped any telltale fingerprint smudges from the portrait's glass with my sleeve. Behind me, I heard the hellish rattle of a key in the lock, followed by the faint squeak of hinges.

Too late to duck under a table. Heart pounding, I rounded the banister post and crouched on the carpeted stairs.

Monica's querulous voice came through. ". . . I still don't understand why."

Patronizing Mavis voice. "You're not paid to understand things, my dear."

Risking a peek, I saw Mavis shed her jacket and drape it over a chair. Monica, casually attired in a peach jersey and white twill slacks and looking mightily miffed, wrestled a key out of the back door. To my surprise, she dropped it in her own purse.

That was mighty white of Mavis, giving her congressman boss's mistress free run of her home. Then again, the isolated Heisler farmhouse made a pretty handy love nest.

Just then, Mavis's face turned my way. I ducked out of her line of sight and kept right on listening.

"But we need Mary Beth Tolliver," said Monica.

"No, we don't. That farm's not going anywhere."

*"Caramba!* If you don't get that signature, the deal won't go through. Andrea told me so herself."

"That's not my concern. My job is keeping Wayne in Washington. The way I see it, Deer Cove is fast becoming a liability."

My skin prickled at the fury in Monica's voice. "You can't do this to me, Heisler!"

"Open your eyes, dear. That deal is political poison." Faint squeak of cupboard doors. "It's high time somebody did a little long-range thinking around here. If we develop the cove now, there are bound to be questions, whispers, rumors. It's a tailor-made issue for that Jeff

Cantrill. Wayne has a tough campaign coming up in the fall. Lakeside must keep a low profile. Suppose we begin this project, and the rumor gets started that Jerry had something to do with Brian McCann's death. A rumor like that could sink Wayne in November." Running water from the faucet. "Go slow. That's all I'm saying. No contracts between Lakeside and Deer Cove Enterprises until after January. And no purchase agreement for that farm until I give the word."

"What about Andrea Porter?"

"What about her?" Shrill annoyance on Mavis's part. "Andrea needs us, dear, not the other way around. Let me talk to Jaswell. He'll keep that girl hopping. You pass the word to Jerry. Forget about Mary Beth Tolliver."

I heard the clatter of toppling kitchenware, punctuated by Monica's rage-filled voice. *"Maledito sea!* This isn't what I planned on!"

"Look, I don't give a shit what you planned on. You are here because Wayne wants you here. And that's the only reason you're here."

"You can't talk to me like that! *Perra gorda!* Jerry will —"

"Jerry will do nothing. That man has more sense than you'll ever have." Contempt sizzled Mavis's voice. "Now, you listen to me! The only reason I've put up with your extracurricular romance is because I've found it amusing. But if it gets in the way of Wayne's reelection, I'll put a stop to it. Just like that!" Finger snap. "What will Donald Pierce think after he's seen that video of you in action? What happens to the wedding bells then, eh?"

A harsh, inarticulate yowl stung my ears. A feline sound of absolute fury. I held my breath, ready for anything, and then I heard the staccato of angry heels and the slamming of the back door.

My recon peek showed Mavis alone in the kitchen, trembling all over, staring at the back door, and twisting a dish towel in her hands. From the look on her face, you'd have thought she'd been on the receiving end of that diatribe, not the other way around. What had she seen on Monica's face, I wondered, to produce such fearful anxiety?

I had no time for reflection. Mavis was heading for the hallway. I ducked below the stair step's horizon, wary as a doe on the first day of hunting season, hoping to catfoot it upstairs without being seen. For once, though, I lucked out. Mavis veered into the parlor at the last second. Flattened against the steps, I heard the tinkle of a lamp chain, the hum of a warming TV, and then Regis and Kathie Lee discussing the finer points of bathing infants.

Time for a soundless Anishinabe retreat. Fingertips against the carpet, I pushed myself into an upright position. Moccasin soles sought out each descending step one by one. Blending against the paneled hallway, I padded along in absolute silence. Tiptoe, tiptoe. Duck beneath the Wyeth. Halt at the parlor doorway. Another peek.

Mavis seemed totally absorbed in her talk show. Holding my breath, I pitterpatted through the empty kitchen, halted at the back door, and turned the latch ever so slowly.

I was always good at sneaking out of the house. Ask Chief.

As I hiked back to my car, I mulled over the ladies' kitchen debate. Obviously, the Deer Cove project meant a lot to Monica. No doubt she intended to marry Donny and use those project revenues to stay affluent until old man Pierce had passed on. Then a competent team of lawyers could crack the old gent's will.

I tried not to think about Donny. Thinking about him always left me with a persistent hollow ache between my breasts. My throat felt as if it were full of warm cement. I told myself I was not going to cry. Fact is, I told myself that all the way to the aspens. But I was wiping away tears long before I got to the Mitsubishi.

Face facts, I told myself. You have no time for the sniffles. You have a mission to complete. Donny isn't in love with you. He doesn't even know Angie Biwaban exists. He's interested in some lady realtor.

Oh-kay, so limit your thoughts of your darling heir apparent to that final fond image of him. The two of you together in that late morning motel room. Discreetly drawn shades and rumpled sheets and the faint miasma of love scents in the air-conditioned chill. He is barechested, tousle-haired bristling with morning stubble. And his eyes are full of love as he smiles at me and reaches for that wrinkled undershirt.

Freeze-frame that image, Miss Biwaban, and store it in the vault of most-treasured memories. For it is all you shall ever have of him.

Minutes passed, and so did the tears, and I found myself back at the car. I shed my moccasins in favor of the Bandolinos and cleared away the brush. Then I steered the Mitsubishi back onto the asphalt.

I had much to do. Whoever killed Jim Tolliver had also killed Mary Beth's father, and for the exact same reason — to obtain ownership of Deer Cove. With Veeder and Mavis eliminated, that left only one player with the motive, the temperament, and the opportunity to commit both murders, the same player who had set up a phony Detroit alibi the day of Tolliver's death — Jerry Carmody.

I was beginning to understand Carmody's motive. Jerry had been in deep shit when the Justice Department had begun their investigation of the Toolmakers. Oh sure, Jerry could have softened the blow by discussing Toolmaker politics with Uncle Sam. But I don't think that would've gone down too well with Jerry's boss in Detroit.

There's not much future at the bottom of Lake St. Clair.

So enter Monica Lonardo, high-class call girl and erstwhile employee of Jerry's. From Monica, Jerry learns about the congressman's labor troubles up in Tilford. With the mob's blessing, Jerry builds himself a storm shelter in the U.P. He resigns from the Toolmakers, goes to work for Burdick, and, with the aid of some Detroit muscle, settles the strike.

231

Everybody thinks the congressman has Jerry on a leash. But it's the other way around. Using Monica to influence Burdick, Jerry calls the shots in the Lakeside family. He's using Burdick's corporation to build his own fortune, with Deer Cove as the jewel in the crown.

I remembered what Jerry had told me after that first planning meeting. *I have long-term plans for that area.* Jerry had been after Brian McCann's property all along. He had orchestrated the efforts to sabotage the Tollivers. And he had been mighty receptive to your Angie's little moneymaking scheme.

As I turned onto County Road Seven, I couldn't quite shake the feeling that I'd overlooked something. It was a nagging, disquieting feeling, sort of like a subtle itch between my toes.

Come on, I told myself. The state of Michigan has sent people to the electric chair on less evidence than this.

And yet . . .

Okay. Like a complete idiot, I would stick out my neck one last time. I'd drop by the Carmody house and go looking for the smoking gun. Also known as the camel hair coat.

But first I had to make a slight withdrawal at the bank.

Suddenly, I experienced a familiar icy tremor at the nape of my neck. That old prison awareness of hostile intent.

Instantly my gaze flitted from one rear-view mirror to another, seeking unfriendly onlookers. I saw only tall roadside weeds, peeling white birches, and Mavis's farmhouse far down the road. I shook off that sudden wild anxiety, chalking it up to nerves badly frayed by the impending conclusion of the sting.

And I drove on.

Bad mistake, princess. Genuine warnings are of no value unless you heed them.

# Chapter Thirteen

Knuckles rapped my lacquered office door. I looked up at once, grateful for the interruption. I had just returned to the bank, right in the middle of their end-of-the-day tally, and my blotter was littered with telephone messages.

My teller friend Audrey lounged in the doorway. "We're just about ready to lock up for the night, Andrea."

I shuffled pink message slips. "Go ahead and lock up. The night janitor can let me out. I've still got some calls to make."

Flashing a broad grin, she leveled her forefinger at my phone. "You come across that one from Mr. Jaswell, gal, you'd better answer it quick. The man wants to talk to you."

"Uh-oh! Sounds serious."

"It is!" Audrey's voice had a merry boy-are-you-gonna-get-it lilt. "Mrs. Hartshorn got all bent out of shape when you didn't come back after lunch. She called Mr. Jaswell at the Rotary. I don't know what you're going to tell him, gal, but, whatever it is, it had better be good." She waggled her fingers in farewell. " 'Night."

"Thanks, Audrey. See you tomorrow."

I was lying, of course. If all went well, by this time tomorrow, I would be down in Detroit, withdrawing Mary Beth's four million from Pontiac Bank and Trust in the form of bearer bonds. I would never, ever see Dick

Jaswell's florid face again, a prospect that brightened my mood considerably.

Peering through my open doorway, I saw the night janitor busily mopping the lobby floor. I waited until he had finished, till he had gone off to clean the other offices, and then turned to my desktop computer.

Eleanor Hartshorn hadn't wasted any time. She had ratted me out to Jaswell. Told him all about my unauthorized peek at the spreadsheets. No wonder Dickie was so eager to talk to me. I glanced at my wall clock. Fourten. Pontiac Bank and Trust would be closing soon. If I was going to grab Mary Beth's four million, it was now or never.

Facing the viewscreen, I typed in the First South Shore access code. The electronic spreadsheet instantly appeared. I accented the Deer Cove Enterprises account and punched the Enter tab. Alphanumerics transformed themselves into the Deer Cove general ledger.

I felt as if there were an invisible rubber band around my chest. My face turned hot and moist. Fingers trembling, I picked up the telephone receiver and tapped out Pontiac's number.

Harried woman's voice. "Afternoon. Pontiac Bank and Trust."

"Good afternoon. This is Andrea Porter at First South Shore Savings Bank in Tilford. I have an electronic funds transfer order on behalf of one of your depositors. A savings account."

"Miss Porter, we're getting ready to close."

"Look, it's only a single transaction. A deposit. I'm sending it through via modem."

I had just said the magic word — *deposit*. No matter how close it is to shutdown time, no bank ever refuses an offer to put money in their vaults.

She hesitated only a few seconds. "It is rather late, but . . . very well. Please give me your institution's Federal Reserve number."

I rattled it off. Miss Professional, that's me.

"Depositor's name and account number?" she asked.

"Mary Anne Medicine Horse. Two-two-two-four-six-seven-nine-six."

I heard a keyboard clacking at the other end. "Excuse me, that name. Medicine — ? Is that one word or two?"

My gaze found the clock. Its second hand was whirling like an airplane propeller. My heart began pounding. Time was running out. That woman had to establish the computer hookup before their system automatically shut down.

"Medicine Horse," I replied, resisting the urge to shout. And I spelled it for her.

"Thank you."

I found myself listening to elevator music. The Mantovani version of "Have to Believe We Are Magic."

With the receiver between my ear and my hunched shoulder, I punished my own keyboard, frantically typing in the funds-transfer commands. I stared anxiously at the clock. Four-fifteen.

Come on! Come on, you moron. Give me access.

I had this horrifying vision of their system switching off at any second. I could almost hear that woman's apologetic voice urging me to try again tomorrow morning.

But there would be no second chance. First thing tomorrow, Dick Jaswell would order this terminal removed. And then he would want to know why I'd been poking around in his general ledger.

My knees quivered uncontrollably. It hurt to breathe. Without that computer hookup, there was no way I could transfer that money. And the clock's second hand had just started yet another fatal sweep.

Suddenly, a raucous honk assaulted my ears. Pontiac's modem was saying hello.

"Hallelujah!" I whispered, flicking on my own unit.

After placing my telephone receiver in the modem's cradle, I faced the display screen once more. The blinking prompt made me grin.

Account 22246796 Ready to Transfer

Typing like a demented graduate of Katie Gibbs, I performed the careful minuet of recognition with Pontiac's computer. Their system rewarded me with an onscreen presentation of their transfer form. I zapped it down to the clipboard and studied the Deer Cove Enterprises ledger one last time.

I had the weirdest feeling of déjà vu. It was as if I were back in the Cameron Tax Assessor's office again, siphoning off those tax payments. I had stolen that money to save my mother's life, and today's repeat offense was designed to restore the wealth of the woman who had been more than a sister to me.

Jerry Carmody had wanted Deer Cove back when Mary Beth's father was still alive. He had made a followup pitch to Jim and Mary Beth, and when that failed, he had used his considerable leverage in the Tilford establishment to drive McCann & Tolliver Construction into receivership.

That's going to cost you, Jer. Extract the proper amount from Deer Cove. Ouch! What a dent! Looks like the corporation is headed for Chapter Eleven. Break out the golden parachutes, everyone.

Now, put it all on the Pontiac entry format. There's your four million, Mary Beth. Try to hold on to it this time, eh? Whoops — mustn't forget Angie's commission. Let's make that four million, seventy-five thousand. After all, I deserve a little something for my efforts. Hmmmmm. Keep it in round numbers, princess. One, no, *two* hundred thousand. Properly dispersed among dozens of passbook savings accounts in the Midwest, that two hundred K will keep my wardrobe fashionable while I'm working those crummy minimum-wage jobs for Paul Holbrook.

When I finished typing, the entry format vanished, replaced by a blinking message. *Initiate Procedure.*

Trembling fingertips hovered above the keys. Taking a deep breath, I thumped the Enter tab.

And it was gone. Mary Beth's stolen legacy. Four million plus teleported to Detroit in less than an eyeblink. If all went well, from there it would travel back into the hands of Mary Beth.

If all went well.

I picked up my telephone receiver. The honking cleared, replaced by the Pontiac woman's voice.

"Miss Porter? Are you there?"

"Right here." I studied the screen. The message *Funds Transferred* winked at me repeatedly. "Sorry to make you work so late."

"No problem. That was a sizeable deposit, wasn't it?"

"Mary Anne Medicine Horse is a very wealthy young lady."

My screen reflection showed a glorious Angie smile with enhanced dimples.

"Shall I mail the signature copy to her home address?"

"Oh, save yourself a stamp. Fax it up here right now. I'll get her in here tomorrow for signature."

"Thanks, Miss Porter. That's very helpful of you."

"Don't mention it."

I gave her my fax number, thanked her for her time and cooperation, and put the receiver in the fax machine's cradle. Two minutes later, my beige unit began its alto whine. The transfer authorization form curled out of the aperture.

Unable to stop grinning, I folded the document and tucked it away in my shoulder bag. I had the lunatic urge to stand out in the empty lobby and take a bow. With the help of modern technology, I had just pulled off the biggest bank robbery in the history of upper Michigan. Paul Holbrook would have a fit.

Instead, I contented myself with a girlish giggle of delight and dashed over to my IBM typewriter to finish the con. Seating myself, I rolled a fresh paper into the machine and considered a number of incriminating statements.

And then it happened.

There I was, sitting with my back to the door, hunched

237

over the keys, mulling the proper words. And then an all-too-familiar baritone snapped at me.

"Damn it all, Andrea! Where have you been?"

My chin nearly hit the space bar. Whirling in my seat, I saw Dick Jaswell in the doorway, with a tan topcoat over his arm.

"I have been looking all over for you. Someone told me you went to Shoreside Plaza." Dick was in no mood for any nonsense. "Damn it! I would appreciate an explanation."

"My—my aunt got sick." Lousy, I know, but it was the best I could come up with on such short notice.

"The last I heard, there are pay telephones in the Soo." Strolling purposefully into my office, he scowled. "You should have called in. You can't just breeze in and out of here. Eleanor has a real problem with that. And frankly so do I."

Too angry and impatient to remain in one spot, Dick began to roam. Each step brought him closer and closer to my monitor. A rancid shimmer ran through me as I remembered what was still onscreen.

Inching my way over there, I babbled, "I'm sorry, Dick. I wasn't thinking. She has these dizzy spells, you know, and—"

"The first thing tomorrow, young lady, you, me, and Eleanor are going to review the bank's policy and procedures manual. The Deer Cove board hasn't voted on any yet. Until they do, we're following the bank's policy. Understand? From now on, you report directly to Eleanor before you leave this building."

"Yes, sir." I shadowed him across the office, sidling to his right, hoping to get behind my desk before he noticed the live screen.

"You're not a free agent anymore, Andrea. You're an employee of Deer Cove Enterprises, and I want to know your whereabouts during business hours." Jaswell discovered my stack of phone messages. "And I would like to have our clients' calls returned the same day, if you don't mind!" My luck ran out. The glowing alphanumerics

238

captured his irritated gaze. "What are you working on?"

I rushed to the keyboard. Too late! Jaswell gave the screen a quick determined scan. His expression shifted to puzzlement. "Funds transferred? Andrea, who gave you authorization to — ?"

I slapped the Escape tab. Bad move! Instead of clearing the screen, the computer reverted to the previous entry. We both found ourselves staring at the Deer Cove general ledger.

"Oh shit!" I yelped.

Jaswell didn't hear the profanity. He was much too interested in the numbers onscreen. Trained accountant's eyes ran down the table of entries. When he came to the bottom line, the color drained from his face.

He swiveled to face me. "Did you take money from this account?"

"*Me!?* Of c-course n-not!" Panic made me a soprano. My denial was even less convincing than the sick aunt story.

Grabbing my shoulders, Jaswell forcibly plunked me in my swivel chair.

"Sit right there, young lady! You're not budging until I get this matter cleared up."

I sat there, stunned, unable to believe this was actually happening. Caught in the act! The one thing I had never planned on. But who could have foreseen Dick Jaswell walking in on me seconds after I had illegally pilfered the money? I was well and truly caught. With that diminished account in the ledger and the transfer agreement in my purse and Jaswell's eyewitness testimony, the Finlayson County D.A. would have no trouble obtaining a conviction.

Desperation stimulated my imagination. Taking Jaswell by surprise was the only chance I had. Only how does a five-foot-four Anishinabe princess take out a former football player twice her size? I had to come up with something, and I had to come up with it quick. Because if I was still here when the police arrived . . .

The prospect of years and years in a Michigan wom-

239

en's prison sent my gaze scurrying around the room like a frightened mouse. From Jaswell thumbing through my phone book to the incriminating computer monitor to the surge protector at the bottom of my desk. A ticklish scheme took shape in my mind. I slid my left foot toward the surge protector.

Jaswell never noticed. He was too busy tapping out numbers on my phone. "Hello. I'd like to speak to Sheriff Hendricks, please."

Lifting my left foot slightly, I caught the power cable on my instep.

"Yes, I'll wait. This is very important."

The cord tightened against my instep. Flexing my ankle, I gave it a sharp yank. The computer's plug popped out of the surge protector. The monitor screen went blank.

Jaswell did a doubletake. With a gasp of dismay, he dropped the receiver and began frantically tapping the keyboard, trying to call back the lost information.

Bolting from the chair, I lunged at my desktop fax machine. Jaswell was still leaning over as I charged him, the bulky unit in both hands, adrenaline stiffening my muscles. I hoisted the fax unit high overhead. Cavewoman killing the saber-toothed tiger.

Spotting me at the last second, he opened his mouth to yell. But the fax machine was already on its way down, propelled by two arms conditioned by years of laundry duty. And whose panicky owner had no desire to repeat the experience. The hard plastic casing tagged him just above the temple. The impact shattered the unit, leaving my palms full of transistors, wires, and plastic shards. He toppled to the floor, groaning like a grizzly with indigestion, taking my telephone, lot applications, and mailing basket with him.

Dropping the electronic debris, I grabbed my shoulder bag and fled. Dick's groans were louder now, and they hinted at an early pursuit. Dashing across the lobby, I gave the door handles a mighty tug. Locked! No doubt

Dick had his own key, but I really don't think he was in the mood to hand it over.

Fortunately, adrenaline rushes do wonders for my creativity. Spotting the fire alarm on the wall, I reached it in two seconds flat, flipped open the tiny trapdoor, and pulled down hard on the plastic hook.

Clanging firebells rattled my teeth. Still clutching a pushbroom, the janitor came running out of the employees lounge. "What's going on!?"

"Fire!" My anxiety was by no means theatrical. "There's a fire back there!" I pointed at Eleanor's empty office. "Mr. Jaswell's hurt!"

The janitor started to move, but I clutched his arm like a bride leaving the church. "The door's locked! We'll be roasted alive!"

With his free hand, the janitor produced a ring of keys, turned one upright, and thrust the jingling cluster into my grasp. "Get out of here, Miss Porter! I'll get Mr. Jaswell out!"

Well, if he wanted to be a hero, who was I to deny him? So I took the gentleman's advice, secure in the knowledge he'd find the wounded Dick Jaswell soon enough. Even if he was initially headed in the wrong direction.

Once outdoors, lingering on the bank's doorstep, I inserted the proper key and turned the deadbolt lock. That would hold Dick for a few extra moments. Stepping onto the front walk, I tossed the key ring onto the roof.

All at once, I had the irresistible desire to do something cute. Pulling out my lipstick tube, I grinned at my reflection in the huge plate glass window and thought of all those Roger Moore reruns I watched as a little girl. Since the stick figure was copyrighted, I knew I'd have to come up with something else.

Bold smile of inspiration.

I drew a stylized tomahawk on the glass.

As I was driving down Armistice, I heard the *whoop-whoop* of fire sirens and spotted flashing red lights in the oncoming stream of traffic. Pulling up to the curb, I watched Ladder One and Engine Three of the Tilford

Fire Department whiz by on their way to the bank. Excellent response time, fellas. You'll do well at muster next year.

As for me, I had one last stop to make.


Five minutes later, the Carmody house appeared in my windshield. A Chevy station wagon sat serenely in the driveway. No sign of Jerry's Beemer. So far, so good.

I eased the Mitsubishi up against the sidewalk. After switching off the engine, I turned the rearview my way. A brief session with the brush and compact soon had me presentable again. I found a blank scrap of paper in my glove compartment, then scribbled out a plausible Exhibit B, to be concealed on the premises.

*Jerry — Jaswell caught me making the transfer. I got away. Have no fear. The money's clear. Get in touch — Andrea.*

Then it was tock-tock up the front walkway. Touch the shoulder pads. Straighten the skirt. Press the doorbell. I gave the mailbox a long look, wondering if I ought to deposit my incriminating note in there. But the front door opened before I could decide.

Evelyn Carmody blinked at me from behind the screen, features flushed, her sandy blond hair a little mussed, her blue eyes dulled by sleep and alcohol. Lint sprinkled the shoulders of her drape-neck blouse, and her charcoal trousers were wrinkled at the hip.

"Yes?" It took her a few seconds to come up with the name. "You're . . . Andrea, aren't you?"

Broad polite smile. "Is Jerry here, Mrs. Carmody? I need to talk to him."

"He was called away a half hour ago." Even sedated by alcohol, there was no hiding the bitter tension in her voice. I gathered Jerry was out tomcatting. She pushed open the screen door for me. "Won't you please come in?"

"Thank you. I really can't stay too long." I looked around, hoping to find a suitable hiding place for my note. "Will you please tell Jerry I've taken care of the money?"

And do be sure to tell the sheriff, Evvie, that I mentioned money when I came to the house.

Always the perfect hostess, the lady Evelyn gestured at the parlor sofa. "Please make yourself comfortable." She cast a sharp longing glance in the direction of the kitchen. "Would you like something to drink?"

"A Kentucky Colonel would be lovely, Mrs. Carmody."

The lady thought so, too. She set off at once in that prim, tightly controlled inebriate's stride. Rounding up some bourbon, benedictine, and lemon juice would keep her occupied for a while, at least long enough for me to plant that note.

Once Evelyn Carmody told Sheriff Dave that I'd been here, chatting about money, he would go fetch a search warrant. I wished I could be here to see the look on Jerry's face when the sheriff unearthed this note.

That hallway closet looked promising. I was looking for a man's raincoat, something Jerry would not normally wear to work. I'd slip the note into the handiest pocket, have a quick drink with the lady Evelyn, and then tool merrily away to Music City to claim that waiting four million.

However, the moment I pulled open that closet door, I spotted a tawny sleeve back there in the shadows. My scalp prickled. No—couldn't be! Breathing in shallow gulps, I thrust a shaky right in there and withdrew one very stylish camel hair coat. The smoking gun, at last!

I brushed the lapel with my fingertips, rejoicing in the slightly oily feel. Identical to the tuft I'd found in Tolliver's car. And I'd seen those basswood buttons before, too, in Eleanor Hartshorn's Christmas photo.

As I studied the coat, however, I couldn't quite shake the feeling that this wasn't Jerry's coat. Ridiculous, I told myself. Those are his clothes in the closet. He had hidden this one in the back.

And then I noticed it. Those basswood buttons were all on the left hand side.

*Buttons on the left.* There was no denying the evidence of my own two eyes. I blinked in surprise at the coat's narrow shoulders, at the nipped-in waist. A *woman's* camel hair coat.

Turning over the front hem, I snuck a peek at the satiny label. Weinberg's of Detroit, eh? A very classy women's boutique.

"Do you like it?"

Evelyn's furious voice turned my head at once. She was standing in the dining room, her features contorted with hatred, swaying slightly from side to side. Putting out a hand to steady herself, she rasped, "I said . . . do you like it?"

"Very nice," I mumbled. How long had she been standing there? Had she seen me going through the closet?

"You want it?" Evelyn ripped the coat from my grasp, bunched it up good, and hurled it in my face. "Well, then, take it!"

I peeled camel hair away from my nose. "Mrs. Carmody —"

"Take it!" Screeching, she slammed the closet door. "He'll buy you one, anyway! Good old Jer. He buys things for all his women. Take it and get the hell out of my house!"

For a split second there, I thought she was going to attack me, but Evelyn turned her alcoholic fury on the coat. Veins sprouting on her temples, red-faced and yowling, she grabbed the garment and threw it on the floor. Jumped on it and mauled it with her heels. Kicked and twirled with the mad rapidity of a flamenco dancer.

"He had the nerve — he actually had the nerve to bring *that* here!" she shouted. "To *my* house! *Hers!* Does he think I don't know!?"

"Evvie —"

"I won't have it here! I don't care what he said! I won't! Not in my house! Not *hers!* Let him hit me — I don't care any more. Fuck him! Fuck all of you!"

Bursting into tears, she sank to her knees on the tattered coat. I tried to help her up, but she pushed me away with a demented savagery. Wailing like an abandoned child, she crouched and pummeled the fabric. All

244

through that dreadful keening, I kept hearing the same mournful refrain. "My house . . . mine . . . !"

I let myself out very quickly and quietly. Closing the screen door, I heard the sound of breaking glass, the thumping of overturned furniture. Poor Evvie. I was half tempted to go back in there and comfort her. I wanted to thank her, too, for putting it all into perspective at last. In her drunken rage and jealousy, she had just told me who Tolliver's killer was. And I thought I could find enough hard evidence to put her away.

Suddenly, I remembered the handwritten note in my grasp. I was sorely tempted to leave it in that mailbox, to ensure that Jerry took the fall for my embezzlement, to help spare the lady Evelyn from another thumping by those merciless fists. Then I decided against it, folded the note, and slipped it into the pocket of my suit jacket. Burdick's defeat in the coming election would take care of Jerry. Without the congressman's protection, he'd be fair game for the Justice Department.

In the meantime . . . on to Mary Beth's old farm.

Axel Killinen sauntered out of the farmhouse as I pulled into the driveway. He still had that antediluvian Milwaukee Braves ballcap. Wending his way through the tall weeds, he beamed and lifted a hand in greeting.

"Evenin', Miss Porter. What brings you out here?"

"Hi, Axel." I shut the car door behind me. The building lake breeze pushed a few raven strands across my brow. "Didn't Dick get in touch with you?"

"Me? Hell no. I ain't heard from Mr. Jaswell since I got paid. What's up?"

"Oh dear!" I feigned a troubled expression. "I'm showing this place at seven o'clock. You should have gotten a call."

"The bank has a buyer?" Axel paced me up the pathway to the house, lowering his cap against the wind.

"Uh-huh. Murray Industries. Their survey party came out from New York this morning. They're having supper at the Caribou right now. The company's interested in the house and"—like a bishop at benediction, I chopped my hand left and right—"four hundred acres on either side. Got the keys to the place?"

"Right here, miss."

"Great!" Accepting the keyring, I glanced at the lowering overcast, at the bronze sky just above the horizon, at the myriad whitehorses on the Big Lake. "They'll probably want to talk after I've shown them around. I'd just as soon not have them standing around outside."

"I've got me one of them Mr. Coffee things in the kitchen. Case any of them button-down-collars needs to ward off the chill."

"Thanks, Axel. You're a doll." My palm touched the bristly stubble on his jaw. Sidelong smile. "Do you really want to stick around for this?"

"It's what Mr. Jaswell pays me for."

Snapping open my bag, I thought of that convenience store three miles back down the road. I'd noticed a Coors sign in their window. "Tell me, do they sell doughnuts at that general store?"

Axel's grin showed plenty of silver. "You bet they do."

I took a twenty out of my wallet and waggled it in invitation. "What say we make it an official errand, eh? You go fetch me some doughnuts. And take your time coming back. Okay?"

He licked cracked lips. Andrew Jackson disappeared into his grasp. "You want 'em plain, sugar, or chocolate-covered, Miss Porter?"

"Plain, Axel. I hear they're calorie conscious at Murray."

A few minutes later, I watched him rattle down the road in a rusting Ford pickup. I stood my roadside sentry post until he had vanished behind a stand of red maples. Then I did what I should have done the first time I had visited Mary Beth's old homestead.

I gave the house a thorough search.

I found what I was looking for in the cellar. Dusty and cobwebbed, it stood upright against the masonry, half hidden by a venerable oil furnace. It was forty inches long, with a splitting oakwood handle and a pitted, rusting steel tip. The gaff that had killed Brian McCann.

I carried it outdoors, brushed away the webbing, and examined it in the rapidly fading daylight. Sure enough, there was a small, oval, flattened area near the handle's bottom, where Brian's skull had compressed the wood.

I handled the murder weapon with a handkerchief, determined to leave no fingerprints, and marched downhill to the wharf. The rolling waves of Kitchi Gammi sloshed against its pilings. Chilly spindrift caressed my face. Remembering my first near-spill on this wharf, I borrowed a trick from Mary Beth's dad. Used the gaff to probe for rotten wood.

Learned something interesting, too. On the solid planks, no matter how hard I tried, I couldn't punch a hole in that weatherworn wood. Those Big Lake winters had made it as hard as flint.

I hastened down the wharf, heading for those two circular craters Axel had pointed out to me, the holes he claimed Brian McCann had made with this gaff before falling into the lake. Bandolino heels beat out a brisk rhumba on the planking. You know, that was probably the last sound McCann heard the day he died, the drumroll of that woman's spike heels on wharf wood.

Two familiar holes greeted me. Hefting the gaff like a harpoon, I struck at one. The tip didn't fit.

Excitement rippled through me. The sweet, sure knowledge that the quarry is near at hand. No, the tip of Brian's gaff did not fit the little round hole. But I knew what did. The killer had shown me herself that evening in the Lynx River locker room.

I remembered reading somewhere—maybe it was *Reader's Digest*—about how many pounds of pressure are exerted by a woman's elevated heel. Put a hundred-pounder like me in Bandolino spikes, and you have five hundred pounds of pressure radiating downward from the stiletto tip. Now, let's take an enraged Hispanic ex-hooker, three inches taller and twenty pounds heavier than me, and put her on this wharf, digging in her heels, winding up for the lethal stroke. Now we're up to nine hundred pounds of pressure, which is more than enough to dent even the most weather-toughened plank.

Jerry must have told Monica about his run-in with Brian McCann at the country club. McCann's refusal put a real crimp in Monica's plans to develop Deer Cove. So she came out here that March afternoon on her own, hoping to undo Jerry's damage and talk turkey with Mary Beth's dad.

Looking back at the farmhouse, I leaned on the upright gaff. So what did you see, Mr. McCann, when you began arguing with the hot-tempered lady? Did you see the same expression of murderous rage Mavis Heisler had seen earlier this afternoon? Unfortunately for you, Monica had failed to rein in her temper that time.

When Jim and Mary Beth began to follow in Mc-Cann's footsteps, Monica pressured her old boss and part-time paramour, Jerry, or perhaps her congressman to grease the skids under McCann & Tolliver.

Ah, but Jim Tolliver fought back. And then came the fateful Saturday when Jim buttonholed Glenn Veeder in Shoreside Plaza — the same plaza which houses Monica's Form Fantastique — and learned the truth about Lakeside's efforts to sabotage him. What do you want to bet Monica looked out the window of her fitness joint and spotted Jim with Veeder?

So Monica knows that Mavis Heisler will be leaving Tilford the afternoon of February seventh. And Mavis has obligingly given her a key to her house. From there Monica telephones an angry Jim Tolliver, hinting that she's willing to sell out Jerry, sweetening her trap with just enough inside information to whet Jim's appetite.

Okay, Biwaban, so you have your incontrovertible proof. Now what are you going to *do* with it? You can't very well walk into the courthouse and hand over the gaff to Sheriff Dave. Not after that little misadventure at First South Shore.

Gingerly I stepped ashore, wobbling as my soles

slipped on a rocky outcrop. Hmmmmm — perhaps I could work a passable scam on the sheriff, one that would ensure I didn't end up running a washing machine in the Huron Valley Women's Institute.

In my imagination, I began dress rehearsals for a future five-minute phone call. *Hi, Sheriff. It's me, Andrea Porter. I'm ready to give myself up. I wasn't in it alone. Jerry and Monica made me do it. That Monica is crazy! She shot Jim Tolliver and made it look like suicide. She also killed Tolliver's father-in-law. She told me she came up behind him and split his skull with a gaff. Look, can I meet you someplace? I don't dare show my face in daylight. She'll kill me! Meet me at —*

Of course, I would be nowhere near the proposed meeting site. But the gaff would be. Plus a letter instructing the sheriff where to find Monica's heel indentations. There was enough physical evidence in the McCann murder to tempt Sheriff Dave into taking a second look. I knew he'd build an airtight case against Monica for that killing.

Cloaked in the reveries of satisfaction, I started up the path to the house. If I'd been listening, I would have heard that faint scraping of shoe leather on ledge rock, that rustling of disturbed branches.

No, not me. Not your Angie. She was too busy congratulating herself on the cleverness of her latest scam.

The only thing I heard was Jerry's adenoidal voice saying, "Hello, babe. What brings you out here?"

# Chapter Fourteen

"Hello, Andrea . . ." There he stood, just to the left of a young maple — short, wiry fellow in a boxer's wary crouch. Leather cap, denim jacket, and broad, merciless smile. "What's that in your hand, there?"

His eyes sparkled in anticipation. I could sense the progression of his thoughts. Dark night. The lovely lady realtor all alone. And the familiar kitchen counter up there in the farmhouse.

I lashed out at him, swinging the gaff with all my might, trying to put a two-inch dent in that mobster skull. Jerry ducked beneath my speeding gaff, then popped up again like some leering jack-in-the-box. Never had I seen a human being move that fast. I had a split-second glimpse of his grinning face, followed by a fleeting close-up of this big, clenched, male fist. And then a fireburst of agony exploded on my chin.

Spectacular pain! It mushroomed like a nuclear blast, extinguishing every last iota of consciousness.

Next thing I knew, I was floating in absolute darkness, listening to the roar of Tahquamenon Falls. The cataract sounded as if it was right beside my head. No, not beside — *inside* my head!

As my consciousness began to crystalize, I tasted bleeding gums, winced at the excruciating pain emanating from my chin. I couldn't believe a man's fist could hurt so much. I realized, too, that I wasn't really floating.

I was draped facedown over something warm and muscular. The sensation was vaguely familiar. I recognized another sensation, as well. A warm pressure across the back of my knees. A man's arm. I was being carried.

Up came my eyelids, slowly and majestically, like Broadway curtains on opening night. Strange nighttime images swam into focus. Balsam trees with their lofty spires pointed downward. Way up there in the left-hand corner of the sky, a darkened lake hovered.

I blinked in disbelief, then realized I was upside down. Now the images made some sense. I was being carried up a hillside path, deep in the evergreen woods. That waterfall noise was merely the sensation of blood running into my head. My chin felt like it was broken.

I tried squirming a bit, just to see what bodily parts were still operational. And Jerry's voice admonished me. "Hold still. If I drop you now, it's a helluva slide into the lake."

That hateful voice brought it all back — our surprise encounter at the McCann farm, Jerry's knockout punch. The awareness of peril sent a frosty shudder through me. Jerry had me, and he was taking me . . . *where* was he taking me, anyway?

Corkscrewing my head to the left, I could make out the yellowish white lights of the Caribou Lodge blazing away on the lake's far shore. That put us at Tamarack Lake, among the rocky bluffs on its western side. I did some quick mileage arithmetic. Okay, so it's twenty miles to Tilford. I couldn't understand Jerry's motivation. If rape was his intent, then why had he carried me all the way out here?

Loose pebbles scrabbled away under his feet. That muted sound gave way to solid footsteps thumping along a plank floor. My eyes took in plenty of upside-down imagery. Birch railing, plywood deck, night-shrouded aspens, the bevelled corners of a modern log cabin, and beyond, the faint outline of a ramshackle barn.

Jerry's knuckles did that old shave-and-a-haircut routine on wood. Rusting hinges squeaked in reply. Cold slurry filled my stomach as I heard the familiar contralto voice of Monica Lonardo.

"It's about time you got here" — Shrill cry of dismay — "*Fijese!* Jerry, are you *crazy!?*"

"You want to know what she was doing snooping around Heisler's, don't you? Get me some clothesline."

So I hadn't been suffering from paranoia, after all. Monica must have doubled back after leaving. She saw me drive away, then she headed for the nearest pay phone. She's the one who had called Jerry away from the house.

I listened to the clatter of Monica's retreating footsteps. My topsy-turvy gaze traveled the cabin's interior. The cedar paneling gave it the proper rustic atmosphere. The room itself was warm and stuffy. Evidently it hadn't been ventilated in a while. There was a battered couch in a fading floral pattern, yellowing gauze curtains, an empty gun rack, Colonial-style straight-back chairs, and a rosewood coffee table seriously marred by an endless procession of smoldering cigarettes.

All at once, Jerry's grip tightened behind my knees. I did a sudden violent backflip, one that ended with me bouncing on the dusty cushions of the couch. My shoulder blades thumped solid armrest. And I just missed breaking an ankle on the coffee table's hard edge.

Pulling myself upright, I pushed unruly raven hair away from my face and demurely lowered my hem. Monica returned from the kitchen, still wearing that peach jersey and those white slacks, ferrying a coil of graying clothesline and looking quite perturbed.

"Why on earth did you bring her *here?* If anybody saw you —"

"Relax, will you? I'm not exactly a virgin at this, you know." Jerry accepted the rope and played out a long strand. "Keep her covered."

Crossing the room, Monica retrieved her purse from the top of a varnished cabinet. She took out a small, snub-nosed pistol. I kept telling myself that it was only a .22, inaccurate as hell at any range beyond fifty feet. But when she trained that muzzle on me, that black hole seemed as big as Jewel Cave.

Grabbing me by the scruff of the neck, Jerry force-marched me over to one of the straight-back chairs. I put up a struggle, making two or three attempts to kick like a Rockette. With his scrotum as the bull's eye. But he was too quick and too strong. Clutching my wrists, he wrestled me into that chair.

Looking on with undisguised amusement, Monica kept the gun on me. I heard the soft *snick* of a switchblade knife. Then felt the rasp of manila hemp on my skin. In a matter of seconds, he had me securely lashed to the chair.

Monica scowled. "I don't know why you even bothered."

"You were the one who wanted to get together, doll."

"I didn't tell you to bring *her* here. Wayne's cabin, for Christ's sake! What if you were seen?"

"I wasn't, so quit bellyaching!" Stepping in front of me, Jerry folded the gleaming blade and tucked the knife in his pants pocket. "I waited around until the caretaker split. Then I dumped her in her car and brought her over here."

"*Her* car!? *Idiota!*" The gun wavered in Monica's grasp. "Why didn't you just do it there?"

"Because I found this in Sweetie Pie's pocket."

Jerry slipped my folded note out of his own breast pocket. Dark eyes gleaming in curiosity, Monica came forward. My stomach turned over as I listened to the rustle of unwrapping paper. Now I *really* wished I'd left that note in Jerry's mailbox.

Holding the note in her free hand, Monica gave it a quick read. Lovely features crinkled in bewilderment. "I don't get it. What's all this about money?"

"That's what I'd like to know." His feral grin in full blossom, Jerry turned to me. "Were you planning to give me some money, Andrea?"

Swallowing hard, I said nothing.

"You and me are going to have a private little chat, babe." His knuckles tenderly stroked my cheek. "I really

253

hate to spoil such a pretty face. But I will—and I'll spoil it real bad—unless you tell me what this is all about."

"Stubborn little thing, isn't she?" Gun in hand, Monica loomed over me. Her face was a strange blend of ardor, anticipation, and impending violence. "Maybe we ought to put her to work at the Chain & Anchor, Jerry. We'll make her the Blue Light Special. A dollar a fuck."

Jerry found the prospect infinitely amusing. "Hear that, Andrea? Monica wants to turn you into a working girl."

Coy smile. "Evvie never gave you any trouble afterward."

"True enough. Know something? Even today she still can't say the word divorce without stuttering like some fucking retard." Squatting before me, Jerry gave my sore chin a playful tweak. "I guess that week upstairs left her with some bad memories, eh? You're looking at the same kind of week, babe, unless you tell me what I want to know."

Monica knelt beside him. "See if she's wet yet, Jerry."

Showing me a hearty lascivious grin, Jerry rolled my skirt hem all the way back. Then, while a gleeful Monica looked on, he ran his palms up my nyloned thighs. He paused to admire the triangle of white cotton at the top, the slight moist pelvic bulge.

"What do you think, Monica?" His thumb caressed the labia beneath that thin veil of cotton. I let out a gasp of fury. "Think she's hiding the money in there?"

"Why don't you slice it open and find out?"

I gasped again as Monica's varnished fingernails tap-tapped my mound. Looking into those dark, filmy, soulless eyes, I began to shiver. I was remembering our encounter in the Lynx River locker room. Her expression of furtive pleasure. Her sudden intimate touch. There were a few of Monica's weird breed in my gender. And they can be a hundred times crueler than their male counterparts.

"Has Donny been in there, Andrea? Has he? Huh? I'll bet it was fun, wasn't it?" Her hot, damp breath tickled my ear. "Did he make you come? Did he? Did you scream? Did it sound like *this?*"

Her fingernails drove into those tender vaginal tissues. I gave off a piercing soprano shriek, slamming against the chair's spine. Mind-warping pain! I couldn't even feel my battered face. Monica's agonizing pinch seemed to last for centuries. Then, as she drew her claws away, I slumped forward in the chair, red-faced and whimpering and streaming tears of anguish.

*"Querida,* you are going to be sorry you ever laid eyes on him." She gave my stinging womanhood a jovial slap. The impact ignited a fresh surge of lancinating pain. Writhing in my seat, I screamed. Monica responded with a mischievous smile. "I'm going to *peel* that onion *raw!"*

Jerry pulled her away from me. "Christ! Take it easy, will you? I want to find out about the money."

"I know what I'm doing."

"Yeah, right. But sometimes you get carried away. Like with that Sandra, remember? Use your head, asshole. It ain't so easy to unload a stiff up here."

I took advantage of that momentary respite, blotting out the blinding pain and coming to terms with the realities of the situation. Trussed up in front of a rape enthusiast like Jerry was bad enough. But the real danger was Monica. She was one sick little puppy. How many Sandras had Jerry been forced to dispose of as a result of Monica's murderous amours?

Yes, I was trapped in this cabin with the murderess of Brian McCann and Jim Tolliver. Tied up and at the mercy of a sadistic whore who knows every way there is to hurt a woman. A whore who thinks I tried to steal her meal ticket.

I had to get out of there. Sooner or later, Jerry would tell her what I'd been doing on the McCann wharf. And then Monica would know I was on to her.

But maybe there was a way out. Jerry and Monica didn't know why I was really in Tilford. I might just be able to throw them a curve.

That's it. Think positive, princess.

A brand-new con game took shape in my mind. I was beginning to feel like Scheherazade. My survival hung on my ability to entertain the sultan just one more time.

Jerry towered over me, swatting my head with the note. "Come on! Let's hear it. What's all this shit about money?"

When you really want to confuse them, tell the truth.

Tearful gasp. "I-I embezzled money from Jaswell's bank. F-Four million in all."

You know, I don't think I'll ever forget that goggle-eyed expression of befuddlement on Jerry's face. "You *what!?*"

"I rigged Jaswell's computer. Transferred out four million." Lowering my chin, I whimpered. "There is no consortium back East. There never was. It was all a scam to get me into the bank."

"You mean there's no fucking industrial park!?"

"N-never was." Shook my head slowly. "O-Oonly a story."

"So you could rob the bank." Jerry's face turned uncommonly thoughtful. "Shit! So that's what the excitement was all about."

"What excitement?" asked Monica.

"After you called me, I staked out the bank. Next thing I know, bells are ringing, and she comes running out of there." Fuming, Jerry waved the note before my eyes. "That still don't explain why you dragged *me* into it! What's the story, eh?"

Elation pumped new strength into my torn, strained muscles. Jerry was going for it. I had to give him just enough information to make the scam believable. With any luck, his own fears would do the rest.

I had seen enough Debra Winger movies to give my voice just the right touch of professionalism. "I'm a federal agent, Jerry."

"Bullshit!" Monica wasn't buying it.

Carmody was another story, though. He stared at me as if I was his worst nightmare come to life. "No! Those

256

bastards! They wouldn't — !"

"My name is Mary Anne Medicine Horse. I'm a computer programmer for the Bureau."

Jabbing the pistol in my direction, Monica shouted, "Don't tell me you believe this crap!?"

"Shut up! Just shut up!" Jerry stiffarmed her across the room. And then, grabbing a fistful of my hair, he yanked my head back. Fire danced along my scalp. I grimaced upward at his face, just an inch or two from mine. "Who's your contact, goddammit!? Who are you working for?"

Jackpot, Angie! Now give the man a terrified look — very easy to do, considering the circumstances — and let the buffalo excrement flow.

"I'm with the field office in Butte, Montana. Mr. Holbrook — he's the chief agent — he recruited me for this job."

"Who are you working with? How many of you are there?"

More frightened tears. And an imagination working overtime. "I-I don't know. Honest! Mr. Holbrook told me to get a job at Jaswell's bank. A sting operation, he said. He told me a lot of Mafia money was moving through that bank. The Bureau wanted to put it out of business."

"What else?" Jerry snapped.

"That's all, I swear! Mr. Holbrook told me to transfer four million, leave that note behind, and go undercover."

"She's lying!" Monica shouted. "That's not the way they operate!"

Turning savagely, Jerry clipped her a good one. Hearing that fleshy smack triggered a twinge of sweet satisfaction in me.

"What the fuck do *you* know!?" Jerry screamed, his features reddening in rage. "How do you think they made Hoffa? Huh? That's exactly how they operate. They always use people the Outfit doesn't know. Motherfucking Bureau *set me up!*" Whirling, he kicked over an empty chair. "This is some kind of fucking Abscam deal. They couldn't nail me for the pension fund, so they dreamed up this. A theft that big—there's no way Burdick could keep the lid on. I'm fucked!" Squeezing my face in the web of his hand, he snapped, "What else, Andrea or Mary Anne or whatever your name is? I want it all! Everything!"

I had to keep playing on Jerry's paranoia. He was half convinced that an FBI strike force was shadowing his every move. That fear had fueled his move to Tilford in the first place. I had to keep feeding that belief, stoking that fear. For, so long as Jerry thought he could use me as a bargaining chip with the feds, he wouldn't let Monica harm me.

Shrill gasp. "The Bureau knows about Jim Tolliver." I did some educated guessing. "Monica's the one who shot him. But you covered it up."

"Shit." Jerry released my hair. "So they're going to hang that on me, too, eh? Yeah, she did it—"

"Shut your mouth!" Monica yelled.

"What for? It's common knowledge now." He crumpled the note and threw it away. "I was at my office. Just getting ready to go over to the Chain & Anchor. Had a little budget work to do. Then the phone rings." He nodded at Monica. "She has a car phone, you know. Asked me to come out there. She'd tried to make it look like suicide, but that scene wouldn't have fooled a Boy Scout. I had to clean it up a little."

A trickle of blood marred the corner of her mouth. Wiping it away, she muttered, "I didn't have any choice. I had to do it. He'd been talking to Veeder."

"You couldn't wait, could you? You couldn't wait and let me handle it. Who cares what Veeder told him? My way, we would've had all of it. We would've split it right down the middle. Just like I promised." I marveled at the regretful tenderness in Jerry's voice, and all at once I understood why he had brought her with him to Tilford, why he had covered up that woman's murder back in Detroit. "No, not you. You rush out there and blow him away. You must think you're fucking Wyatt Earp!"

They began squabbling like an old married couple.

"I *called* you!"

"You sure as hell didn't try the office!"

"I told you I had Tolliver —"

"You didn't tell me he was *dead!*" Jerry interrupted, aiming an indignant glance at me. "She suckered me right into it. When she called up, I figured to have a heart-to-heart with the guy. And when I get there, Asshole presents me with a fucking stiff!" He thrust an accusatory forefinger at Monica. "I should have known from the tone of voice. That oh-Jerry-help me tone of voice. I should have known there'd be another mess to clean up. Just like that fucking Sandra."

"Shut up about that!"

"No, *you* shut up! You're stupid, Monica. You always were stupid. From now on, you stick with the fucking and let me do the thinking. Okay?" Shrewd glance at me. "How'd the Bureau tumble to it?"

More brilliant prevarication. "Mr. Holbrook had the Toyota wired that night."

"Ahhhhhh-*shit!*" Features convulsing with anger, he glared at Monica. "You stupid, stupid . . . I should've let you sink back in Detroit. I should've knocked you over. You are more fucking trouble —" Bad memories choked his voice box. "Have you any idea what I spent greasing Burdick? That suicide verdict cost me plenty! Oh shit, and those fucking feds have it all on tape!"

Well, that explained why the canny sheriff had taken such a lackadaisical approach to Tolliver's death. Jerry had indeed put the squeeze on his pet congressman. Just another in the long line of clean-up jobs Jerry had done on behalf of his murder-minded girlfriend.

I leaned forward, twisting my wrists this way and that, trying to get some slack. Tightening hemp bit into my skin. My fingertips were turning numb. Jerry knew his work. Those knots were more secure than a pair of stainless steel handcuffs.

Monica's gaze drifted away from me. She watched Jerry pick up his leather cap. "Where are you going?"

"As far fucking away from here as I can possibly get!"

"You can't run out on me!" It was the same outraged yowl I'd heard at Mavis's. "I saved you, remember? I gave you Burdick —"

"Yeah, and a possible accessory rap!" he interrupted. "Don't you get it, Monica? You've fucked up everything. There's no way I can fix this mess. No fucking way!" He lightly tapped his left temple. "I've got too much information up here. If I get picked up, with this kind of rap hanging over me, the boys downstate are going to assume I'm talking to lighten the load."

Monica's face blanched suddenly.

"Yeah, you've got it. They'll put the whack on me. Maybe you, too. You don't get into the fucking Witness Protection Program when you're tied into a murder."

The pistol wavered in her grasp.

"You're not going to leave me with *her!*" she cried.

"Why not? You've wanted to get into her pants for days. Now's your big chance," Jerry said, striding across the room. "Try not to kill her, though. Uncle Sam kind of frowns on that."

I froze in my seat. Alone in the cabin with Monica Lonardo was not the outcome I'd had in mind when I started this scam. But I had no time to react. All at once, a cold round metallic object burrowed into my right ear. I winced at the sudden unfamiliar pain, then paled in terror as I smelled the gun oil and realized what it was.

"Jerry . . ." Monica's teasing tone brought him up short. "Surely you're not leaving without getting a piece of this."

His hasty speculative grin made me sick. "I'm tempted, doll. But I ain't got the time."

"Go on, Jer. Indulge yourself. You've told me often enough what you'd like to do to her."

He lingered at the door for several breathless moments. Then . . .

"Yeah . . . why not." He started back. "You want to do this one in stereo? I'll do the top hole. You do the bottom."

Delighted laughter from Monica. "No thanks. For

260

now, she's all yours. I'll have my fun with her later." The pistol's stubby barrel gouged my ear. "Come on, Andrea. I want you to show Jerry a real good time."

I clenched my teeth shut.

"I don't think you understand me." For emphasis, Monica's pistol gave me five solid taps above the eyebrow. "If you want to live, you have to earn the privilege. Do it, *querida*. Open wide!" The muzzle came to rest against my right temple. I trembled, engulfed by thoughts of Jim Tolliver's gruesome death. "Come on, Andrea. Open your mouth. Jerry has a surprise for you. Ooooooooh, such a prissy señorita!"

"I'll fix that," Jerry snickered, hastily unzipping his fly.

I don't quite remember all of it, just a crazy quilt of nightmarish sounds and imagery. Jerry swaggering my way. His hateful chuckle. The feel of that pistol muzzle against my head. Monica's merry laughter. That burgeoning phallus emerging.

Jerry's erection surged with every step. When he confronted me, his shaft was a reddish serpent sidewinding to bite at my nose. Broad hands lowered to grab my face.

And, all at once, the metallic pressure at my temple was gone. Something round, slick and steely grazed my cheekbone. I saw the snub-nosed pistol in Monica's delicate hand and suddenly realized what she was doing. The barrel came to rest against Jerry's abdomen, an inch below his belt.

My gaze shifted upward at just that second. I saw Jerry looking down in disbelief. Caught his horrified expression of betrayal as Monica's forefinger tightened on the trigger.

*Bah-whoom!*

They say a .22 caliber pistol doesn't make much noise. Don't you believe it! Up close and personal, it's like a cluster bomb going off. Tiny gobbets of gunshot viscera spattered my face. My eyes shut instinctively. All I can really remember are the smells. Those dreadful smells. Acrid scent of gunsmoke and coppery stink of spurting blood. Odor of scorched flesh and whiff of emptying bowels.

Opening my eyes, I saw Jerry backpedaling away from my chair, his right hand feebly clutching the streaming wound. He seemed to be toppling in slow motion. He was screaming, but I couldn't hear him. The gunshot had deafened me.

When I was ten years old, I saw Daddy shoot a moose on the Gunflint Trail. A bull moose with an eighteen-point rack. Jerry went down the same way as that moose. The same hopeless, rubber-legged, inevitable way. The tender flesh of his eyelids quivered at the onslaught of indescribable pain. His desperate gaze looked to me for help. But it was too late. The gleam was gone from Jerry's eyes before his body struck the cabin floor.

My ears were humming like twin transformers. Features livid, Monica entered my field of vision. Her lips contorted into strange shapes. I gave her a blank, uncomprehending look. She took umbrage at it. Up came the pistol muzzle.

"I can't hear you," I shouted. "I can't hear."

The humming subsided gradually. I was very lucky. A larger caliber gunshot might have left me permanently deaf. Monica took a moment to relieve Jerry's wallet of its contents. Hooker habits die hard, I guess. Then, facing me once again, she began mouthing faint unintelligible phrases.

All of a sudden, her voice came through loud and clear. ". . . doing at the McCann place, eh?"

Determined to hold onto the Mary Anne identity as long as possible, I replied, "I-I thought th-there was something funny about McCann's death. Mr. Holbrook didn't believe me. S-so I went looking for proof."

"Bucking for a promotion, were you?" The pistol's hot muzzle caressed my throbbing chin. "What were you looking for? Tell me!"

"The gaff," I rasped. "I figured you had the most to gain from the completion of the project. I thought it strange they found Mr. McCann without it. I couldn't see him putting it down and then reaching for a boat."

"Clever!" Monica's expression radiated a kind of vile intimacy. I could guess what she'd intended to do with her share of the Deer Cove money. Thoroughly armored by money and the privacy it bought, she could spend the rest of her life looking for Sandras, for more young flesh to suit her deviant appetite.

Kneeling beside me, she stroked my face with her fingertips. "I'll let you in on a little secret, *querida*. That *pachaco viejo* never even had the gaff with him. I found it propped against the cellar door when I arrived." Coy giggle. "That bastard McCann was down there on the wharf, tying the rowboat to one of those pillar things. I looked at him, and I looked at the gaff. And I thought, it'd be so easy. Just like rolling a john, you know? I'd kill him, and then his fat wife would have to sell. I'd roll the body into the lake, and everybody would think it was an accident. That he'd had a dizzy spell. Something like that." Glossy lips formed a petulant moue. "It all went wrong, though. The old man heard me coming. He started to get up — asked what I was doing there. So I hit him. I hit him as hard as I could. *Caramba!* He wasn't knocked out. He started yelling and tried to get up. It wasn't like TV at all. When you hit them, they're supposed to be out cold." She uttered a shrill nervous chuckle. "So I rushed at him to hit him again. And he backed away from me. Then his foot slipped on the ice. A big wave hit the dock, and he fell right into it. He kept yelling at me, begging me to go get help. I watched him get tossed around out there, tossed around on the lake, you know? Then I dropped the gaff and started walking." Shaking her head ruefully, she added, "Turns out it was the best thing I could've done. They all thought McCann brought the gaff with him. Nobody ever guessed I'd even been there . . . except you. Not even Jerry." Mild look of regret. "Jerry knew about all my cupcakes, but he didn't know about McCann."

Not that I was feeling particularly chatty, you understand. I just didn't want this thick-witted sadist, who had

263

so easily appropriated murder into her bag of tricks, nominating me for the role of *cupcake*. That's why I asked, "Why did you kill Jerry?"

"He was right. If your boss knows about Tolliver, then there's no way for the Outfit to fix it." Standing up, Monica cast one last look at her one-time lover and mentor. "This is the only way out for me. It has to look as if Jerry dragged you here for some fun and games. After you're dead, I'll untie one of your hands and leave the gun on the floor." Licking her lips, she ran the gun muzzle down the front of my blouse. I could feel its fading heat through the fabric. "It's going to look like Jerry tied you up and got a little rough. You grabbed the gun and killed him. The Outfit will buy it. They know Jerry better than anybody. Once I've lined up a good alibi for myself, I'm pretty sure the cops will buy it, too."

So was I, but I didn't want her knowing that. "Keep dreaming, bitch. That sheriff's no fool. He's going to wonder why I didn't untie myself."

"No, he isn't." Cool smile and petulant shake of the head. "Not after he sees the damage. I'm going to make it very, very convincing."

Without warning, Monica jammed the hot gun muzzle against my pudenda. My breath erupted in a ululating scream. Somewhere beyond this crimson universe of agony, I heard her teasing giggle. "That's called previews of coming attractions, cupcake!"

Slowly I came back to full consciousness, wreathed in shimmering pain. I tried to reach beyond my aching face and numbing hands, beyond my violated womanhood, hoping to string some intelligent thoughts together. No doubt she would make the torture look convincing. And sometime before the constant agony overwhelmed my sanity, she would have me telling her all about Chief and Mary Beth and Tettegouche.

My nostrils detected the pungent aroma of burning balsam, and I heard the pinging of a warming cast-iron stove. Tilting my head to the left, I grabbed a peripheral glimpse of the kitchen. A smiling Monica puttered around an old black Victorian stove, feeding wood into the firebox, carefully arranging a handful of steel utensils. Perched on top of the firebox was an old-fashioned flatiron. Its bottom was just taking on a rosy hue.

I had a nightmarish mental image of that sadistic whore gliding into the living room, a dreamy smile on her lovely face, showing me the iron's fiery surface. See what I have for you, *querida*. . . .

Teeth clenching, I rotated my wrists in opposite directions. Dammit, I had to get out of there. For the sake of Chief and Mary Beth and, most of all, for Paul Holbrook's favorite Anishinabe client . . . me! More struggling and wiggling. Shit! If only I could free a thumb — get to work on Jerry's knots. How long did it take one of those old-time flat irons to heat up, anyway?

The rope held firm. I was on the edge of my chair, straining like a German shepherd trying to slip his leash. A warm, wet stickiness trickled over my hands. A dull burning ache asserted itself through the veil of numbness. No good! I was shredding my wrists, but that was about it.

Jerry Carmody lay three feet in front of my toes, mouth agape, with soddened red fabric covering his whole torso front. Those sightless blue eyes seemed to mock me. Silently I berated him for his cursed expertise. I wondered how many dissident Toolmakers had dived into Lake St. Clair secured by Jerry knots. Wondered, too, if any of them had been Monica Lonardo's cupcakes.

And then a recent memory bubbled to the surface of my mind. The sound of Jerry's switchblade flicking open. My gaze zeroed in on his jacket pocket. The slight bulge triggered a fresh surge of hope.

Somehow I had to get myself and the chair over there without alerting that sick, sick lady in the kitchen. One more hasty peripheral glance revealed Monica stocking the firebox with split wood. No doubt she was daydreaming about the fun to come. So much the better. Daydreamers are notoriously poor listeners.

One by one, I kicked off my pumps. I needed all my

balance for this stunt, and I couldn't do it perched on stiletto heels. Pressing my stocking feet to the floor, I grabbed the chair's wooden seat with all ten fingers and leaned forward ever so slowly.

The chair's weight settled on my spine. Bending at the waist, I let it slide forward. Its rear legs left the floor without sound. I was beginning to look and feel like a Ninja turtle.

The intervening distance felt more like three miles. I took it one step at a time, hunched over, my calf muscles straining, the heavy chair wobbling all over my stern. Packhorse Angie. Perspiration streamed down my face, blurring my sight. My fingers felt as if they'd been touching off two dozen mousetraps. And if you're scoffing, friend, why don't you stretch your arms all the way back and try carrying a full-sized chair around the room?

My hands sank beneath the weight, and I knew I was losing it. Trying to compensate, I bent lower, using my fingers to push the weighty chair toward my shoulders. I choked back a yelp. Damn, that chair weighed a ton! Taking a deep breath, I gave it an all-or-nothing shove.

And, as usual, I overdid it. The chair smacked the back of my head. My nyloned foot skidded on the polished floor. And I pitched forward, diving straight at Jerry.

Compared to me, the Three Stooges are the epitome of grace.

No doubt the boys' coach at Central would have approved of the way my shoulder slammed into Jerry's ribcage. Me, I was horrified by the dreadful *bumpetty-thud* and that ghastly exhalation of dead air from Jerry's lungs. Monica had to have heard that!

But she didn't. Jerry's slowly cooling corpse had muffled the noise just enough.

I found myself facedown on Jerry's remains, my face on his left bicep, my knees in the bloody pool near his belt. Blinking away the tears and perspiration, I gripped the chair and performed a slow roll along the dead man's torso. Chair legs mashed his middle, quickening the flow of blood. I felt it soaking into my jacket and skirt. Shuddered in disgust. Churning my legs, I managed to wheedle myself into the correct position. I wound up staring at the cabin ceiling, with my hands wigwagging in a frantic attempt to locate Jerry's pocket.

My fingertips located Jerry's belt, rode the leather like a freeway, and made a turnoff at the pocket. Burrowing both hands into the aperture, I examined the contents by touch. My index and middle fingers made contact with smooth ivory. I got my thumb over there, and together we all withdrew that slender switchblade knife.

*Snick!* The opening blade raked my jacket sleeve, eliciting a whispered gasp of pain. The razor-sharp tip had broken my skin. Blood dampened my blouse. Ignoring the cut, I twirled the ivory handle in my fingers, in the best majorette tradition, taking care to keep my left fist clenched — I didn't want to lose any fingers — and went to work on the rope binding me to that chair. First things first, you know. First you get free of the chair, then you can make a run for the door, if necessary. Your Angie is nothing if not practical, especially in moments of life-threatening danger.

Suddenly, the restraining rope went slack. Still gripping the knife, I slid down Jerry's corpse and rolled face-down onto the floor. Within an eyeblink, I was up on my knees, sawing away at the cluster of cords binding my wrists, facing the kitchen doorway and ready for anything.

As my wrists came free, I experienced an agonizing pins-and-needles sensation in both hands. The bonds had almost cut off my circulation. My hands felt like catcher's mitts, huge and puffy.

Clutching the knife, I tiptoed past Jerry and made my way to the door. One anxious glance at the kitchen. So far, so good.

With some effort, I managed to get the knife closed, then thrust it into my jacket's side pocket. Squeezing my eyes shut I masked them with one hand, pulled open the door, and made my rabbity exit. The second I heard the latch click, I exposed my eyes to darkness. Perfect! My night vision showed me a grayish barn looming in sharp relief against a star-filled sky, shadowy aspen groves, and a sleek automobile shape in front of the barn.

I figured Jerry must have left my Mitsubishi at the bottom of the hill. With luck, I could hotwire Monica's wheels over there, leave her stranded out here, make the switch, and be on my way. I'd find a lonely public telephone somewhere between here and the Big Mac bridge. Call the state police and report gunfire at Burdick's cabin. Even if Monica managed to get away, there was enough evidence at the scene to guarantee her speedy conviction.

Assuming, of course, that the Outfit let her live long enough to come to trial.

Up the path I went, crouching whenever I passed a cabin window. Angie on the warpath. I felt bold and wary and tricky and apprehensive. It was not unlike sneaking into Aunt Della's house following a college mixer.

I paused at the cabin's corner. Made a cat-footed dash across the backyard to Monica's Camaro. Rough rhyolite pebbles persecuted my toes every step of the way. Grimacing, I wished I had my moccasins.

I dropped below the horizon of the car's roof. Paused and listened. Nothing. Slowly I dropped to my knees, my hand reaching for the driver's side doorlatch.

Suddenly, I heard a mechanical *chunk-chunk-chunk* noise coming from the top of the barn. A flood of high-intensity light irradiated the yard, showcasing me in midgrab.

Shading my dazzled eyes, I made out an array of spotlights on the barn's roof. A high-tech security device for a privacy-minded congressman. Motion sensors automatically flicked on the yard lights whenever someone entered the cabin's backyard. I stood erect fast, feeling like a Rockette at center stage.

And then I heard the crash of a flung-open screen door, followed by the resounding *thunk* of something hard punching into the Camaro's door and the piercing *craaack* of Monica's .22 caliber pistol.

268

# Chapter Fifteen

Whirling, I saw Monica on the cabin's back steps, holding the pistol in the approved one-handed firing range stance. Orange flame winked at me from the muzzle. The bullet shattered the Camaro's side window, peppering my sleeve with tiny shards.

And I was off and running. One scared shitless Anishinabe princess making a beeline to the barn. It was twenty-five feet up a slope as gentle as a cow pasture's knoll, but for me it was like running all the way to Denver. My shoulder blades went numb, tensing in expectation of the inevitable bullet strike.

Instead the bullet whizzed right on by and cratered the barn door. Another one clipped the button from my jacket's cuff. Its friction heat sizzled the back of my hand. Ahead lay the slight opening between the barn doors, a vertical pillar of darkness no wider than a desk drawer. A noisy sequence exploded behind me — two loud gunshots, followed by the oh-so-sweet sound of a hammer clacking on an empty chamber.

I side-skipped through that narrow opening. It was a tight squeeze, even for my schoolgirl figure, but I couldn't pause to widen it. Not with that maniac on my heels. Once inside, I stopped, turned, and grabbed the aluminum door. A blend of panic and adrenaline had my muscles working at peak capacity. Gimbals rumbled as I slid the door shut. The locking mechanism engaged with a sonorous clang.

*"Puta Indianita! Te mataro para ese!"* Monica began with that, and her screaming crescendoed into a high-pitched jumble that far exceeded my prison Spanish. Sinking to my knees, gasping for breath, I listened to her fists pounding the door. There was one final burst of ear-sizzling profanity, then the fading drumroll of retreating footsteps. She wouldn't take very long to find the keys to this barn. I had maybe four, five minutes to find a way out.

Damp straw and cold cement tickled my soles. Whitish glows flickered up in the rafters, places where the illumination from that spotlight array had leaked into the barn. I groped in the darkness, my hands patting circular wooden posts, drifting along the horizontal gate beams of abandoned stalls.

I had the weirdest feeling I'd used up the last of my luck in that wild ass dash to the barn. Had not Monica become caught up in the chase, had she paused to take careful aim instead of firing on the run, I might now be lying out there on the ramp, my bleeding body showcased in that two-hundred-watt gleam.

I had to be extremely careful. I couldn't count on Monica being so careless the next time.

I had to find another way out — a feed chute, a corral door . . . hell, I'd even settle for the pigpen. Anything to get me closer to those aspen woods. Once in the forest, I'd have no trouble eluding Monica.

My eyes gradually adjusted to the barn's absolute gloom. The interior resolved itself into a film noir mosaic of ghostly grays and ebony shadows. I spotted a fuzzy gray structure off to my right, tall and slim and soaring upward. My hand touched cold metal. I let my fingers roam, and they halted abruptly at a flat, perforated surface.

Ladder step, I thought. All right! That meant the hayloft was directly overhead. Glimmer of an idea. If I did this right, I just might be able to turn the tables on Monica.

As I climbed the steel ladder, the sharp verdant smell

of fresh-cut hay enveloped me. My legs jostled big square bales as I groped my way through the loft.

Dropping to my hands and knees, I crawled very slowly to the edge of the loft. A night breeze tickled my face. I guessed on a fifteen-foot drop to the cement floor. All right, gentlemen, synchronize watches and begin Plan A. I grabbed the nearest hay bale and used it to mark the edge. Toppling over the rim would have ruined my whole day. I wrestled another bale across the floor and placed it on top of the first. Then another. And another. It was just like stacking blocks in the playpen.

By the time I finished, I had six hay bales stacked haphazardly on the loft's rim. I had to reach overhead to place the final one. Six bales. Each weighed in at about fifty pounds. That gave me three hundred pounds of dried vegetable matter. Plenty of ammo for Operation Hay Drop.

Feeling very sly and dangerous and desperate and frightened, I crouched behind my makeshift stack. As I did so, I felt a gust of warm air billow up from below. Groping around behind me, I touch-felt a series of ruler-straight crevices, the rectangular outline of the hayloft's trapdoor. Burdick must have used it to slide hay bales down into the horse stalls.

Okay, so let's suppose the hay avalanche doesn't render that murder-minded hooker *hors de combat*. What if she comes up that ladder, intent upon shooting off my knee-caps. It might be smart to have an escape hatch handy, right?

By touch I located the trapdoor's retaining bolt. I broke a thumbnail trying to slide it back. The crumbly substance beneath my fingertips told me it had long since rusted shut. I needed a ten-pound sledgehammer to knock it back.

Sigh of frustration. So much for that idea. Then again, maybe it could still work. If I removed the hinges, I'd still be able to kick the trapdoor open in an emergency.

I pulled Jerry's switchblade from my pocket, flicked it

271

open, and used it as an impromptu screwdriver. Wiggling the knife's sharp tip into the slots, I winkled out three of the four stubby wood screws. Grunting beneath my breath, I labored to extract the fourth. The builder must have used an air-powered drill to insert that one. But it came free at last, and I grinned as I threw the hinge away.

On to the second hinge. Two wood screws came free after much sweating and twisting and cursing. I had just started on the third when I heard the rattle of a key in the barn door's lock.

Again the gimbals rumbled. A flashlight beam swept the empty stalls. Monica's teasing voice announced, "Come out, come out, wherever you are."

Jamming Jerry's switchblade into the floorboard, I skittered across the loft on all fours, flattened out beside my makeshift hay high rise, and peered over the edge.

"You really can be quite trying, you know." The flashlight beam thoroughly probed the downstairs area. Behind the glow stood Monica's silhouette, holding the pistol upright. "You'd better come out, Andrea. If I have to come after you, I am going to be very, very angry." The beam slid from left to right and back again, illuminating the dark hulks of abandoned farm machinery. "Where are you, little cupcake?" Monica emitted a naughty giggle. "Did you enjoy that little love touch? There's a lot more where that came from. If you don't come out, *querida,* I'll make it hurt twice as much and ten times as long. You know I will. So get out here."

The beam played over a cobwebbed tractor. Monica was rapidly running out of downstairs space. Soon she'd be aiming that shaft of light up here. I was tempted to push and hope for the best. But I knew she had to come just a little bit closer. Fighting down the surge of panic, I crouched and waited.

"Would you like to hear what I'm going to do to you?"

Not really, I thought, willing her to come closer. The backglow lit up Monica's face. She looked as if she was about to have an orgasm. The lady had a vile and vivid imagination. Slowly she raised her flashlight, intending to sweep the loft.

I crawled back from the rim, put my shoulder to the stack, and pushed!

I had envisioned the stack toppling like a tree. Timmmmmmber! Instead, the damn thing buckled in the middle. Three bales plunged over the edge. One cartwheeled over my head, crashing on the trapdoor. Baling wire parted with a musical twang. My feet and Jerry's knife were suddenly awash in hay. The rest of me wound up draped over the bottom hay bale, feeling like a perfect fool. My yelp was one of dismay and disappointment.

Judging from the enraged scream downstairs, I had scored at least one direct hit. But it wasn't enough. Not nearly enough. Gunfire reverberated through the rafters. A bullet thunked into the hardwood pillar on my left. Stiffening in alarm, I heard Monica's hasty footsteps on the ladder. *Tank-tank-tank-tank-tank!* I struggled to push myself upright.

"Ohhhhh, you little bitch!"

Time to make use of that escape hatch, I decided. But I botched it. My stockinged foot skidded on the loose hay. I landed two inches short of the trapdoor, my chin rapping the loft's floorboards. Another feline scream, this time from me.

The flashlight pinpointed me. Its backglow gave Monica's features a gargoyle cast. Straw littered her jersey and frosted her unruly dark hair. She moved stiffly, favoring her left shoulder, a refugee from a Saturday matinee *Creature Feature*. The Incredible Scarecrow Woman.

"Oh, you are going to pay for *that,* cupcake!" Monica's lips shaped a lascivious pout. "Get up and follow me down the ladder."

I rose on all fours, blinking and gasping. My gaze frantically searched the loft, seeking a weapon. I couldn't let her take me. I couldn't let myself die like that.

The beam momentarily highlighted Jerry's upright knife, still rooted in the loft floor.

"Do as I tell you, Andrea. If you don't, I'm going to cripple you right this minute. Then I'll get my utensils and do you out here. *Comprende?* Now, get up . . . slowly."

With an expression of tearful resignation, I pretended to obey. And when I saw her grin in satisfaction, I threw myself at the knife. Monica saw what I was up to and dived at me. In seconds, we were a screaming female tangle on top of that trapdoor, kicking and clubbing, clawing and punching. Adding the strewn-about hay, our combined weight was maybe two hundred and thirty pounds. Light enough for the kitchen table but far too much for two measly wood screws to support.

The remaining hinge erupted from the wood with an anguished screech. The trapdoor and Monica vanished instantly. Still in midroll, your Angie found herself sailing through the air like a stray Frisbee.

My carnival training took over. Hurling myself forward, I thrust both hands at the embedded switchblade. Straining fingers closed around its ivory handle. Somewhere down below, in the impenetrable darkness, I heard a hellish *rattle-de-bang*, then crescendo screaming. Monica's voice traveled upscale, finishing in a shrill, mindless ululation that must have shattered her vocal cords.

The shaky handhold halted my plunge, converting it into a clownish, one-handed trapeze act. Swinging back and forth, legs churning, heart hammering, I could feel the upright knife wilting like tulips in June. Way, way off balance, I windmilled my free arm and lashed out at the trapdoor's rim.

Just in time, too! For as my fingertips made contact with the wood, the switchblade gave way completely, cartwheeling into darkness. My fingertips skidded toward the rim. Wailing in dismay, I got my right hand up there and doubled my grip.

"Oh shit!" I gasped.

There I dangled, soaked in sweat, my legs still doing that freewheeling bellclapper swing. Adrenaline rampaged through my system. I hoped the uncontrollable trembling wouldn't dislodge my tenuous fingertip hold.

My aching fingertips told me I weighed as much as Roseanne. I suffered this indignity in silence, intent upon maintaining that grip, gathering my strength for the tricky climb back over the rim.

A dreadful silence filled the barn. No longer was Monica screaming. I was in near-total darkness, drooping from the trapdoor's frame, with the only sound audible being the frenzied pounding of my own heart.

My biceps began to burn. Time to risk an ascent. While I still had the strength. Chin-up time. One elbow over the rim. My jacket sleeve popped beneath the armpit. This linen suit was a total loss. Then the other elbow. Uttering whispery grunts, I baby-crawled forward, wiggled my waist over the rim, and managed to get one knee into the loft.

Minutes later, I was flat on my back on that hay-littered floor, sighing in relief and thanksgiving, with my forearm across my brow. Believe me, the next time Angie the Magnificent does a trapeze act, she will be clad in sequinned tights, and there will be a sturdy safety net down below.

Lifting myself on one elbow, I spied Monica's flashlight on the floor. Its beam washed over a stack of Blue Seal feedbags. Picking it up, I wondered what had happened to its owner. So I aimed the beam through the trapdoor. And nearly fainted.

Monica's bulging, sightless eyes stared back at me. She lay spread-eagled on the steel fangs of a spike-tooth harrow. Bloodied upright prongs ran the length of her torso. A single spike protruded from her gaping lips, and a stream of red ichor leaked out of her blood-saturated mouth.

I dropped the flashlight. Thought of myself dropping through that trapdoor. Landing on the rusty tines. Bile surged into my throat. That horrendous view of Monica seared its way into my mind. I tried to blot it out, but it wouldn't budge. It kept replaying itself over and over again, like a jammed slide projector. And, for the first time, I became aware of the stench of all that blood.

That did it! I experienced a flash of disorienting weightlessness. Reeling on my feet, I watched some hay bales come flying straight at me. Then I passed out.

When I came to again, it was still night. The coppery stench was less noticeable. Already the blood was coagulating on the cement. Crawling over to the ladder, I let the night air bathe my flushed, overheated face. The chill roused me. When I felt strong enough, I made a shaky descent down the steel ladder.

I shielded my face on the way out. Like Jerry in the cabin, Monica Lonardo was beyond any help. One view of her impaled remains was enough, thank you.

I lingered on the barn's outdoor ramp. The security spotlights had long since winked off. Far across the lake, I saw the Caribou Lodge cloaked in darkness, barely distinguishable from the surrounding countryside.

I made it fast. I had no idea how much time I had left until daylight. When Jerry and Monica failed to show, there would be questions. Sooner or later, the Michigan law was going to show up. Better for all concerned if they found no trace of Angie.

I broke off an aspen branch and swept away the footprints, both mine and Monica's. Then, entering the cabin, I retrieved my shoes and that false incriminating note. Averting my face, I kicked the chairs away from Jerry, knocked over the coffee table, gathered up the clothesline fragments, and tossed them into the blazing stove. I did the same with the aspen branch, as well.

Shoes in hand, I carefully picked my way down the hillside trail, hopping from one moss-covered rock to another, leaving little trace of my passage. Another Native American could have followed my trail with ease, but, fortunately, there were none of them on the Finlayson County force. Sheriff Dave would be mightily interested in the puzzle I had left behind. The toppled furniture indoors suggested a fight. And he would scratch his head in puzzlement over those clumsily-erased footprints. Had there been one intruder here? Or fourteen?

The law would find Jerry Carmody shot to death in

Burdick's cabin and the murder weapon out in the barn, inches from Monica's lifeless hand. Questions, questions. Did Monica go berserk and shoot her one-time lover? Or did Jerry's mob buddies come north from Detroit and silence them both?

Over to you, Sheriff. This Anishinabe princess has business downstate.

June the twenty-second found me in Silver Bay, Minnesota, looking and feeling a whole lot better than I had in days. At least I no longer felt like bursting into tears every time I looked into a mirror. The chin swelling was gone, and pancake makeup did much to conceal the saffron bruise.

Mary Beth and I were having an early lunch at the Northwoods Café. She had just finished her visit to the obstetrician. She had changed a bit during the weeks I'd been away. Her smile was brighter, her belly much bigger, and the summer sunshine had lightened her hair to a rich brownish blond.

"If it were up to me, I'd stay," she said. "But Doctor Toftey says my blood pressure is up a little bit, and he thinks I ought to be somewhere a little more accessible than Tettegouche. So he's making arrangements to have me admitted to Miller-Dwan when the labor starts." She sipped milk from a tall glass. "Are you sure your Grandmother Biwaban won't mind having a houseguest?"

"Not at all," I replied, putting my half-eaten hamburger back on the plate. "Fact is, it's her idea. She brought it up while I was down in Duluth. Just a word of warning, McCann. Don't take over the kitchen the way you did with Chief. That's her turf."

"No problem. I'll be otherwise occupied." She proudly patted the tummy bulge.

"Well . . . ," I said, reaching for my shoulder bag. "If you're headed for Duluth, I'd better give you this now."

After zipping open the bag, I withdrew two laminated cards and laid them side by side on the checkered tablecloth. They were bank identification cards, one showing my face, the other displaying a Polaroid portrait of Mary Beth. Both bore the name *Mary Beth Tolliver*.

Wiping her hands on the napkin, she remarked, "They're identical."

"You bet. The printer did a great job." I pointed to the corporate logo of Timberland National Bank. Three days earlier, I'd walked into their branch bank in Aitkin, Minnesota and opened a safety deposit box in Mary Beth's name. Into this box went four million dollars in the form of payable-upon-demand bearer bonds. That's how I'd asked for them at Pontiac Bank and Trust, when I closed out the Mary Anne Medicine Horse account. The manager had nearly had apoplexy, but she handed over the loot just the same.

"See? He printed a larger copy of the Timberland logo," I explained, "and then added your photo underneath. Then he photo-reduced the whole thing down to ID card size. A friend of mine in Two Harbors did the laminating. All you have to do, Mary Beth, is wait a while. Give those tellers plenty of time to forget my face. Then you walk in, flash that ID card, and claim your money."

Mary Beth picked up the card and studied it for several moments. Then she quickly placed it facedown on the table. Her mouth quivered, and her eyes misted as she looked at me.

"What's the matter?" I asked.

"Nothing's the matter, Angie. Nothing at all." Her mouth curved into a lopsided smile. "You know . . . last winter — after Jim . . . was killed — when I — I was all alone in that farmhouse, and I was losing it — losing *every-thing* . . . I thought, it's all gone. Everything we worked for — me and Jim and Daddy. It was all gone. And now you've given it back to me."

Making a steeple of my fingertips, I grinned. "It was a cinch, McCann. Like Mr. Barnum says, there's a sucker born every minute."

"Don't!" Eyes blinking rapidly, Mary Beth squeezed

278

my forearm. "Don't give me that bravado routine. I know what you went through to get this money. Your grandfather told me what Carmody and that woman did to you."

I patted her hand in turn. "That grandfather of mine has a big mouth."

"Angela, what you've done for me . . . I can't ever repay you. You know that, don't you?"

"If you really want to repay me, you can do me a favor." She nodded vigorously. "Name it!"

"Raise him right," I said, pointing at the prenatal bulge. "See that he turns into a good man. Like his father."

"I will," she promised, smoothing the front of her maternity smock. "And I want your promise to come see us when we're settled. I don't want his aunt to be a stranger."

Sheepish smile. "Uh, I'm a little hot in Michigan."

"No problem. I'm not going back to Tilford."

"What about the house?"

"I'll let it sit for a year or two. Then I'll pay the back taxes and have it listed."

"If I were you, Mary Beth, I'd try to do that long-distance. Sheriff Dave might be a little bit curious about your improved financial status."

Her jaw tightened in determination. "I can handle Dave Hendricks. If he ever asks, I'll tell him Aunt Johanna died and left me a modest inheritance." Concern softened her features. "It's *you* I'm worried about. If you get arrested, you get word to me right away. Understand? I'll hire the best lawyers to defend you."

I thought of a certain lonely attorney in Sault Sainte Marie and decided to do my good deed for the day. Angie the Matchmaker.

"You mean Whatzisname . . . Andy from the Soo?"

"Andy Capobianco." Even as she said it, her expression turned thoughtful. She was wondering whether or not to get in touch.

I gave her a prod in the proper direction. "You know,

279

Mary Beth, I'll bet he could handle the sale of that farmhouse for you."

"Now that's an idea." She looked down at the empty dishware. "Delicious! Say, hadn't we better round up Charlie and head home?"

"I'll second that," I said, reaching for the check.

"Oh no you don't!" Deflecting my grasp, Mary Beth took custody of the check. "You've done enough for me, Angie Biwaban. More than enough! This one is my treat. Go fetch Charlie, would you?"

I breezed past the checkout stand and stepped into the afternoon warmth of Silver Bay's central shopping plaza. Watched a quartet of grim senior citizens troop through the doorway of the one-story, pastel green post office. I ambled down the shaded walkway. Cheerful Anishinabe princess in her white oversized short-sleeved jersey and light blue denim shorts. Stopping in front of Zup's Food Market, I gave myself the once-over in the window.

Well, in another day or two, I'd no longer need the pancake makeup, if my reflection was any indication. My face was coming along nicely, thank you.

A battered face does not inspire confidence. But it does have its uses. To be specific, those bruises had been very helpful to me during my getaway. I don't think the intake clerk at that women's shelter in Saginaw bought my story about the brutal, two-fisted boyfriend, but at least she didn't turn me in. The center's staff chipped in and bought me a brand-new outfit of hand-me-down clothes and a bed for seven days. After that, I put the Minnesota plates back on the Mitsubishi and dropped in at Pontiac to collect my winnings. I took my time getting back to Tettegouche, drifting from reservation to reservation, resuming my Angela identity as soon as I reached Anishinabe turf.

Chief came out of the market while I was preening. He had a plastic sack of groceries in one hand and a rolled-up newspaper in the other. His smile was one of exasperation.

"What are you doing?" he asked.

Proud and pleased Angie smile. "Waiting for my horse."

"Horse!?" he echoed.

"Yeah, the big white stallion. The one that runs at the speed of light." Leaning against the Coke machine, I folded my arms and grinned. "I have this irresistible desire to mail Sheriff Hendricks a silver bullet."

"Feeling proud of yourself, eh?"

"Damned right! Why, I might even change my name to Kemo Sabe."

"I wouldn't."

"Why not?"

"Kemo Sabe is Paiute for horse's ass." Trying hard not to smirk, he handed me the newspaper. "On second thought, maybe that is kind of appropriate. Take a gander at page four."

I obeyed. The paper was the *Duluth News-Tribune,* and there on page four was a huge headline reading NO CLUES YET IN BIZARRE DOUBLE MURDER. Just beneath was a disturbingly accurate artist's sketch of your Angie and a smaller headline, SOO WOMAN SOUGHT FOR QUESTIONING.

Hands trembling, I folded the paper and aimed a sickish smile at my grandfather. "I'm open to suggestions."

"If I were you, missy, I'd be thinking about a fast exit from the Northland. *Before* somebody opens their mouth about the remarkable resemblance to Charlie Blackbear's granddaughter."

Together we crossed the parking lot.

"Think Aunt Della would be happy to see me?"

"Now don't you go getting Della mixed up in this. One accessory in the family is enough."

"Oh, knock it off, Chief. You know you're not really mad."

"Oh, I'm *not,* am I!?" He made a pretense of indignation and just as quickly abandoned it. Genuine affection glimmered in those obsidian eyes. "No, I guess I ain't. I've been reading about that Carmody fella. Paper's been full of stuff about him. You did good, Angie, greasing the skids under that guy."

281

"It wasn't my doing, Chief. Monica's the one who put him out of circulation. And she was every bit as rotten as he was."

"Don't sell yourself short. You got Mary Beth's money back when there was no hope. No hope at all. The law may frown on it, but . . . I think you did all right." He ruffled the back of my neck. "Just don't go making a habit of this, okay?"

"I'll be good, Chief. I promise."

"Seems to me I've heard that one before."

As I opened my mouth to reply, I caught a glimpse of a two-tone sedan suddenly slowing down on Outer Drive. A cruiser of the Minnesota State Patrol. The passenger window came down, and a trooper in mirrored sunglasses gave me a long, lingering, emotionless look.

Chilled invisible fingertips tickled my spine. Adrenaline set my knees atrembling. Casually I averted my face, letting a windblown swirl of raven hair cloak my features.

Don't get paranoid, Biwaban. Maybe they're just stopping for pizza at the Food Shop. Maybe the trooper just wants a better look at the pretty girl.

Yeah. Uh-huh. So what are they doing off the highway? And why were they driving so slow? And why doesn't he smile or whistle? And, most importantly, has he seen today's paper?

Just then, I spotted a tall, earnest, brown-haired man striding my way, approaching from the Norwest Bank. Sudden panic kindled a frantic desire to run. I squelched the impulse, then relaxed when I realized he was dressed too casually to be an FBI agent.

"There you are!" cried a familiar baritone voice.

Blinking in disbelief, I yelped, "Paul!"

"I have been looking for you for *days!*" Paul Holbrook's face tensed in irritation. "I've been up every dirt road between Two Harbors and Grand Marais."

Sickly smile. "Oh, Paul, what a pleasant surprise. Uh, this is my grandfather, Charlie Blackbear—"

"Pleased to meet you, sir." Paul nodded respectfully,

then started in on me again. "Where is this cabin of yours, anyway? Everybody up here seems to know you. But no two people gave me the same directions."

"Chief, this is my parole officer, Paul Holbrook. Also known as Kemo Sabe." I wanted to hear Chief laugh, but of course he didn't.

"Somebody said you were up on the Gunflint Trail. I spent two days driving around up there. Every other mailbox had the name Kerfoot on it. Where the hell have you been?"

If he wanted to think I'd been on the Gunflint, I wasn't about to disillusion him. Hands on my hips, I snapped, "Look, Kemo Sabe, if you can't find Odeimin Lake on a map, that's not my problem."

"No, you have a more serious problem, young lady." Paul rummaged in his blazer's inner pockets, then produced a folded document. "Do you know what today is?"

"Sure do. June the twenty-second."

"That's right, Miss Biwaban. And that is thirteen days after you were supposed to report to my office." Fuming, he lifted the document. "Well, I've had it."

"What have you got in mind, young fella?" Cool as ever, Chief blocked his path. "You thinking about hauling my granddaughter off to jail?"

"No, sir, I'm not. I don't believe in incarceration. Your granddaughter needs to learn self-discipline, and that's not going to happen with her sitting around in jail." Paul slapped the document against his palm. "You're not getting off that easily, Angie. I haven't lost a client yet, and I'm not going to start with you. You're going to make this parole work." He grabbed my wrist and smacked the folded document into my grasp. "There! Formal service and notification!"

Peeling it open, I skimmed through all the heretofores and hereunders.

Paul caught my scowl of confusion and added, "That is a fugitive warrant, Miss Biwaban. As of June ninth, you've been in violation of the terms of your parole. I haven't submitted it to the Department yet. And that's because I'm giving you one more chance. You're accompanying me back to South Dakota — *today!*"

I cast a surreptitious glance in the direction of the cruiser. Both troopers stood beside their vehicle, watching us with mild, dispassionate interest. Chief had said I needed a fast exit from the Northland. And with Paul's help, I just might get one.

But I couldn't let him think I was too eager.

"Today!?" I bleated. "You mean . . . right now!?"

"You've got it." Paul nodded in satisfaction. "The minute your bags are packed, we are going back to South Dakota. Otherwise, I'm going to file this with the Department, and they will begin formal extradition proceedings with the state of Minnesota. In which case you *will* go back to prison. You're getting a choice, Angie. What's it going to be?"

"What about Clunky?" I saw Paul's face register confusion and added, "My car. I left it with . . . friends on the Gunflint Trail."

"No problem," Chief said. "I'll drive it out there. I can always fly home."

"That's a fine idea, Mr. Blackbear. Angela needs plenty of positive family support while she's paying her debt to society. I'll give you the address in Pierre."

"Pierre!?" I echoed. "But I live in Rapid City!"

"Not any more you don't." Paul reclaimed the fugitive warrant. "I took the liberty of paying off your landlady. Your furniture is all crated up and waiting for you — at the Department's halfway house in Pierre."

"Paul!" I bellowed. "You didn't! Oh, you rotten bastard! You are the biggest turd —"

"In South Dakota. Guilty as charged." His forefinger tapped the end of my nose. "And you, princess, need a little more structure in your life. Once you're a free woman again, you can gallivant to your heart's delight. Until then, you're going to learn to obey orders."

"I can't live in Pierre. You can't even find the mall. They hid it in a gulch."

"I'll happily provide you with a road map."

"Pierre sucks!"

"Is that any kind of language to use in front of your grandfather?"

"Oh, Paul, be reasonable."

"Look, you're getting off pretty easy for a parole violator."

And even easier for a wanted woman embezzler, I thought. A notion that made it hard for me to retain my fussbudget face.

The troopers got back in their cruiser. A ripple of relief ran through me.

"You're going to live in Pierre, and you're going to be a model parolee. And if the prospect distresses you, Angela, I'm sorry. You brought it on yourself. You broke the rules, and now you have to pay the penalty. One year in Pierre."

That idiot rhyme coaxed a grin from Chief. "Man has a point, Angie."

"Damned right I do," Paul added. "Just wait till you see the job I have lined up for you. You're going to wish you kept that appointment, Miss Biwaban."

No doubt it was a vile, menial, low-paying job, typical of those in Paul's Work Experience program. But the thought of my Tilford booty salted away in banks throughout Minnesota would do much to make it bearable.

And I found the prospect of a year in Pierre a whole lot more pleasant than serving hard time in a women's prison.

Most importantly, the halfway house would provide a welcome and much-needed sanctuary, permitting me to relax and wait out the long months until my final discharge. Months during which the trail would grow cold, and the memories of Andrea Porter would fade, and the law enforcement agencies would turn their energies to more pressing matters.

One year in Pierre. I would be marking time, cherishing my own precious memories of my Andrea days, rehearsing the words I would say on the inevitable day I again confronted the man I loved, my darling heir apparent, Donald Winston Pierce.

You should never worry about me. You see, I always land on my feet. Except when I land on my head.

Now, if only I could think of a clever way to lure Donald out to South Dakota. . . .

With an inward smile, I watched the cruiser tool away. Then I glanced at Chief and caught his fleeting expression of relief. Our gazes locked momentarily, and I knew he knew what I was thinking.

Paul frowned. "Well, Angie?"

Feigning a look of demure contrition, I made fists and presented both wrists in tandem. Submission to the handcuffs' embrace. A visual gesture of surrender.

"Your prisoner, Kemo Sabe."